WHAT'S
LEFT
UNTOLD

SHERRI
LEIMKUHLER

What's Left Untold
Red Adept Publishing, LLC
104 Bugenfield Court
Garner, NC 27529
http://RedAdeptPublishing.com/

This is a work of fiction. Names, characters, places, and incidents either are the product of the author's imagination or are used fictitiously, and any resemblance to locales, events, business establishments, or actual persons—living or dead—is entirely coincidental.

For my husband, my daughters, my parents; the reason for everything.

CHAPTER 1
February 2006

The envelope slid from between the pages of the book and fell to the floor, landing between my feet. The sudden familiarity of it—the pink paper slightly yellowed with age and the masculine, angular lettering in sparkly purple ink—was like a slap in the face. I bent to retrieve it and pinched it between my thumb and forefinger as if it were something distasteful, possibly dangerous.

Lia. The name rose from my subconscious as mist rises from water at dawn—hazy, intangible. It had been nearly twenty years since I'd last seen or spoken to the girl who had once been like a sister to me. Before she'd willfully disappeared, vanishing into thin air, Lia had been my best friend.

The back flap of the envelope was ragged and torn from where I'd ripped it open in a hurry on that hot summer day long ago. I slipped my fingers inside and retrieved the soft pink sheet of paper. I unfolded it, and my eyes skimmed over the cursive L embossed at the top of the page. One by one, long-forgotten memories began to crystallize in my mind, making my head throb and my heart ache.

Wiping my sweaty palms on my jeans, I sank to the hardwood floor of my home office. My pulse raced, so I drew on my yoga practice. *Calming breaths.* I pulled in a deep, cleansing breath through my nose, filling my lungs, and exhaled through my mouth in a long, steady stream.

Then I began to read.

I SHIFTED RESTLESSLY on the faux-leather chair, crossing and uncrossing my legs, as I cast envious sideways glances at the young women with swollen bellies, glowing complexions, and glossy hair. Abstract paintings of mothers and children adorned the walls of the mauve-hued waiting room. I absently wondered whether, perhaps, my age had caused my recent inability to conceive, or maybe it was some sort of karmic punishment for being so greedy. Jack and I had already been blessed with three beautiful, healthy daughters. Was it selfish to want another child? In my heart, I didn't think so. *Maybe we should adopt.* I paused to consider an adorable towheaded boy from Russia or an exquisite Somalian boy with big brown eyes and skin the color of burnt umber.

"Anna Wells?" the nurse bellowed, interrupting my reverie.

I gathered my green hobo bag—I'd overheard the stylish art teacher at the elementary school saying no one used the word "purse" anymore—and followed the short, squat lady to the dreaded scale. I shed my jacket, shoes, and bag before stepping up for the moment of reckoning.

"One thirty-nine," the nurse announced as she recorded the number in my chart.

I frowned as she wrapped the blood pressure cuff around my upper arm and made a mental note to skip dessert. I was still carrying an extra seven pounds of baby weight, even though my four-year-old Helene had long since left babyhood behind.

"Pressure's good," the nurse said, handing me a sealed plastic cup. "Bathroom's around the corner. Place the cup in the window when you're finished."

I stepped into the small room, rolling my eyes at the water-scapes that strategically bedecked the walls—a myriad of flowing rivers and cascading waterfalls. Holding the cup between my thighs, I hovered over the toilet. When my mission was complete, I placed the warm cup in the window as instructed and washed my hands with the abrasive, industrial-strength soap.

The nurse, who had a bored, slightly impatient expression on her face, was waiting for me in the hallway. She escorted me to an exam room and handed me two large blue crepe-paper squares. "Remove all your clothes. Top opens in the front. Place the other one across your lap. Dr. Preston will be with you shortly."

Reluctantly, I complied with the nurse's directive, with the exception of my socks, which I left on. Inwardly pleased by my small act of defiance, I tucked my legs beneath me. The tissue-thin paper covering the exam table crackled under my bare behind. Warily, I eyed the tray of gleaming metal instruments on the countertop. The plum-colored walls, which undoubtedly bore witness to the vast display of emotions that filled the room—hope, despair, joy, sadness—were closing in on me. I exhaled slowly, trying to relax.

Gyno visits were the worst. And I'd forgotten to shave my legs.

"EVERYTHING LOOKS GOOD," Dr. Preston declared. She leaned back in her chair, snapped off her latex gloves, and tossed them into the trash can. "As you get older, conception can become tricky—elusive, even—despite the ease with which you've conceived before. At nearly thirty-five, you're approaching advanced maternal age, crazy as that sounds." Dr. Preston snorted and rifled through a cabinet. Her large round glasses gave her kind, intelligent face an owlish appearance. "Look this over." She handed me a brochure detailing the risks associated with conception and pregnancy beyond the age of thirty-five. "It's also possible, though not as likely, that your husband could be experiencing decreased sperm quality or motility issues. We can run some tests, maybe start you on Clomid—"

"Fertility drugs?" I never imagined I would have to consider taking drugs to get pregnant, nor did I fancy the idea. I didn't even like to take ibuprofen for a headache.

"It's an option if another pregnancy is what you want." Taking in my blank expression, she continued. "Or you can simply wait and let nature take its course." Dr. Preston rested her hand lightly on my shoulder, her dark eyes filled with clinical compassion. "Call me if you have any questions." She slipped out the door, leaving me alone in my flimsy gown to ponder my options.

The distress I felt over what she'd just said—advanced maternal age and fertility drugs—rendered Lia's letter silly by comparison. *Inconsequential high school drama.* In my haste to make the appointment on time, I'd shoved the letter back into the yearbook and thrust it onto my office bookshelf once again. Out of sight, out of mind.

"ADVANCED MATERNAL AGE," I reported to Jack over dinner as I mindlessly twisted strings of whole-wheat linguine around my fork. "When did I get old?"

"You're not old. You're beautiful." Jack leaned over and kissed the tip of my nose.

"I'm serious, Jack. The first three times were so easy, effortless. And now we've had five negative pregnancy tests in two years. I'm having a hard time wrapping my head around it."

Jack placed his large masculine hand over mine, and his thumb gently stroked my knuckles. His wavy dark hair gleamed beneath the glow of the handblown-glass pendant lights.

"Besides," I whispered, "I know how much you want this."

Jack adored our daughters, but I sensed a quiet yearning for a son. I could see it in the wistful way he watched fathers in the park, playing catch with their sons and pushing dump trucks through the sand. I knew he'd envisioned a future filled with fishing trips, camping, football games, and Boy Scouts—the very things he'd missed out on as a boy.

"Anna, I have everything I want." Jack's mesmerizing ocean eyes bored into mine. "You, the girls. It's everything I need. I'm happy."

I let out a long, shaky breath. "But what about a son? I want that for you. For *us*."

Jack glanced at the brochure I'd brought home. A frown creased his brow as he regarded the charts and the lines representing the multiple risks associated with pregnancy after the maternal age of thirty-five angling sharply upward. "We have three beautiful, healthy girls, Anna. We have each other. What more could we want?"

That was Jack—eternally positive and always the voice of reason.

"Nothing," I agreed, anxiously wringing my hands in my lap as I searched his face. "I love you, Jack."

"I love you too, Mrs. Old Lady." A wicked grin crept across his handsome face. "How 'bout we head upstairs and let nature take its course? Doctor's orders."

CHAPTER 2
November 2006

My breasts were tender, and I craved salty tortilla chips and carbonated beverages, all of which I attributed to my impending period. But it never came. *I'm pregnant!* My heart leapt with joy. I rifled through my calendar, counting forward and back, to make sure I hadn't miscalculated. I was never late. *It's nothing*, I convinced myself instead. *Probably stress.* After so many disappointments and false alarms over the past two years, I didn't want to get my hopes up. But then, a few hours later, I spotted the familiar pink-and-white box while rummaging through the cabinet beneath the bathroom sink in search of a new tube of toothpaste. I peeked inside. One test stick remained.

"What the hell?" I muttered. I peed on the absorbent end of the stick and carefully placed it on the edge of the sink to wait for the expected "not pregnant" line to appear.

"Mommeee!" Helene's shriek was followed by a crash and another howl.

The sound sent a jolt of adrenaline through my body. I yanked up my zipper and raced downstairs to find Helene sitting on the kitchen floor in a puddle of milk. A metal kitchen stool was overturned beside her.

"I was thirsty," Helene explained, a pitiful expression marring her lovely, upturned cherubic face. Already in kindergarten, she

6

had yet to outgrow her plump baby-pink cheeks. A full gallon of organic milk—plastic carton split wide open—gurgled and belched liquid onto the tile floor.

"Are you okay?" I knelt beside Helene and swiped away a fat tear that tumbled down her round cheek.

"I'm home!" Evelyn bellowed and slammed the mud room door behind her.

I glanced up in time to see eight-year-old Evelyn making a bee-line for the kitchen, full speed ahead as usual. "Watch out!" My warning came two seconds too late.

Evelyn skidded across the slick tile and landed in a heap beside us, bashing her chin on the stool as she went down. Drops of blood dribbled from her lip where she'd bitten it and then splashed onto the floor, mixing with the milk and turning the liquid a sickly Pepto-Bismol pink. At the sight of her own blood, Evelyn became hysterical, which made Helene sob harder.

"I'm s-s-sorry," Helene said, stuttering through her tears.

"It's okay, girls. Accidents happen." My body sagged with exhaustion as I surveyed the mess, but for my girls' sakes, I forced a half-smile and a chipper tone. "You know what Grandma always says..."

"There's no crying over spilt milk," the girls mumbled.

"That's right. So how 'bout we get you cleaned up, okay?" I heaved myself to a standing position.

"Okay," Evelyn said.

"Leave your clothes here, and I'll run a hot bath for you." I bent to collect the broken carton from the floor and deposited it into the sink.

"With bubbles?" Helene asked.

I dabbed at Evelyn's lip with a clean cloth. "Yes, with bubbles."

"Woo-hoo!" The girls shrieked and peeled off their wet clothes, the spilled milk and split lip instantly forgotten.

"Last one's a rotten egg!" Evelyn yelled as she dashed upstairs.

By the time the girls were bathed and dressed in fresh pajamas, the milk-saturated and bloodstained clothes tossed into the washing machine, and the kitchen floor mopped, it was time to make dinner. It would have to be something quick and easy. I decided on spaghetti, Kathryn's favorite.

Kathryn, my firstborn, who was already mature and responsible beyond her eleven years, had arrived home from a friend's house just as I was soaking up the last of the milk. She'd immediately pitched in—helping me carry the sopping towels to the washing machine and refilling the mop bucket with fresh soapy water—without being asked. Cooking her favorite meal was my way of saying thanks. I glanced at the digital clock on the stove. Jack wouldn't be home for two more hours. His work as a sports therapist often kept him at the office late. But his long hours were also part of the price we paid for me quitting my full-time marketing job in favor of occasional freelance writing work so I could stay home with the girls. I sighed and filled a large pot with hot water, added a teaspoon of salt, and set it on the stovetop to boil.

I WAS READING BEDTIME stories to the girls when I heard the rumble of the garage door. Jack was home.

"Daddy!" the girls shouted, instantly eradicating the peaceful vibe I'd been cultivating for the past half hour.

Jack dropped his work bag on the floor and tackled the pogoing girls to the ground, tickling them wildly. The girls giggled and shrieked with delight. *Why is it that dads are such experts at getting the kids riled up right before bed?* My own father had always done the same.

"It's all you!" I threw my hands up in surrender, leaving Jack to re-tame the shrews. I wandered downstairs, put on the kettle, and curled up with a book, enjoying my first quiet moment of the day.

"ANNA!" JACK SHOUTED, startling me awake.

My book lay askew on my lap. I hadn't made it three pages before I'd dozed off. Jack bent down, swept me into his arms, and planted a big smacker on my lips.

"Wow! What's that for?" I stifled a yawn with the back of my hand.

"Why didn't you tell me?" Jack's expression was a mix of shock and delight. He whipped a white plastic stick from his back pocket and waggled it in front of my face.

"Oh my God!" The two pink lines were blurred by the happy tears gathering in my eyes. Consumed by the chaos of the afternoon, I'd forgotten all about the pregnancy test. "I don't believe it!"

Confusion furrowed Jack's brow. "You didn't know?"

"No. I mean, yes. I mean, I thought maybe..."

Jack's dark-blue, emerald-flecked eyes sparkled. "We're going to have a baby!"

"We're going to have a baby," I repeated, letting the words sink in. Having decided to forgo fertility treatments, I'd resigned myself to the fact that I might never become pregnant again. But now the promise of another baby made my chest swell with happiness. I wrapped my arms around Jack's broad back and squeezed tightly, hoping with all my might that we would finally have a son.

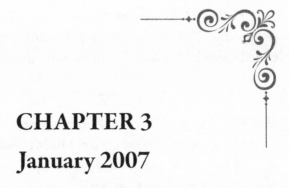

CHAPTER 3
January 2007

I dreamt I was swimming in the Caribbean Sea, the warm turquoise water lapping at my legs, then I woke with a start as the dreamlike wetness morphed into cold reality. I whipped back the covers and was horrified to discover the red-stained sheets.

"No." A low, guttural moan escaped my throat. "No, no, no, no, no." I stumbled into the bathroom and sank onto the toilet, where I discharged a stream of urine and blood thick with clots. I buried my face in my hands as my despair grew by the second, threatening to swallow me whole.

"What's wrong, Mommy?" Helene asked. She looked sleepy and adorable in her pink princess pajamas, her favorite stuffed animal clutched to her chest.

"Oh, sweetie, it's nothing. A bad dream. Go back to your room, and I'll be there in a minute." I choked back a small sob. *Bad dream, indeed. More like a nightmare.*

I turned the shower on full blast and stepped into the punishing stream. Hunching my shoulders, I let the steaming water sear my skin. The water turned salty with the tears I sobbed into the mist. When the water ran cold, I toweled off and listlessly searched the cabinets for a pad. My vision blurred as I affixed the pad to an old pair of underwear then tugged on stretchy black yoga pants and a long-sleeved T-shirt. With shaky fingers, I dialed Dr. Preston's office and was instructed to come in immediately. My next call was to Jack, and my heart broke as I punched the numbers.

"Hello," answered the deep, soothing voice.

"Jack." My voice cracked as I squeaked his name. It was all I could manage.

"Anna? What's wrong?"

"The baby... I'm so sorry, Jack." I began to sob in earnest. "I think I'm losing the baby."

There was a brief, heavy silence that cut me to the quick before Jack replied. "I'll be right there."

My throat constricted. I dropped the phone into its cradle and numbly went about the usual morning routine of sipping herbal tea and packing lunches. Kathryn and Evelyn, lost in their own early-morning preteen rituals, seemed none the wiser. But Helene, who'd witnessed my distress, slipped her small hand into mine as we walked slowly to the bus stop.

Jack's shiny black Ford Explorer careened into the driveway just as the yellow school bus disappeared around the corner. Tears frosted my cheeks, and my teeth chattered in the early-morning cold as I stood waiting in the driveway.

"Anna." My name became vapor in the crystalline air. Jack unfolded his body from the car, pulled me to his chest, and held me until the ends of my damp hair began to freeze. Then he gripped my elbow to steady me as I climbed into the SUV. I avoided his eyes, fearful of the worry and regret I would see etched on his face. After three years of trying and failing to get pregnant and finally accepting that our family was complete, that we would never have a son, we'd discovered the joyous news of the pregnancy and allowed ourselves to celebrate and plan. We'd allowed ourselves to hope. The pain and disappointment of the loss was unbearable. I was crushed beneath the weight of it.

We drove to the doctor's office with Jack's white-knuckled left hand gripping the wheel. His right hand rested on my thigh, fingers interlaced with mine.

Dr. Preston confirmed our worst fears. The pregnancy had spontaneously terminated, and I was experiencing a natural miscarriage. A D and C would not be necessary. Dr. Preston warned that the bleeding could last up to two weeks and that a follow-up appointment would be required to make sure my uterus was clear and my hCG levels back to normal. "You can try again in a few months," she consoled.

Wordlessly, we left the office and rode home in silence. Not the worried and fearful silence in which we'd arrived but a silence heavy with sadness, emptiness, and loss. Hot tears leaked from my eyes and slid down my cheeks. I brushed them away with the back of my hand, gazing impassively out the window as the world rushed by in a blur of dead brown grass and stark trees. The depressing landscape was a cruel, mocking reflection of my own physical and emotional state. *Barren*.

At home, Jack put fresh sheets on the bed and closed the blinds, engulfing the room in darkness. I was suddenly exhausted. My limbs felt like lead. I climbed into bed and buried myself under the covers. Jack took the rest of the day off and climbed in beside me. He held me tightly as I cried myself to sleep.

CHAPTER 4
March 2007

I wallowed in darkness.

In the weeks following the miscarriage, loneliness and emptiness were my constant companions, pervasive and relentless. Sleep was my only escape. All I wanted to do was sleep. Most days, I couldn't even manage to shower or get dressed. I responded to the girls' occasional questions and entreaties with monosyllabic mumbles and pretended not to see the worried sidelong glances they cast in my direction. Jack had told them I wasn't feeling well, that they should be on their best behavior and let me rest.

After escorting the girls to the bus, I would retreat to the shelter of my still-warm bed. Like a vampire, perpetually cold and pale, I slept fitfully during the day and restlessly roamed the house at night, blatantly ignoring my freelance magazine and newspaper column deadlines.

Jack had been a loving and compassionate caretaker, picking up the slack around the house and in our lives, doing the grocery shopping and the laundry, and shuttling the kids to their various activities. He'd patiently allowed me time to heal but, ultimately, he refused to continue as an enabler.

"This isn't healthy, Anna," Jack said one Saturday morning. He opened the blinds in our bedroom, and the late-morning rays streamed in. Dust motes danced in the sunlight. "This has gone on too long. You need to talk to someone."

I drew the covers over my head.

Jack sat on the edge of the mattress, and my body tilted sideways. "There's a sports psychologist that works in my office on Wednesdays. I can ask him for a recommendation. Maybe he knows someone who specializes in... these things."

"What things?" I responded listlessly. "Like what it feels like to lose a child? To fail? To be utterly empty inside? To have disappointed the one person I love most of all?"

Jack rubbed my back. "Exactly those things. But you are not a disappointment, Anna. Far from it. You are strong and brave. And you did not fail. This was not your fault."

I twisted to the left, turning away from Jack. "I don't want to talk to anyone."

"We can't go on like this. The kids need you. *I* need you. We have three children who love you, who need their mother."

I burrowed deeper into the covers. A small part of me, deep down below the layers of sadness and grief, knew Jack was right. He sat quietly for a moment then let out his breath in a long, slow exhalation and gave me a comforting kiss on the crown of my head, as a parent would kiss a small child. Wanting nothing more than to close my eyes and shove the encroaching world back into the closet of my mind, I was relieved when he stood to go. The dreamless, fitful sleep to which I'd become accustomed was reaching for me, pulling me back into its depths. I anticipated the click of the bedroom door, signaling Jack's departure and the burden of expectation retreating with him.

Instead, I heard Jack's voice, firm and insistent. "Evelyn has a lacrosse game in an hour. Why don't you get up and take a shower? I'll bring you a cup of tea."

Behind closed eyelids, I desperately searched for sleep. When Jack returned fifteen minutes later, I was still in bed.

"Damn it, Anna!" Jack set the mug of tea on the nightstand with a thump. He whipped back the covers, leaving me exposed and vulnerable in my stained, oversized T-shirt. "You are going with us to this game!" He stormed across the room and into the bathroom. I heard the shower hiss to life. Then, suddenly, strong arms were prying me from the comfort and safety of my bed.

"Jack, no." I protested weakly at first then with more strength. "No!" I pushed against his chest, trying in vain to free myself from his grasp.

"We have to move on, Anna. Miscarriages happen all the time. It's sad and painful, but it's part of life. We've been so fortunate."

I began to weep. "It's so unfair."

"Shh." Jack smoothed my tangled hair with his palm and gently released me to stand on wobbly legs in front of the shower.

Tears streamed down my face. Jack gently lifted the shirt over my head, tossed it into the overflowing laundry bin, and kissed me on the back of my sweaty neck.

"You're so beautiful, Anna. I've missed you. I've missed us." Jack closed and locked the bathroom door. Then he spun me around and kissed me on the lips, tentatively at first and then with more urgency. His mouth was pleading, hungry with need, and aching with worry.

My love for this man fractured the walls I'd erected around my broken heart. We continued kissing as he unbuckled his belt and dropped his pants to the floor. The steam from the shower engulfed the room, creating a film on the glass. I unbuttoned his shirt, slid the palms of my hands along the familiar curves of his torso, and slipped his shirt off his shoulders. Together we stepped into the steaming water. The scorching liquid soaked through my pain and cleansed my soul, easing the sadness that resided within and held me captive.

CHAPTER 5
April 2007

"Anna Wells to see Dr. Barrows," I said to the receptionist. I had been feeling better, making small, positive strides each day for the past month since my mini breakthrough in the shower with Jack, but my bout with depression and grief had left me feeling broken and fragile. Some days, I walked by my bedroom and longed to draw the blinds and climb back into bed, but I knew that was a slippery slope.

I was escorted down a short hallway and directed to a room on the right. Dr. Faith Barrows stood behind an orderly desk of glass and wood. As I entered the office, she walked toward me, arm extended. About my age, she had a trim, athletic figure and wore her sable hair in a loose chignon. Ruby-rimmed glasses framed warm, kind eyes. The air smelled of sandalwood and vanilla, the décor reminiscent of the sitting area at my favorite spa. Two plush white couches and an overstuffed armchair formed a semicircle in the center of the room. Each was adorned with a multitude of soft pillows in comforting hues of lavender and sage, and a lush violet throw was elegantly draped across the back of the chair. An enormous saltwater fish tank graced one corner of the office, and a petite stone fountain trickled in another. I immediately felt comfortable and relaxed, which, I realized, was the point.

"You must be Anna," she drawled in a deep Southern twang that made me cringe. Yet, somehow, Dr. Barrows exuded just enough grace and charm to counter that grating effect. "Nice to meet you. Can I get you anything? A glass of water? Mint tea?" She pronounced it "tay."

"No," I replied, unable to stifle a giggle.

Dr. Barrows arched her perfectly shaped brows, her expression a mixture of curiosity and amusement. "It's not often a client finds the suggestion of mint tea so humorous."

"It's just that—" I lapsed into another fit of giggles. "You look just like Tina Fey."

"And sound like Dolly Parton, right? I get that a lot," she said with a wry grin.

My shoulders relaxed, and an easy smile crept across my face. Dr. Barrows was down to earth, straightforward, and had a sense of humor. I wasn't sure what I'd expected—perhaps a rigid, analytical type that would view me as little more than a problem to be solved—but Dr. Barrows was a pleasant surprise. She made me feel as though we were old friends, two women simply getting together for "tay." That was ironic considering I hadn't had a close female friend in ages, not since Lia vanished from my life nearly twenty years ago.

Lia. She was nothing more than a faded memory dusty with age and neglect. It was almost as if I'd imagined her. Then I'd discovered that letter, the one that had fallen at my feet, the one I hadn't so much as glanced at again since I'd learned about advanced maternal age, secondary infertility, and miscarriages.

Dr. Barrows motioned toward the couch. "Why don't you have a seat?"

I settled stiffly onto the edge of the cushion, attempting to appear unflappable, but quickly abandoned the ruse and slumped against the soft pillows.

Dr. Barrows nonchalantly kicked off her nude peep-toed heels and nestled into the couch perpendicular to mine. She tucked her bare feet beneath her, a surprising but endearing gesture. "Let's start with why you're here."

I opened my mouth to speak, and to my horror, emotions tumbled out instead of words. My carefully constructed dam suddenly burst, and the tears began to flow.

Dr. Barrows handed me a tissue and patted me on the back. "Take your time."

I dabbed at my tears and blew my nose. "I had a miscarriage."

Dr. Barrows nodded solemnly and jotted a note on the pad of paper balanced on her lap. For the next twenty minutes, she peppered me with gently probing questions about my marriage, family, friendships, and hobbies. By the end of the session, it became abundantly and shockingly clear to me that, despite the pain of my miscarriage, there were other underlying factors contributing to my sadness: lack of purpose, for one. I'd spent the past decade raising my family, but now that the girls were all in school, my focus and priorities needed to shift along with theirs. Accepting occasional freelance writing work was not enough to fill the empty gaps in my days. I needed to set new goals and challenges for myself.

"Many women at this phase of their lives dive into their careers again or explore new hobbies," Faith said. "In fact, it's a great time to schedule yourself a girls' weekend or reconnect with friends."

Friends. A small but complicated word. When Lia walked out on our friendship all those years ago, she broke my heart. I promised myself I would never let anyone hurt me like that again. When I moved to Ohio, I made mostly acquaintances instead of friends, which had suited me fine at the time. I'd become jaded and carried a healthy dose of skepticism about friendships in general. Jack and I eventually returned to Maryland, but I hadn't kept in touch with anyone from high school. So I focused on work and starting a family. Despite all the love and support from Jack, I'd been lonelier than I'd realized or had been willing to admit.

"First thing you need to do is get right with yourself," Dr. Barrows counseled. "Find a hobby, do some things you love to do, challenge yourself."

I gave a slow, reluctant nod. "Okay."

"I also want you to rethink your outlook on friendship. You know what we say in the South, don't you?"

"No."

"Why, good friends are better than cheese grits, of course. And that's saying a lot. I love me some grits!"

I couldn't help but laugh, but it did get me thinking about hobbies and about Lia and the shock of finding that letter from her. *Maybe I should read that letter again.*

CHAPTER 6

September 2007

My therapy sessions with Dr. Barrows—*Faith*, as she'd invited me to address her—had been like sailing into a safe harbor to escape raging storms. After five months with Faith, I'd been able to unfurl my sails of peace and hope and allow her gentle guiding breeze to carry me into my season of healing.

By June, the fog of depression had lifted, and darkness had turned to light. I was more positive about the future and more care-free. I felt lighter somehow just having someone besides Jack to talk to and confide in.

Therapy sessions no longer seemed necessary, but Jack had en-couraged me to continue. "Just to chat," he'd said. I hadn't argued. The truth was, I liked Faith. I enjoyed her company.

"Tell me about your typical day," Faith had prodded during one of our first sessions together.

"WELL, I GET UP, PACK lunches, and walk the girls to the bus stop. Then I work until the girls get home from school. The after-noons are a blur of homework, dinner—"

"I said to tell me about *your* day," Faith interrupted.

"I *am* telling you about my day."

"Anna, all I've heard so far is what ya do for everyone else. What do ya do for *you*?"

I sat dumbfounded, embarrassed that I didn't have my own list to rattle off—places to go, people to see. "I enjoy my work," I ventured. "Writing fulfills me. Taking care of my family fulfills me. Being a mother and a wife and a writer is who I am."

"But that's not all ya are. You owe it to yourself—and your family—to make your own interests a priority."

I tugged at a loose thread on the hem of my shirt. The din of the usual background noises in Faith's office—the gurgle of the fountain, the bubbling of the fish tank, the tick of the clock—filled the silence.

"What do you like to do, Anna?"

Memories of Jack and me before we had kids came back in a rush. Thoughts of activities we used to enjoy crowded my mind—going on long hikes, dabbling in triathlons, listening to live music, traveling, exploring small towns, and discovering quaint bed-and-breakfasts. I dusted off each image one by one, relishing the shine.

"I used to run. And dance," I blurted. "And I read a lot too."

"Why don't ya do those things anymore?"

"I don't know," I whispered. I felt like an archaeologist, digging up ancient artifacts. "The kids, I guess. We got busy raising the girls. And Jack's practice really took off..."

"Okay, here's your assignment. I want ya to choose something ya used to love doing, or something new ya wanna try, and find a way to do it. Make it a priority in your schedule. And when I see ya next, I wanna hear all about it."

For five consecutive mornings after that session, I'd sat on my patio—coffee mug in hand, dogs lying at my feet—and contemplated Faith's assignment. Finally, after hours of intense soul-searching, I knew what I wanted to do. What I *had* to do.

The storage bin was in the basement, shoved into the back of a closet and buried under piles of life's detritus: old work boots, winter coats the girls had outgrown, neglected toys, and abandoned stuffed animals. At the bottom of the bin, beneath the malodorous cleats, funky shin guards, partially deflated soccer balls, and too-small lacrosse sticks, I found the box I was searching for. The word Brooks was printed in bold blue letters on the side. I opened the lid, and the smell of aged rubber hit my nose.

Before I could change my mind, I extracted my running shoes from the box and slipped them on my feet. The feel of them was like encountering a forgotten acquaintance, vaguely familiar and somewhat awkward.

I leashed Chessie and Bay and walked two brisk laps around the neighborhood. The sun was warm on my face, but the spring air was tinged with the early-morning chill, not yet choked with the humidity that would soon blanket the mid-Atlantic with thick, oppressive heat. Pre-kids—and pre-Faith—running had been my therapy. I'd been a tomboy growing up, and running had always been second nature, my skinny arms and legs pumping as I gleefully outran the boys during our backyard games of tag and football. As a young adult, running had allowed me to clear my mind and collect my thoughts. It had allowed me to be my best self. But over the years, life, work, and kids had been thieves of time, and responsibility had replaced running. Now I would have to work to regain the fitness I had once taken for granted and possessed with ease.

Walking quickly became a daily habit. Afterward, I would feel great—alert and energetic in a way coffee couldn't mimic—and the dogs were delighted by the new routine. When the novelty of pounding the pavement wore off, I hit the trails. The dogs cavorted through the nature preserve that bordered our property while I walked at a steady clip along the stream.

Faith had applauded my efforts, and her support, along with Jack's, despite his worry over the isolation of the trail, spurred me on. The kids, however, were slightly less enthusiastic because carving out time for myself sometimes meant that their needs weren't immediately met, and some of our usual household routines were altered.

"Mom," Kathryn yelled one morning as I was packing lunches for school. "Where is my blue shirt?"

"I don't know," I replied as I smeared almond butter on whole-grain bread.

"Did you do laundry yesterday?" she asked as she raced down the stairs and darted through the kitchen en route to the laundry room.

I licked a blob of sweet raspberry jam off my thumb. The laundry baskets were overflowing with dirty clothes, but after three straight days of rain, the weather had been so gorgeous the previous day that I'd opted to hit the trails when I'd finished working rather than run errands or do chores. "No, I didn't."

Kathryn whirled to face me, her mouth gaping in surprise. "But today is picture day, and my favorite blue shirt is dirty!"

"I'm sorry to hear it." I shrugged, refusing to feel guilty. "I guess I'd better teach you how to do the laundry."

My response was met with an indignant huff as Kathryn stomped up the stairs to find something else to wear.

Taking time for myself meant that dinner was sometimes served later than usual or a trip to the grocery store was postponed, prompting regular complaints from the girls that there was "nothing to eat." But daily exercise helped sharpen my focus, increase my productivity, and lift my spirits.

"When Mom's happy, everyone's happy," Jack would say when we were finally gathered around the dinner table. When he said that, the girls' howls of starvation were replaced by eye rolls as they forked food into their mouths.

I spent two weeks walking the neighborhood loop before I was ready to run. I was nervous—I hadn't run in twelve years—but my body remembered what to do. I was awkward and ungainly at first, but eventually, my stride evened out, and my gait became more natural. I felt alive, euphoric. But there was a price to pay for my joy.

"Ungh," I groaned when my feet hit the floor the morning after my first run.

"Sore?" Jack asked with a chuckle.

"That's an understatement," I muttered as I gently palpitated my quads.

"Let me do that for you." He knelt in front of me and expertly stroked and kneaded my aching thighs with his strong, skilled hands. I flopped back on the bed and sighed with relief. Then the cool, firm touch of his hands was unexpectedly replaced by the soft warmth of his lips as he trailed gentle kisses up my inner thigh. His chin pressed into the softness between my legs as his lips moved toward my belly, and my sigh morphed into a small groan of pleasure. My whole body was warm and tingly, and my back arched in response to his touch. Jack laid the full length of his body atop mine and brushed my hair back from my forehead. He planted small kisses all over my face—my forehead, cheeks, eyelids, chin, and nose—until he finally pressed his lips against mine. I responded hungrily, my mouth urgently exploring his.

"Gross!" Evelyn yelled from the doorway. She stood with her back to us, arms crossed.

"Evelyn, you know you're supposed to knock!" I scolded.

Jack laughed and gave me a parting peck on the cheek. "Kissing's not gross," he said, standing. "I love your mom."

"It's still gross," Evelyn insisted.

"Well, then, knock next time," I reiterated.

Jack grabbed my hands and pulled me to my feet. "Rain check?" he whispered against my ear.

I gave his backside a discreet squeeze. "Definitely."

Jack winked at me then dashed toward Evelyn. She shrieked and playfully banged her fists against Jack's broad back as he lifted her up and over his shoulder. As the two of them disappeared down the hall, Chessie and Bay came bounding into the room, tails thrashing. Chessie held her red leash tightly clamped in her mouth.

I laughed and patted the dogs. "Okay, okay." I reached for my running shoes. "We'll go."

Faith had been right. In the short time since I'd started tending to my own needs, we were all happier, even the dogs.

MY LEGS, DECIDEDLY sore after my first few runs in more than a decade, were nothing compared to my feet. Angry blisters had sprung up on my heels, and my toenails were bruised. My Brooks were like new—I'd only worn them a few times—but as I entered the sporting goods store, I wondered if the shoes had somehow shrunk during their years in storage.

"Nine and a half," the clerk announced after measuring my feet.

"What?" I shrieked. "You've got to be kidding! Maybe we should measure again."

"Nope. You're definitely a nine and a half."

"How is that possible?" I gazed at my feet. "I've always worn an eight."

"Feet change," the balding clerk said with a shrug. He was stocky, likely a former athlete. Judging by his imposing size, I would guess a football player. But he'd grown soft. His limbs were loose, and his round belly protruded over the waistband of his pants. *An armchair athlete now.* "When's the last time you bought shoes?"

"Um..." My cheeks burned. "A while ago."

He gave me a knowing grin. "You have kids? My wife said her feet grew a half size with each pregnancy."

I did a quick mental calculation and frowned. Given that logic, nine and a half was spot-on. "So that's really what I'm measuring? A nine and a half?"

"Actually, you measure a nine. But you should always go up half a size in running shoes to give your toes some room. Plus, these run a bit small." He hoisted my old Brooks into the air.

I spent an hour trying on a variety of shoes in various styles, sizes, and brands before deciding on a lightly cushioned pair of Saucony Kinvaras, size nine and a half. I'd always loved my Brooks, but the Kinvaras just felt right on my feet. They were so much lighter than my old shoes. Or maybe, having let go of the grief that had been weighing me down, it was me who was lighter.

FOUR MONTHS OF RUNNING had molded my shoes to my feet, and my Kinvaras fit like a glove. Over the summer, I'd worked hard to gradually increase my endurance and pace, and soon I'd longed to expand my running horizons beyond the short, familiar trails in the nature preserve behind my house. Jack—still nervous about me running trails alone, especially in more isolated areas—suggested I take the dogs to Patapsco Valley, a nearby state park popular among runners, hikers, cyclists, and horseback riders. The gorgeous park—with its lush forests, neatly groomed trails, and winding streams—quickly became my favorite running destination. By September, I'd made it a point to get there at least three days each week.

The early-morning sun bathed the park in soft, dappled light, and a woodpecker hammered an unseen song in the canopy overhead. I was up to running six miles and had decided to forgo my usual loop in favor of a longer, more scenic trail. The serpentine path traversed a thicket of trees. The leaves whispered of the autumn glory to come as I splashed through mossy-banked streams that bisected the trail. The dogs—panting happily by my side—occasionally veered from the trail to swim and splash in the bubbling creek.

After an hour of running, I returned to the parking lot and doubled over—hands on knees—to catch my breath. A sheen of sweat coated my skin, and my shoes were wet and covered in dirt, the soles caked with mud. The dogs lay sprawled on the ground at my feet, panting, as I removed my shoes and banged the soles together to dislodge the mud.

"Hey there!" The voice was familiar, but I didn't immediately recognize the lean, toned woman walking toward me. Her wavy brown hair was pulled back in a ponytail and threaded through a baseball cap.

I lifted my sunglasses as she approached, and her sharp features came into focus. "Faith! What are you doing here?"

"Enjoying this gorgeous day, same as you." She smiled and leaned down to scratch Chessie and Bay behind the ears. Their tails wagged frantically, but both dogs were too spent to stand.

"You going for a run?"

"Nope. I'm fixin' to ride." She motioned toward the Outback parked in the lot. A mountain bike was strapped onto the rear rack.

"Jack and I used to mountain bike when we were in college. Now our bikes are gathering dust in the garage. His work schedule doesn't leave him much time for riding."

Faith was quiet, her expression pensive. "We should ride together sometime."

"That would be great! I'd like that," I said, wondering about the implications of trail riding with one's shrink.

A truck rumbled down the gravel road, kicking up a cloud of dust, and parked in the lot. Two fine-looking college boys hopped out of the cab and busied themselves strapping on helmets and backpacks, eating granola bars, and taking swigs of Gatorade, while casting surreptitious glances in our direction.

Faith appeared conflicted, as if deciding something, then let out a long, noisy breath. "My fiancé and I used to ride. I've been going it solo since we called off the engagement a year ago. Therapeutic, ya know?"

We both laughed at the tired stereotype of therapists being the ones most in need of therapy. "I wouldn't want to impose on your solitude," I said.

"I'd enjoy the company. Besides, you'd probably love it. Maryland has some kick-ass single tracks, especially if ya don't mind getting wet!"

I gestured toward my sopping socks and shoes, and Faith laughed. "Well then, it's settled." She gave the dogs another pat. "I best skedaddle if I'm to get this ride in. See ya in two weeks?"

"Two weeks," I said, confirming my next appointment.

The college boys pedaled their bikes across the parking lot toward the trailhead. "Hey," the first one greeted as he passed, his eyes sweeping over us appreciatively.

"Hey," we replied in kind.

"How's it going?" the second one asked, foolishly eyeing us instead of the trail. He rode smack into a tree and toppled over. His friend nearly fell off his own bike as he hooted with laughter.

"Are you okay, sugar?" Faith drawled in her syrupy Southern voice.

"Yeah. I'm fine," the boy replied, dusting himself off as the tips of his ears grew bright red. He collected his water bottle, which had been ejected, and quickly pedaled away. As soon as he was out of sight, we busted out laughing.

"Oh my Gawd!" Faith said. "That is too funny!"

"Hilarious!" I agreed, giggling at the flirting fail.

"That poor guy. I hope he's okay."

"Maybe bruised his ego a bit," I said, still laughing.

"That'll teach him to watch where he's going!" Walking backward, Faith waved her hand in a half circle. "See ya 'round!"

"Have a good ride!" I called after her as she jogged toward her car. I retrieved an old towel from the back of the van and began drying the dogs. A goofy smile was plastered on my face, and a warm, happy feeling was zinging through my body. It wasn't the post-workout buzz I'd grown accustomed to but a different kind of high.

As I drove home with the windows down, the wind whipping my hair into a frenzy, I tried to pinpoint the sensation—a mixture of contentment, anticipation, and glee. I was almost home before I could identify what these feelings meant: *friendship*.

I parked the car in the driveway and switched off the ignition as images of Lia bombarded my brain. I tipped my head back against the seat and closed my eyes. I could see her smile, almost hear her laugh.

Before I'd started running again—after the session with Faith in which she'd encouraged me to pick up a hobby or reconnect with friends—I'd read Lia's letter again. And I had felt nothing. But now, still floating on a friendship high—a feeling that Faith had reawakened in me—I remembered the teenage bliss of lazy summer afternoons. Lia and I would eat ice cream cones as we sat on the splintered boards of the city dock, our feet dangling above the water as we gossiped and laughed.

The dogs began to whine, anxious to get out of the car, and their restlessness cast a shadow on my rose-colored reverie. Once again grounded in reality, I remembered the drama and betrayals, the pain of Lia slowly pulling away from me, until she was simply gone from my life altogether. No explanation. No forwarding address. Nothing.

Frowning, I opened the liftgate to free the dogs and pushed all thoughts of Lia from my mind, unwilling to let my memories mar the new happiness and contentment I'd found.

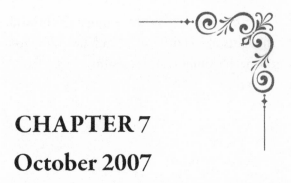

CHAPTER 7

October 2007

"Hey there!" Faith said as I entered her office. She'd long ago abandoned the formality of a handshake, greeting me with a warm hug instead. A steaming cup of chai stood waiting for me on the side table.

"How are you?" I plopped onto the sofa, kicked off my shoes, and tucked my legs beneath me.

Faith laughed as she settled into the armchair across from me. "Aren't I the one who's supposed to be asking that?"

Nonplussed, I took a grateful sip of the spicy tea. "How was your ride?"

"Which one?" Taking in my quizzical expression, she continued. "I've been out three times since I last saw ya. You look great, by the way."

"Thanks. I finally lost the last of the baby weight. I'm feeling pretty good."

"That's great! Keep it up!" Faith tapped a few keys on her laptop then removed her glasses and leaned toward me. "So let's talk about friends. Girlfriends in particular."

"Faith. You know I'm married," I deadpanned.

"Oh, get outta here. You know what I mean. I reviewed my session notes last night and not once did ya mention spending any time with friends."

I took another sip from my mug. "I don't really have time for friends."

Faith gave me a stern look over the ruby rim of her glasses.

"What? I'm too busy." Working from home, I didn't have coworkers to interact with, and our sprawling, sparsely populated subdivision didn't exactly lend itself to community connections beyond a smile and a wave as someone drove past. My girls—easily the youngest in our neighborhood—were the only kids at their bus stop. And while I did tend to see the same cluster of moms at various sports practices and games, the groups seemed exclusive, tight-knit. Introvert that I was, I was always content to stick my nose in a book rather than insert myself into the conversations swirling around me, and no one had bothered to reach out and invite me in either. "Friendships take time. And besides, Jack's my best friend. Always has been."

"Anna, ya know that's not enough. Jack can't be your everything. It's not realistic. Never mind that it's not fair to him and not good for you. Women need other women in their lives."

"I consider you a friend."

"Likewise. But I'm also your therapist. Now tell me, who else do ya spend time with?"

I averted my gaze. Jack was a family man through and through. After long, grueling hours at the office—save for the occasional post-work happy hour, at which I sometimes joined him—he was content to come home and spend time with the girls and me. We were both homebodies. It was one of the common ties that bound us. Over the years, I'd had plenty of acquaintances and casual friendships with women, but there was no one I'd considered a true friend, at least not since high school.

"I haven't exactly had the best track record with girls," I scoffed.

Faith regarded me intently over the rim of her glasses. "Go on."

I exhaled loudly, shifting in my seat. "We moved a lot. And I was a tomboy. I liked sports. I wasn't really into the whole Easy-Bake Oven and Barbie thing." I wrinkled my nose at the memory.

"How did that make you feel?"

"Like I didn't fit in. And girls just seemed so complicated, you know? And... evil, untrustworthy." Faith was doing that whole silent bit, so I cleared my throat and continued. "When I was in fourth grade, a sixth-grade girl stole my diary and read it aloud on the bus."

"Tell me more about that."

"It was horrifying. I felt so betrayed. And then there was this girl in high school, the first girl I ever really clicked with. We were best friends. But after graduation, she just disappeared without a word. Totally abandoned our friendship, like I'd never meant anything to her." Traitorous tears gathered in my eyes, and I angrily blinked them away. "I never did understand what happened. Still don't. Anyway"—I waved my hand dismissively as if clearing cobwebs—"it was a long time ago. It doesn't matter."

"Sounds to me like it does matter. What was her name?"

"Lia."

"How did you meet?"

My shoulders relaxed, and my lips involuntarily curled into a half-smile at the memory. "How much time have you got?"

"You're it until lunch," Faith said.

I pivoted on the cushion, extended my legs, and, in true stereotypical psychotherapy fashion, reclined fully on the couch. My back sank into the soft plush pillows, and I laced my fingers behind my head. Gazing up at the cornflower-blue ceiling, I inhaled deeply, appreciating the soothing, lavender-scented air. I could remember it all, every detail, like it was yesterday.

CHAPTER 8

August 1986

I lounged on a futon in the covered bed of my parents' Chevy pickup. My eyes were shielded against the bright morning sun by my favorite pair of sunglasses—white with palm trees etched on the lenses. I'd found them in Ocean City two months earlier at a cheesy boardwalk shop overflowing with lewd T-shirts, cheap towels, and rubber flip-flops. As we traveled west toward Annapolis, I watched the twin spans of the Chesapeake Bay Bridge and the choppy water beneath it recede in the distance.

Tank, my five-year-old golden retriever, sat contentedly by my side. His pink tongue tumbled from his gently graying muzzle, and his silken ears flapped in the breeze. I fiddled with the dial on my silver boom box and adjusted the antennae. "Cruel Summer" by Bananarama blasted from the speakers. In the back of the truck, surrounded on all sides by my family's remaining belongings that wouldn't fit into the small moving van, I leaned back against the cushions and tapped my bare feet to the music.

Most fifteen-year-olds might think it a cruel summer indeed if their parents up and moved to a new town right before the start of high school. Not me. I welcomed the change. I held no particular love for my previous school and had no strong ties to Cambridge, Maryland. It was just another small fishing town among many that we'd lived in.

Two hours later, we pulled into our new neighborhood, Tide-water Estates, which featured a collection of quaint Cape Cods nestled along the Severn River. Though weather-worn and aging, the water-privileged community was clearly undergoing a transformation. Young children played on front lawns while fathers trimmed the hedges and meticulously applied thick coats of fresh paint to wooden fences. Mothers watered flowers and weeded overgrown gardens.

My dad had been tapped to manage and operate a new "boatel" called Harbor Cove, essentially a hotel for boats in need of over-winter storage, and my mom had landed a plum part-time job at a local bookstore. The diversion was good for us all as we struggled to adjust to my brother's recent departure from the nest. A walk-on football recruit for the Tigers, Jeff had left two weeks prior to begin summer training before his freshman year at Clemson. In all the years of moving from town to town, Jeff had been the one thing that was sure and constant in my life. Though we were complete opposites—Jeff was outgoing, blond, athletic, and popular, whereas I was quiet and shy with my dad's dark coloring and sharp features—my brother had always been my defender and hero. My friend. He'd only been gone fourteen days, but we were a tight-knit family, and his absence was already deeply felt. On autopilot, my mother would sometimes set the dinner table for four instead of our newly three, a mistake that always brought tears to her eyes.

All Tidewater residents had private access to the community beaches as well as a local swimming pool, though my parents couldn't fathom the necessity of a pool when the whole town was a stone's throw from the river. Nevertheless, they'd been swayed by the dirt-cheap rate for an August-only membership and had ultimately forked over the cash so I could spend the last few weeks of summer "getting to know some of the kids in the neighborhood." With indulgent smiles on their sweaty, summer-tanned faces, my parents shared that news with me during our first dinner in our new house as we sat on the floor, eating pizza from cardboard boxes. I knew they were trying. They knew I missed Jeff, and they wanted me to be happy in our new home—one that, my dad promised, we would stay in until I graduated. And so, for their sakes, I arranged my face into an expression I hoped resembled happiness—or at least gratitude—and resigned myself to spending what remained of my summer at the community pool.

For the next three weeks, I obediently slathered on sunscreen and made the short trek to the pool. The sidewalks were forced upward at odd angles, like a mouthful of crooked teeth, by the large roots of the towering beech trees that flanked the walkway. But my acquiescence ended there. Instead of socializing, I spent my days with my nose in a book and tried to tune out the bits of gossip that floated to me on the occasional sunbaked breeze. As the first day of school loomed, the frenzied conversation among a gaggle of bikini-clad blondes lounging in the grassy area was focused on the students from the rival junior high who would be joining us at Bay View.

"I hear there's this one girl who's slept with every guy in her class," one of the blondes announced as she pumped Sun-In onto her already platinum hair.

"Oh yeah! I've heard about her!" a curly-haired girl interjected. "She's got some weird name, like Amelia or Leah or something."

"It's Lia, and I heard she has a VD," Stephanie, the group's queen bee apparent, accused.

A girl named Renee curled her lip. "Eww."

I gnawed on my straw as the gossip swirled. The paper cup containing my beloved Cherry Coke sweated in my hands. I tried to focus on my book, yet I couldn't help but keep one ear on the conversation. Though I was intrigued, I had no desire to get involved. I'd known girls like this before. They were the popular crowd, the ones who gossiped and whispered and pretended to be nice to your face but wouldn't hesitate to stab you in the back. The girl who'd stolen my diary and read it aloud on the bus had been one of those girls.

"But I hear she's really pretty too. Like, totally beautiful," Curly Hair said, pulling a compact and a tube of cherry ChapStick from her bag. She smeared the gloss onto her thin lips and made a kissy face in the mirror.

"Whatever," Stephanie said, rolling her eyes. Clearly bored by the less salacious turn the conversation had taken, she feigned a yawn and reclined on her towel, prompting the other girls to follow suit.

With peace and quiet restored to the pool deck, I returned my attention to my book and made a mental note to steer clear of these girls at school.

THE FIRST DAY OF SCHOOL dawned hot and muggy. The thick morning air enveloped me like a damp woolen blanket. I emerged from the sweltering bus and heard a shriek of laughter from the student parking lot. Stephanie, the queen bee, was leaning against the hood of a bright-blue Iroc-Z, looking impossibly tanned and pretty in white shorts, sandals, and a sleeveless teal shirt with the collar upturned. A tall, lanky boy stood in front of her, twirling a set of car keys around his index finger. Two more of the pool girls climbed out of the car's back seat and followed Stephanie and the boy to the side entrance of the school. I ducked my head and entered through the main doors, acutely and uncomfortably aware of my knee-length denim shorts, baggy T-shirt, and sneakers. The slightly cooler air inside the building was both musty and sterile. The faint remnants of chalk and bleach stung my eyes.

From the back pocket of my shorts, I withdrew a damp, index-card-sized piece of paper. My first class was in P002. The hallway perpendicular to the office was lined with doorways labeled with the letter A. Halfway down the hall, I turned left and found myself surrounded by rooms beginning with the letter C. The school was packed with sweaty pink students laughing, hugging, and high-fiving one another. Someone rammed into my side and knocked my purple backpack off my arm.

"Ow," I complained, rubbing my shoulder.

"Sorry," a rotund boy apologized as he hurried past.

The first bell rang. I bent down and unzipped my backpack, frantically searching for my map of the school. The halls began to empty as I rifled through the pages. "P, p, p, p," I muttered as I ran my index finger across the page. Beads of sweat popped out on my forehead, and I began to panic.

"Portables are outside," said a singsong voice behind me.

A short, smiling strawberry-blonde hooked her thumb over her shoulder before disappearing into a classroom. I snatched my bag from the floor, retraced my steps, made a left, and bolted for the door that led outside.

"Walk!" a teacher reprimanded as I flew past his classroom.

I slowed my stride enough to satisfy him then dashed out the door. P002 was the second of four portable classrooms located behind the school and adjacent to the tennis courts. I ascended the short ramp to the portable and pushed open the door just as the final bell rang. The heavy August air smacked me in the face. The excited chatter emanating from the stifling room came to a halt. Every face pivoted to stare at me.

A short man with a graying beard and an impressive potbelly stood at the front of the room, his shirtsleeves rolled up to his elbows. He slid his glasses down his long nose and peered at me above the frames. "Nice of you to join us, Miss..."

"Clark," I said, breathing heavily. I tried to ignore the muffled tittering in the classroom.

"Ah, yes. Here you are," he said, consulting a notebook on his desk. "Dianna Clark."

"Anna," I corrected.

"Oh. Got it," Mr. Snowden muttered as my face burned. "Have a seat, Miss Anna."

I pushed my way down the narrow center aisle, and my sweaty legs brushed against the moist knees and thighs of my classmates. I grimaced and shuddered in disgust as I scanned the classroom. Every seat was taken except for a single chair wedged into an airless back corner. Two of the pool girls, seated side by side in the middle row, whispered as I passed.

The intercom crackled to life as I settled into my corner seat. The backs of my thighs stuck to the chair, and a rivulet of sweat trickled down my back. A scratchy female voice instructed us to stand for the Pledge. My heart thumped wildly beneath my palm, and I tried to ignore the sweat that pooled at my lower back, dampening my shirt and the waistband of my shorts. A tiny puff of air floated through the stuffy room, and the class collectively issued a brief sigh of relief.

As the morning announcements droned on, I tapped my pencil eraser against the desktop and wondered if I might actually pass out from the heat. My eyes had begun to swim in their sockets when Mr. Snowden's sharp, nasally voice jolted me to attention.

"Volunteers?"

"For what?" A boy across the aisle whispered toward the splotchy red neck in front of him.

"School store," Splotchy Neck replied with a snort.

"If there are no volunteers to manage the store, I'll have to assign someone," Mr. Snowden warned.

The curly-haired pool girl's hand shot into the air.

"Thank you, Miss Jacobs. You'll report to—"

"No! Not me!" she clarified. "Anna said she wanted to do it, being new and all." The girl innocently batted her eyes at the befuddled teacher.

"Okay, ah, Miss Clark, then."

My face burned as all eyes swiveled in my direction. *What just happened?* I had no idea what the school store was or what I'd been volunteered to do. But given the reaction of my classmates, it was not a job anyone wanted.

The pool girls bent their heads together, unsuccessfully attempting to stifle their laughter, and a boy sitting next to them cast a disdainful glance in my direction. "Geek," he muttered loud enough for me to hear.

Hoping to opt out of the assignment, I raised my hand.

"Yes, Miss Clark?"

"I'm not sure about the school store—"

"Yes, right," Mr. Snowden interrupted. "New girl. Stop by after class, and I'll fill you in. Now, if everyone would take a worksheet and pass it around, we'll get started."

I slunk down in my sticky chair and closed my eyes. The year was not off to a good start.

THE NEXT MORNING, I reported to the school store, which was adjacent to the cafeteria and little more than a glorified broom closet overflowing with blue-and-white Bay View High School supplies and apparel. Three senior boys loitered by the door. Their deep baritone voices mingled with a melodious giggle. I coughed lightly into my fist, and the boys who were blocking my way faced me with their eyebrows raised expectantly. They looked me up and down, shrugged, and reluctantly dispersed, leaving me face-to-face with the most beautiful, enchanting girl I'd ever seen. Her lopsided grin was instantly familiar. She was the girl who'd directed me to the portables.

"Hi. I'm Lia," she said, smiling brightly.

The Lia? The one the pool girls had gossiped about so relentlessly? *Impossible.* The way the girls had talked, I would have expected a salivating, man-eating, amazon-sized trollop. The petite girl who stood smiling before me was more like Christie Brinkley. I was glad to finally see a friendly face.

I wiped my sweaty palms on my plaid shorts. "Anna," I replied. "I'm new here."

Lia cocked her head to the side. "We're all new here, aren't we?"

That single comment put a definitive chink in my self-protective armor. I liked her immediately. Lia was short—elfin, almost—with tiny ears and hands, a delicate, pointed chin, and a mischievous twinkle in her green eyes. But she was also exceptionally curvy, with thick strawberry hair that tumbled to her waist. A smattering of cinnamon freckles graced her otherwise porcelain skin, and I noted that both her short nose and her tiny white teeth were slightly crooked. Most notable, however, was the slight gap between her two front teeth. The flaw would have made anyone else look like a hillbilly, but Lia pulled it off with ease, like a miniature Lauren Hutton. Piece by piece, Lia was nothing exceptional. All put together, she was stunning.

My eyes swept over her white polo shirt, acid-washed denim Guess miniskirt, and pink Keds, and I was immediately self-conscious about my own attire. I ducked my head and pushed past her, hugging my notebook to my flat chest.

"Tigers, right?" she asked.

I whirled around, bewildered. Lia laughed, filling the small room with a merry, tinkling sound. She tossed her long, wavy hair over her shoulder. I caught a whiff of Cinnabon.

"Your shirt." She reached out to lower my notebook. "Clemson Tigers?"

"Oh. Yeah. My brother goes there. He plays football."

"Awesome! I love football!"

"You do?" I asked, stunned.

"Of course! Don't you?"

A slow smile spread across my face. "Um, yeah. I grew up playing backyard ball with my brother and his friends."

"Cool," Lia replied. "There's a home game on Friday. Bay View's playing Annapolis. We should totally go!"

"We should definitely go," I said.

Lia returned my smile, dimples flashing, and plucked two blue-and-white pom-poms from the shelf. "Guess we'll be needing these." She stuffed two one-dollar bills into the cash box. "My treat."

FAITH WAS STARING AT me expectantly, waiting for more, but words suddenly escaped me. My memories floated away. I really didn't know what else to say.

Then I remembered. "I found an old letter from Lia about a year ago." I'd thought of the letter occasionally but hadn't bothered to read it again, at least not in the six months since I'd filed it away for good. I'd read it after one of my sessions with Faith last spring then tucked it back in the yearbook. "She gave it to me the summer after we graduated from high school."

"Go on," Faith encouraged.

"It fell out of my yearbook when I was flipping through the pages."

"What did it say?"

"Nothing, really. Lia wrote that she had something important to tell me." I snorted and hooked my fingers into air quotes around the word "important."

"And what was that?"

I shrugged. "I don't know. Probably nothing. Lia was always so dramatic. Anyway, it was a long time ago. I've moved on."

"Have you?" Faith's eyebrows were arched into question marks above her inquisitive gaze.

I resumed an upright position on the couch and met Faith's eyes. "Of course." But my cheeks burned with the lie. *If I have truly moved on, why haven't I been able to trust women and make friends more easily? And why do my conversations with Faith keep coming back to Lia?*

"Anna, lots of people like to forget the past, preferring to focus on the future and moving forward, which is not a bad thing. But our past is important. It makes us who we are today."

Faith put her glasses on and leaned back in her chair, regarding me intently. "This is good stuff, Anna. You should continue down this path, see where it leads ya. But not with me." She began tapping away on her laptop, her brow furrowed in concentration.

"What do you mean?"

The copier whirred to life behind me, and Faith stood to retrieve the piece of paper the machine spat out. "There's a lot of things at work here. First, you said you wanted to go riding with me sometime. Here's directions to the Cliff Trail at Catoctin Park." She handed me the paper. "I'm heading there Friday morning if ya wanna join me. It's a real fun ride. Second, if we're to start hanging together outside the office, then I do see that causing a problem, professionally speaking. Ya know, conflict of interest 'n' all."

Then she handed me another sheet of paper with a name and telephone number on it. "This here's Darlene," Faith explained. "She's a doll. I think you'd really like her. In my opinion, I don't think you're needing these sessions anymore. But if ya do need to talk to someone, Darlene here's your girl. 'Less, of course, you don't wanna go riding with me." Faith gave me a challenging look, one eyebrow cocked expectantly.

My breath caught in my throat, and for a moment, I felt as if I were free-falling. For the past six months, Faith had been my life-line. More than that, she'd become my friend. But as her words sank in, I realized that while she was severing the ties of our professional relationship, she was fully extending her hand in friendship, and my heart swelled with joy. I'd known for a few months that I no longer needed a therapist. Jack and I had discussed it. But I did need Faith.

Automatically thinking I would need to pick up Helene from school at noon, I exhaled slowly, disappointed to have to decline her invitation to go riding. Then it hit me: for the first time in more than a decade, I was no longer bound by such a rigid schedule. Helene, my baby, was now in first grade. Knowing she would spend the whole day in school, I'd cried when she'd boarded the bus a few weeks ago, but she hadn't even looked back. She, along with the rest of my family, was spreading her wings while I'd been content to sit back and watch them all fly.

"You're on," I said, smiling widely. "See you at the Cliff Trail on Friday." Maybe with Faith in my life, I would finally, truly, be able to move on.

CHAPTER 9
March 2008

The rich, complex aroma of coffee beans and spices greeted me as I pushed through the front door of Muddy Waters Café. I scanned the cozy, inviting space in search of Faith's signature chignon but didn't see her. I spied only the regular knitting circle of gray-hairs, the weather-beaten watermen, and the harried young mothers who were constantly wiping tiny fingers and plump faces and retrieving fallen objects from the floor.

I gazed longingly at the lovely outdoor patio overlooking the river, but the bright March sunshine was no match for the winter chill that still clung to the air. Sighing, I sank into a plush, wine-hued chair facing the fireplace and tried to imagine what Faith's reaction would be when I told her the news. The recently opened café had become my weekday refuge for writing and occasional get-togethers with Faith, but that day I had an ulterior motive.

Faith and I had been trail riding regularly until snow and ice had rendered the trails treacherous. Determined to stay outdoors despite the plunging temperatures, I'd convinced her to go running with me. We'd discovered Muddy Waters while running along an abandoned railroad track bordering the quaint historic town of Ellicott Mills. My workouts with Faith had become my best and only therapy. Faith had been right: I no longer needed standard therapy sessions. What I needed was to pursue passions and hobbies of my own, get regular exercise, and focus on building new friendships. Riding and running with Faith had accomplished all three. But my steadily growing bond with Faith also caused me to think of Lia more often. As a result, I'd read Lia's letter once more. The question of what she'd needed to tell me that warm summer day so long ago still occasionally haunted me. But ultimately, I decided it wasn't important. It couldn't possibly still have any relevance or impact on my life. So I'd slipped the letter back into the yearbook where it belonged, just another relic of my past.

"The usual?" Dixon, the head barista, called from behind the counter. Dix, who was attractive in that scruffy, twentysomething way, bustled about, humming to a tune only he could hear, as he brewed and frothed with admirable efficiency.

"You bet," I replied. Then, on second thought, I said, "Better make it decaf today."

Dix grimaced and shook his head disapprovingly as he frothed my milk and drizzled sauce into the cup. I knew he considered decaf coffee as pointless as nonalcoholic beer.

"Decaf, extra hot, minus the shot, freckled zebra latte," Dix said as he deposited the drink onto the low wormwood table in front of me.

"Thanks." I took a quick sip of the steaming beverage, a delectable mix of white and dark chocolate with a dash of cinnamon—a concoction Dix had created himself. In my haste, I burned my upper lip. I dunked the corner of my napkin into a cup of ice water and pressed it to my mouth. The cubes clanged against the glass in time with the bells on the front door as Faith bustled in.

"So sorry I'm late," she drawled. Then she noticed the bits of damp shredded paper I was peeling from my lip. "You okay?"

"Hot," I explained, scowling at the offending beverage. I could already feel a blister forming.

"Coffee?" Dix called as he pulled shots from the espresso machine.

"Earl Gray for me, please," Faith replied, casting an appreciative glance at Dix as he strode toward our table. The muscles of his forearms flexed as he poured amber liquid into Faith's teacup. Her eyes never left Dix's retreating form as she plunked two sugar cubes into her tea, took a tentative sip, grimaced, then added a third cube. "Better," she declared, settling into her chair. "So what's new?"

"You'll never guess what showed up in my inbox this week," I prompted.

"A coupon to get you some clipless pedals for your bike?" Faith teased. She was constantly campaigning for me to ditch the toe cages and upgrade to bike shoes that clipped into the pedals.

"I like my pedals just fine, thank you." In truth, the idea of being stuck to my bike freaked me out.

"So what, then?"

"A save-the-date for my twenty-year high school reunion."

Faith clapped her hands. "That's wonderful! Though I had no inklin' you were that old," she said with a wink. Her expression became serious when I remained silent. "You *are* gonna go, aren't ya?" Faith pursed her lips and blew gently across the surface of the tea, causing the steaming liquid to ripple and shimmer.

"I highly doubt it."

"Well, why the heck not?"

"I haven't seen any of those people in ages. It would be really awkward."

"I think it would be good for ya. Not to mention it's one of life's great milestones. I think you'll regret it if ya don't go. When is it?"

"Not until next summer." I bit my lip and tried to imagine what it would be like to walk into a room full of people I once knew, people who were now mere strangers. The idea wasn't the least bit appealing.

"Besides," Faith continued, "wouldn't it be nice to reconnect with some folks? You know, maybe rekindle some old friendships?"

I immediately understood the hint and gave a dismissive shake of my head. "I doubt she'll even be there." The mere thought of seeing Lia again tied my stomach in knots.

"Would it be so bad for old friends to become new friends?"

"What do I need new friends for? I have you."

Faith frowned and lowered her eyes. She replaced the teacup in its saucer and wiped her palms on her denim-clad thighs. An odd sense of foreboding washed over me, and my fingers went cold despite being wrapped firmly around my warm mug.

"Anna, there's something I've been meaning to tell ya." The somber tone of her voice made my heart race, and my mind conjured up a slide show of unpleasant possibilities. "My daddy's not doing so well. Since Mama's passing, he just ain't been the same. Absentminded. Forgetting things. His friends down there say he's needing more regular care." She sucked in her breath before lowering the boom. "I may have to move back to Mobile."

My mouth dropped open. I couldn't imagine my life without Faith. It had been a long time since I'd had such a strong connection with a woman. I'd embraced my friendship with her. I'd allowed myself to be open and vulnerable. And now that vulnerability threatened to expose me to a hurt and loneliness I had known before, one I'd vowed never to experience again. I swallowed my selfishness and summoned the courage to speak. "I'm sorry about your dad," I said weakly as I patted Faith's knee. I felt sorry for myself and ashamed because of it.

"It's not like I've gotta go right away," Faith said, her expression brightening. "I'm gonna take a trip down there, assess the situation myself. Anyway, I know you didn't ask me to meet ya here to talk about my daddy. What's up with you?"

"I'm... pregnant."

CHAPTER 10
APRIL 2008

A month after I'd shared my happy news with Faith, I was strolling through the grocery store and had just taken the first sip of my Starbucks chai latte when razor-sharp fingers of steel gripped my abdomen. The pain was intense. I clutched my stomach as a warm, creeping wetness seeped into the crotch of my favorite jeans.

Seized by fear and yet oddly detached, I abandoned my full cart of groceries and walked on numb legs into the parking lot. I fumbled in my bag for the keys to my new minivan and sank heavily into the driver's seat. A maniacal laugh escaped my lips and disintegrated into a sob as I realized, with perverse satisfaction, that the blood would not stain the charcoal-gray leather. Jack had wanted fabric seats. He'd complained that leather made his legs sweat. But bloodstains would have been difficult to remove from fabric upholstery.

Tears blinded my eyes as I drove. Within five minutes, I'd hastily parked the minivan in the driveway, wobbled into the house, and made my way across the expansive foyer to the powder room. I unzipped my jeans, barely recognizing my ghost-like reflection in the mirror, and lowered myself onto the cold porcelain seat. Thick, dark fluid oozed from between my legs as hot tears streaked down my cheeks.

I was losing our baby. Again.

Jack and I hadn't been trying for a baby. But when I'd counted backward on the calendar, I realized I must have become pregnant during our ski trip in February. I allowed myself a brief moment of self-pity and grief as my brain ticked off the cute, unique names we could have given the baby, names befitting his Colorado conception: Denver, Hayden, Ridgely, Rocky. I knew in my bones it was a boy. I closed my eyes and let the tears fall. This time around, the tears felt cleansing rather than destructive, a way to mourn and move on instead of the gateway to an abysmal downward spiral. My sessions with Faith had taught me a lot about myself and about how to "grieve constructively." Instead of wallowing in sadness and loss, instead of isolating myself in darkness, I would seek the light. I would reach out to my family and wrap myself up in their unconditional love. And if I ever felt alone or especially weak and desperate, I would slip on my running shoes and hit the trails with Chessie and Bay faithfully by my side. Between Faith and my family, I knew I had people in my life I could count on, people who cared about me as much as I cared about them. It hadn't always been that way.

October 1986

LIA WAS A SHAMELESS flirt, and the school store was routinely visited by a steady stream of boys who stopped in simply to chat with Lia and admire her. But homecoming weekend was the first time I considered the possibility that some of the rumors I'd heard about Lia over the summer might be true.

Shortly after my date and I climbed into a Ford Bronco with two other couples to head to the dance, Lia climbed onto her date's lap and promptly stuck her tongue down his throat. She and Derek made out the whole way to the school and, throughout the evening, received multiple warnings for having their bodies smashed too closely together. The gym was hot and crowded, and my date—a senior Lia had introduced me to just a week before—was never anywhere to be found. Rumor had it he was sneaking into the boys' bathroom to smoke weed with some of his senior friends. Though Lia was too busy with Derek to notice, I was miserable and couldn't wait to go home.

After three tortuous hours—during which I'd officially ditched my absentee date and told him to find his own way home—the five of us tumbled out of the school in a sweaty heap and, thankfully, climbed into the Bronco. I'd barely shut my door before someone produced a half-pint of Smirnoff from the glove box and began passing it around.

Lia tipped her head back and took a long swig. "Whooee!" she bellowed, passing the bottle to her date.

He helped himself to a deep gulp then gritted his teeth and dangled the bottle over the back seat. "Snead's?" he suggested, referring to the post-homecoming bash at Bill Snead's twenty-acre farm. Bill's parents were rumored to be in Belize for the week.

I was the single dissident voice among the otherwise unanimous yesses. "I'm ready to head home," I said, waving off the bottle. My feet were killing me, and my date and I hadn't exactly hit it off.

"Aw, c'mon, Anna. Don't be a party pooper," Lia said.

"Yeah, Anna. Besides, your house is in the opposite direction of Snead's," the driver complained.

I pushed away the bottle of vodka that was again being thrust in my face. "I don't care. Just take me home."

Amidst a chorus of groans, the driver reluctantly turned toward my house. And instead of defending or supporting me, Lia faced forward and took another sip from the bottle. "Your loss."

THE MONDAY AFTER HOMECOMING, Lia flounced into the school store with a satisfied smirk. "You missed out," she announced. "Snead's party was totally awesome."

"What'd I miss? Getting drunk and watching you make out with Derek?"

She gave me a sly sideways glance. "We did more than make out."

"Like what?"

"What do you think?"

"No way!"

"Yes way! Why wouldn't I? That makes three conquests this year." Lia smiled proudly, stowing her backpack beneath the counter and retrieving the cashbox.

My mouth dropped open. "This year?"

"Yep. It's my big F-you to society's double standard. You know how boys are heroes for getting laid but girls are sluts? Like that's fair."

"How many guys have you slept with?"

"I dunno." Lia shrugged. "Lost count." She gave me a playful wink and knelt on the floor to unpack a box of Bay View sweatshirts.

I watched her in shock. "That's probably not the best idea."

"What? Opening another box of sweatshirts?"

I crossed my arms. "You know what I mean."

"No. I don't."

"It's not a game, Lia. You shouldn't sleep around like that."

"What are you, my mother?"

"No."

"Then stop judging me."

"I'm not. It's just—"

"It's just what, Anna?" Lia crossed her arms and jutted her hip. "Not morally okay? Says who?"

"Don't you care about your reputation?"

Lia tossed her head back and cackled. "No! Why would I care about that?"

"And... it's not safe!" I suddenly remembered the rumors I'd overheard at the pool. "You could... catch something."

Lia glared at me, her eyes blazing. "So you believe the rumors? You think I have some sort of disease? Well, I don't! I'm not stupid, Anna." She unzipped her backpack, reached inside, and produced a handful of condoms, which she threw at me. The foil squares skittered across the floor. "I thought you were different!" she said through clenched teeth. "I thought you were my friend."

"I am your friend." I stepped forward and placed my hand on her arm. "I just don't want you to get hurt."

"Too late," Lia murmured as she walked out of the store and slammed the door behind her.

CHAPTER 11
May 2008

Faith had been in Alabama, visiting her father, when I miscarried. We'd talked on the phone, and she'd sent flowers and a fruit basket, but it was the first week of May before I saw her again.

Spring was in full bloom, and unlike the last time Faith and I had met at Muddy Waters, winter's oppressive chill was a distant memory. Instead, the air possessed an insistent oven-baked quality. The gentle breeze blowing off the river was briny and warm, redolent of the marigolds and wildflowers in bloom. We sat on the outside deck and watched sailboats glide by on the glistening water. I watched wistfully as a toddler stood at the water's edge. Her white-blond hair was in pigtails, and her sandals were dangerously close to becoming sodden as she joyfully threw handfuls of pebbles into the river. An elderly woman—perhaps the girl's grandmother—stood by her side, maintaining a careful grip on the girl's free hand. A kayaker, skinny and bare-chested, paddled in and out of our line of sight as he explored the shallows and the marshy nooks and crannies of the wetlands. The morning was deliciously languid and serene.

Much to our disappointment, Dix was not working that day. However, the girl who delivered our drinks—iced mocha for me, sweet tea for Faith—was essentially a female version of him, young and attractive in an unassuming way. Her long dark hair cascaded down her back in loose dreads, and her eyes were the color of violets. A tiny piercing on the side of her nose glittered in the sun. As she disappeared into the darkness of the café, Faith launched into one of her lectures.

"So, have you given any more thought to your reunion?"

I tucked a loose strand of hair behind my ear. "No. Not really. It's still a year away."

"Well, I really think you should go." Faith paused to lick bits of blueberry oat muffin from her fingertips. "I went to mine four years ago, and it was... cathartic. People from our past are the key to our future, Anna. These are the people who knew ya before ya even knew yourself. It's good to reconnect with people who knew the girl you used to be."

I aggressively slurped my mocha as Faith pressed on.

"Introduce them to the woman you've become and open your mind to their transformations as well. It'll change your life in ways ya can't imagine."

"Are you finished?"

Faith's eyes widened innocently. "What?"

"You sound like a shrink, you know."

"I *am* a shrink."

"Not *my* shrink. Not anymore, thank goodness! Which was *your* idea if I recall."

"True. But I'm still your friend, and I can't help but give ya good advice—free of charge, I might add—when you've got your pretty little head up your hiney."

At that, we both laughed then lapsed into companionable silence, munching on our muffins and making small appreciative grunts of pleasure. Muddy Waters had the best muffins in town. I was relieved to be off the topic of the reunion. I marveled at the fact that nearly twenty years had passed since I graduated from high school, but I really had no desire to attend the supposed milestone event. I wasn't that person anymore, nor did I want to be. But Faith was always so oddly insistent that I attend. It was as if there was something she wasn't telling me.

A blue heron beat its long, elegant wings and lifted off from the marshy riverbank where it had been quietly nestled. The kayaker whipped out a camera and quickly snapped a few pictures as the great bird took flight.

"So, tell me about Alabama. How's your dad?"

Faith took a long sip of her tea. "He's happy as a lark," she said with a rueful laugh. "But his friends were right. He's constantly misplacing his slippers, and he kept reading the same magazine article over and over. One evening, the tea kettle started whistling, and it scared the bejeebers outta him. He'd no recollection of putting the water on." Faith frowned, and a shadow passed over her face.

"I'm sorry, Faith. Is there anything I can do?"

"Aw, sweetie, just pray for him. And me." She averted her eyes and began fidgeting with her teacup. "I'm fixin' to move south at the end of the summer. God knows I'll be needing some prayers if I'm gonna be living with my daddy again." She laughed, but the smile didn't reach her eyes.

"Well, we still have the summer," I replied with false cheer. My chest constricted at the thought of losing Faith. I inhaled a deep breath and swallowed the pain that struggled to rise up and swallow me. Before Faith moved to Alabama, I would make it my mission to spend as much time with her as possible. Together we would tackle new adventures and make memories we would never forget. I was determined that our friendship would last, unlike my friendship with Lia, which had burned as bright as a star before vanishing from sight.

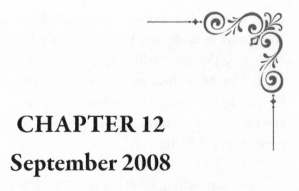

CHAPTER 12
September 2008

Faith's Outback was packed to the gills. Sweat trickled down my back as I helped her stuff the last of her belongings into the car. The heat—combined with a stomach that was clenched in uncomfortable knots because of Faith's imminent departure—served to make me irritable and edgy. To override my physical comfort, I breathed slowly and deeply, trying to focus on all the fun Faith and I had had that summer. We'd managed to get three races under our belts: two duathlons and a mud race in Richmond, where we'd raced as a team. We had alternately run and ridden a mountain bike over a six-mile course until reaching the final obstacle, a tandem belly crawl in a pit of mud beneath menacing coils of barbed wire.

After the mud race, we'd returned to our hotel to shower, attempting, with only a modicum of success, to scrub away the mud packed beneath our fingernails and caked in the crevices of our ears. Then we had headed to the Shockhoe Slip Historic District for window-shopping and lunch. With bellies full of fried yellow tomatoes and pan-seared mahi-mahi, we'd spent the afternoon exploring Maymont Park and the botanical gardens. Finally, we had strolled along the canal walk adjacent to the James River.

Later that night, we'd slipped into our pajamas, ordered pizza, and giggled like schoolgirls, laughing until our stomachs ached. It had been a long time since I'd experienced friendship like that. Perhaps I'd *never* experienced it.

March 1987

WHEN LIA SLEPT OVER at my house, which was often, we were routinely awakened by the sound of pebbles pinging against my window. Some random audacious boy was always hoping to get Lia's attention and, more likely, into her pants.

"Lia, no," I would protest as she wiggled into her jeans. "My mom will kill me if she finds out." But Lia would simply plant a kiss on my forehead, tiptoe out of my room, and creep down the hall, leaving me to lie awake, restless with worry and seething with irritation. I didn't understand why she couldn't be content to just stay with me. It was always as if she was trying to prove something. And she was seemingly unconcerned that her actions might get me into trouble with my parents.

Once, however, Lia silenced my protests with a fierce, withering gaze, her eyes glowing in the ambient moonlight. "At least your mom gives a shit," she said, a hint of melancholy softening the sharp edge of her anger.

I thought Lia was crazy, yet I envied her freedom. But later, in the wee hours of the morning, it dawned on me that perhaps she *wanted* to get caught. Perhaps she wanted to know there was an adult in her life who actually cared that she was sneaking out with boys at night.

June 1987

MY PARENTS WERE SO pleased with my final report card—thanks mostly to Lia doing my math homework for me—that they allowed me to invite Lia to join us for our family vacation in Ocean City. As an added bonus, my brother, Jeff—who I'd missed terribly—was coming home from Clemson and bringing his roommate, Danny, with him. But next to Lia, I barely existed. She was all skin and charm in her skimpy bathing suits, and the boys couldn't keep their eyes off her.

"Don't even think about it," I whispered to Jeff during dinner as I passed him a slice of pepperoni.

My brother heeded my advice, but Danny followed Lia around like a lost puppy, eagerly lapping up whatever scraps of attention she tossed his way. During the day, they flirted and wrestled while my mother peered disapprovingly over her sunglasses. Lia would squeal and jump on Danny's back in the ocean then wrap her short, shapely legs tightly around his waist.

At night, the four of us would catch the bus to the boardwalk, share a bucket of Thrasher's fries, then buy tickets to the Zipper. The goal was not to hurl as the erratic motion of the ride whipped us forward and back and sent us somersaulting through the sky.

Later, in the wee hours of morning, well after our midnight curfew, Danny would come knocking on our bedroom window, and Lia would tiptoe back out into the night.

"What are you doing?" I asked as she slid open the window, the hum of the outside air conditioning unit suddenly loud in our small room.

"Going out to have some fun."

"I don't think it's a good idea." I knew how upset my parents would be if they found out.

"Just go back to sleep." Lia ducked through the window and giggled as she thumped to the ground, bumping into Danny.

"Lia..." I sat up in bed, angry and ready to insist that she stay in, but she'd already slid the window shut, engulfing the room in silence once again.

On our last evening at the beach, we decided to skip the board-walk and take advantage of our condo's amenities: indoor and out-door pools, tennis and volleyball courts, an ice cream shop, a beach grill, a deli, and a game room.

At ten minutes to midnight, I dutifully rode the elevator to the fourteenth floor while Lia lingered defiantly by the pool, assuring me that she would be upstairs "in a minute." I'd spent the first part of the day ignoring her, still angry that she'd snuck out with Danny the night before. But as usual, she'd used her wit and charm throughout the day to wear down my defenses, giving me her undivided attention, making me laugh, and surprising my whole family with a picnic lunch she'd prepared.

"When did you make this?" I'd asked as I plucked a strawberry from a bowl of fresh-fruit salad and popped it into my mouth.

"Last night," she'd replied, treating me to a lopsided grin. "It was really windy on the beach, so Danny and I made a midnight run to the grocery store. When we got back to the condo, I was too keyed up to sleep." She'd winked and bit into a cucumber sandwich.

But now Lia was up to her usual tricks. I entered our condo at precisely midnight, and my parents—who were typically in their pajamas by ten—were still fully dressed and sipping wine on the balcony, presumably enjoying the balmy summer night. More likely, they were keeping an eye on us. I joined them on the balcony, which overlooked the pool and tennis courts. Peering over the railing, I squinted into the darkness, trying to locate Lia.

"Hi, sweetie," my mother said, her smile fading when she realized I was alone. "Where's Lia?"

The night breeze lifted my hair from my neck. "She's, uh, still down on the deck. I think she wanted to say goodbye to Danny."

Dad glanced at his watch and cleared his throat. "A little late, isn't it?"

"She should be up in a minute." I leaned over the railing and scanned the deck for signs of Lia.

My mother and I spotted her at the same time, standing atop the walkway leading to the beach. She and Danny were illuminated by floodlights from the volleyball courts, making it clear to see that they were making out. Lia's hands were stuffed into the back pockets of Danny's jeans. The whereabouts of Danny's hands were unknown. My face flushed with anger and embarrassment. To have my mother standing beside me as we watched Lia and Danny suck face made me want to shrivel up and disappear. But it also pissed me off that Lia could be so considerate one minute and so self-centered the next. I felt foolish and manipulated, but I also felt the need to defend her to my parents. I wanted them to like her. For all of Lia's shortcomings—and we all had them—she was still the best friend I'd ever had. She might have been inconsiderate at times, but she was also fun, smart, and adventurous. I was certain—if the situation were reversed—she would always have my back.

My mother stiffened at my side. "She's a little too fresh with the boys."

"It's also not very respectful of her to disregard our curfew," my dad said, glancing at his watch again.

"I don't think she means to be disrespectful. She probably just lost track of time," I explained, rising to her defense. "Besides, Jeff and Danny are still out."

"Jeff and Danny are in college. They don't have a curfew." My dad gave me a big bear hug then ducked into the condo. At six foot five, he had to be careful not to hit his head on the doorframe.

My mother eyed me carefully. "I know it's been difficult, with as much as we've moved, for you to make friends. But I'm really not sure what you see in her." She tipped her head back and polished off her Riesling. Her blond hair fluttered in the breeze.

The tennis court lights clicked off, and we glimpsed Lia and Danny making their way, hand in hand, down the walkway. At the bottom of the steps, Lia hopped on to Danny's back and kissed his neck as he piggybacked her toward the building and out of sight.

"I hope you realize the sun doesn't rise and set on that girl," my mother said. She kissed me on the cheek, bent to retrieve the empty Riesling bottle, and followed my dad into the condo.

WITH THE LAST OF FAITH'S boxes loaded into her car, I mopped my sweaty brow with the back of my hand and wiped it dry on my T-shirt. It may have taken thirty-seven years, but in Faith, I had finally found a true friend. And she was leaving. I was determined to remain strong, but when Faith wrapped her arms around me, my stoicism melted into a sappy puddle. The tears flowed freely between us as roots of sorrow burrowed into my soul.

"Aw, don't cry," Faith drawled. She tenderly wiped the pads of her thumbs beneath my wet eyes. "It's not like I'm dying. Just moving south a ways. We'll still see each other."

I wanted to believe her. But I couldn't suppress the sadness that washed over me, stealing my breath and my words, so I simply nodded and hugged her as my tears wet her hair.

Faith blew me a kiss and ducked into the driver's seat. As she backed out of the driveway, honking her horn and waving frantically out the window, I knew she was taking a piece of my heart with her. The emptiness and hollowness that enveloped me as I watched her drive away was painfully reminiscent of my miscarriages. The difference was that with my miscarriages, I mourned the loss of what could have been. With Faith, I mourned the loss of what already was.

CHAPTER 13
January 2009

The flight was packed. A toddler screamed somewhere behind me, but it didn't faze me at all. *Not my kid, not my problem.* Besides, I'd been there, done that.

I reclined my seat, careful not to encroach on the leg room of the passenger behind me, and flipped open my book. *The Kite Runner* had been collecting dust since I'd received it as a birthday gift nearly a year ago. I couldn't remember the last time I'd read an entire book. I resolved to add reading to my list of goals for the new year.

In the weeks following Faith's departure, Jack had been especially attentive. I knew he was fearful of losing me again to the darkness of depression, but I wasn't worried. The miscarriage, painful though it was, had forced me to see things in my life that I'd never noticed before or had chosen to ignore. I'd been so wrapped up in an obsessive cycle of pregnancy, nursing, and mothering that I'd lost myself somewhere along the way. Perhaps my introversion and isolation had been early warning signs of depression. Perhaps my miscarriage and subsequent therapy sessions had actually *saved* me from falling into an even darker and more dangerous abyss.

A round-trip ticket to Mobile had been my Christmas gift from Jack and the girls. It was the most thoughtful and perfect gift I could have imagined. I hadn't been that excited on Christmas morning since Santa brought me an Atari when I was seven years old. I was like Charlie receiving a golden ticket to the chocolate factory, only better. Not only was I going to see Faith, but I would also get to escape to warmer climes during the thick of Maryland's bone-chilling winter.

After four ridiculously relaxing hours, including a stopover in Charlotte, the plane touched down in Mobile. I'd left my laptop nestled in my shoulder bag and allowed myself to get lost in my book instead of hammering out my columns that were due next week. The CDC had recently published new guidelines regarding children's physical activity, and one newspaper editor—considering the topic timely to coincide with the current spate of New Year's resolutions—was particularly keen on receiving my article in time to run in next week's edition. As far as I was concerned, New Year's had already come and gone, and I would still have time to submit the piece before my deadline after I got home. So for now, it could wait.

I retrieved my carry-on suitcase from the overhead bin and walked at a leisurely pace up the jetway toward the exit. Following signs for ground transportation, I exited the terminal and scanned the cars idling along the curb, searching for Faith's familiar Outback.

"Anna!"

I heard Faith's voice and pivoted toward the sound. She was standing next to a matador-red Mustang convertible, smiling and waving her arms overhead, but her smile was not the joyful one I remembered. Her face was pale, and her cheeks were hollow. Her mouth and eyes were drawn at the corners. Caring for her father was clearly taking its toll. But her thin arms were as warm and welcoming as always, wrapping around my neck in a big hug. "It's so good to see ya! Thanks for coming."

"Are you kidding? I couldn't wait to get here!"

"It was so sweet of Jack and the girls to spare ya for a few days. He's one of the good ones, ya know."

"The best," I agreed. "Nice car, by the way."

"You like? It was my gift to myself when I moved back to Mobile. Besides, you only live once, right?" She popped the trunk and struggled to lift my suitcase.

"Here, let me help." I relieved her of the bag and deposited it into the trunk.

"Well, let's get on home and get ya settled. I'm excited for ya to meet my daddy." Faith's cheerful voice was incongruous with the way she gripped the steering wheel tightly and pressed her lips into a thin white line.

"How is he?" I ventured.

"Good days and bad. But I'm glad I can be here to help."

It was a bright, sunny day in Mobile, with temperatures hovering just above sixty degrees, not quite warm enough for shorts or riding with the convertible top down, but it was a welcome change from the biting cold and freezing temperatures at home. I peeled off my fleece sweatshirt and rolled down the window, enjoying the feel of the warm sun on my bare arm.

"Nice, huh?" Faith asked with a laugh. "I'd forgotten how much I love the South."

Faith's father still lived in the same house where she had grown up, a handsome three-bedroom rancher on a quiet cul-de-sac dotted with sweetgum and hickory trees. Four white wooden rockers graced the front porch, upon which a gray tabby lounged, meticulously licking her paws.

"Home sweet home, Alabama!" Faith cheered as we climbed out of the car.

I retrieved my suitcase from the trunk and ascended three narrow steps to the porch. As we crossed the threshold into a comfortably furnished living room, I was greeted by a delectable aroma that made my mouth water. "What is that delicious smell?"

An older woman with snowy-white hair shuffled into the room. "Homemade apple pie," she said.

"Hey, Mabel," Faith said, greeting the woman with a kiss on the cheek. "This here's my friend Anna. How's Daddy doing?"

"Nice to meet ya, dear," Mabel warbled in a Deep South accent to match Faith's. She smiled and patted my arm. Plum-hued lipstick stained her front teeth. "He's taking a nap. But he did call me June again today." Mabel sighed. "I think my being here's upsetting him."

I shot Faith a quizzical look.

"June was Daddy's sister," she explained. "She died when they were teenagers. Hit by a car while riding her bike."

"That's awful. I'm so sorry."

"It's all right. It was a long time ago. Daddy never spoke of it until recently, though." Faith frowned and turned back to Mabel. "Thanks a ton, Mabes. I really do appreciate it. Will you stay and have lunch with us?"

"I'm afraid I can't today. I'm off to market to pick up some nibbles for my bridge game tonight." Mabel's eyes widened slightly and went misty as she gathered her large rose-colored handbag and a light floral-print jacket. "You young ladies enjoy." Mabel sniffed and closed the screen door behind her.

"I've known Mabel since I was a little girl," Faith explained. "She and my mama were the best of friends. They played bridge together for years before my mama passed."

"Oh." I didn't know what else to say. My own parents were healthy and thriving. My dad had done very well for himself in the Boatel business. A week earlier, they'd departed from Miami—where they snowbirded during the winter months—for a six-month cruise that would take them from Columbia and Aruba to

Africa, Sri Lanka, India, the South Pacific, and Australia before arriving in San Francisco. From there, they would travel to Seattle to spend a month with Jeff and his fiancé, Amy. I made a mental note to check the calendar and see if it might be feasible to fly out to Seattle to meet up with them. Not only had my parents been busy traveling the world, but it had been ages since I'd seen Jeff. Faith's circumstances were reminding me that family was precious and life was short. Tomorrow was never a guarantee.

"So!" Faith rallied, clapping her hands, her voice full of false cheer. "I know ya don't eat land-dwellin' meat, so how 'bout some tuna salad on rye?"

"Sounds perfect. I'm starved!"

I left my suitcase at the foot of the stairs and followed Faith into a cozy kitchen that was reminiscent of a fifties-style diner with its checkered tile floor and stark white countertops. Four metal chairs with red vinyl seats encircled a small round table that basked in the sunlight streaming in through a picture window.

Faith retrieved the tuna salad from the refrigerator and dished a heaping spoonful onto a slice of toasted rye. She filled two tall glasses with iced sweet tea and joined me at the table, where a small vase of daisies sat between us.

I took a huge bite, and my stomach rumbled gratefully. "This is delicious!"

"Why, thank you," Faith replied, taking a small, delicate bite of her own sandwich.

I eyed her suspiciously. "You've lost weight." Faith had always been trim and athletic without an ounce to spare. Now she just appeared gaunt.

"It's been a little crazy 'round here—moving in with Daddy, starting a new job..."

"I'm sure it's been hard, seeing your daddy this way."

Faith frowned, sniffling, and I covered her thin hand with mine.

"He's not good." She reached for a tissue and dabbed at her eyes. "Sleeping's the only thing that gives him any peace. It's the only time he's not feeling scared or confused. The worst part is that he was so happy to see me just a few months ago, and now he's startled when I walk into the room, like he doesn't even remember who I am."

"I'm so sorry, Faith. I wish there was something I could do."

"Just ya being here helps. And believe me, we're not gonna sit around moping. We're gonna have us some fun." She suddenly brightened. "I have a surprise." Her mood shifted so quickly, it was hard to keep up. Faith disappeared from the kitchen, and when she reemerged, she was carrying an envelope with a green ribbon tied around it.

"Faith!" I scolded. "We agreed, no presents."

"Well, this here's a gift for the both of us, compliments of my wonderful new colleagues."

Curious, I tore open the envelope and withdrew a glossy color brochure for a condominium complex in Gulf Shores.

"So? Whaddaya think? Pretty sweet, ain't it?"

"You mean we're going *here*?" I asked, waving the brochure in the air. "This weekend?" I was simultaneously excited and perplexed by the generous gesture. A weekend at the beach was always welcome, but I'd been looking forward to seeing Mobile and exploring Faith's hometown with her. Besides, Faith seemed exhausted. I would have expected traveling to be the last thing on her mind. But I'd been excited to escape from my normal routine. Maybe Faith needed to get away too.

"Of course, silly. Surprise! Or Merry Christmas, or whatever you wanna call it. We're getting the hell outta Dodge for a few days."

"But what about—"

"Daddy's gonna be fine. I've arranged for a nurse to stay with him, and Mabel will be stopping by, too, so we're all set."

I eyed Faith carefully. "Are you sure you're up for it?"

Faith stood with her arms akimbo and jutted her chin. "What do you mean?"

"It's just... you look tired. I know you have your hands full here, but I hope you're making time to take care of yourself too."

Faith dropped her thin arms to her sides and let out an exasperated huff. "Of course I am."

"Have you seen a doctor?"

At this, Faith let out a ragged chuckle. "Girl, I don't need no doctor. I'm up to my *eyeballs* in doctors with Daddy. Besides, I'm finer than frog hair split four ways." She leaned across the table, plucked two apples from the fruit bowl, and tossed one at me. "As my grandmama always said, an apple a day keeps the doctor away." She winked and sank her teeth into the fruit. "Now just be gracious and say thank you already."

"Thank you." I ducked my head and bit into my own apple. "It's an awesome gift. But I hope you didn't spend a lot of money."

"Not a red cent. My boss owns a condo in that there building and lets us girls use it any ol' time we want. She claims it's good for staff morale and whatnot. I'd have to agree, wouldn't you?" Faith didn't wait for my answer before rambling on. "As soon as I heard you were coming, I went right to the book to sign us up and thanked my lucky stars this here weekend wasn't taken."

I couldn't help but laugh at how much more pronounced Faith's Southern drawl had become since she'd moved back to Alabama. "Well then, I guess we're going to Gulf Shores!"

I PROPPED MY BARE FEET on the dash and let my wind-whipped hair lash my face as we drove to the resort town of Gulf Shores. Faith popped in a Jimmy Buffett CD, and we sang along at the top of our lungs, badly off-key, caterwauling about cheeseburgers and latitudes and volcanoes.

An hour after leaving Mobile, Faith wheeled the Mustang into a large covered parking area beneath a gleaming white building. Our two-bedroom oceanfront condo was comfortably furnished in a tropical theme, all white wicker and palm trees. The first thing we did upon arrival was change into running gear and head out for a five-mile run on a paved path parallel to the sea. For the final mile, we shed our shoes and strolled along the water's edge, our toes sinking into the sand as the brisk Gulf nipped at our ankles.

Faith sighed. "I needed this."

"Me too," I agreed. Warmth and sunshine—and spending time with Faith—were always good for the soul. "What do you want to do when we get back?"

"I vote for beer and hot tub before heading out to dinner."

"Excellent plan." I silently hoped I would fit into the bathing suit Faith had loaned me for the trip.

"Race you back to the condo!" Faith challenged.

"You're on!"

Three hours later, our limbs were soft from the hour-long, post-run soak we'd enjoyed while sipping Coronas with lime. Once we were freshly showered, we strolled along a boardwalk lined with an eclectic mix of shops filled with trendy beachwear and old-school kitsch. The early evening air was cool and dense, and the light Gulf breeze raised goose bumps on my skin.

We ducked into a lively Mexican restaurant and, within minutes, were feasting on flaky tortilla chips and chunky homemade guacamole. For dinner, I ordered fish tacos, and Faith chose spicy chicken enchiladas. We were on our second pitcher of sangria when a high-pitched Southern twang rang out.

"Well, I'll be! If it ain't Faith Montgomery!"

A tall brunette made a beeline for our table. Her lips and fingernails were painted a bright shade of coral, and her cleavage and wrists were adorned with thick strands of beaded jewelry. I could hear her jangling approach from several tables away. In her perfumed wake followed an equally tall, rail-thin blonde with close-cropped hair, wearing jeans and a tight white T-shirt.

"Emmaline?" Faith asked, her brown eyes popping wide with surprise. She stood to greet the new arrivals.

"How the hell are ya?" the brunette woman asked, her voice rising and falling in exaggerated octaves.

"I'm fine," Faith replied. "And it's Faith Barrows now."

"You're married?" The brunette looked skeptically at Faith's naked ring finger.

"Divorced."

The woman gave Faith a knowing smile before pulling her in for a hug. Then she held Faith at arm's length. "Let me take a gander at you! Aren't you just a sight for sore eyes! And as beautiful as ever, I must say!"

Faith gracefully pivoted from the woman's enthusiastic grip. "This is my friend Anna Wells. She's visiting from Maryland."

"Oh, good gracious me, where are my manners?" The woman fixed me with her bright-green gaze and extended her hand, bracelets jangling. "I'm Emmaline."

"Nice to meet you," I replied, shaking Emmaline's hand. For such a large woman, her grip was surprisingly dainty.

"And this here's my girlfriend, Carla." Emmaline gestured toward the Annie Lennox lookalike, who was leaning against the wall, examining her cuticles.

"Hey," Carla responded with a half-hearted wave of her thin, pale hand.

"Please, won't you join us?" Faith invited, tapping into her deep-seated Southern manners. "We were just about to order another pitcher of sangria."

"It sure as heck would be great to catch up with ya," Emmaline declared, taking a seat next to Faith. Carla sauntered over to the table and settled into the chair opposite Emmaline. A brief, awkward silence descended.

Irrational jealousy pinched my stomach. I was intrigued by these new arrivals, but I was also enjoying having Faith to myself. Now that she'd moved away, time with her was precious. I wasn't sure I wanted to share. But with Emmaline and Carla now seated—effectively turning our table for two into a four-top—I knew I had to put on my big-girl pants and play nice. "How do you two know each other?" I asked Faith, dunking a tortilla chip into the heaping bowl of guac.

"Emmaline and I went to high school together. Hadn't seen each other in years—"

"Until she showed her sweet face at our reunion," Emmaline cut in.

"You never told me you went to your reunion!" I scolded, shooting Faith an accusing glare.

"Ya never asked."

My own reunion was now a mere five months away. The initial save-the-date had soon morphed into an official Evite, according to recent emails from the reunion planner. I'd asked Jack if he wanted to go, but he was completely ambivalent about the whole thing. "Whatever you decide is fine with me," he'd said. But I was still on the fence.

"Was it some sort of secret?" Carla inquired, her first contribution to the discussion.

"I think we were the ones with a secret!" Emmaline guffawed and winked playfully at Carla, who rolled her eyes.

"Emmaline went to the reunion with her husband," Faith confided in a hushed voice.

"Ex-husband," Emmaline corrected.

"And Carla arrived on her own, without a date," Faith continued.

"And the rest is history!" Emmaline exclaimed, reaching across the table to grasp Carla's pale hands.

My head bounced back and forth between Faith and Emmaline like I was watching a tennis match.

"Anna here has a reunion coming up this summer," Faith said, peering at me over the salted rim of her glass. Though a margarita with salt was fairly common, Faith was the only person I knew who liked her sangria salted.

"Are you gonna go?" Carla asked.

"Oooh, you should definitely go," Emmaline interjected before taking a delicate sip of her sangria.

"I don't know." I shrugged. "It just seems pointless." I ran my finger around the salt-free rim of my glass. "I haven't kept in touch with anyone from high school." I could feel my words starting to slur as the sangria worked its way into my bloodstream.

"But it's so much fun!" Emmaline exclaimed, clapping her hands.

"And it's her twentieth," Faith volunteered.

"Your twentieth? That's like a rite of passage. A milestone!"

"That's what I told her," Faith said, her eyelids starting to droop. Her cheeks were slightly flushed from the alcohol, a stark contrast to her overall pallor.

"You might regret it if you don't go," Carla added.

"I told her that too. But she's stubborn, ya know?"

"I'm not stubborn!"

"Well, bless her heart. Ain't she just the cutest thing when she's angry?" Emmaline teased.

"I'm not angry!" I huffed. "I'm just... undecided."

"Well, you'd better get on it, missy. You don't wanna miss the boat on this one, trust me," Emmaline said, helping herself to our chips.

I leaned back in my chair and crossed my arms as Faith and Emmaline lapsed into excited gossip, commonly known in the South as "spilling the tea." Carla tapped her foot in time to the beat of "La Bamba," which was being played by a mariachi band squeezed into a dark corner of the crowded room.

Emmaline and Carla were undoubtedly entertaining, but I found myself wishing they hadn't intruded on my evening with Faith. I also wasn't sure I welcomed Emmaline's bossy directive about my reunion, and I was even less thrilled that her words had robbed me of my carefree state of mind. I sipped my drink and silently weighed the pros and cons of attending my reunion... and of possibly seeing Lia again. The mere thought made my pulse race. I drained the rest of my glass and reached for the pitcher to pour myself another.

WE STUMBLED INTO THE condo, and Faith made a beeline for the sink. She filled a glass with water, chugged it, and filled it again. "You want?" she asked, pointing at her glass.

"Please!" I called, racing for the bathroom and making it just in time. I could hear Faith retrieving a second glass from the cabinet, the rattle of the ice maker as it whirred to life, and the clinking of cubes dropping into the glass.

When I returned to the kitchen, we both leaned against the counter, hydrating in companionable silence. "So what's the deal with Emmaline and Carla?" I asked, curious to know more about the interesting pair.

"Emmaline and I go way back," Faith reflected. "We were in grade school together but never ran in the same circles, ya know? She was real popular in high school—cheerleading captain, homecoming queen, the whole bit. Went on to be a sorority girl at Auburn, had a fling with one of her professors, and eloped with him after graduation—much to her parents' dismay, I might add. The way Emmaline tells it, she and her husband were already on the outs when she bumped into Carla at the reunion. Rumor has it the two of 'em got it on in a bathroom stall. Really set tongues a-wagging down here. Emmaline up and divorced her husband soon after and has been with Carla ever since. It was all terribly scandalous."

"Well, that settles it. If random hookups and scandalizing the neighbors are par for the course at reunions, count me out. I like my utterly boring suburban life just fine, thank you."

Faith chuckled. "Oh, don't be such a stick in the mud. You don't have to be the one *causing* the scandal. Just go and be entertained by it." Her laughter dissolved into a body-wracking cough.

I rubbed her back until the coughing subsided. When she looked up, I was startled by the puffy bluish circles that shadowed her rheumy eyes. "Maybe the whole 'apple a day' thing isn't doing the trick."

"All I'm saying," Faith continued in a rasp, ignoring my subtle nudge toward seeing a doctor, "is that if you go to your reunion, you might be surprised how much people have changed over the years. At the very least, it'll be a fun night of people-watching for you and Jack."

I pursed my lips, considering this possibility. "True."

"Besides, people are supposed to come in and out of our lives at different times for different reasons." Faith held my gaze for a long time before standing and stretching her arms overhead. "Well, I for one am ready to get outta these clothes and into my jammies."

As Faith retreated to her room to change, a sudden longing for Jack and the girls drew me to my laptop, which was still sitting open on the kitchen table. I opened my email and wasn't surprised to see twenty-six messages. My inbox was constantly overflowing with messages from editors as well as newsletters and announcements from the girls' schools and sports teams. I began sorting through them until I got to one from Jack that made my heart leap. I devoured his words, my cheeks flaming at the suggestive prose.

"Well, my, my!" Faith teased, unabashedly peeking over my shoulder.

"Faith!" I scolded. "This is private."

"I'll say!" She pulled out a chair and joined me at the table. "The only messages I ever saw like that were the ones my dickhead ex-husband used to send his slutty little girlfriend." Faith's rueful smile softened the sharp edges of her words. She was not a bitter person, not one to hold a grudge. "Those kinda feelings will suck the soul right outta ya," she'd once said.

I saved the message from Jack. Clearly, I wouldn't be able to send a suitable reply with Faith sitting beside me. The last email in my inbox was from Tammy Adams, the reunion planner. I opened the attachment, and a graduation-themed Evite with the number twenty superimposed over a blue cap and gown filled the screen.

"Well, this sure is serendipitous," Faith said, scooting her chair closer. "Well?" She impatiently drummed her fingertips on the tabletop.

"I told you," I replied, annoyance creeping into my voice. "I haven't decided."

"Well, why the hell not, Anna? Surely Emmaline and Carla are example enough as to how much people can change in twenty years. It'll be a hoot! You should go."

I made a noncommittal shrug and let out a long sigh, which sent the pen atop my notebook rolling across the table. I tried to grab for it, but my arm seemed to move in slow motion, my reflexes hindered by the copious amounts of sangria I'd consumed. The pen pitched off the edge of the table and onto the floor. As I bent to retrieve it, the room swayed slightly.

"Easy there, girly," Faith said, but her words were accompanied by a snort.

I was suddenly hysterical, consumed by peals of riotous laughter. The two of us giggled and laughed and snorted for no reason at all until tears were streaming down our faces. I grasped my aching belly, aware on some level that I was in the throes of the most amazing ab workout of my life, and gasped for air, pleading with Faith to put an end to the madness, which only made us laugh harder. When my daughters got to laughing like that, one of them inevitably peed their pants. The notion had a sudden sobering effect. My pelvic floor muscles were not what they used to be after pushing three babies into the world. I hadn't been able to jump rope without soaking my drawers since Helene was born.

"You're just afraid of seeing that Lia girl again, aren't ya, ya chicken?" Faith blurted.

"I am not!" But the idea of seeing Lia again admittedly filled me with loathing. I sometimes imagined what it would be like to come face-to-face with her. I envisioned trying to muster fake smiles and forced pleasantries while battling the hostile feelings that roiled inside of me. The possibility that she might still wield that much power over my emotions was disconcerting.

"Well then, whatcha waiting for?" Faith challenged, gesturing toward my laptop.

I drew in a deep breath and jutted my chin defiantly. "Fine." With a quick jerk of my hand, I guided the mouse to the green rectangle that read, Like, Totally! in response to the question, *Will you attend this event?* and then froze. One hundred seven people had already confirmed. What if Lia was one of them? I closed my eyes. I couldn't bear to look.

"Go on," Faith prodded, nudging my arm with her elbow.

I could feel my resolve faltering as I eyed my alternatives: Undecided and Totally Lame. Before I could lose my nerve altogether, I abruptly clicked the green box and yanked my hand back as if bitten.

"See, that wasn't so hard now, was it?" Faith teased, a huge, satisfied grin on her face.

I narrowed my eyes and wondered yet again why Faith was so insistent that I attend my reunion.

Ping! A new message arrived in my inbox. I hesitated, wondering if it might be Jack sending another saucy email, but decided to chance it. The message was from Tammy Adams, thanking me for my RSVP and sending a link to join the BVHS Class of 1989 Facebook page.

"Ooh, that sounds interesting," Faith said, looking over my shoulder again. "Let's check it out."

"I dunno, Faith. I'm pretty tired."

"Girl! My hot flashes have more stamina than you!"

"You do not have hot flashes," I protested, calling Faith on her lame exaggeration.

Faith cocked her head and contorted her face. Her raised eyebrows and pursed lips created a *"maybe I do, and maybe I don't"* expression. "C'mon. It'll be fun."

I had to admit, I was intrigued. "What the hell." I clicked on the link and held my breath as a stream of dialogue, comments, and pictures filled the screen. Tammy's name appeared next to a tiny thumbnail of two freckle-faced, ginger-haired boys. I clicked on her personal page, which detailed her education, employment history, and current city, and provided links to her photo albums. Within minutes, I was privy to all the recent highlights of Tammy's life. She and her family had vacationed at Walt Disney World that summer. For her birthday, they had dined at The Cheesecake Factory. And she and her husband, Donald, had celebrated their twelfth anniversary by taking a weekend trip to Virginia Beach.

Facebook virgin that I was, the wealth of information I was able to obtain with the click of a mouse was both frightening and mesmerizing. It seemed similar to rubbernecking at the scene of an accident—I knew I shouldn't be looking, but it was impossible not to.

I exhaled, long and slow, and leaned closer to the screen. Tammy had not changed much since high school. She was still a large girl with an infectious grin and bright-red hair, but that fleeting moment of recognition was tainted by the realization that I was gazing at a complete stranger. The pictures and tidbits of information conspired to create a false sense of knowing someone who, in truth, I didn't really know at all—not now and not even in high school. The juxtaposition of knowing and not knowing was chilling, uncomfortable.

"Looks like a fun girl!" Faith commented, though I found myself thinking, *How would I know?*

I navigated to the BVHS Class of 1989 home page and, under a random banner of pictures, saw there were ninety-four members. I clicked on the member link, and the screen filled with faces and names of people I once knew. I was fascinated by the images staring back at me, faces simultaneously familiar and foreign. It was like recognizing someone at a distance then realizing, as they drew closer, that they were not who they appeared to be.

My eyes swept over the page, and my body slumped against the chair when I realized Lia's face was not among the images. Mostly, I felt relieved, as if I'd dodged a bullet. But a pang of disappointment also gnawed at my gut. I shrugged and chalked it up to morbid curiosity. Part of me was dying to know where she was and what she was doing. *Is she married? Does she have kids? What does she look like? Will I even recognize her anymore?* Some people on the screen looked exactly the same as I remembered. Others, sporting glasses, wrinkles, and receding hairlines, appeared to have aged far beyond our nearly forty years. Hair colors had changed, waistlines had expanded, noses had shortened, and breasts had been cartoonishly augmented, but one thing always remained the same: the eyes. The windows to the soul.

I began choosing classmates at random and felt a voyeuristic rush at my freedom to anonymously browse through people's lives, glimpsing the worlds they'd created for themselves. My chest swelled with compassion and goodwill toward these people that I suddenly felt connected to, as if glimpsing was akin to knowing.

But in the next instant, like a balloon popped with a pin, the bubble burst, leaving me deflated with regret and the wilting certainty that I didn't know these people at all. It had been too long. I'd simply been drawn in for the moment, swept up in the excitement, wooed by the access I had to information I really had no right to know, despite people's willingness to post it publicly.

"So, is she going?" Faith asked.

With the deadline to reply quickly approaching, and Lia not exactly being known for her dependability or punctuality, it seemed highly unlikely she would be going. "No."

Faith shot me a half-lidded sideways glance. "Well, that's a good thing. Right?"

"Sure, whatever. It really doesn't matter." I gave a dismissive wave of my hand and closed my laptop. Lia had tossed our friendship away like yesterday's garbage, cast me aside without explanation, and waltzed off without looking back. I'd spent the second half of my freshman year at college tending the wounds she'd inflicted, cleansing them with tears and sealing them with a thick layer of protection against further injury. So as I tried to convince Faith—and myself—that I was happy Lia was not going to the reunion, a small kernel of regret had embedded itself in the soft lining of my being. The mixture of conflicting emotions created a sickening stew in my gut. Or maybe it was the sangria.

"You never did tell me what happened between you two."

"It's a long story."

"We've got nothing but time, sugar." Faith sauntered to the sofa, nestled into the soft cushions, and propped her fuzzy slipper-clad feet on the table. "Why don't ya change into your jammies and tell Auntie Faith all about it."

It wasn't a request. The therapist in Faith was determined to talk it out and get to the bottom of things. I was exhausted but open to wading through the emotional stew with Faith. It was nice to finally have a girlfriend to confide in.

I bobbed my head and stumbled toward my room, bumping my shoulder against the wall along the way. When I returned, dressed in yoga pants, a tank top, and my favorite hoodie, I could smell the salty breath of the sea and feel its cool embrace as the air crept into our condo through the open balcony door. Faith's head was tipped back against the cushions, her eyes closed as she listened to the soothing rush and retreat of the water. On the table in front of her stood two glasses filled with a dark-crimson liquid.

"That better be grape juice," I opined, indicating the glasses.

Faith sat up, laughing. "'Course not. It's cabernet. You know, hair o' the dog? My grandmama swore by it." She took a hearty sip to prove her point.

The mere sight of the wine made my stomach clench. I retreated to the kitchen, refilled my water glass, and retrieved a bag of pretzels. I upended half of the thick sourdough twists into a fish-shaped plastic bowl and tucked it into the crook of my arm.

"I don't know 'bout your grandma, but my idea of a preemptive hangover strike involves lots of water and salty snacks." I pushed Faith's feet aside and deposited the fish bowl onto the table.

Faith snatched several pretzels from the bowl. "Mmm, good choice," she mumbled through a mouthful. "So, spill it, sister."

I let out a long, slow breath. "In a nutshell? Lia hurt me, flat-out abandoned me, and walked out on our friendship without a word, and not once in almost twenty years has she so much as called or written. Nothing. Nada."

Faith raised an eyebrow and silently sipped her wine.

"All I know is that once we went to college, she started avoiding me—wouldn't return my calls, wouldn't see me—and then she was just... gone. I've never felt so... disposable. It was a dark chapter in my life, one I'd just as soon forget."

"But it doesn't make sense. Something must have happened."

"I told you, I have no idea, which is partly why it hurt so much."

Faith plucked another pretzel from the bowl. "Did you try to find her?"

"When I got home for winter break, I went to the marina where she used to live, and she wasn't there. Strangers were living on her boat. They had no idea who Lia was. So I went into the marina restaurant, and the bartender told me Lia had come in to collect her last check and left." I shrugged and frowned. "That was all anyone knew."

"What about before she disappeared? What's the story—*her* story?" Faith popped a pretzel into her mouth and watched me intently, expectantly, as her jaw worked the pretzel like a cow chewing her cud.

"Well, she never knew her father. Her mother was an irresponsible flake who slept with Lia's first boyfriend to prove, in some twisted, sadistic way, that men were scum and only wanted sex."

"Wow!" Faith exhaled in a long, low whistle. "I hope she had a good therapist." Her words were flippant, but her face had gone from white to gray as she gulped her wine while the abandoned water glass was leaving a wet ring on the table. She flicked her fingernail against the pretzel in her hands, knocking fat grains of salt to the floor.

"On that note, I know it's a huge bomb to drop, but I'm exhausted." I made an unsuccessful attempt to stifle a sudden yawn before surrendering to the fatigue that enveloped me.

"It's one helluva bomb, all right, but I'm with ya. Stick a fork in me. I'm done."

I leaned over and gave Faith a sloppy hug. The tangy smell of fajitas clung to her hair. "Thanks for a fun night out."

"Don't menshion it," she slurred, rising from her chair to follow me down the hall to her room.

It was 2:43 in the morning. I was drunk, bone tired, and emotionally weary. My limbs felt too heavy to manage the small task of brushing my teeth. Thankfully, I was already in my pajamas. I took two steps into the bedroom and collapsed onto the bed—the seashell-motif comforter scratchy against my cheek—and had fitful dreams about Lia.

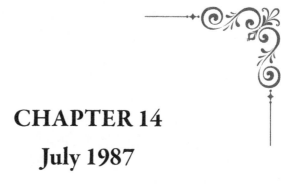

CHAPTER 14

July 1987

Lia lived, literally, on the water. When her mother, Rose, could no longer afford the rent on their duplex, she and Lia had moved into a decrepit houseboat docked at Harris Point Marina, a ramshackle establishment located on a murky inlet off the Severn.

It was a muggy, late-July afternoon when I pulled into the parking lot at Harris Point. Gravel and seashells crunched beneath my white Sperry knockoffs as I walked toward the crumbling dock. I resisted the urge to clamp my hand over my nose—the air enveloping the marina was thick with the smell of fish, garbage, and gasoline.

"It's about time you got here!" Lia bellowed from atop her boat, waving her arms overhead. She was wearing cutoff denim shorts and a halter top. Her long tangerine hair was gathered into a high ponytail.

The boat creaked gently beneath Lia's weight as she scampered from the top to meet me at the boat's bow. She unlatched a small gate, stretched out her arm, clasped my hand, and hauled me aboard.

"Nice place you got here," I said, sweeping my eyes over the vessel.

"Shut up!" Lia replied, nudging me playfully.

"No, I mean it. It's so cool that you live on a boat!"

"It's not as cool as it seems," Lia admitted, handing me an open, half-eaten box of Bugles. "And the smell! Ugh!" She wrinkled her crooked little nose. "*Eau de marina.*"

I pressed my lips into a firm line, refusing to confirm or deny her assessment.

"C'mon. I'll give you the grand tour." From the bow, Lia opened a sliding glass door and stepped into the boat's stifling interior. To the left was a captain's chair. The brown leather seat was faded and torn.

"Do you take it out on the river?"

"Hell no! This hunk o' junk hasn't left the dock in two decades."

Further along the starboard side was a kitchenette with a small sink and cooktop. A mini refrigerator was tucked beneath the countertop, and a tiny sliding window was positioned above the sink. A small clip-on fan, whirring uselessly, was attached to the curtain rod. The port side contained a cramped U-shaped seating area with a removable table. Beyond the kitchen, Lia showed me the "head," a miniscule bathroom with a handheld shower nozzle suspended from the opposite wall.

"So you can shit and shower at the same time," Lia deadpanned, demonstrating the pumping action required to flush the toilet. "And don't throw your pads or tampons in there. That'll totally screw us over."

I nodded and swallowed audibly. An accordion-style door at the end of the narrow hallway opened to reveal a double-decker rack.

"Ta da!" Lia cheered, opening the door to the boat's sleeping quarters, which she shared with Rose. The bedroom consisted of two padded sleeping areas on the bottom, and two more aloft—miniature bunk beds. On the floor, another padded piece leaned on its side.

"What's that for?"

Lia expertly righted the triangular insert and wedged it into the space between the two lower beds, creating one larger sleeping area. "Comes in handy," she said with a knowing wink.

"Hopefully, by that, you mean it gives you more room to stretch out."

"Sure, whatever," Lia said with a shrug, indulging me. She knew I considered her promiscuous behavior reckless and not necessarily in her best interest. I cared about Lia, but she'd made it clear that this particular brand of caring was unwelcome. As far as Lia was concerned, we simply had to agree to disagree on that topic.

Two small, square-shaped windows and one overhead pop-up hatch were the only sources of light or air in the tiny room. Claustrophobia was kicking in, so I was relieved when Lia led us back to the kitchen. The boat was a nice enough place to visit—interesting and unique—but I was glad I didn't live there.

"And that's all, folks," Lia said, opening the fridge. She tossed me a Cherry Coke and grabbed a can of Mountain Dew for herself then popped the top and took a long swig.

"No AC?" I asked.

"A window unit, but it doesn't work. Rose hasn't bothered to have it fixed. And why should she? She's never here."

"Where is she now?" It was one o'clock on a Saturday afternoon.

Lia shrugged. "Work, I guess."

"Where does she work?" I took a long swig of my soda, savoring the sweet, fizzy sensation of the lukewarm liquid on my tongue. Lia never wanted to talk about her mother, and I knew she was embarrassed by the way they lived, so it was a huge step forward in our relationship that she had invited me to her boat.

"The lawn and garden shop. She's some kind of plant specialist. But weed is the only plant I've ever known her to specialize in." She snorted and shook her head. "Let's go above deck. It's stifling in here." Lia looped around to the port side of the boat and climbed a ladder to the upper deck. I followed suit, giving the rusty ladder a good tug to make sure it would hold before I began climbing.

Up top, Lia unfolded two beach chairs. From a canvas bag, she produced two ratty towels and draped one over each chair. I settled into the chair covered with a faded, rainbow-striped towel, closed my eyes, and tipped my face toward the sun. Foul fishy smells aside, it was pure bliss, and the view from the marina was sensational. Sparkling water and bright afternoon sunshine bathed the shoreline in dappled light. Lia sat beside me and positioned the box of Bugles between us. We munched in companionable silence, listening to the clank of metal beating against sailboat masts and the caw of seagulls as they flapped overhead.

"My aunt is the only reason we can even afford this place," Lia muttered, her bitter words bruising the serenity. "She sends money when she can, for my birthday and holidays, but if I don't get my hands on it first, Rose blows it all on pot. Or uses it to fund her spontaneous road trips and spiritual retreats." As if the mere mention of her name conjured the woman herself, Rose suddenly appeared on the dock. "Speak of the devil," Lia grumbled.

"Did I hear someone say pot?" Rose asked and chuckled. The sound of her laugh was uncannily similar to Lia's. She unlatched the gate and moseyed onto the boat, turning sideways to fit her wide hips through the narrow space.

Lia scowled at her mother. "Hi, Rose. Nice of you to show your face."

"Aren't you gonna introduce me to your friend?"

Lia reluctantly stood and motioned for me to follow. A portly, flame-haired woman stood, swaying slightly, on the bow. The spaghetti straps of her sundress accentuated her meaty arms, and the thin fabric clung to her undulating flesh.

At the sight of her, my mind flashed back to the horrific tale Lia had told me a few months ago about her mother. Lia and I had just had our first fight. We'd gone on a double date with two boys from another school, and the boy Lia had set her sights on—the cute one, of course—was interested in me, a turn of events that surprised us both. Lia responded by giving me the cold shoulder at school, saying everything was fine but making it clear, by her actions, that it wasn't. I knew her ego was bruised, but I didn't deserve to be treated like that. I hadn't done anything wrong. So after a few days of receiving the silent treatment, I waited for her in the school courtyard and confronted her on the way to lunch. At first, I thought she was going to ignore me and keep walking. Instead, her face crumpled, and she dropped a bomb I'd never seen coming. It was her way of making me understand her need to be chosen and to be the center of attention, her need to be in control, to be loved.

"There was this boy," Lia said, leaning against the brick courtyard wall, her voice breaking. "I met him in eighth grade. He was a junior, and he was totally beautiful and reckless, a troublemaker. He told me I was the prettiest girl he'd ever seen, and he asked me to be his girlfriend."

"What did your mom say about you dating a high school guy?"

Lia gave a derisive snort. "Rose? She doesn't have a motherly bone in her body. But I started dating Tony, and suddenly she was interested in my life. She told me Tony was no good for me, which only made me want him more, of course. So I started sneaking around, seeing Tony behind her back. And he started pressuring me to have sex. He said if I wouldn't do it, there were plenty of other girls who would. But I put him off, made excuses. I was scared. I'd never had sex before." She sat down in the grass and rested her back against the wall.

I sat down beside her. Still a virgin myself, I hung on Lia's every word. "So, did you?" I asked, breathless.

Lia snorted and shook her head. The lunch bell had rung, and the courtyard was quiet and empty, save for the sound of a robin chirping in a nearby tree. "Rose forgot my fourteenth birthday. She actually left for work the night before and didn't come home for two days, which wasn't unusual, but she'd never forgotten my birthday. I ran straight to Tony, and we did it in the back seat of his car. Afterward, he drove me to 7-Eleven and bought me a cherry Slurpee for my birthday. He told me he loved me, and I was stupid enough to believe him." Lia's eyes filled with tears. "We had sex a few more times, and then he just stopped calling. I heard rumors that he had a new girlfriend. I was crushed. I felt so used." She swiped at her tears with the back of her hand.

"Then one day, after school, his car was parked in front of my house. I was so happy. I thought he was there to apologize. Instead, I found him and Rose screwing in my room."

"Oh my God, Lia!" I gasped and leaned against her. "What did you do?"

"I ran outside, but I couldn't get the sounds of them having sex out of my head. I stayed out all night, climbed the fence of some golf club, and slept on a stack of lounge chairs. When I got home the next morning, Rose was sitting on the front steps, smoking a joint."

"What did she say?" I asked gently.

Lia smiled sadly. "She said, 'I told you he was no good for you.' That was it." She hung her head, and a fat tear splashed onto her acid-washed jeans, leaving a small, dark ring. My heart broke for her. "Swear you'll never tell anyone," she pleaded.

I choked back the huge lump in my throat. "I promise."

Lia's ruddy complexion had gone gray. I put my arm around her, and the girl who was known for being effusively affectionate went rigid. I pivoted to face her and held her hands instead, struggling to find the right words to console her. "It wasn't your fault,

Lia. You didn't do anything wrong." She closed her eyes, and I squeezed her hands tighter. "What your mother did was horrible. Unforgivable."

Lia snatched her hands away. "Rose was only trying to protect me." Her eyes were narrowed, her tone defensive. "She'd warned me that Tony was a loser, and she was right."

I recoiled. Lia's response was like a slap in the face. Then her defenses crumbled. She rested her forehead on my shoulder and began to sob. I wrapped my arms tightly around her and held her as she cried.

Many years would pass before I would learn that it was common for people to express extreme loyalty and love for the very people they loathed and feared, the very people that hurt them the most. In the end, we had decided that no boy was worth risking our friendship, and neither of us saw those boys from the other school again.

I shook my head and struggled to cast the memory from my mind. But as I gazed at the enormous woman before me, an unwelcome image of her naked and straddling a high school boy defiled my brain. I thought I might be sick.

"Anna, this is Rose," Lia introduced.

"Charmed," Rose said, extending a pudgy hand. When she smiled, I could see Lia in her features. They shared the same fair skin and catlike green eyes, though Rose's were currently red-rimmed.

I reluctantly returned the greeting.

"And what have you two been up to? No good, I hope!" Rose's laugh tinkled merrily, like Lia's. She stepped closer and put both hands on my shoulders. "Are you feeling ill, child? Or haven't you gotten your sea legs yet?"

My skin must have turned green at the sudden mental image of Rose atop her daughter's boyfriend.

Lia put her hands on her hips and narrowed her eyes. "Are you just getting home from work?"

"Aw, hells no!" Rose threw her head back and cackled. "Just making a pit stop. Off to St. Mary's City. Charlie Daniels is in concert tonight," she rasped. "Now where'd you stash the cash from Auntie Ivy?" Rose raised one ruddy eyebrow, an exact replica of Lia's trademark expression.

"Rent's due next week," Lia argued.

"And Harris pays you on Friday, correct? Now hand it over."

On top of her AP courses and extracurriculars, Lia worked twenty hours a week at the marina. Next to her—with my standard-level classes and two four-hour shifts at the Pizza Palace—I felt like a slacker. Defeated, Lia disappeared into the cabin to retrieve the money. I wondered if I should say something—rise to her defense—but my own parents had taught me to respect adults, and I didn't feel as though it were my place to butt in to the confrontation between Lia and her mother. So I simply watched the sad and awkward dynamic unfold.

Rose gave me a triumphant smile. "Is that your hot rod parked in the lot, Annie?"

I ignored the fact that she'd gotten my name wrong. "I wouldn't exactly call it a hot—"

"Would you mind dropping me at the mall? I've got a ride to St. Mary's from there."

"Uh—"

"Thanks. You're a dear."

"After you snap a picture for us," Lia demanded, emerging from the cabin with a disposable camera in one hand and a wad of bills in the other. She handed both to Rose then slung her arm over my shoulder.

"Say weed!" Rose prompted.

I DEPOSITED ROSE IN front of the J.C. Penney, where a painted Volkswagen van awaited.

"That was... interesting," I said to Lia, who was climbing from the back seat of my Monte Carlo into the front, squeezing herself between the two ivory leather bucket seats.

"Story of my life," she muttered.

"Let's go back to the boat and order pizza. My treat." I shifted the car into drive. "Buckle up!"

Lia rolled her eyes but obliged. The traffic light turned green, and I followed the car in front of me as it made a left. "Shakedown" by Bob Segar was blasting from the radio. Lia and I were singing along. Then, suddenly, Lia screamed.

The car came out of nowhere. A brown sedan was barreling toward us. The driver was wearing a newsboy cap. All I heard was grinding metal and shattering glass. I felt the jolt of the impact and then spinning. Followed by stillness. And eerie silence.

I opened my eyes to sparkling light. Glass was everywhere. Blue-green shards rained down as I lifted my head to see Lia beside me. Her face was scratched and bleeding, and her eyes were wide as she pulled a shard of glass from her hair. I glanced at the rearview mirror and saw matching facial lacerations of my own. Time stood still. The silence pressed down upon us. Then there were sirens, shrill and screaming, cutting through the deafening hush.

I don't remember how I went from sitting in the car to sitting in the back of an ambulance, with an ice pack pressed to my forehead. Time was warped, ebbing and flowing in strange fits and starts. My foggy brain struggled to comprehend the scene. Flashing lights. Heat shimmering above the pavement. Traffic snarled in all directions. A smashed-up sedan with a hat embedded in the dazzling spiderwebbed windshield.

"That's a nasty bump you've got," a disembodied voice said. "We should take you in, have it checked out."

"No," I heard myself say. My voice sounded thin, far away.

"You really should go to the hospital."

The mangled Monte Carlo was jacked up on a concrete island. Paramedics scurried around. *Where is Lia?* "No," I repeated with more force. "I'm fine."

"So you're refusing treatment?" the voice asked, sharper now.

"I'm fine," I repeated. Then I began a new mantra: "My father's gonna kill me. Oh my God. My dad. The car!"

"Just so we're clear, if you step away from the ambulance and collapse, we are not liable." The voice was harsh, abrasive, like steel wool.

I slid down from the ambulance. My legs wobbled. I began to walk, slowly, in a daze.

A man with dried blood on his face and a bandage taped to his bald head approached. He looked confused, haunted. He'd been crying. "I'm so sorry. I didn't see you girls. Your car, it came out of nowhere. Are you all right? You poor girls..."

Then the man was gone, and my parents were there, their faces crumpled and hoary. Someone must have called them, though I didn't recall giving anyone my number. But it didn't matter. They were there.

I collapsed in their arms, my defenses crumbling. "Dad, your car," I whispered, my voice catching. "I'm so sorry about the car." I buried my face in his chest and sobbed.

He hugged me tighter. "Don't worry about the car," Dad soothed. "The car can be replaced."

"We're just glad you're okay," Mom cried, plucking shards of glass from my hair.

AN HOUR LATER, WE WERE inside the mall, sitting in a red vinyl booth and eating ice cream sundaes. Lia and I were scratched, bruised, and shaken, but otherwise okay. The adults talked in hushed tones.

"Thank God for the Monte Carlo," my mom said.

"The officer on the scene said the big, sturdy car and the steel door saved them. He said if they'd been in a smaller vehicle, they'd probably be—" Dad's voice cracked.

Mom squeezed his hand, silencing him.

Lia and I zoned out, eating—but not tasting—our sundaes as our parents droned on in reverent tones, as if they were at a funeral parlor instead of a Friendly's restaurant.

"I was on my way to St. Mary's when I heard the squeal of brakes and a loud crunch, like beer cans being stomped on," Rose explained. "And I had a bad feeling about it. The universe told me I should go back to the mall. It was divine intervention. The goddess guided me."

"Too bad your goddess didn't intervene *before* the crash," Dad lamented.

"All that matters is that the girls are okay," Mom said, giving Dad's hand another reassuring squeeze.

The waitress brought our check. I excused myself to the restroom and was shocked by my reflection. My face looked as if it had been attacked by an angry cat. Tiny bits of glass winked from my tangled hair, and a bluish golf-ball-sized lump rose from my forehead. I winced as my fingers grazed the tender flesh.

Outside the restaurant, in the mall parking lot, Rose declined my dad's offer of a ride, claiming she had a friend waiting to take them home. Lia shrugged and pulled me in for a hug, whispering, "It's fine," in my ear as we said our goodbyes.

I followed my parents to their car and gingerly climbed into the back seat. On the ride home, I tried to stay awake, but my eyelids weighed a ton.

"Maybe you shouldn't sleep yet," Mom fretted, but the pull of slumber was too powerful. I let my dreams carry me away.

"RISE AND SHINE, SLEEPYHEAD!" Faith sang as she swept into my room and twisted the blinds open. The light streamed in through the slats, and the gentle beams were like a bolt of lightning to my brain.

"Ungh." I moaned and rolled onto my stomach, pulling a pillow over my head.

"It's a beautiful morning in Gulf Shores. Time to seize the day!"

I heard a soft clink beside my head before the acrid smell of coffee hit my nostrils. My stomach did a somersault. I fought to crack open one eye—the tacky remnants of mascara had glued my lids together—and was met with the blurry porcelain image of a smiling yellow starfish on a periwinkle mug. The angry red numbers of the digital clock—7:18—seared my retinas and forced my eyes closed again. The red digits danced on the inside of my eyelids. I'd only had four and a half hours of sleep. My entire body thrummed and buzzed. Slowly and carefully, I eased myself into a sitting position. My head throbbed in protest. My mouth was foul and fuzzy, as if a small dead animal was decaying on my tongue. I chanced a tiny sip of the black coffee—anything to wash away the vile taste in my throat—and my mouth filled with saliva. I lurched to the bathroom as sweat popped out of my pores. Trembling, I sank onto the edge of the tub and rested my forehead against the cool tile.

Faith poked her head into the tiny bathroom. "You okay there, sugar? Need me to hold your hair for ya?"

No one but my mother had ever offered to do that for me. A sudden wave of tenderness toward Faith replaced my budding annoyance with her chipper mood. Apparently, she could handle her liquor much better than I could.

Bits and pieces of the previous night came floating back, and I groaned anew as I remembered that I'd accepted the reunion invite. Well, it wasn't like I'd paid a nonrefundable deposit. I could always change my reply.

"I'll be okay. I think." I stood on shaky legs. The wave of nausea subsided, and I splashed cool water on my clammy face. I brushed my hair and teeth, dumped the coffee down the drain, and tossed back three Advil before tottering toward the kitchen.

Faith had retreated to the balcony and was flipping through the pages of a *Psychology Today* magazine. Moving slowly, cautiously, afraid of upsetting the apple cart in my stomach, I toasted a cinnamon raisin bagel and topped it with a smidge of peanut butter and a few slices of banana. I hazarded a tentative bite, hoping to keep it down, and joined Faith on the balcony. She was right—it was a beautiful day. The turquoise waters of the Gulf crashed gently onto the shore. The sun shone brightly, its caressing warmth beating back the occasional cool breeze that raised goose bumps on my bare arms.

"Aren't you going to eat?" I asked Faith.

"Already did. Had a cup of coffee, went for a short meander along the beach, then came back and toasted myself a bagel while you snored away for a hundred years like Sleepin' Beauty."

"I don't snore!" I protested.

Faith smiled knowingly. "Of course ya don't. It wouldn't be ladylike."

I took another tiny test bite of the bagel, and to my relief, my stomach accepted the offering with a small, appreciative growl.

"Well, eat up, so we have time for a run before brunch."

"You can't be serious." I couldn't decide which sounded worse, the idea of running beneath the glaring sunlight or heaping piles of oily breakfast foods jiggling on my plate.

My eyes swept over Faith's attire, which had, until now, escaped my notice. She was decked out in a white visor, a white performance tee with the Savannah Rock 'N' Roll Marathon logo emblazoned on the front, and a teal running skirt. Her thick chestnut hair was swept back in a ponytail, and her beloved Asics were ziplocked onto her feet. She looked as if she'd just bounded off the cover of *Runner's World*. She was definitely serious. I was happy to see her so relaxed and chipper, a marked improvement from the haggard, stressed-out woman who'd greeted me at the airport. Escaping to Gulf Shores for a few days had been the right thing to do.

Faith flashed a wicked smile. "And here I was thinkin' *you* were the runner, not me." She laughed then changed tack, taking a more compassionate approach. "It'll make you feel better, I promise. Take the edge off a bit. Hair of a different dog."

I shrugged, doubtful, yet resigned to my fate, and retreated to my room to suit up for my morning torture. As my mom liked to say, "You make your own bed, you lie in it."

"Let's get this over with," I muttered, wrapping the remainder of my half-gnawed bagel in a paper towel. "Just take it easy on me, okay?"

"Not a chance," Faith scoffed.

I followed her listlessly out the door, like a petulant child trailing her mother, down three flights of stairs, and into the vibrant day.

FRESHLY SHOWERED AND ravenous, Faith and I relaxed on the oceanfront patio of Marlin Moe's, a seaside café that served breakfast all day. I sagged in my chair, stuffed to the gills from my satisfyingly greasy, calorie-laden feast.

A flock of seagulls screeched noisily overhead, and sandpipers pecked at the crumbs scattered across the patio. The first ten minutes of running had been painful. My head ached, and my body leaked fruity-smelling perspiration. But somewhere around the two-mile mark, the throbbing began to recede, and I inhaled deep lungfuls of salty sea air as the sweat purged the toxins from my body. By the time we had returned to the condo forty minutes later, I was a new person—cleansed, purified, and rejuvenated. Jack's encouraging mantra rang in my ears: *The only workouts you'll regret are the ones you skip.*

Faith flagged down our waiter to request the check, or so I'd assumed. Instead, she surprised me by ordering a plate of homemade cinnamon rolls and two lattes. "Gotta live life to the fullest while we can." Her wide grin lit her whole face.

When the plate of sweet, sticky pastries arrived, I couldn't resist. I tore off a chunk and groaned with pleasure as the soft, sweet dough melted in my mouth. My gaze drifted across the sea as several would-be surfers paddled out beyond the modest breakers, their wetsuit-clad bodies bobbing in the Gulf. The azure water slashed across the robin's-egg horizon, and a scarlet banner-towing biplane buzzed overhead. A jaunty UB40 tune emanated from a shell-shaped speaker and mixed with the din of the busy café and the roll of the surf.

"So," Faith said, licking the glaze from her perfectly manicured fingertips, "what are you gonna do if Lia does show her face at the reunion?"

I chewed slowly, letting the cinnamon and sugar dissolve on my tongue. The sweetness in my mouth soured as the memories came flooding back. "I honestly don't know." It was hard to imagine the moment. So hard, in fact, that I was inclined to avoid it altogether. The difficulty of facing Lia in that moment—if she even bothered to show up at the reunion—and the stress the idea of it was causing me would likely not be worth whatever half-baked reason she might offer for her disappearing act. She had proven herself untrustworthy, unreliable. *Her mother's daughter after all.*

The day was too lovely to spend it dwelling on the reunion or Lia. I would have plenty of time to mull it over and discuss it with Jack when I returned in just a few short hours to icy-cold Maryland. Pushing the topic from my mind, I leaned back in my chair, tilting my chin toward the warm sun, and slung my arm across my full belly. My watch glittered in the bright afternoon sunlight, catching Faith's attention.

"Shit, girl!" Faith shrieked, ripping me from my brief repose. "We gotta get going, or you're gonna miss your plane!"

FAITH WHEELED HER MUSTANG convertible up the ramp to the departure terminal and skidded to a stop at the curb. I gave her a hasty but heartfelt hug and leapt from the car to grab my suitcase, weave through the thankfully short security line, and make a mad dash for the gate.

A flight attendant stood sentry at the entrance to the jetway and clicked the door shut behind me as I made my way, panting and sweating, down the ramp and into the aircraft's cabin. I stowed my carry-on in the overhead bin and settled into my seat. Closing my eyes, I took long, slow breaths to calm my racing heart. Then I made an unsuccessful attempt to read.

Unable to concentrate, I gazed out the window and sipped absently from a plastic cup of cranberry apple juice. The sky beyond the small oval pane was a swirl of soft colors, like an opal or a delicate freshwater pearl. Suddenly exhausted, I rested my head against the seat and closed my eyes, letting my dreams carry me away.

When I opened my eyes again, the sky had darkened, not yet to the deep black of night but to the rich eggplant that preceded it. We were making our descent into Baltimore. The flight attendants bustled about, collecting trash and ensuring that everyone's seatbacks and tray tables were in the upright position.

Baltimore greeted me with its frigid winter breath. The chilly air deftly penetrated the thin jetway walls and seeped into my very bones as I exited the plane. Inside the terminal, I wheeled my small carry-on bag out of the stream of foot traffic and hastily retrieved my fleece jacket. I donned it and zipped it up to the neck in anticipation of the frigid task ahead: waiting outside to catch a shuttle to the long-term parking lot.

After zigzagging endlessly through the lot, the shuttle finally deposited me at my car, which was dishearteningly blanketed in a thin veil of snow. Grumbling, I unearthed the ice scraper from the depths of the trunk and dislodged the frost and ice with un-gloved hands. I was almost home before my red, wind-chapped fingers quit aching.

An hour later, I pulled into the driveway and paused to appreciate the sight before me. Our lovely home rose from the frozen ground like a glowing beacon of safety, warmth, and light. I closed my eyes and conjured the cozy scene: Jack, calm and focused as he whipped up a pot of his signature seafood chowder; Helene reading a book in front of the fire; Evelyn playing with the dogs; and Kathryn practicing the piano, filling the house with the soothing, melodious music. The image warmed me from the inside out. I'd enjoyed my girls' weekend with Faith, but I was glad to be home with my family where I belonged, where my heart was truly happiest.

As I parked the car in the garage and headed for the door, I realized that Faith was right. I had nothing to lose by going to the reunion, and I might actually enjoy it. I was no longer the timid high school girl who'd been content to live in someone else's shadow. I was proud of the woman I'd become and of the life I'd built with my family. I would go to the reunion, hold my head high, and introduce all the people who'd known the wallflower Anna Clark to Anna Wells, the woman who was basking in a light that was all her own.

CHAPTER 15
February 2009

After efficiently hustling the girls through homework and dinner and shuttling them to their respective evening sports and activities, I arrived home with grand plans to relax with a magazine and a cup of herbal tea before beginning the pickup rounds. But then I heard the subtle *ding* from my laptop, and like Pavlov's dog, I abandoned the magazine and returned to the kitchen, where I saw I had five new messages: two emails from the school and three notifications from Facebook. My pulse quickened.

The initial Facebook frenzy had slowed as the deadline to register for the reunion had come and gone. As expected, Lia had remained MIA. Powerless against my rising curiosity, I'd done a quick search for Emilia Clay, Lia's full name in high school. But the search had proven futile, producing only two results: a teenager in Texas and an Asian woman in San Francisco. I'd felt slightly disappointed but unsurprised... and also relieved. Part of me wanted to see Lia, but the other part knew it was what I feared most about the reunion.

But then, in response to desperate pleas from delinquent classmates, Tammy had extended the deadline, prompting another flurry of activity as new attendees were added to the class Facebook page. The Facebook notification informed me that Lori Jacobs Hudson and two other people had joined the class reunion page.

I clicked on the notification and studied each new addition: Lori Jacobs, the curly-haired pool girl who looked exactly the same save for the fine lines that now framed her mouth and eyes, a boy whose name sounded vaguely familiar but whose face I didn't recognize, and the very name I'd been dreading—and anticipating—for weeks. *Lia.*

Emilia Clay Nelson. The letters jumped out at me as if they'd come to life, ready to strike. I recoiled in shock, hot tea splashing onto my wrist. Every cell in my body was flooded with fear, loathing, and anger. And *relief.* I reached for a napkin and sucked on my burnt wrist. My eyes remained glued to the screen, my heart pounding. With a shaking hand, I guided the mouse over Lia's name and clicked.

I didn't recognize her at first. I wondered if I would have recognized her if we'd passed on the street. Maybe we *had* passed on the street. According to her profile, she now lived just south of Baltimore, an hour away. Her once shiny strawberry-blond locks had darkened to a dull rusty brown. She wore her hair short, the ends angled sharply toward her chin. Her face was rounder, her smile more reserved. Her teeth had been coerced into a neat, orderly line, perfectly straight. The trademark gap was gone.

I leaned closer, squinting at the picture in front of me. It was definitely Lia. I would have known those eyes anywhere—bright green and angled upward like a cat's. The cute, slightly crooked nose and Cupid's-bow lips were the same, yet the teenage girl of my memories had morphed into the middle-aged woman on my screen. I smiled despite the ache in my heart.

Hastily clicking through Lia's photos, I gleaned that she was working as an engineer for Lockheed Martin, that she was married—*Good for you, Lia*—to a short, balding man, and she had two children, twin boys. *Figures. I can't manage to have one boy, and Lia has two.* Irrational jealousy stabbed my heart as the chiming clock announced my tardiness.

"Shit!" I hissed through my teeth as the grandfather clock chimed six. I'd completely lost track of time and would be late picking up Kathryn from dance. *Again.* Facebook had sucked me into a black hole, a bizarre time warp with fascinating age-progression technology. I snatched my bag off the countertop and flew out the door, knowing I would be greeted by the dance company director's reproachful stare and a five-dollar late fee on the next month's tuition.

As I rushed through town toward the dance studio—speeding through lights so yellow, they were orange—it dawned on me that if I'd been privy to Lia's Facebook profile, then surely she'd already rummaged through mine. Icy tendrils of doubt infiltrated my veins. I suddenly felt violated, exposed, and irrationally protective of my family and my privacy. I cursed myself for putting my life on display for all the world to see. At least that was how it seemed.

With Lia, I had always been in the shadows, cocooned in a shroud of invisibility. But without her, I'd emerged a butterfly. I didn't know what had happened to her or what kind of life she'd led for the past twenty years, but I suddenly felt triumphant, superior. I believed with all my heart that, in the game of life, I had ultimately won. And I didn't want to share my victory with her. I didn't want to have it tarnished in any way by her judgment or her proximity to it. It had taken a long time for me to forget her and move on. The looming reunion, the classmates crawling out of the woodwork, and the existence of Facebook had conspired to shine a probing spotlight onto parts of my life I'd considered ancient history. It had reawakened old memories that had been tucked away in the deep recesses of my mind for decades. For the most part, I had forgotten about Lia. But I'd never forgiven her. And now Pandora's box stood before me, the lid cracked open on rusted hinges, daring me to open it wider and peek inside.

What have I done? I parked the car and bounded up the front steps of the dance studio. Kathryn and her teacher stood glaring at me through the glass doors. Being late occasionally was inconsiderate but tolerable. Being late three weeks in a row—mostly because of my newfound fascination with Facebook—was flat-out unacceptable. Not only would I be subjected to the wrath of the director, but my precocious fourteen-year-old would likely take me to task as well.

Kathryn, in typical firstborn fashion, had always strived to achieve and perform beyond her years. She always wanted to excel. She appreciated structure and routines. She was reliable, conscientious, and a little bit controlling. "Bossy," her sisters would say.

A pang of guilt struck me as I strode into the lobby. I'd spent so many years obsessed with having another baby that the babies I already had had grown up before my eyes. And I'd nearly missed it. I choked back a sob and made the snap decision to treat Kathryn to something special.

Mrs. Alder, a frown on her stern, sharp face, pushed open the studio door. Kathryn stood beside her. My daughter's dark hair was slipping from her ponytail, and her slender arms were crossed over her budding chest.

"Late fees double after the third infraction, Mrs. Wells."

"I know. I'm sorry. This is so unlike me," I babbled. "It won't happen again."

Mrs. Alder forced a tight smile and locked the door behind us.

Kathryn had walked ahead and now stood on the sidewalk waiting, her foot tapping impatiently. "I was the last one again," she admonished. Her cheeks were rosy from exertion and indignation. Her blue-green eyes blazed under the light of a full moon.

"I know. I'm sorry. I lost track of time. I've been a bit distracted lately, but I'll do better. I promise." I made a mental note to set my clocks ten minutes ahead. Maybe that would help. "How 'bout I make it up to you over dinner?"

"Sushi?" she asked hopefully. It had been one of her favorites since preschool. I smiled at the memory of her kindergarten classmates openly gawking as Kathryn expertly worked the chopsticks that came with the bento box I'd brought to school for her sixth birthday.

"Sushi it is." I reached out to take her hand in mine, thankful that she would let me.

WITH THE GIRLS FINALLY tucked into bed and Jack not due home from work for another thirty minutes, I raced to the phone and punched in Faith's number. I held my breath as the phone rang three times, four...

"Hello?"

"Faith?" Her voice sounded strange, raspy. "Is that you?"

"Hey, girl!" she exclaimed, the attempt at cheerfulness falling flat. "Of course it's me. Who else would it be?"

"Is everything okay? You don't sound like yourself." I began to pace, the dogs watching me intently as I wore a path into the living-room carpet.

Faith exhaled, abandoning all pretense. "Daddy's not doing so well. We had to move him into a home last week."

The news stopped me in my tracks. "Oh, Faith. I'm so sorry. Why didn't you call?"

"I meant to. It's just been so busy, and I'm just so darn tired. Completely whooped."

"How can I help?" I gnawed at a hangnail on my thumb.

"Thanks, girl, but all we can do now is wait. Pray. It's up to Daddy now. And God."

"I could plan another trip down, help you with meals and the house."

"Bless your heart. But really, I'm doing okay. And Mabel's helping out. Besides, I'm sure you've got your hands full up there."

"The girls do keep me hopping. That's for sure." I laughed and resumed my pacing.

"So what's up with you anyway? Hearing what's going on up there is likely the best medicine. Take my mind off things 'round here."

"Lia's going," I blurted. I knew Faith would understand. I expected she would be surprised, aghast, excited, or even offended on my behalf. But as the silence dragged on, I began to wonder if she'd heard what I said.

Finally, she sighed loudly, sounding exasperated. "Anna, if ya wanna go to the reunion, go. It really shouldn't make one whit of difference whether Lia's there or not. Just go. Eat, drink, be merry. Make small talk with the others and forget about her. Lia is part of your past, not your future, 'less you want her to be. Life's too short for you to keep fretting 'bout this damn reunion."

Ouch. Faith was most definitely not herself. But she was right, of course. I hung my head, ashamed, like a dog that had piddled on the carpet and been rightly chastised. *What's my problem anyway? Why am I still so hung up on Lia?* She'd hurt me. I'd moved on. It was over. Ancient history. End of story.

"So is this session going to cost me?" I was desperate to lighten the mood. Faith didn't bite.

"'Course not," she said, exhaustion seeping back into her voice. Things were probably worse with her father than she was letting on. I was about to bid her goodnight, but she beat me to it. "Well, I'm pooped, girl. Gotta hit the hay. Keep me posted, though, okay?"

"You bet!" I replied with false enthusiasm. Her father's failing health aside, I had the nagging feeling that something else was up with Faith. I just couldn't put my finger on it.

I sank onto the floor between the dogs and scratched them behind their ears, making their tails thump. Cuddling with Chessie and Bay always made me feel better. I actually wrote a column about it once, the health benefits of playing with or petting an animal, both of which increased the levels of oxytocin and decreased cortisol, reducing stress.

I was worried about Faith. I felt protective of her, the way I'd once felt protective of Lia. Like Faith, Lia had been larger than life: bold, outgoing, strong, confident. But inside, she was as fragile as the rest of us. I closed my eyes and let my fingers trail through Bay's silky black fur as another memory of Lia came floating back.

August 1987

ON THE FIRST DAY OF our junior year, Lia arrived at school, proudly toting a new monogramed L.L. Bean backpack. It was pink, with her initials, ELC—for Emilia Lillian Clay—stitched in purple. "Compliments of my aunt," she said with a bright smile.

We linked arms and walked toward our first-period class. Three boys followed closely behind, snickering in an evil way that made me feel like I had a "kick me" sign on my back. Or maybe toilet paper was stuck to my shoe, or my skirt was tucked into my underwear. But then we heard their hurtful words.

"Easy Lay Clay," the boys chanted, hooting with laugher and gleefully high-fiving each other, celebrating their supposed ingenuity.

Anger flooded my veins and set my face on fire. I clenched my fists and racked my brain for nasty retorts I could hurl at the boys.

Lia, however, remained outwardly passive. Her composure and utter lack of reaction denied the boys any satisfaction, and they eventually sauntered off. But everyone had heard, and everyone was staring. With all eyes on her, Lia straightened her back and held her head high—appearing taller than her diminutive five feet, one inch—and tossed her long hair over her shoulder. She waltzed into the classroom without a backward glance. I was the only one who saw the tears in her eyes.

The next morning, despite what had happened the day before, Lia wore her monogrammed backpack and was up to her usual antics—*perhaps hiding her humiliation with humor*—making me laugh until I cried with her running commentary on the anatomy of our fellow classmates.

"See that guy?" she asked, peering out the school store window. "He's got a mole the size of a quarter on his penis. And that one"—she tilted her head toward a skinny boy with sandy hair—"he's got the skinniest peter I've ever seen. Every time I see him, all I can think is Pencil Peter."

"Stop!" I pleaded. My stomach hurt from laughing so hard. Then a tall, dark, gorgeous stranger passed the store and ducked into a stairwell. "Who's that?" I panted, trying to catch my breath.

"Grrr," Lia said, making the word sound like a purr. She leaned over the counter, craning her neck to get a better view. "I don't know. But I plan to find out."

CHAPTER 16
March 2009

It was an unseasonably warm evening in March. After driving the girls to their friends' houses for sleepovers, I poured two glasses of wine and beckoned to Jack, who was in the office finishing up patient reports, to join me outside on the patio.

The air still held a hint of winter's chill, but a warm, delicate breeze carried the promise of the balmy spring days ahead. In the fading daylight, I glimpsed tender green buds gracing the trees. Just the week prior, the branches had stood stark and barren, etched in fine point against the gray winter sky.

"What's the occasion?" Jack asked, reaching for a glass and taking a generous sip of Shiraz.

"Nothing, really."

Jack raised one thick, dark eyebrow. He knew me too well.

"Okay," I admitted. "I signed us up for the reunion."

"Ha!" Jack grinned, his eyes crinkling at the corners. "You're full of surprises. I thought you'd rather have a root canal than go to the reunion."

"I changed my mind."

Jack continued to stare at me over the rim of his glass. "You changed your mind, or Faith changed it for you?"

I punched him playfully on the shoulder. "Very funny."

Jack reached for my hand and tugged me closer, mischief dancing in his eyes. "I'm just teasing."

"Okay, to be honest, it was actually copious amounts of sangria that changed my mind." I laughed and shielded my eyes from the setting sun. "I'm a little anxious about it, but I was worried I'd regret it if we didn't go. I hope you don't mind." I sat on the lounge next to Jack, our thighs touching.

He slipped his arm around my waist. "Nope. We'll go. I told you I was fine with whatever you decided."

"Are you sure? I know it's not your cup of tea."

"*You're* my cup of tea." Jack slid the thin strap of my top down my arm and kissed me lightly on the shoulder.

Inspired, I reached over and released the back of his lounge chair then climbed atop him. After draining the remainder of his wine, Jack abandoned the glass and set to work untying the drawstring of my cargo pants. Our once-voracious sex life had been temporarily diminished by our struggles with infertility and by my miscarriages and depression. But slowly, patiently, we'd found our way back to each other. I tugged down his zipper and lowered myself onto him. Our bodies moved in unison as the sun slipped below the horizon, painting the early evening sky in majestic shades of indigo and violet.

ON MONDAY, AFTER SEEING the girls off to school, I dashed to the yoga studio to try an Ashtanga class and emerged feeling focused and energized.

At home, Chessie and Bay greeted me at the door with their usual enthusiasm and followed closely on my heels into the mud room, their tails wagging expectantly. Not one to disappoint, I produced two repugnant bully sticks from the box overhead and shooed the dogs outside. Spoiling the dogs was a guilty pleasure of mine. I enjoyed how happy it made them.

I stowed my yoga mat in the closet and made a quick detour into the office to check my laptop before heading upstairs. I was stunned to find more than a dozen Facebook notifications, including eight friend requests from former classmates. Tammy had posted a chipper message designed to drum up excitement for the most "kick-ass reunion ever!" I snorted, recalling the wholesome, studious high-school version of Tammy. She would have sooner stuck a pencil in her eye than utter the word "ass."

Over the past several weeks, I'd gotten more comfortable with Facebook and had carefully crafted my personal page to reveal only the details of my life I wanted to share. Curiosity getting the best of me, I occasionally clicked on Lia's page to see if I could glean any additional information about her. But like me, she kept the personal details to a minimum and had not added any new posts or pictures since initially establishing her account.

I deleted the message from Tammy and quickly accepted all the friend requests, enthusiastically poring over the pictures and personal information of people long lost to me. It was a time-consuming habit that, I was ashamed to admit, had become a bit of an addiction.

It amused me to learn that Dean, a shy, geeky Dungeons & Dragons–playing classmate, was now a successful business owner, regularly traveling to exotic locations all over the world. His photo albums boasted pictures of the great pyramids, the Taj Mahal, and the Colosseum.

And Renee—in a move that surely incensed her wealthy, controlling parents—had dropped out of college to pursue an acting career in Hollywood. Five years later she'd slunk home sans career but with a new nose and breasts. Now twice divorced with three kids, she toiled as a cosmetologist by day and attended community college by night. *Couldn't have happened to a nicer person.* She'd wasted no time trying to sink her claws into Jack when he'd first started at Bay View.

In addition to being one of the pool girls and disgustingly wealthy, Renee had probably been most notorious for the raucous parties she'd thrown at her parents' bayside mansion. Our junior year, her much-anticipated post-homecoming bash had been the talk of the school for weeks.

October 1987

RENEE'S GIGANTIC TUDOR-style home sat perched high atop a cliff, the back yard a sheer drop into the bay. Through the large arched windows, we could see hordes of people crammed inside. An overflow of revelers spilled onto the meticulously landscaped front lawn and milled about like ants. Cars densely lined both sides of the street. We cruised the block twice before finding a place to park and then huffed our way up the steep driveway to the front door. Two guys toting a beer bong barreled past Lia, me, and our dates—Mark, Lia's boy toy of the moment, and Jason, my friend and fellow Pizza Palace employee—as we edged our way into the crowded foyer. An enormous crystal chandelier dangled overhead. The stench of cigarettes and cheap beer overpowered the underlying refined notes of sandalwood and leather.

High on excitement, which was fed by the animated crowd and thumping music, we pushed our way through the mass, slithering between bodies, until we found a small pocket of space just outside the kitchen. Jason nudged me with his elbow and peeled back one lapel of his dark-gray jacket to reveal a silver flask as he waggled his eyebrows. Lia squealed and clapped her hands. She grabbed me by the wrist and tugged me through the crowded kitchen in search of some Cokes. We didn't make it far before one of Lia's many admirers playfully accosted her, grabbing her around the waist. She giggled in mock protest, and I left her to flirt as I carried on with our mission, shouldering my way through the throng.

At the back of the kitchen—stationed in front of a bank of French doors—were two stainless-steel ice buckets stocked with sodas. By the time I'd nudged and elbowed my way through the room, there was only one Coke left among the remaining cans of Sprite, Mug Root Beer, and Orange Crush. I leaned sideways, stretching my arm between layers of polyester and tulle. Just as my hand made contact with the icy can, warm, strong fingers wrapped around my own. Startled, I yanked my hand back and peered up into the most breathtaking eyes I'd ever seen—rich, chocolate-brown irises ringed in sapphire and flecked with bits of emerald were presided over by an enviable spray of thick, dark lashes.

My own eyes did a quick circuit of the chiseled face: square jaw, full lips, and strong nose were neatly arranged beneath a mop of shiny dark-brown hair. The boy's gaze locked onto mine, and a deep flush crept up my neck, lighting my cheeks on fire. The way he was staring at me—like he wanted to eat me alive—sent waves of heat rolling through my body.

"It's all yours," he said, extending the can toward me as his smoldering eyes bored into mine. I must have looked ridiculous, like a fish with my mouth gaping open. *Catching flies*, my brother would have teased.

The boy's smile widened, exposing a row of perfectly straight white teeth and a deep dimple creasing his right cheek. Before I could speak or even accept the proffered can, a slender, fake-baked arm snaked through the crowd and snatched it from his hand.

"*There* you are, Jack! I've been looking *all over* for you," Renee scolded in a nasally, high-pitched voice. She linked her arm through his and tugged him in the opposite direction. As they disappeared into the crowd, I could hear Renee whining about how thirsty she was as she popped the top of the Coke. *My* Coke.

So that's the infamous Jack Wells. I made my way back through the kitchen, which was overrun with sweaty teenage bodies pressed together like sardines. Since the day Lia and I had caught our first and only glimpse of Jack at the school store, he was all the girls at Bay View had been talking about—the gorgeous new guy from New York.

Lia had regrouped with Mark and Jason on the front patio, the bluestone alight with tiki torches and a row of solar tea lanterns. I shook my head as I approached, raising my empty hands to indicate the mission's failure. Jason simply shrugged and swigged directly from the flask, shivering as the potent spirit burned its way down his throat.

"That new guy? Jack? Did you know he's dating *Renee*?" I asked Lia.

"Nope. Guess she wasted no time pouncing on him."

Mark passed the flask to Lia.

"Can't say I blame her, though. He's hot!" She took a hearty sip and choked on her next words. "But she better hold on to him while she can. She's got some competition!"

SUDDENLY, THE FRONT door burst open, and the dogs began to bark, startling me. I banged my knee on the underside of the desk. The girls were home from school already!

"Hi, Mom!" Helene bellowed, slinging her backpack onto the floor and racing for the bathroom.

"We're home!" Evelyn announced unnecessarily.

I could hear the sink running and knew she was washing her hands so she could dig into her favorite afternoon snack: Goldfish crackers, a cheese stick, and an apple. Helene would opt for yogurt and granola. Kathryn was at piano practice and would need to be picked up in an hour.

I glanced unbelievingly at the clock and realized, with disgust, that I'd wasted nearly three hours trolling Facebook. *Again.* I was still in my sweaty yoga clothes and hadn't eaten lunch or written my columns. Clearly, the real danger of Facebook was not how it permitted others a peek into my cherished private life but rather the toll it exacted in terms of hours wasted.

I sighed as I pushed back from my desk, knowing I was in for a long night, and dragged myself wearily into a witching hour of my own making.

CHAPTER 17
June 2009

"You wouldn't believe how flexible this guy's toes were!" Jack shook his head and chuckled.

We were ensconced in The Tack & Jibe, a cozy little dive bar a few blocks away from the Marriott, for a round of pre-reunion cocktails. I sipped my Godiva white-chocolate martini and listened to Jack recount the highlights of his week. His work as a sports therapist and its regular intimate contact with the public provided an endless supply of conversation fodder. He often regaled me with tales of women who spanned the spectrum from harried, unkempt mothers who fretted over unshaved legs and chipped toenails to college coeds who primped and perfumed before appointments. But at least the women cared. The men, he would tell me, were the worst when it came to personal hygiene: filthy feet that stank; socks that literally had to be peeled from the flesh; and bodies that reeked of stale sweat, extreme odor, and the sour tang of urine. "Oh, the humanity!" Jack would sometimes exclaim after work, and I would know he'd likely spent the bulk of his day tending to the unwashed masses.

I flicked my tongue against the chocolate rim of my glass, savoring the sweet contrast to the bitter bite of vodka.

"Keep that up, and we may not make it to the reunion," Jack threatened, placing a hand on my bare knee exposed by the long slit in my black skirt.

Preferring to stick bamboo shoots under my fingernails rather than go shopping, I'd raided my closet for something suitable to wear, settling on what Kathryn called my "Egyptian dress." The cropped, V-neck top ended an inch above the skirt's low-rise waistband, revealing a strip of taut abdominal flesh. All the running and cycling I'd been doing had paid off, and I was secretly pleased to be able to show off my fit, firm body. A pair of strappy, high-heeled sandals adorned my feet, and I'd painted my toes a metallic Bay View blue. Dangling sapphire earrings, with a matching necklace and bracelet—anniversary gifts from Jack—completed the ensemble.

"You look *hot*," Jack had murmured in my ear while helping me fasten the necklace.

I'd leaned back and pressed myself against him, delighting in the feel of his strong, hard body. "You're no slouch yourself," I'd said as I turned, wrapped my arms around his neck, and planted a kiss on his mouth. Jack was always handsome, but he looked especially striking that night in a perfectly tailored black suit and crisp white shirt. A Bay View-blue tie was his nod to school spirit.

After months of dread, fear, and anticipation, our twentieth high school reunion was finally there. Jack and I had enlisted my parents to take the girls overnight so we could make a weekend of it. Knowing I would be too nervous to eat at the reunion, we'd made reservations for an early dinner at the Chart House, a high-end steak and seafood eatery famous for its classy atmosphere and stunning views. Afterward, with bellies stuffed full of the most delectable, mouthwatering shellfish on the planet, we'd wandered the historic cobblestone streets of Annapolis. The briny scent of the bay mingled with the greasy smell of fried seafood served at the waterfront cafes.

Strolling past the gates of the naval academy and along the bricks in front of Lee's Homemade Ice Cream Shoppe transported me to my carefree high school days. I vividly recalled the summer evenings Lia and I had spent there at the docks. She would gleefully drag me from bar to bar, flirting her way inside and then sweet-talking some poor chump into buying us drinks, all part of her quest to find a vulnerable, lonely midshipman to take advantage of. Meanwhile, I would be feigning irritation but secretly enjoying her antics, knowing we would ultimately end up sitting on the bench at the end of the pier. Gazing at the inky water and the city lights reflected in its smooth, black surface, we would lap at ice cream cones from Lee's—strawberry cheesecake for her, mint chocolate chip for me. The cool creaminess on our tongues had always been a welcome relief from the heat.

A sharp pang of longing had pierced my insides as Jack and I strolled the cobblestones. Thinking of all Lia and I had missed, all that had been lost between us, filled me with regret. There was a time when I couldn't have pictured any part of my future without Lia. I'd envisioned her as my maid of honor, godmother to my children, the person I would meet for lunches and pedicures and go on girls' weekends with. But none of that had happened. Lia had denied us those opportunities. That night, however, presented a new opportunity. But I planned to play it cool. If Lia approached me, I would greet her with an aloof but pleasant smile. And if she wanted to talk—to explain—I would listen. That was all I was willing to commit to.

After dinner, Jack and I had ducked into the bar. We'd stumbled upon The Tack & Jibe as we'd strolled toward the Marriott. A chalkboard sign on the sidewalk advertising the martini specials and the sound of live acoustic music had drawn us in like moths to a flame. Despite the slightly unpleasant odor of stale beer and bleach, the tiny, narrow bar was dimly lit and cozy. I was relishing a rare night out with Jack—one I was in no hurry to exchange for an awkward evening of forced pleasantries with a hundred virtual strangers. The thought had entered my mind more than once to skip the reunion and simply stay put. Though Jack was looking forward to catching up with a few of his high school swim team buddies that he'd lost touch with over the years, the only people I might have liked to reconnect with—Becky, Kim, and Kelly, my former dance teammates—weren't going to be there. Mostly, I was dreading the inevitable encounter with Lia. My stomach twitched nervously at the prospect of seeing her.

In an effort to relax, I focused my attention on the grungy guy sitting on a stool near the front of the bar. He languidly strummed a decrepit guitar and warbled a barely coherent rendition of "Hotel California," but the crowd loved him. The martini had generated a pleasant buzz that flushed my cheeks and eased the tension from my muscles. I let myself go, swaying to the music, my joints loose, my limbs pleasantly heavy and boneless.

From the corner of my eye, I saw Jack glance at his watch and beckon the bartender with a causal lift of his arm. He settled the bill and placed his hand gently, intimately, on the small of my back. He leaned close, his familiar, masculine scent making me dizzy with desire. "Time to go."

Sucking in a deep breath to clear my head and steel my resolve, I slid carefully from my stool and onto the worn wooden floor. "Let's do this thing."

Perhaps the night was meant to be, destined to be. Perhaps it had been scripted this way all along, my estrangement from Lia somehow necessary and intended in this game called life. The reunion would be our turning point, the pivotal moment when our

separate paths would collide, the setting of a joyful reunion between two long-lost friends.

Get a grip. I was getting way ahead of myself. My thoughts were
going amok, my imagination running wild. For starters, Lia might
not even show. She'd certainly established a track record of bailing
at the last minute. And for me to give my friendship to Lia again
would require a huge leap of faith on my part and complete honesty on hers. As my brother would say, "The girl has some 'splainin'
to do."

A LARGE GILDED SIGN welcoming the Bay View High School
Class of 1989 was prominently displayed in the elaborate lobby of
the Annapolis Marriott Waterfront Hotel. From the entrance, we
could see all the way through the building to the terrace overlooking the bay. The grand entrance was reminiscent of the Caribbean
resorts I'd visited. But instead of the clear turquoise waters of the
islands, we were met by the murky greenish-gray of the bay. In
the distance, the Chesapeake Bay Bridge etched an inky silhouette
against the crimson summer sky. The bridge, fondly known as "the
gateway to the beach," connected Maryland's eastern and western
shores, just as it had connected my past to my future, delivering me
from Cambridge to Bay View High School. To Lia and to Jack.

My palm was sweaty in Jack's comforting grasp. We circum-
vented the large ornate fountain and made our way to the registration table, my stilettos clicking loudly on the marble floor. An elegant couple stood before us. The woman was exotic, with loosely
plaited long black hair. She casually rested a bejeweled hand on her
date's back. I didn't recognize her, but there was something vaguely familiar about the man. He chuckled politely in a pleasant baritone as one of the women working the registration table thumbed
through a huge stack of name tags. Bay View was an exceptionally

large high school. Our class alone had more than four hundred seventy graduates, and more than a third of those were expected to be in attendance at the reunion.

The man leaned toward his date, and my mind raced to put a name to the handsome face. His kind, intelligent eyes were framed by round, wire-rimmed spectacles, and his hair had gone a distinguished gray at the temples—a tribute to the twenty years that had passed. I squinted, desperately trying to see the boy hidden within the man. A nudge to Jack's ribs prompted him to subtly shrug, and the movement caught the woman's attention. She glanced over her shoulder, the long braid swishing across her back, and smiled politely, displaying perfect Chicklet teeth, square and blindingly white. The man then pivoted to face us, his features momentarily drawn in contemplation before his eyes popped wide with recognition.

"Well, I'll be damned!" he exclaimed, pulling me in for a rough hug and then releasing me to give Jack's hand a vigorous shake. "Anna Clark and Jack Wells! I haven't seen you two in, ugh, twenty years!"

Dean Melby. The shy, nerdy Dungeons & Dragons–playing bookworm and captain of the chess team had morphed into a sophisticated, well-dressed, attractive man with an exotic woman on his arm. His ebullient greeting surprised me, making me blush. Dean and I had been friends in the sense that Dean was friendly to everyone. We waved and said hello to each other in the hallways, but—his intelligence level being far superior to mine—we hadn't had any classes together. Lia, on the other hand, had shared many of the same classes with Dean, and she'd spent many a school store morning opining about his studious sexiness. But despite her musings, Dean was one of the few boys in our class Lia *hadn't* hooked up with. And not for lack of trying.

Dean introduced us to his companion. "This is my fiancée, Nishtha."

Nishtha extended her hand. "Nice to meet you."

I couldn't help but notice the enormous rock on her ring finger.

A moment of awkward silence followed our cursory greetings, and the four of us stood bobbing our heads and smiling. Finally, Dean cleared his throat loudly and said, "Well. See you inside?"

"You bet!" I replied, my voice unnaturally high.

"Right-oh," Jack added.

"Right-*oh*?" I whispered, amused. In fifteen years of marriage, I'd never heard Jack utter the words "right-oh."

Jack shrugged, flashing me a sheepish grin as we refocused our attention on the registration table. Tammy, the reunion planner, was handing out name tags and reunion favors: a blue leather bookmark with our school name, graduation year, and mascot—a blue crab—embossed in white.

"Anna! Jack! So glad you could make it," Tammy enthused, handing us our swag.

"Hi, Tammy. Nice to see you. You've done a wonderful job with the reunion."

"Thank you." Her broad smile morphed into a tiny pout. "I'm afraid you've just missed cocktail hour, but dinner is about to be served in the ballroom." She gestured to the right, the flesh of her upper arm swinging.

Outside, the Marriott wait staff was busy clearing dirty appetizer plates and empty glasses from the tall, linen-covered cocktail tables that dotted the terrace. A gentle breeze filtered in through the open doors, momentarily lifting my hair from my shoulders, and I shuddered—less from the draft than from the prospect of walking into a room full of vaguely familiar faces.

Sensing my unease, Jack squeezed my hand reassuringly as he made small talk with Tammy. The peel-and-stick name tags featured our senior photos, black-and-white images lifted from the yearbook. Jack laughed uproariously at my extremely dated picture.

"Look at that 'do!" he teased. Despite his hair being more closely cropped and newly sprinkled with silver, Jack looked almost exactly the same as he had in high school. It was so unfair. Men aged so gracefully.

Time had not been nearly as kind to me. I frowned at the smiling image in my hands, taking in the sky-high bangs and the permed brown hair that framed a much fuller, rounder face. The hair, of course, was an unequivocal disaster, as were all things style- and fashion-related in the eighties. But I gazed longingly at the smooth, unlined skin devoid of the bags and crow's feet that now framed my eyes, compliments of three daughters, who had, as newborns, delivered sleepless nights to temper my new-mother joy. Decades of smiles and laughter had given birth to the creases around my mouth, and the constant worries over how to protect my babies and raise them well had etched furrowed ruts into my brow.

We thanked Tammy again and made a beeline for the bar, which stood opposite the ballroom. With most of our classmates already seated, there was no line. My martini buzz had completely evaporated, and I was parched.

Jack knew, without asking, that I would want a glass of red, which he ordered along with an IPA for himself. I gratefully accepted the generous pour of an oaky cabernet and peered into the ballroom. Jack, waiting for his beer, stuffed a few neatly folded bills into the tip jar.

At least eighty sharply dressed couples sat chatting and laughing at round tables bordering a small wooden dance floor. The tables were clothed in royal blue. Small votive candles resting atop mirrored squares encircled vases filled with white daffodils. Blue and white balloons were gathered in bunches, and soft instrumental music was playing in the background.

I fidgeted nervously on the threshold, taking quick, short sips of wine while I waited for Jack. Boisterous laughter erupted behind me. Several guys from Jack's swim team had convened at the bar, the group of them engaging in the enthusiastic backslapping, hand shaking, and closed-fisted hugging that were the rituals of men.

I was about to join them when I caught movement out of the corner of my eye. A figure was emerging from the restrooms at the far end of the hall. She was dabbing at the front of her shirt, a flashy, jewel-toned camisole subdued by a dark, tailored blazer. *Lia.* My muscles went rigid. My pulse raced, and my heart hammered in my chest, but I couldn't move. *Run! Turn around! Look away!* But my feet remained traitorously rooted to the spot, my eyes wide and staring, glued to Lia's approaching form. I didn't want to blink for fear she might disappear once again. She continued to move toward us, slowly closing the gap.

Lia was ten feet away before she looked up. Her eyes, unseeing at first, went wide, and her mouth formed a small circle. Time stood still for a long, agonizing moment before Lia broke the stalemate. Her features cracked: anguished eyes above a face-splitting grin. "Oh my God!" she shouted in a high, slightly hysterical voice, as if she might burst into tears. "It's you," she whispered. "You're here. I wasn't sure you would come. And that's really the only reason I'm here. To see you." She hesitated then stepped closer, her eyes locked on mine.

I broke contact first, my gaze sweeping over her, taking in the familiar shapely calves and neat, delicate ankles. She was heavier in person than she'd appeared in her Facebook picture, but I would have recognized her face anywhere. Short, rust-colored hair was tucked behind one ear. Pudgy cheeks concealed the once-defined lines of her heart-shaped face. But the short, crooked nose and sparkling green eyes were exactly the same. My throat constricted, forming a hard, uncomfortable knot, and I was seized by panic, my mind pleading with me to take flight. *Leave! Leave now! This is a mistake. Just turn and go!*

But Lia was standing directly in front of me. I absently registered the silence that engulfed us. The swim team reunion, that only moments before had been a raucous affair, had quieted. For one insane, slippery moment, I hovered on the lunatic fringe. I imagined drawing my arm back and slapping Lia full across the face. My limbs twitched uncomfortably at my sides, and I battled oscillating urges to assault her and embrace her. Lia solved the dilemma by lurching forward and wrapping her arms around me in a fierce hug. I stood stock-still. And then, hesitantly, I reciprocated, cautiously drawing my arms around her. Lia still possessed a certain magnetism that made her difficult to resist. And she still only came up to my chin.

She released me and stepped back, her green eyes brimming with tears. "My God. You're beautiful," she said, making no attempt to conceal her obvious surprise. A single tear escaped and slid prettily down her round cheek. She didn't bother to wipe it away. "I'm so glad you're here. I was afraid you wouldn't come," she repeated in a whisper.

Jack came to my rescue, sidling up beside me and slipping a strong, supportive arm around my waist. I drew strength from his solid, reassuring presence but still couldn't manage to find my voice.

"Jack," Lia said, shifting her gaze to him. She stepped toward him and leaned in for a brief, formal embrace. "So good to see you again."

"Likewise. Can I get you a drink?" Jack offered, ever the gentleman.

"Chardonnay?"

Jack slipped away again but not before I drained what was left of my cabernet and handed him the empty glass, silently indicating my urgent need for a refill. I was desperate for something to calm my jangled nerves and dull the sharp edges of the encounter with Lia, which threatened to shatter my emotions and shred my resolve to remain stoic. Having something to do with my hands would also prove useful, I realized as I anxiously twisted my fingers into sweaty knots. Angry with myself for exhibiting such a lack of composure and grace, I sucked in a deep breath and dropped my arms to my sides. "Lia," I whispered, feeling like I was in *The Twilight Zone*. One moment, the years yawned between us, gaping and insurmountable. The next, time was but a small, insignificant crevice of little consequence, easily traversed.

"How have you been?" Lia asked.

I bristled at her casual tone. My best friend lied to me, avoided me, then disappeared for twenty years without a word. *How does she think I've been?* I wasn't ready for this. I would not be able to tolerate such small talk and false pretense as if everything were peachy keen, as if nothing had ever happened. We simply could not just pick up where we'd left off.

"I'm very well, thanks." I replied, flashing a forced, bright smile. I'd once read a book that deemed happiness and a life well lived were the best revenge.

"That's good. Great!" Lia replied, her voice climbing an octave. "You and Jack look great. Happy."

"Thanks. We are." I hated myself for being so bitchy, even if she deserved it.

Thankfully, Jack reappeared with our drinks, and we all sipped in silence, at a loss for what to say or do next until Chris and Ryan, Jack's swim-team friends, joined our awkward little gathering.

"A toast," Ryan said, lifting his beer aloft. "To twenty years."

"To twenty years," we chorused.

"I'm told we're to head inside," Chris said, stepping back to make room for Lia and me to pass. "Ladies first."

Jack placed his hand, familiar and comforting, on the small of my back, and we followed Lia into the ballroom. Our small party of five, arriving late, made quite the entrance. All eyes were on us. Four of the pool girls—as I'd forever referred to them—had commandeered a table near the door. Next to them was a table of men sans wives or dates. They were all former jocks, mostly lacrosse players. One was eyeing Lia wolfishly. Two others hooted appreciatively as she passed, staring unabashedly at her cleavage.

A wave of revulsion curled in my stomach, and I was unexpectedly gripped by a fierce sense of loyalty and protectiveness toward Lia. I couldn't imagine what it must've been like for her to walk into a room full of men she'd slept with, men who had intimate, carnal knowledge of her. As it was, my own face flushed as we passed. Of the eight men at that table, I'd briefly dated one and made out with two others. Lia, however, had screwed them all—an act that, in high school, was a supreme source of pride and power for her, a slap in the face to society's double standard. Now, however, her previous actions served only to humiliate her. I shot a sideways glance at Lia, admiring her dignified posture, her purposeful stride, and the way she held her head high, pretending not to notice the heckling and catcalls. The tips of her ears, however, had gone scarlet, and her fingers were curled into fists at her sides.

Lia turned to me then and said simply but loudly enough for the Neanderthals to hear, "My *husband* couldn't make it tonight. Mind if I sit with you?"

I wondered if Lia's husband knew of her free-spirited past. Perhaps he'd chosen not to attend, unwilling to abide the knowing looks and Cheshire grins that would be directed toward his wife. Or maybe Lia had encouraged him to stay home, fearful of the muttered words and whispered tales that might make their way to his unsuspecting ears.

"Not at all," Jack replied, his grip tightening on my hip. Jack's mother had been abandoned by his philandering father, so I knew Jack was likewise disgusted by the boorish antics on display. These arrogant, immature former jocks, who'd behaved like entitled jerks in high school, apparently had evolved little during the intervening decades. *Some things never change.* I wondered if the idiom would also apply to Lia.

I wasn't exactly thrilled by the prospect of sharing a table with Lia for the entire evening, but given the circumstances and her direct request, I didn't feel I had another option. I sighed, resigned to my uncomfortable, unexpected fate, and hoped it wouldn't be as awkward as I anticipated.

As most of the seats in the ballroom were already claimed, the five of us weaved our way toward the far end of the room, dodging white-gloved servers delivering salads, until we arrived at a table that was only half full.

"Are these seats taken?" Jack asked a skinny girl with glasses.

I didn't immediately recognize Mary Stewart, a girl who'd been a permanent fixture in the drama club and another classmate I'd really only known in passing. An equally skinny man sat beside her. His name tag identified him as Theodore.

Mary gestured toward the empty seats. "It's all you." Her keen obsidian eyes made a quick sweep of our name tags. The athletes and thespians at our school, while cordial, did not exactly mix. "This is my husband, Theo," Mary introduced. The men shook hands while Lia and I smiled politely.

Jack and Lia sat on either side of me, Ryan and Chris across from us. "Jack and Anna were high school sweethearts. Anna and Lia were best friends. And Jack, Ryan, and Chris were on the swim team together," Mary explained to Theo, neatly summarizing us.

The sluggish cog of memory began to turn, and I suddenly recalled that Mary had gone to college in Boston. Theo pushed his chair back, half-standing, and extended his hand to each of us. With his other hand, he held his yellow seersucker tie against his chest to keep it from dangling in his soup. "Nice to meet yous," he said in a nasally voice, his Adam's apple bobbing above the neck of his baby-blue shirt. The bones of his hand were fine and delicate, like a bird's, his palms soft and smooth. I resisted the urge to pull my hand away from his weak, clammy grasp. "The clam chowdah's great," he remarked, settling back into his chair as the attentive wait staff delivered soup and salads to us latecomers without delay.

Dean Melby and Nishtha appeared with fresh drinks, taking the two open seats between George Kent, the loud and pompous former class treasurer, and Mary. Moments later, George's mousy wife, Leslie, appeared, perplexed by the loss of her chair. George did not even acknowledge her presence.

"I'm sorry. I must have taken your seat," Ryan apologized, standing to retrieve an unoccupied chair from a nearby table. We all scooched closer together to make room.

Our table was composed of a motley crew, indeed, a mixing bowl of people who never would have shared a lunch table in high school. Banal pleasantries were exchanged all around. George blatantly ogled Lia's boobs, undoubtedly recalling any number of steamy sessions he'd shared with her on her boat. Lia and Leslie both ignored George's disrespectful behavior.

The arrival of the main course provided a welcome distraction. Jack and I had requested the salmon, which was served on a bed of spinach with a side of green beans and mushroom risotto. The rest of the table, with the exception of Nishtha, who was a vegetarian, had ordered the chicken with carrots and red-skinned potatoes. Everyone tucked into their food in silence, ignoring George's distasteful attempts at humor as he made fun of one of the bus boys.

Though artistically presented, the salmon was dry, and the beans were overcooked. The risotto, however, was surprisingly flavorful, but I was too edgy to eat much of it. Mostly, I pushed the grains around the plate with my fork. Lia was clearly struggling as well. She'd barely taken three bites of her meal. I mentally patted myself on the back for having the foresight to make reservations at the Chart House. I was thankful I'd eaten a proper meal beforehand. Jack, however, was having no such problems. He downed his second dinner of the evening with ease.

"Finished?" he asked through a mouthful, aiming his fork at my plate. At my nod, he speared the remainder of my salmon and deposited it neatly atop the remains of his risotto.

As dessert was served, Tammy sidled up to the podium and clinked a spoon against her glass. "Welcome, Bay View Class of 1989. Thank you all for coming and for making our reunion such a success."

Tammy prattled on for the next fifteen minutes, offering gratitude to every person who'd volunteered and every company who'd sponsored the event. She then coaxed several former chorus members to lead us in singing "Blue and White Forever," of which I couldn't remember a single verse, and then directed our attention to the screen behind her. The lights dimmed, and the opening chords of Alphaville's "Forever Young" echoed throughout the room. On the screen, a slideshow sprang to life, launching a montage of embarrassing photos from our teenage years, replete with big hair, pimples, pegged jeans, pastel colors, and upturned collars.

I'd apathetically, yet purposefully, neglected to submit any photos, but that did not spare me from seeing my face on the big screen. Pictures appeared of me talking with Jack in the school parking lot, performing a dance routine at halftime, and hanging out with Lia on her boat on a vibrant summer day—a photo I vividly remembered. Rose had magically appeared that day, returning from work to collect some cash for one of her weekend jaunts, and snapped our picture. In the photo, Lia and I looked happy, young, and hopeful. Our tanned arms were draped lazily around each other's shoulders, our heads tipped together, and our smiles bright.

I gave Lia a sharp, questioning glance. She lowered her eyes but couldn't hide her smile. "It's my favorite picture of us," she murmured.

So she hadn't forgotten about me. My heart leapt at the thought, only to be squashed again by the questions I'd tortured myself with so many times before. *Why did you disappear? Where did you go? How could you abandon me like that?*

Watching the pictures flash by was like viewing a photographic time capsule. The clothes and hairstyles instantly dated the images, as did the upbeat eighties music that accompanied the pictures. Young, hopeful, smiling faces filled the screen, and I gazed wistfully upon the pictures of Lia and me as they bloomed to life then faded from sight. A candid shot of Jack and me at prom, regarding each other sadly, warily, made me uncomfortable. Beneath the table, Jack reached for my hand. I fidgeted anxiously in my seat and wished for the slideshow to come to a swift and merciful end.

The final image was an aerial view of our entire class on graduation day, a sea of blue and white gowns rippling across the gymnasium, our caps gleefully flung from our heads, suspended in midair.

"And without further ado," Tammy announced amidst a thunderous round of applause, "I invite you to enjoy the rest of the evening as we celebrate the best class to ever grace the halls of Bay View High School—the class of 1989!"

The DJ cued C+C Music Factory's "Gonna Make You Sweat," and the drunkest of our classmates descended onto the dance floor.

"Refill?" Jack asked, noticing my empty glass.

"Please." I was admiring Jack's broad shoulders as he made his way toward the bar when small, cool fingers pressed into my forearm.

"So," Lia shouted over the music, "what have you been up to the past, oh, twenty years?" Despite her shorter hair and stouter body, Lia's smile still lit up her face, making her eyes sparkle.

Here we go. I doubted we would be able to dig below the superficial layers of "fines" and "goods." Lia had never been one for in-depth conversations or serious heart-to-hearts, which, at the moment, suited me just fine. Despite the many questions burning in my brain, I was too nervous to dig deep just yet, and I was determined to remain cool and collected. I would not be the one to cast the first stone. But it was obvious we would have to touch on some difficult topics for there to be any chance of salvaging a friendship that had long ago been forsaken.

To be honest, I wasn't even sure I *wanted* to rekindle a friendship with Lia. I'd done just fine without her. In fact, I'd probably done better, judging by the sadness in her eyes that her smile couldn't hide. I had married the love of my life and had three amazing daughters, a beautiful home, and interesting, flexible work. And I had Faith.

Faith. Friendship with her had been the icing on the cake, the cherry on top. She had filled a gap in my life that I hadn't acknowledged had been there. But her moving to Alabama had exposed that gap again. Faith was as dear to me as ever, but she was no longer near. Communicating across the miles and seeing each other only a few times a year wasn't the same. *Maybe someday Lia could fill that gap again.* Realizing I had nothing to lose, I lowered my defenses and decided to play along, see where things would go.

"Do you want the long version or the short one?" I asked.

"I'll take whichever one you're willing to give me," Lia shouted as the last chords of Tone Loc's "Wild Thing" blasted from the speakers.

"Well..." I began, raising my voice above Billy Idol's as he belted out the opening line of "Mony Mony." My ears were ringing, and my throat was getting scratchy. "Do you want to go outside?"

"Great idea." Lia stood and collected her jacket. "Gets chilly on the water at night. Remember?"

I nodded, realizing I'd forgotten to bring a jacket, and followed Lia through the crowd. Jack was congregating with a group of swimmers near the bar, a beer in one hand, a glass of wine in the other. I made a beeline for him and eagerly relieved him of the wineglass, taking a greedy gulp. Over my shoulder, Jack spotted Lia standing by the doors to the terrace. I followed his gaze, and Lia gave us both a small, self-conscious wave.

"Everything okay?" Jack asked.

"So far," I replied between two more swigs of wine. "We're headed outside to chat. Too loud in the ballroom."

"Good luck. Should I wander out soon to rescue you?"

"Uh, yeah. That's probably a good idea. Twenty minutes?"

"In twenty," Jack confirmed, kissing my cheek.

Lia was perched on the edge of a stone wall overlooking the bay. Her features were silhouetted in the moonlight. I felt a moment of tenderness toward her as some of our happier moments flashed through my mind. But then, just as quickly, I forced myself to remember the times she wasn't there for me, the times she'd taken me for granted, and I steeled my heart against these dangerous emotions. I inhaled deeply and sat stiffly beside her.

Lia sipped her chardonnay with a wistful expression. "I've missed you," she said, startling me with her candor. "There's so much I want to tell you, so much to explain. I don't know where to begin."

I pressed my lips together to suppress the numerous complicated questions that vied to escape. Instead, I forced myself to remain in safer, more neutral territory. "Let's start with the basics. Break the ice a bit?" Lia gave an agreeable bob of her head, so I pressed on. "I saw on your Facebook page that you're married. And you have kids?"

"Yes." Her shoulders relaxed. "I have twin boys, Nathan and Nicholas. My husband, Neil, couldn't make it tonight."

"That's too bad. I would have liked to meet him."

"Actually, this really isn't his scene." Lia exhaled and shook her head. "He would have been miserable trying to mingle with all these people."

There was an edge to Lia's voice as she spoke of her husband, so I steered the conversation toward her kids. "Did you bring pictures of your boys?"

Her face brightened. "I did!" She rummaged through her cream-colored leather bag and extracted a thin pink wallet.

Of course it's pink.

She flipped open the wallet to reveal a recent family photo of her, a diminutive, balding man, and two towheaded boys. The man had sharp features and beady eyes hidden behind square, dark-rimmed glasses. The boys wore happy, confident smiles and, like their mother, boasted a smattering of gold freckles across their small noses.

"This is Nick," Lia said with a smile, pointing at the blonder of the two boys, who was the spitting image of his mother. "And this one"—she shifted her fingertip to hover above the other boy, who, bless his heart, was less fortunate, having inherited his father's thin lips and weak chin—"is Nate. They're ten. Almost eleven."

"What a beautiful family," I complimented, uttering the expected reply. "I have a ten-year-old too. Evelyn. She'll be eleven next month." My face flushed with pride.

"And you have two more girls, right?" Though she'd clearly perused my Facebook page, as I had hers, Lia's uncharacteristic interest surprised me. The Lia of old would have preferred to talk about herself.

"Yep. Kathryn and Helene. Fourteen and eight."

"Lovely names!" Lia exclaimed.

"Unfortunately, I get the bad mommy of the year award because I didn't bring pictures."

Lia laughed, easing my guilt. "You and Jack always said you were going to have a big family," she mused. "So where are you working?"

I was irrationally irked that Lia didn't ask anything more about my girls. The godmother I'd once envisioned her to be would have wanted to know everything about them—their favorite foods and colors, their hobbies and interests, their unique quirks. I swallowed my irritation and replied to her question. "I'm a writer. Freelance. Newspaper columns, a magazine article here and there." I clamped my lips together and crossed my arms over my chest. I was already giving away more than I'd intended. *Where is Jack? Hasn't it been twenty minutes already?*

"So you decided on journalism after all. Good for you," Lia said, a faraway look in her eyes. "Remember when you were undecided, agonizing about what school to go to, what to major in?"

"I was never as confident as you were," I lamented. "And I never fully decided. I dual-majored in marketing and journalism. What did you end up doing?" I was anxious to shift the focus back to her.

"Got my engineering degree, worked for Lockheed Martin. Now I run my own business, Ivy Consulting."

The name sounded familiar. "Wasn't Ivy your aunt's name?"

"Yes. But I like the name. It grows on you." She sipped her wine. "Get it?"

I smirked at the witty pun.

"Business is going really well," Lia continued. "I'm currently building my client base in Northern Virginia, which would be great if it weren't for the hellish commute around the beltway." Lia easily reverted to our familiar pattern of her talking and me listening. It dawned on me that by staying in control of the conversation, she could steer the discussion any way she wanted and avoid topics she would rather not discuss.

"Tell me more about Neil," I interrupted, hoping to glean some insight into her whereabouts the past two decades.

Like me, Lia seemed reluctant to divulge too many personal details. She twirled a strand of hair around her finger. "He's a good guy, into sports, the kids..."

I let the silence hang between us as Faith had taught me to do, relying on its uncomfortable presence to nudge Lia onward.

Lia snorted and shook her head. "I know he doesn't seem like my type."

"He's not exactly the big, beefy type you used to go for," I agreed. Though, truth was, I never really knew Lia to have a type. If a guy had a penis, he was her type.

"I didn't always make the best decisions, did I?" Lia gave a rueful chuckle and shifted her gaze to the horizon, where the twin spans of the bridge had become a beacon against the darkening sky. A gentle breeze ruffled her short hair, nearly whisking away the words she whispered next. "Neil was there for me when I needed someone."

A cool breeze floated off the water, and I began to shiver in the night air. As if on cue, Jack materialized behind me and draped his jacket over my shoulders. "Getting a bit chilly out here," he said, flashing me a conspiratorial wink.

Lia glanced up. "Hey, Jack." The two of them had more or less ignored each other during dinner. But now, alone on the terrace, their lack of interaction was simply awkward. Jack had never been a big Lia fan, but being outright rude wasn't his style.

"Hi, Lia. How have you been?" he asked stiffly as he pulled me close. But we both knew his real question was not "*How* have you been?" but "*Where?*"

"I'm good, thanks," Lia replied, touching Jack lightly on the arm. Her lips slowly curled into a smile. "And you're as handsome as ever." I narrowed my eyes and gave my head a quick shake. *Once a flirt, always a flirt.* "What are you doing with yourself these days?"

"Running a sports therapy practice, enjoying my girls." He draped his arm lovingly and protectively around my shoulders.

I closed my eyes, and a memory bloomed behind my lids. I remembered the way Lia had relentlessly pursued Jack in high school, the way she'd flirted with him. Unlike so many other boys at Bay View, Jack had been immune to Lia's charms. He had not been interested in her. Jack had chosen *me*.

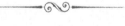

November 1987

THE BOYS' SOCCER TEAM had advanced to the playoffs, and the bleachers were packed as Bay View played host to Broad Creek. Typically, Lia kept her attention on the field, her eyes glued to the guys' muscular thighs. "Soccer players have the best legs," she would often utter in an appreciative purr. That night, however, she was restless. I watched from the corner of my eye as her sharp gaze flicked over the bleachers. Jack had broken up with Renee a few weeks after homecoming, and since then, there was no shortage of girls angling to take her place, Lia included.

Lia's face suddenly brightened. "Be right back," she announced with a sly grin.

She weaved her way through the crowd and wrapped her arms around Jack from behind like they were old pals. She then wedged herself between Jack and his friend, latched on to Jack's arm, and towed him to where we were sitting. Jack's eyes met mine as Lia plopped down in front of me and motioned for Jack to sit beside her. I'd continued to admire Jack from afar, carefully orchestrating my walks between classes to catch glimpses of him in the hallways, and sharing a smile when he passed by the school store in the morning. I secretly hoped he would stop to buy a notebook or pack of pencils, giving us an excuse to talk, but he never did.

Throughout the game, Lia giggled and whispered into Jack's ear, her hand resting casually, possessively, on his thigh. Jack humored her but didn't respond. At halftime, uninterested in playing spectator to the game unfolding on the bleacher in front of me, I wandered to the concession stand. The savory scents of grease and bread gave me a sudden craving for a soft pretzel and a soda. I reached into my pocket, extracted a few crumpled bills, and was about to hand the money over when I spied several dollar bills flapping overhead.

"Make it two." The voice was deep and smooth, black velvet. I could feel the heat of his breath on my neck. *Jack*. I looked over my shoulder and was once again struck dumb by his ridiculous beauty. As a rule, high school boys were simply not supposed to be that gorgeous.

Jack flashed a shy grin. "I believe I owe you a Coke."

Snacks in hand, we weaved our way through the bodies amassed along the walkway and ascended the bleachers as Bay View shot the ball into the net on a penalty kick. The metal stairs groaned beneath our sneakers as the crowd leapt to their feet to celebrate the goal. Lia, unused to being disregarded, stared at us in astonishment. Her glare was a mixture of fire and ice as Jack and I squeezed into the open seats in front of her. I bit into my pretzel and could feel Lia's eyes boring into the back of my skull as I chewed the thick, salty dough. Shrinking beneath Lia's withering

gaze, I lied about seeing someone I needed to talk to, thanked Jack
for the Coke and pretzel, and disappeared into the crowd.

ON NEW YEAR'S EVE, Lia insisted we go to a party at Chris
Miller's house. Chris and Jack were both on the Annapolis Aquat-
ics Swim Team, so Lia was convinced Jack would be there. She
boasted that it would be the night she "made her move." I scowled
and shook my head in disgust. Lia had been putting the moves on
Jack for two months already. *Can't she take a hint?*

My crush on Jack had continued to grow, like a living, breathing beast taking up space in my chest, but I didn't breathe a word
of it to anyone. Convinced Jack was out of my league and that he
would make a move if he was interested, I continued to watch from
the sidelines as other girls threw themselves at him and flirted relentlessly, to the point that they seemed desperate. Jack humored
them, laughing at their jokes and flattery, which only made me like
him more. But he'd remained decidedly single despite his many admirers.

Chris's house pulsed with energy. Music thumped, and drinks
flowed. The minute Lia and I walked in the door, someone handed
us two plastic cups filled with chunks of fruit floating in a rosy liquid. I took a tentative sip. It was crisp and sweet. Kool-Aid with a
twist.

We circuited the room and polished off our drinks. Lia
snatched the cup from my hand and returned it to me filled to the
top with the potent juice. "He's got to be around here somewhere,"
she fretted, scanning the crowded room. She quickly downed her
second cup, disappeared into the kitchen, and reemerged with a
pitcher. She filled her cup a third time and dangled the pitcher
above the plastic lip of mine.

"I'm driving!" I protested, protectively covering my cup with my palm.

Lia shrugged. "Suit yourself." She tossed back a hearty swig of her drink and slithered into the gyrating fray on the makeshift dance floor.

"There you are!" someone shouted.

A pair of hands snaked around from behind and covered my eyes, and the scent of apple hit my nose. "Guess who?"

I whirled around, admittedly disappointed that it wasn't Jack, but relieved to see that Becky and Kelly had finally arrived.

"Where's Lia?" Becky asked.

I inclined my head toward the dance floor, where Lia was grinding with abandon, sandwiched between two guys.

"God," Kelly grumbled. "Does she ever give it a rest?"

I shook my head and rolled my eyes—accustomed to Lia's antics by now—and the three of us broke into a fit of giggles. Becky grabbed my wrist and tugged me toward the kitchen. "C'mon. Let's find something to eat."

We rummaged through the pantry and unearthed a bag of chips and a box of frosted blueberry Pop-Tarts. I'd just ripped open the last package of cardboard-tasting pastries when Chris stuck his head into the kitchen. His disembodied face floated in midair, and we giggled at the apparition.

"You might want to check on your friend," he suggested.

Chris's tone was sobering. We quickly stashed the remnants of our snack on the pantry shelf and scurried into the crowd. Lia was passed out on a couch. I sank to my knees and hovered near her head. Her sour exhalations warmed my ear. I sat back on my heels, relieved that she was still breathing and hadn't vomited on herself. I reached out and gently shook her shoulder.

"Lia?" When I received no response, I shook her again. She mumbled something unintelligible and rolled over, pressing her face into the velvet color-blocked cushions. I wobbled to my feet and gazed down at her, unsure what to do.

"Let her sleep it off," Kelly suggested. She bent across Lia's body to retrieve the dingy brown-and-orange afghan that was haphazardly draped over the couch and tucked it around Lia's sleeping form.

Still uncertain, I glanced at Becky and saw that her gaze had shifted to something beyond my shoulder, her eyes wide. The hairs on the back of my neck stood on end. Someone was behind me. I could feel the heat of him before I could see him. Then a deep, sexy voice murmured something about Lia not being able to handle her liquor.

I spun around. "Lia can handle just about anything," I said as I stared into those breathtaking eyes.

"But not everything," Jack corrected. He flashed his dazzling smile. "Pizza's here. Do you want a slice?"

I glanced worriedly at Lia, and Becky plopped onto the couch near her feet. "I'll sit with her," she offered with a wink.

Jack reached for my hand, and my heart hammered in my chest. We weaved through the crowded, noisy living room—ignoring the pizza boxes stacked ten high—and wandered into a quiet den adjacent to the kitchen. I sat on a couch, and Jack closed the door then sat close.

"The mysterious Jack," I said stupidly, involuntarily inching away as my nerves got the best of me. I inhaled deeply, willing my galloping heart to quiet. I was certain Jack could hear it beating wildly against my chest.

"Why would you say that?"

"Well, no one seems to know anything about you." *Except that you're gorgeous and aloof and mysterious.*

"What do you want to know? I'm an open book."

"Okay. Why did your family move to Maryland?"

Jack grimaced and sipped his beer. "My mom is from here. My parents split up when I was really young. Apparently, she'd had enough of New York."

I suddenly felt guilty for prying. "I'm sorry."

Jack shrugged. "Don't be. From what my mom says, we're better off without my dad anyway. I don't even know the guy." His voice was calm, his face placid. But I was certain I detected a flicker of regret in his eyes.

"Everyone deserves to know their father." It was a heavy conversation, but the words flowed easily between us.

The cacophony of the party suddenly ratcheted up, and the television volume was cranked full blast. Dick Clark began the countdown to midnight, and Jack edged closer, his eyes intense, searching mine. I could smell his cologne, a spicy, peppery fragrance that blended nicely with his own earthy, masculine scent.

My palms were sweating, and I was pleasantly tipsy, drunk on alcohol and Jack's attention. When his soft lips tenderly met mine at the stroke of midnight, a fizzy sensation exploded inside of me, like fireworks on the Fourth of July. I battled to control the conflicting emotions that raged between my desire for Jack and my loyalty to Lia. Knowing how angry she would be if she knew I was sitting there, kissing Jack, was sufficient to spoil the moment.

I pressed my palm against Jack's strong, broad chest and pushed him away. "What about Lia?"

Jack frowned. "What about her?"

"She's, uh, really into you," I stammered. "In case you hadn't noticed. I don't want to get in the way of anything. If you're interested in her..."

My hand was still resting on Jack's chest. He placed his large hand over mine and held it tightly. "Does it look like I'm interested in Lia?"

I attempted to withdraw my hand from his grasp. "But..."

Jack released my hand but held my gaze. "I'm not the least bit interested in Lia. I'm interested in you." Then his lips were on mine again, more urgent but with a respectful restraint, a question.

I am in big trouble. It was the only thought in my mind as my mouth answered his.

THE BREEZE FLOATING in from the bay kicked up a notch, and I leaned into Jack's warm body. A roar of laughter and voices exploded behind us as a boisterous crowd of sweaty, drunken classmates stumbled out of the ballroom and onto the terrace, their shirts soaked through with sweat and spilled beer. The party had clearly moved outside.

"Lia!" Tammy shouted, grabbing Lia by the hand. "I saw on Facebook that you're an engineer. My husband is an engineer too, but he's trying to find a new job..."

Tammy's voice was swallowed by the crowd as she towed Lia toward the opposite side of the terrace, causing us to become separated in the throng.

"You ready to get out of here?" Jack whispered against my ear.

"More than ready." My head was pounding, and my cheeks were aching from the forced smile that had been plastered on my face all evening. The effort to speak above the thumping music and din of the crowd had taxed my vocal cords, rendering my voice deep and raspy.

"It sounds sexy like that," Jack teased.

Spying Lia across the crowded terrace, I caught her eye and waved, intending to duck out without further ado. I didn't get the answers I was hoping for, but the fact that Lia and I were even talking again was a miracle in itself. As the saying went, Rome wasn't built in a day. I lifted my foot to massage my aching arch. *Nor was it built while wearing stilettos.*

Jack kissed me on the cheek. "I'm going to hit the men's room before we head out."

"Okay." I sank onto a padded bench near the terrace doors. "I'll wait here."

Through a gap in the crowd, I saw Lia skillfully extract herself from a particularly rowdy group that had tried to reel her in. She caught my eye and made a beeline for me. Sitting alone, I felt like a deer trapped in the headlights.

"Anna, I'd really like to see you again," Lia blurted. Then she giggled at the pickup line.

I dropped my guard and allowed myself to imagine the possibilities. Twenty years had been wasted—there was no changing that. But perhaps this could be the start of something new. Perhaps there was the possibility, however remote, of decades of friendship still ahead.

"Okay," I was surprised to hear myself whisper.

Lia smiled, relieved. "I'll email you. We'll set something up."

I stood from the bench. "That would be good." Then my arms were around her. I missed my friend. I missed her deeply, yet I was still angry for all that we'd lost. But instead of mourning all that hadn't been, I was suddenly aware of all that could still be. Lia and I could still become old ladies, wrinkled and gray, rocking in chairs on my front porch, sipping tea, talking about our grandkids, and laughing at our foolish teenaged selves.

I desperately wanted to understand why Lia had disappeared, if for no other reason than to have a sense of closure. But more than that, I wanted to forgive her. I wanted to free my soul of the burden it carried, and I wanted to salvage any possibility of rekindling a friendship with Lia while there was still time. As we embraced, the years we'd lost melted away, filling the yawning gap between us and mending the tattered edges of my heart.

CHAPTER 18
August 2009

Two months passed with no word from Lia. The week after the reunion, I checked my email and Facebook daily to see if there was a message from her, but there was nothing. At first, the radio silence was a relief. But as the days passed, I hoped I would see her name in my inbox. By the fifteenth day, I'd given up that hope. *Fool!* I should have known better. Lia was the one who'd abandoned me, wronged me, all those years ago. And she was also the one who'd said at the reunion that she wanted to see me again, that she would email me. I would be damned if I was going to be the one to reach out to her. The ball had been in Lia's court—it always had been—and she'd dropped it. Again.

My disappointment had morphed into frustration then anger—at myself, at Lia—until finally, mercifully, indifference set in. Back-to-school mania was in full swing. The girls needed physicals, haircuts, new shoes, and school supplies. Weeks passed, and I didn't so much as think of Lia. And then, as abruptly as tender shoots burst forth from the earth in spring, she appeared. I was home, working furiously to meet a deadline for *Fitness* magazine. I'd just put the final touches on a piece about triathlons—recently deemed the fastest-growing adult participation sport in the country—when I heard the telltale *ping.*

Lia: *Meet for lunch?*

I stared at the message until the text blurred and the letters transformed into unrecognizable mishmash. I closed the window and resumed my work. Five minutes later, I was interrupted by another *ping*.

Ignore it. Anger flared again as I remembered that Lia had waited two months to reach out. But I couldn't summon the discipline to delete the message without reading it.

Lia: *Sorry it took so long. Neil lost his job.*

I wondered if it were true. *Lia wouldn't lie about something like that, would she?* I drummed my fingertips on the desktop, mentally weighing the pros and cons of meeting with her. Even though the cons were in the lead, I quickly tapped five keys before I could change my mind.

Anna: *When?*

Lia: *Friday, 12:00. Keller's?*

My heart beat rapidly. I hated her. I missed her.

Anna: *OK. C U then.*

I immediately closed Facebook and logged in to my email account. Faith was a stubborn social media holdout. I knew she would prefer I call, but with my deadline looming, I couldn't afford the luxury of a phone call.

I smiled at the memory of the long, indulgent conversation we'd had after the reunion. I'd caught her in the bath—given the nature of her work, she always had her telephone nearby—and she'd demanded that I tell her everything and not leave out a single detail. So while she'd soaked in the tub, I put the phone on speaker and painted my toenails bright pink while regaling her with my reunion tale. Faith gasped, laughed, and interjected at all the appropriate places. I felt giddy and warm as Faith and I chatted across the miles the way I'd always imagined girlfriends did. But Faith was more than just a friend—she was the sister I'd never had but always wished for. That fact alone made me swell with pride and happiness that I'd been able to give my girls each other. *Sisters.*

Faith had also been gratifyingly annoyed on my behalf when I called to vent after months had gone by after the reunion with no word from Lia. Faith said she'd been feeling better, and it was refreshing to hear her in good spirits. The Southern sass had returned to her voice. I jotted a quick message, wondering what Faith would have to say about my pending lunch date. I didn't have to wait long for a reply.

"Don't reveal your whole heart in the first five minutes. Let her do the talking so you can decide if you like what you're hearing. Remember, silence is golden. She who holds the silence holds the power. Good luck!"

A LIGHTWEIGHT NAVY-blue blouse, white linen pants, and a navy pair of espadrilles served as my suit of armor. I'd experienced a strange mix of excitement and apprehension, as one did before a first date, as I dressed that morning. Now, as I drove to Keller's, I just felt sick. I'd fretted the night before about the wisdom of meeting Lia. I also fretted over what to wear, which made me angry. I was no fashionista and wasted no time worrying about my wardrobe or what was "in style." But on that occasion, and for reasons I could not quite articulate, I wanted to look good. I wanted to impress. When we were teenagers, Lia had always been the pretty, fashionable one. It was my turn to shine. But I knew this unusual posturing and this attitude were rooted in a need to boost my own confidence rather than a desire to outdo Lia.

Childishly, I thought it would serve her right if I didn't show up at all. But Jack and Faith had both encouraged me to go, more or less on the grounds of having nothing to lose—a rationale I did not entirely agree with. Not only was my pride on the line, but my heart was too. What troubled me on a deeper level was that I suddenly seemed incapable of making a decision without both my husband's and my former shrink's support and approval. But I'd accepted Lia's invitation then spent the next week obsessing over my outfit.

I parked in the lot at Keller's—our favorite high school hang-out—and sat in the car with the stifling heat rapidly rising. I wondered what the hell I was doing there.

Tentatively, I peeled myself from the oppressive interior of the car and ventured into the building. I was momentarily blinded as my eyes adjusted to the darkness. As my haloed vision settled into definitive lines and shapes, I realized Keller's had changed little in twenty years. Everything was exactly as I remembered but with an extra bit of spit and shine. The pool table had been re-covered—the new felt was a Bay View royal blue instead of the old, faded green—and sleek flat-screen TVs had replaced the bulky box sets. I'd imagined walking in would be like *Cheers*—everyone would know my name—but I didn't recognize a single face. The wait staff bustled about, tending to the lunch crowd, and Mr. Keller himself, a standard fixture at the family-run establishment, was nowhere in sight. Neither was Lia. And I'd purposely arrived ten minutes late.

Recalling that we'd preferred the patio when the weather was nice, I wandered toward the back door, debating if ninety degrees and humid still counted as "nice." In our teens, it would have been ideal. We would have stripped off our oversized T-shirts and dined al fresco in bikini tops and cutoffs. Now that I was pushing forty, I was less fond of baking in the sun and sweating through my clothes. I stepped outside into the smothering heat. A dozen people were seated on the patio, but no Lia. I crossed my arms and glanced at my watch. I would give her exactly five minutes to show. If she didn't, game over. She would never get the benefit of the doubt from me again, no matter the excuse.

I stepped back, taking refuge in a rectangle of shade cast by the building's overhang. My eyes passed over the patrons dining on fish tacos and shrimp salad. It wasn't until an older woman with short rusty-brown hair smiled at me that I realized I'd been scanning the crowd in search of long strawberry-blond locks. I did a double take. *Lia.* She was already there, a glass of water sweating on the table in front of her. I'd been searching for the Lia of twenty years ago. I still couldn't reconcile the image before me with the one etched in my memory. I realized I probably looked different to her too. Two decades had passed after all.

I swallowed, forced a smile, and walked toward an uncertain future. Lia watched me approach. The bay behind her shimmered, its smooth, murky surface deceptively beautiful in the sparkling sunlight. A blue-and-white-striped umbrella bathed the table in shade, and to my relief, a small breeze floated inland from the water, lightly wicking the sweat from my arms.

Lia was stunning in a lemon-yellow sundress with a flowing, calf-length skirt and flat brown sandals. The air gently stirred her hair. Without the weight of her former waist-length mane to coax the locks into gentle waves, her hair was a mop of unruly curls that just grazed her pale, freckled shoulders. She must have blown it out for the reunion, I mused, taken aback by the surprising sight of the springy curls.

Lia laughed and dramatically fluffed her hair with an upturned palm. "Curly, right?" Her smile widened. "I had no idea exactly *how* curly until I went short. Of course, having kids changed it too. Much thicker and darker now."

Her easy candor disarmed me. "I know what you mean. My feet grew half a size with each pregnancy."

Lia laughed again and stood to hug me. She'd lost weight since the reunion.

"You look great," I complimented, feeling ridiculously over-dressed in my blouse and heels. I fought a sudden urge to flee. Instead, I sat stiffly on the edge of the chair opposite Lia.

"Thanks. It hit me one day that my curves were gone and I was simply round, like an overinflated beach ball," Lia said with a self-deprecating chuckle. "My New Year's resolution, like everyone else's on the planet, was to lose weight. I didn't get serious about it until after the reunion, though." She helped herself to a long sip of her water. "I've lost ten pounds since then."

"Well, you look great," I repeated.

Our waiter was gorgeous and deeply tanned. His hair was tousled and sun-bleached, as if he'd just paddled in on a surfboard. His muscular forearms flexed as he gripped the notepad in his hands. "What'll you ladies have?"

"What are the specials?" Lia asked, perusing her menu.

I stared at her, nonplussed. She was a stranger indeed. The Lia I knew would have immediately turned on the charm in the presence of such a fine specimen and said something grossly flirtatious and ridiculous like "I'll have *you* for lunch."

Kai, his name tag read, rattled off the soup and catch of the day, while casting surreptitious glances at the scantily clad teenage girls giggling at the table beside us.

"I'll have the calamari, tomato, and caper salad," Lia ordered.

"Great choice," Kai approved absently, his eyes fixed on the girls.

I cleared my throat loudly. "Crab cake sandwich with a side of Old Bay fries, please."

"Excellent." Kai scribbled in his notepad and headed toward the kitchen without so much as a glance at either of us.

"Some cougars we are," Lia lamented. "Remember the good ol' days? When it was us the boys were staring at?"

"Uh, no. More like *you* they were staring at," I corrected. Feeling fidgety and anxious, I plucked a sugar packet from its holder and tapped it against the table. "I'm sorry to hear about Neil's job. What happened?"

"Budget cuts. Neil's not a full-time teacher, so the school can't renew his coaching contract. He's been a real piece of work this summer." She frowned and shifted her gaze toward the water.

"What's he going to do?"

Lia shrugged. "Dunno. So far, he's been eating Doritos and playing video games. Guess he'll figure something out eventually." She reached for the basket of assorted breads Kai had delivered to our table along with a water for me. "Let's not talk about Neil." She smeared whipped butter onto a warm piece of pumpernickel. "I try to limit carbs, but bread hot out of the oven is hard to resist." She groaned with pleasure as she took a big bite.

I helped myself to a piece of the bread. "Is that how you lost the weight? Cutting carbs?" Running and biking regularly had, so far, allowed me the luxury of enjoying carbs whenever I wanted.

"No. My diet wasn't the problem. Lack of exercise was. I started riding my bike, and the weight started falling off. I've kinda hit a plateau, though. I think I need to add some strength training, shake things up."

"That's probably a good idea." Then without thinking, I blurted, "We should do a triathlon sometime." The *Fitness* article I'd been working on was still so fresh in my mind.

"Are you trying to kill me?" Lia exclaimed. "I knew you were probably mad at me, but not *that* mad. Sheesh."

I rolled my eyes in mock exasperation. The conversation was edging toward dangerous territory.

"You *are* angry, though," Lia observed. It was not a question.

I shrugged, popping a piece of honey wheat into my mouth.

"I don't blame you. I'd be mad at me too. I wasn't sure you'd agree to meet me. Especially here. So many memories..."

The bread hardened into a wet lump in my mouth, and I struggled to swallow it. "*Mad* doesn't exactly cover it, Lia," I croaked around the hunk of bread. Our eyes locked. I refused to blink or speak. Faith's words of wisdom echoed in my brain. *She who holds the silence holds the power.*

Kai appeared with our lunches, interrupting our stalemate.

"So what *does* cover it, then?" Lia asked.

Kai deposited our plates in front of us and beat a hasty retreat. "Can I have some pepper?" Lia hollered at his back.

"What kind of question is that, Lia? Where do I even start?" I asked, my voice rising. "Angry, confused, sad, betrayed, hurt, rejected, disappointed." Each word was laced with years of resentment.

Lia's pretty green eyes widened and filled with tears. *Here comes the drama.* I steeled myself for the lies and excuses that were certain to follow.

"Anna." Lia's shiny eyes searched my face. "I am so sorry. I made so many bad choices. Some good choices and some necessary choices but definitely some bad ones. My biggest regret is losing you. I've really missed you, and I'm sorry... for everything. I just want your forgiveness. This time, I promise I'll be the friend you deserve."

I was speechless. I wasn't sure what I'd expected—excuses, blame, flippant remarks, nonchalance. But not this. A sincere apology might have been what I was hoping for but certainly not what I was expecting. Her ease and willingness to accept responsibility should have filled me with relief. Instead, flames of suspicion and doubt flickered within, making me edgy and tense.

Kai reappeared with the pepper. "How's everything?"

"Great," I replied, popping a fry into my mouth.

"Delicious," Lia added, though I wasn't sure she'd taken a single bite.

"Cool. Let me know if you need anything else."

We both watched as Kai paused on his way back to the kitchen to chat with a cute young waitress who was balancing a tray of crab nachos and two draft beers. Kai relieved her of the pints and whispered something in her ear that made her smile, exposing deep dimples. She was adorable. I sighed, realizing I was probably old enough to be the girl's mother. Not the mother of a toddler—like the two twentysomethings on the opposite side of the patio who hadn't had a moment's peace since they'd arrived—but the mother of a daughter nearly old enough to *work* at Keller's. At my age—closer to fifty than twenty—I was not meant to be nursing, changing diapers, potty training, trekking off to Gymboree once a week, and downing countless mugs of coffee in a desperate attempt to stay awake through yet another *Dora the Explorer* marathon. I was meant to be there, balanced on the precipice of the next phase of my life. My shoulders slumped, and my armor slipped. Right there, at that moment, was where I was meant to be, perhaps *destined* to be. So I took a deep breath and jumped, hoping Lia would catch my fall.

"Why?" I asked, fighting to remain cool and aloof, despising the nervous quiver in my voice. "I want to know why you left. One minute, we were best friends, hugging each other in your dorm room at Maryland, making plans and promises to stay in touch and see each other during the holidays. And then you were just... gone." I'd given up all pretense of stoicism and was speaking rapidly, breathlessly, my words coming in a rush.

Lia sat quietly, patiently, allowing me to let it all out.

"The few times I managed to reach you on the phone that fall, you were so distant, distracted. I was so confused, Lia. I still am. Did I do something wrong? The letter you gave me that day at Maryland, it said you had something to tell me. But it was crazy packing for college, and I forgot. I'm sorry I didn't get to see you, but I did call. And you shut me out. Is that why you ignored me? Is it why you left? Or was it something else? Please tell me. Please help me understand what happened."

Lia opened her mouth—her Cupid's-bow lips forming a perfect O—then snapped it shut again. Absently, she pressed her fingertip into a bead of water shimmering on the table and began tracing a pattern of swirls and spirals on the polished wooden surface. Finally, she spoke, her voice hesitant, uncertain. "It's a lame cliché—it's not you, it's me—but I'm afraid it's true. It was never you, Anna. You didn't do anything wrong. All I can say is I'm sorry."

The remains of my lunch, which had initially made my mouth water, now seemed utterly repulsive. The smell of crab and grease mingled with the fishy, sulfurous smell of the bay and hovered like a thick stew in the humid air. I shoved my plate away and leaned back in my chair, folding my arms defensively, protectively, across my chest. "That's *it*?" I asked between clenched teeth. "You disappear for twenty years without a word, and that's all you have to say: 'It's not you, it's me'? Well, that's not going to cut it!" I stood abruptly from the table, and my napkin tumbled from my lap onto the weather-worn planks. "This was a mistake."

"Wait!" Lia's hand shot out and gripped my forearm, her eyes pleading with me to stay. The young girls at the table beside us stopped giggling and stared. The mothers bounced their toddlers on their laps, offering them fries and shushing them, probably to better eavesdrop on us.

Jaw clenched, I sank into my seat and resumed my defensive posture. I would give her one last chance to say something that made sense, something that was *real*.

Lia chewed the inside of her lip, a familiar, contemplative gesture. She was mulling her options. To hell with Faith and her *silence is golden* bit.

"Christmas break was the worst," I blurted. "We had *plans*, Lia. We were supposed to spend the weekend together in Salisbury, and you just bailed. I was so disappointed. I'd been looking forward to it—to seeing you—for months. And then you just... disappeared! We were *best friends*. I was always there for you. And my family was there for you too. We felt *sorry* for you. I didn't deserve to be treated like that. I deserved better. And now I deserve an explanation."

I was queasy with the adrenaline that coursed through my veins. My limbs trembled, and my hands were clenched into fists. I flared my nostrils and inhaled deeply in an effort to calm down, gratified by the shock on Lia's face. Her typically rosy-pale complexion had blanched a sickly shade of grayish white.

"I didn't need your pity," she shot back, regaining her composure. "I could take care of myself. I'd been taking care of myself since I was three years old, since Rose decided that having a kid was a total drag and she'd be damned if she'd be tied down."

"Rose treated you like crap," I agreed. "But that doesn't give you the right to treat other people badly. When you took off, I was so angry. I never wanted to speak to you again." I laughed bitterly. "And in a nasty twist of irony, I got my wish. You made your choice, and I moved on with my life. The only time it really hurt was on my wedding day. And when my girls were born. I always imagined you'd be there—my maid of honor, godmother to my daughters. Instead, you were already a distant memory. Ancient history."

Lia sniffed, glanced down at her lap, across the bay to the distant shore, anywhere but at me.

"And now," I continued, "just as quickly as you disappeared, you resurface again, like some ghost from the past. I hadn't planned on going to the reunion, but my *friend* Faith said it would be a mistake not to. She was worried I'd regret it. So I decided to hell with it! It didn't matter if you were there because *you* didn't matter. I thought you showing your face at the reunion would have no bearing on my life. But I was wrong. Seeing you again slayed me. So I just want to know—*need* to know—why? The least you could do, after all these years, is give me an answer that makes sense."

I was breathing heavily. I'd said my piece. I greedily sipped my tepid water—the ice had long since melted—and attempted to quench the fire in my throat. The ball was in Lia's court. I leaned back in my chair and stared at her intently, challenging her—willing her—to provide me with an answer that would be the aha moment I'd been waiting for. But she was still looking toward the water, avoiding my gaze. Her forehead was furrowed, her eyebrows drawn together as if trying to solve a difficult riddle.

"Was everything okay?" Kai interrupted, warily eyeing the untouched food on our plates. An eerie hush had fallen over the patio that had been abuzz with chatter when I'd arrived.

"Um, yeah. Fine," I muttered. "We're just busy... catching up."

"Need some boxes?"

"No," we chorused.

"Any dessert today?"

I shook my head. Lia sat in stony silence.

"All right, then. I'll bring the check." Kai quickly cleared our plates. His calf muscles rippled as he walked, and his low-slung cargo shorts clung to his hips.

I held my breath, waiting for Lia's reply. A hot trickle of sweat ran down my back. The sun, having edged beyond the range of the umbrella's protective shade, was beating unmercifully upon my shoulders.

Lia's brow eased. Though her features appeared placid, her eyes remained troubled. "I'm sorry, Anna." Her voice was so soft, the words were nearly carried away on the hot currents that caressed us. "I wish I had a better answer for you, one that would make things right between us. But I don't. I did a lot of things in high school I wasn't proud of, and I needed a fresh start. The only way I knew how to do that was to leave my past behind. Unfortunately, that included you. I didn't mean to hurt you—"

"Forget it!" I snatched a twenty-dollar bill from my wallet and slapped it on the table. "I have to go."

"Anna, please. Don't—"

"It's too little, too late, Lia!" I glared down at her, but my lower lip quivered as I thought of Faith, her anguished cries ringing in my ears. My heart had broken for her when she'd called on Tuesday with the news. "Besides, my *friend* needs me. Her father died this week. The funeral's tomorrow. I'm headed to the airport from here to be with her because that's what real friends do. They support each other. They're *there* for each other."

I stalked toward the patio exit that led to the parking lot. Through blurred vision, I fumbled for my keys and dropped them in the gravel. A puff of chalky dust rose from the ground. Cursing, I knelt and grabbed the keys. I had just yanked the car door open when Lia caught up to me.

Her small, delicate fingers encircled my wrist. "Anna, I'm sorry. I keep messing up. This is just so hard—"

"I don't want to hear it, Lia. Against my better judgment, I decided to give you a chance, hoping that you'd changed. Clearly, I was wrong." I slammed the door shut, shoved the key into the ignition, and stomped on the gas pedal. To my shock and horror, the car lurched backward instead of forward and slammed into the low brick wall in front of the building. My head jerked violently backward before snapping forward and crashing into the steering wheel. A tender lump rose immediately beneath the skin. Dazed, I glanced up to see Lia standing rigid, her eyes popped wide, her hands clapped over her mouth. In my haste, I'd shifted the car into reverse instead of drive. Mortified and shaken, I laid my head against the wheel and let the tears fall, hot and bitter, soaking my sweaty cheeks.

Then Lia was moving, running toward the car. The restaurant manager, several servers, and a few customers trailed in her wake. "Oh my God! Anna!" Lia pounded on my window. "Are you okay?"

I watched in fascination as my hand floated lazily from my lap to the door and my finger depressed the button to lower the window. Lia's face floated in front of mine, her green eyes intense. I couldn't wrap my head around it. Why was she was standing in front of me instead of sitting beside me? It was déjà vu. I'd been there before, covered in shattered glass.

Lia's voice snapped me from my dream and awakened me to the nightmare. "Your head! You're hurt!" She yanked open the door and unbuckled my seat belt.

Strange, worried faces loomed behind her. In the rearview mirror, I could see two waiters studying the back of my car. One was solemnly shaking his head, and the other was rubbing his hand over the day-old stubble on his chin. I imagined I could hear the raspy, scratching sound.

I gazed, unseeing, at the people around me. Their voices were muffled, their movements slow and languid, as if underwater. Then, without warning, the hazy lens of shock clicked into sharp focus and catapulted me into the small clutch of chaos that engulfed me. People were shouting and swarming around the car, asking questions and barking orders. Lia's green eyes were staring into mine, but it was Faith's darker mahogany ones I saw. I had to get to the airport.

"Okay," I mumbled, stumbling out of the car. "I'm okay."

Lia wrapped an arm around my waist to steady me.

"Ma'am, you've got a heck of a knot on your head. Should I call an ambulance?"

"No! Don't!" I shouted more loudly than necessary.

The man glanced from me to his phone to Lia, uncertain.

"Really," I said, managing to steady my legs and work my trembling lips into a slippery, reassuring smile. "I'm fine. I've got to get to the airport. I have a plane to catch."

"Um, I don't think you're getting anywhere in this car," said the muscular, olive-skinned waiter with the five o'clock shadow.

My smile faltered. I twisted out of Lia's grasp and tottered like a newborn deer toward the rear of the car to survey the damage. The sturdy knee wall, soundly constructed of brick and concrete, was no worse for the wear. Unfortunately, the same could not be said of my car. The rear quarter panel was crumpled like a tin can. Jagged strips of metal curled menacingly toward the tire, which was partially deflated. I let the air out of my cheeks and ordered my brain to engage. *Think, Anna. Damn it, think!*

"I'll drive," a soft, tentative voice offered.

I snapped my head around to find Lia looking at me hopefully. Instead of being grateful, I only felt rage. Of course she would use this to her advantage. Anger flooded my body, but the rush of adrenaline it delivered was welcome, serving to get my brain and body moving again. I quickly assessed the situation and weighed my options. Jack was at work, an hour in the opposite direction, so I decided to first call a cab, then AAA. I would fill Jack in later.

I found the number I was searching for and waited for the call to connect. "Yes, I need a cab—" I began, speaking clearly and confidently. Then my phone was rudely snatched from my hand.

"That won't be necessary," Lia said into the phone before snapping it shut.

How dare she! Of all the nerve, the little—

"Anna, it'll take at least thirty minutes for a cab to arrive. You'll miss your flight. Please. Let me drive. I know I wasn't there for you before, but I'm here now. Let me help you. I owe you that much."

You owe me a hell of a lot more than that. I gave a derisive snort. As if she could simply give me a ride to the airport and call it even.

"What's your AAA number?" she asked.

"It's, uh..." I stammered, confused and caught off guard by Lia's take-charge attitude.

"Check your wallet," she suggested.

I retrieved the card from my wallet and rattled off the numbers. Within minutes, Lia had arranged for a tow truck.

"Where do you want them to take it?"

"Um, Performance Auto. Ellicott Mills."

Lia repeated the words into my phone then handed it back to me. "They'll be here in an hour, which gives me just enough time to get you to the airport and back before they arrive." She turned on her heel and waltzed toward a white Lexus parked on the opposite side of the lot.

I bit my lip and shook my head, the reality of the situation sinking in. Since opening my battered trunk was out of the question, I lowered the back seats and leaned in so I could yank my bags forward and out through the door. I draped the canvas messenger bag over my shoulder and awkwardly wheeled my carry-on across the gravel lot to Lia's car as the back hatch yawned open to receive my luggage. I slung the bags into the back and grudgingly settled into the passenger seat like a truculent teenager. A thin sheen of sweat coated my body.

Without a word, Lia backed out of her spot and swung the car toward the exit just as the Italian-stallion waiter emerged from the restaurant, a bag of ice in hand. Lia reached out the window and accepted it with a wink. "Thanks, Leo," she said, referencing his name tag. "I'll be back in an hour to meet the tow truck." And with that, Lia plunked the cold bag of ice onto my lap, making me gasp, and peeled out of the parking lot.

We rode in silence. I gingerly touched the ice pack to my forehead. The quarter-sized lump had darkened to a delicate shade of eggplant.

WHAT'S LEFT UNTOLD

"Some Advil might help," Lia suggested as I gently probed the protrusion.

I frowned but obediently unearthed a travel-sized bottle of ibuprofen from my bag and popped two pills.

"There's water in the back." Lia indicated it with a tilt of her head.

A twelve-pack of bottled water sat on the floor behind me. The liquid inside the bottle was hot against my palm. I cracked the lid and took a large, grateful swig, trying not to think of all the toxic chemicals that had leached into the water from the sunbaked plastic.

The early-afternoon traffic was light, and we made it to the airport in record time, with almost sixty minutes to spare before my flight was scheduled to depart. Lia pulled up to the curb in front of the Delta Airlines entrance and popped the hatch. She sat stiffly, staring straight ahead as I collected my bags. I fought the urge to stalk into the airport without a word, but my manners got the best of me. Faith would have been proud. I leaned in through the passenger window and issued a terse "thank you" that Lia didn't bother to acknowledge. I turned to go, but Lia's urgent shout halted me mid-pivot.

"What?" I huffed.

Lia's lips were moving, but I couldn't make out the words over the din of the airport. I stepped closer and leaned toward the open window.

"Ivy," she whispered, the word barely audible.

I scrunched my face in confusion.

Lia cleared her throat, drew in a large breath, and spoke again, loud and clear. "My aunt needed me. That's why I left. It was the right thing to do, but it meant moving to Florida and losing my scholarship. I didn't think anyone would understand, and I didn't want anyone to try to talk me out of it. So I just... left."

With that, she pulled away from the curb, leaving me to stare open-mouthed. I watched, more confused than ever, as Lia's Lexus merged into the steady stream of traffic and exited the airport.

TWO DAYS LATER, I EMERGED from the cold, sterile interior of the airport into the muggy, warm embrace of the August evening. Jack caught my eye and waved. He left the car idling and climbed from the driver's seat to relieve me of my luggage and wrap me in a welcoming embrace. Safe and secure in his arms, I crumpled against him. An anguished gasp escaped from my throat.

"Aw, sweetie. I'm sorry." Jacked hugged me tighter and kissed the top of my head. "Do you want to talk about it?"

A policeman started toward us, casting a suspicious glance at Jack's car. Lingering at the airport was forbidden. I could sense we were about to be ordered to move along.

"Let's go. I'll tell you on the way," I said with a sniff.

A luminous crescent moon was in the early stages of its ascent. The city lights obliterated any trace of stars from the jet-black sky. We rode with the windows down. The breeze was a pleasant balm for my tear-streaked face. Jack didn't push for details. He sat companionably by my side and hummed along to an REM song on the radio.

I blew my nose loudly and swiveled in my seat to face him. "It was awful," I whispered. The sweet stink of funeral lilies was still sharp in my nose. "So sad." Fresh tears filled my eyes and ran in hot streaks down my face.

Jack clasped my hand and gave it a reassuring squeeze. I told him about Faith, drawn and thin, with sallow skin and dark hollows beneath her eyes. Months of watching helplessly as her father slipped further into the pit of dementia had left her physically wrecked. I couldn't imagine what it was like to see the disease relentlessly increasing its grip, closing the blinds on the windows of her father's soul, until finally squeezing the life from him. "And in the midst of it all, I kept thinking of Lia. Can you believe that? I felt like such a traitor."

"Why?" Jack asked.

"Because I should have been thinking about Faith! It made me angry to be so distracted. But all these years, I thought Lia was just being selfish when, as it turns out, she was helping her aunt. She had a reason for leaving. A good one, it seems. It never crossed my mind that *Lia* might have been the one who was confused or hurting or scared. I should have tried harder to find out what happened. I should have been a better friend."

"You did try. You know that, right? You were only eighteen, and Lia shut you out. That was her choice. She could have confided in you if she wanted to."

"Why do you think she's confiding in me now? After all these years?"

"I don't know. Maybe she has a good reason for that too."

I pondered that for a while as Jack drove. He hummed along to the radio again, his fingers interlaced with mine.

After Lia had left me at the curb at the airport, I'd spent the flight to Alabama mulling what she'd said, which ultimately left me feeling like I owed her an apology for the way I'd behaved at Keller's. My actions had seemed justified at the time, but in hindsight, not so much. I also wanted to thank her again for her help with my car and for driving me to the airport. But mostly, I wanted to hear the rest of the story. I wanted to know what was going on with her aunt—why Aunt Ivy had needed Lia's help—and what Lia's life had been like in Florida. I also knew the ball was back in my court. Lia had tossed it to me like a hot potato, and now I juggled it in my hands, hoping not to get burned.

We pulled into Performance Auto. My silver Honda Odyssey looked shiny and new under the glow of the parking-lot lights. Jack had stopped on the way to the airport to pay for the repairs and pick up the key, which he withdrew from his pocket and handed to me.

"Try not to back into anything, would ya?" he teased.

My fingers instinctively grazed my forehead. A small tender spot remained, but the lump was gone. "Wise guy, eh?" I laughed weakly, punching him in the arm. My heart swelled with affection for him. Jack had always been my rock. I'd spent more years of my life with him than without him. Six more, to be exact.

After that first kiss in high school on New Year's Eve, we hadn't started dating right away. I was nervous and unsure because I found it hard to believe that Jack Wells—the most gorgeous, sought-after guy in school, the guy that every girl at Bay View wanted—wanted me. I also wasn't sure how Lia would take me dating Jack, so I was patient. I let him pursue me. And I pinched myself daily.

February 1988

THE STUDENT GOVERNMENT had launched their annual carnation fundraiser. For a dollar, students could purchase a carnation and have it delivered to another student on Valentine's Day. A red carnation for true love, pink for secret admirer, and white for friendship. Lia had enough flowers, mostly pink and red, to create an entire bouquet. I, however, was content with my four white flowers from Lia, Becky, Kelly, and Kim, and my single pink one. I knew who the pink was from.

"You and Jack will make a cute couple," Lia said, spying my pink carnation, giving me her blessing. By then, she'd set her sights on some other guy, but I still had the uneasy feeling that she hadn't let it go, that it still galled her to have been rebuffed by Jack. She still watched him, her eyes following him as he moved through the halls at Bay View, like a predator stalking her prey, patiently waiting for the right moment to pounce.

A month later, on my birthday, I found a single long-stemmed red carnation on my desk. There was no note, but a note wasn't necessary. Jack and I had spent the past month talking on the phone for hours every night and going out together on weekends. The Saturday before my birthday, he'd told me he had never met anyone like me and that he only wanted to be with me. He asked me to be his girlfriend, and I said yes, my heart soaring. At school, word spread quickly that we were together, but we were not like the touchy-feely couples that held hands constantly and made out in the hallways. So the rose on my desk served as a public declaration of our relationship. After that, the girls at Bay View finally, reluctantly, withdrew their claws.

Toward the end of our junior year, Lia was bragging at lunch about her latest conquest and her prowess.

"You really think you could have any guy at Bay View you want?" Kim asked Lia, calling her bluff.

"Like taking candy from a baby," Lia boasted.

"Even Jack?"

We all swiveled in our seats to see Renee standing behind us, flashing a wicked grin. She balanced her lunch tray on one hand, and the other hand was planted on her hip. Lia's pride and reputation were on the line.

The silence stretched out a beat too long before Lia replied. "I wouldn't go after Jack while he's dating Anna." It was a strange answer. Unsettling.

Satisfied, Renee sauntered off with a smirk. I bit into my apple but couldn't swallow it.

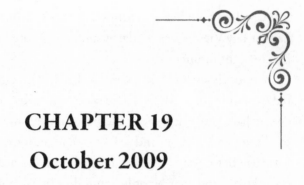

CHAPTER 19
October 2009

Water dripped from the ends of my hair, splattering onto the wooden planks of my front porch, as I rocked anxiously in the large Adirondack chair. I'd gotten up early to finish a magazine article touting the benefits and versatility of quinoa, and then I'd seen the girls off to school before hitting the trails behind the house for a six-mile run.

Now I was freshly showered but too nervous to eat. The run had successfully calmed my mind but hadn't untied the knots in my stomach as I anxiously awaited Lia's arrival.

Part of me wanted to pretend I hadn't heard what she'd said when she dropped me off at the airport. But I had heard, and I'd considered it rather coy and calculating on Lia's part to leave me with that little nugget of information—that she'd moved to Florida to help her aunt—and nothing more. She'd dangled the bait in front of me and waited to see if I would bite. I had. A month after returning from the funeral, I'd sent Lia an email.

"Let's talk. Next Friday, 10:30? My place..."

An hour later, she'd replied, her message equally brief. "See you then. What's the address?"

Now I waited. A fresh pot of coffee brewed in the kitchen. Its aroma was sharp and earthy. A plate of bagels and cream cheese and a bowl of fresh fruit salad stood at the ready. The morning was bright and sunny, the sky a cloudless Carolina blue. The fading heat of summer sighed the last of its warm breath on my neck. Not a fan of hair dryers, I preferred to let my silky brown locks air-dry whenever possible.

An agitated jay squawked noisily as he flitted from branch to branch. A pair of frisky, chattering squirrels played hide-and-seek among the trees. Chessie and Bay slept soundly at my feet until the faint rumble of an engine caught their attention. Gravel popped beneath the wheels of Lia's SUV, intruding on the peace and solitude of the morning. The jay quieted, the squirrels retreated to their hiding spots, and the dogs leapt to their feet, ears pricked and bodies rigid. Their aggressive postures were betrayed by frantically wagging tails.

I watched anxiously as the familiar white Lexus crept toward the house. Jack and I had always viewed our home as our castle, our single extravagance, and we took pride and pleasure in its maintenance and upkeep. But as Lia approached, the grand house, with its meticulously landscaped gardens, suddenly seemed flamboyant, pretentious. My face flushed as I imagined how Lia would see my home. The smug triumph I'd expected to feel at this moment—knowing that living well and being happy would serve as the ultimate revenge—never materialized. With shame, I realized it didn't matter anymore. Lia had her life, and I had mine. Besides, it was no longer revenge I sought, but reconciliation. Lia was my living history. I desperately wanted to understand what she'd been through, which in turn, would help me understand why she'd left.

Suddenly, I could picture Lia and I as old ladies, old friends. She would emerge stooped and gray from her Cadillac sedan, her green eyes still alight with mischief but framed by a whirlpool of wrinkles. We would wrap gnarled fingers around warm mugs of tea and hand-knitted shawls around our bony shoulders, and we would rock on this very porch as we sipped and talked and laughed and reminisced about what foolish young girls we'd been. The thought made me smile.

I descended the steps and watched as Lia's eyes swept across the wide front porch adorned with sculpted pillars, hanging plants, and matching Adirondack chairs. Passion flowers sprang from silk baskets, wind chimes tinkled in the soft, warm breeze, and a porch swing swayed gently, invitingly, in a triangle of sunlight.

"Hey there!" I greeted, hesitating a moment before offering a brief, stiff embrace.

"Nice place," she observed, hugging me back. She glanced around again. Her lips were pursed, and her head bobbed. "You did good." We laughed and cast our eyes toward the porch, where Chessie and Bay obediently sat, their entire bodies trembling with the effort to contain their enthusiasm. "Oh my God!" Lia exclaimed. "Such cute puppies!"

"That's Chessie and Bay," I said. The mere mention of their names set the dogs' tails to wagging even more furiously. Their tongues licked their chops in anticipation, like Preakness horses stomping at the gate. "Okay!" I called, the verbal command releasing the dogs. In tandem, they sprinted down the stairs and bolted across the lawn toward Lia, where they circled and sniffed our new guest.

Lia knelt and was immediately ambushed by the dogs. Their enthusiastic licking and prancing elicited shrieks of mellifluous laughter, which tinkled just as merrily as it had when we were teenagers. I offered up silent thanks to the dogs for so beautifully breaking the ice.

Lia stood and brushed bits of grass from her pants. I frowned at the dirty paw prints smudged across her cream capris and the clumps of pale fur clinging to her brown shirt.

"Sorry about that," I apologized, pulling the dogs back by their collars.

"No worries." Lia giggled. "They're great! Beautiful dogs. I'd love to have a dog, but Neil's allergic." A strange expression pinched Lia's face, but she quickly recovered.

"I think Bay weighs more than you do," I said, glancing from my petite friend to my 105-pound Labrador.

"Hardly." She snorted with an exaggerated roll of her eyes. "Maybe back in the day but not anymore."

"What do you mean? You look great." Though still heavier and rounder than she'd been in high school, Lia was definitely thinner. She'd probably lost another ten pounds since we'd met at Keller's. "What's your secret?"

"Remember that weight training I mentioned? It's working. And there's a spin class at the gym that's kicking my butt."

"Do you ride outside too?"

"Whenever I can. I've been taking my bike to the BWI Trail."

"That's, what, fifteen miles?"

Lia shrugged. We'd reached the kitchen, where the modest brunch stood waiting. My stomach, which had been doubled up in knots just thirty minutes ago, was growling ferociously. "Did you eat?"

"I can always eat," Lia joked. "This looks delicious. You shouldn't have gone to all this trouble."

I waved dismissively and handed her a plate, my mind working overtime as I scooped up several heaping spoonfuls of fruit and motioned for Lia to follow me to the back patio.

As we passed through the morning room, Lia paused and fixed her gaze on a family photo taken that summer at the beach. "Your girls are beautiful."

"Thanks. They look more like Jack every day."

"I see a lot of you in them too, especially the youngest. She's your mini-me."

"Really? I've never thought so. It's interesting what other people see."

"Your oldest favors Jack, but she has your high cheekbones and your smile." Lia gingerly laid a fingertip against the edge of the silver frame, her expression wistful.

"Hmmm." I stepped around her and through the French door that opened onto the back patio, anxious to change the subject. Talking about food and fitness was one thing, but talking about my family was another. I was not yet ready to share with Lia the more intimate details of my life.

We settled onto the padded chaise lounges, the sun shining brightly overhead, and gnawed on our bagels. I chose the seat beside her rather than across from her, so we could both gaze at the trees instead of at each other. The leaves, just beginning to burn with color, rustled and danced on the fragrant fall breeze.

Lia pursed her tiny Cupid's-bow lips and blew gently across the steaming surface of her coffee before taking a dainty sip. "It's good. Thanks," she said, breaking the silence.

"You're welcome." I gulped at my own coffee a bit too eagerly, and the rich brown liquid burned my upper lip.

Lia and I cautiously waded into neutral conversation, discussing the weather, the Ravens' promising football season, and our jobs. Finally, running out of pleasantries, we lapsed into silence again. Even the forest creatures had gone quiet. I began to wonder if Lia was going to pretend she hadn't said anything about her aunt and moving to Florida. Maybe she regretted letting it slip. Maybe there was more to the story. Or maybe she was simply waiting to see if I would bring it up. Curiosity was killing me—it was the reason I'd invited her over, after all—but I would be damned if she was going to put the burden of this conversation on me. It was her story to tell.

Finally, Lia shifted in her seat, cleared her throat, and opened her mouth to speak. A puffy white cloud rose from behind the trees, momentarily obliterating the sun. Lia shivered, her bare arms turning to gooseflesh. I couldn't tell whether she was chilled from the minute drop in temperature or from what she was about to say. Her eyes were on mine, clear and verdant green in the bright sun, unblinking and alight with a fiery new determination. "Aunt Ivy's husband, Roberto, had a heart attack."

"Oh no! That's awful." It wasn't at all what I'd expected. I didn't even know her aunt was married.

Lia gave her head a quick shake, not wanting my sympathy. "They had been running an inn together for years. Aunt Ivy handled the day-to-day operations, and Roberto handled the finances. He never told her they were in trouble. Apparently, they'd been in the red, on the brink of bankruptcy, for years. While Roberto was recovering, my aunt found all the overdue notices and unpaid bills. The debt collectors were breathing down her neck. She didn't want to sell. The Conch Out Inn was her home, her *life*. But she couldn't afford to hire anyone, and she needed help with the accounting and getting the finances in order. She needed someone she could trust, someone good with math. She needed *me*. So I went. It meant leaving Maryland and giving up my scholarship, but I did what I had to do." Lia lifted her chin defiantly.

I was flabbergasted, speechless. Apparently, Lia had been closer to her aunt than I'd realized. I had never known Lia to be so selfless. I furrowed my brow, trying to fit all the pieces together.

Lia stiffened, sensing my hesitation. "I don't expect you to understand or to forgive me for hurting you—even if it was to help my aunt—but I hope you will. Forgive me, that is."

She was right. I still didn't understand why she didn't tell me what was going on. I would have been there for her. I would have supported her decision. But this was the explanation she was offering. I could take it or leave it. I could choose to forgive or not to forgive. Maybe someday she would tell me more. Maybe someday it would all make sense.

Lia's eyes were on me. I could feel the weight of her stare. Mahatma Gandhi had once said, "The weak can never forgive. Forgiveness is the attribute of the strong." And so I decided to be strong.

"You're right. I don't understand," I said.

She dropped her gaze, her chin sinking to her chest in defeat.

I reached out and grasped her dainty hand in mine. "But I do forgive you."

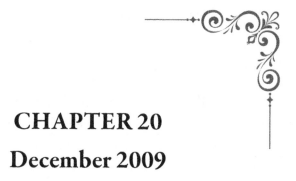

CHAPTER 20
December 2009

"What are you up to today?" Jack asked as he dressed for work, looking utterly gorgeous in jeans and a white T-shirt. The sculpted muscles of his arms flexed as he shoved a comb through his dark, wavy hair.

"Lia's coming over to bake." I yawned, stretching my arms overhead. I could feel his gaze on my breasts as they pushed against the thin silk of my chemise.

"How are things with you two?" With some effort, Jack's appreciative expression rearranged itself into one of concern.

"So far, so good. We're taking it slowly. One step at a time."

"That's probably a good idea," he agreed, shrugging into a navy button-down shirt. The rich-blue fabric enhanced the sapphire rim of his irises.

He circled the bed and attempted a chaste kiss on my forehead, an action I foiled by wrapping my arms around his waist and pulling him close. "Mmmm." I inhaled the familiar scent of him, masculine and earthy with a hint of spice. "Stay with me," I murmured.

Indulging me, Jack dropped his warm lips to my jaw and nuzzled my neck, sending a shiver of delight through my body. Then, to my disappointment, he pulled away. I executed my best pouty face.

Jack chuckled. "I have a client in less than an hour. Rain check?"

"And soon!" I demanded.

He treated me to one of his dazzling smiles, the one that showed off his dimples and deepened the cleft in his strong, square chin, and then left to escort the girls to the bus stop as he always did on Fridays.

Throughout high school, Lia had joined my mom and me for our annual Christmas cookie-baking-day extravaganza. The cutting, rolling, dusting, and glazing—a thin layer of flour coating everything—were among my fondest childhood memories. So inviting Lia to bake with me felt symbolic. The cookies were my olive branch, a sign of my determination to move forward and begin creating new memories.

Last weekend, the girls and I had gotten together with my mom for our traditional mother-daughter-granddaughter baking day and had decided that the original recipe for Lia's favorite cookie—pumpkin-raisin-walnut—was even better with chocolate. I hoped Lia would think so too. Even the revised recipe seemed symbolic of what Lia and I were attempting to accomplish with our friendship: taking something old that had once been good and making it even better.

After Jack and the girls had left for work and school, I dressed quickly, put on a pot of coffee, and switched into festive mode. Making a quick circuit of the family room, I clicked on the Christmas tree lights, lit a few candles, and popped a holiday CD into the player, humming along to "A Holly Jolly Christmas" as I pulled the cookie-baking ingredients from the pantry.

The house was pleasantly redolent of cedar and pine, compliments of our freshly cut tree and the candles burning on the mantel. Lia was due to arrive any minute. In the two months since I'd

last seen her, I'd had time to mull all she'd told me about moving to
Florida and helping her aunt, but I still had so many questions.

When the doorbell rang at, impressively, the exact hour we'd
agreed upon, I greeted Lia warmly, tugging her in from the cold
and into a welcoming, forgiving embrace.

A FEW WEEKS LATER, on Christmas morning, after the girls
had torn through their gifts in record time and dispersed to enjoy
them, Jack presented me with a beautifully wrapped, thin, rectangular box. I was fooled into thinking it was a necklace, perhaps the
jade-and-turquoise stunner Jack had caught me admiring in a magazine. Instead, the box contained a Delta Airlines gift certificate for
one round-trip flight from Baltimore to Mobile. The makings of
another Christmas tradition appeared to be in the works.

"Are you trying to get rid of me?" I teased, narrowing my eyes
at Jack.

"If I wanted to do that, the ticket would have been one-way."
Jack's laughter curled into a howl as I socked him in the arm. "I just
know how much you enjoy spending time with Faith," he added,
rubbing his shoulder. "And I know it's been a long time since you've
seen her." He wrapped his arm around my shoulders and planted a
warm kiss on my temple.

"I really wish she hadn't moved," I lamented, slumping into my
husband's strong, solid body.

"Do you think she'll come back now that her father's..."

"I don't know. She has a pretty good thing going in Mobile.
And she's really a Southern girl at heart. I think she's happy to be
home."

As though her ears had been burning all the way down in Alabama, the phone rang, the caller ID announcing a call from Barrows, Faith. I leapt to my feet and raced to the phone.

Faith sounded merry but tired. It was, after all, an hour earlier in Alabama. I teased her, suggesting that she pour another cup of coffee to perk herself up, then shared the exciting news about my Delta gift certificate from Jack.

"That boy's a keeper!" Faith exclaimed with bark of raspy laughter, as if something had caught in her throat. Faith had battled a seemingly continuous string of colds and viruses since moving to Mobile.

"You okay?" I asked.

"Damn fruitcake," Faith explained with a chuckle. "Well, I'd better get to it," Faith said, begging off the call to go whip up a sweet potato pie for the Christmas dinner she was having with her coworkers.

Before saying our goodbyes, we agreed that a weekend in February would be perfect timing for my visit. I logged on to Delta's website the next day to book my flight, knowing that by February, I would be good and ready to get the hell out of icy-cold Dodge. A dash of warmth in the midst of winter was always a balm for the shivering, vitamin-D-deprived soul.

CHAPTER 21
February 2010

"Well, howdy there, girl! You sure are a sight for sore eyes!" Faith crooned as I wheeled my carry-on bag toward her, dodging a myriad of harried travelers.

I could have said the same to her. She was a sight, all right. Leaning against the open trunk of her Mustang, Faith looked even worse than she had at her father's funeral. Clearly, she was still struggling with the loss. Her clothes hung from her skeletal frame. Her cheeks were sunken. Her skin had adopted a ghastly pallor. When I hugged her, her bony shoulders were as frail as a bird's wings beneath the fabric of her shirt. But outward appearances aside, she was her usual chipper self. She was quick to inform me that going for a run was our first order of business.

I pursed my lips, poised to question whether she was truly up for a run. Judging by her appearance, all signs pointed to no. But Faith was a stubborn, determined woman. I knew her well enough to know that if she said we were going running, we were going running.

"What?" she asked, noticing my hesitation.

"Nothing." I shrugged and smiled as I collapsed the suitcase handle and stowed the bag in the trunk. "I'm just happy to be here." A surge of unexpected emotion swept through me, and my eyes welled with tears.

"I'm happy too," Faith said, blinking back tears of her own. "Now don't go getting all sappy on me." She pulled me into a fierce hug then held me at arm's length. "Let's get outta here. I got some exciting news to tell ya."

As we drove, Faith explained that—though it had crushed her to do so—she'd sold her family home and, with the proceeds, purchased a waterfront condo on Mobile Bay. "It was the right thing to do," she explained. "I mean, what was I gonna do with a whole house to myself? Besides, I like being near the water. It's peaceful."

"I can't wait to see it," I said, though inwardly, my heart broke a little. *She's definitely not moving back to Maryland.*

After a quick stop by Faith's new condo—which was lovely and perfect for her—to drop off my suitcase and change into running gear, we drove to Meaher State Park. We chose a five-mile loop that traversed hardwood ridges, wound through tall pines along the shoreline, and featured spectacular views of Lake Martin.

Faith, who usually bounded along like a gazelle, was huffing with effort at the two-mile mark. By the fourth mile, she urged me to go ahead without her. "Go!" she commanded. Reluctantly, I went. I'd finished stretching and was headed back to the trailhead to find her when she finally tottered into view, breathless and pale.

"Cramp," she explained as she walked past me and plopped down onto the nearest bench.

"Are you okay?"

"'Course I am," she said sharply. Then, she resumed her usual playfulness. "Don't you go gettin' all big-headed now 'cause you were faster today. Got lucky is all." She leaned forward, elbows on knees, and panted to catch her breath.

"Whatever you say." I knew it was useless to try to argue with a shrink. "And to think people accuse lawyers of being righteous and stubborn!"

Faith huffed in mock exasperation. "So Little Miss Yankee here is a comedienne now? Well then, do I ever have just the thing for you!"

"Oh yeah? What might that be?"

"You'll have to wait 'n' see," she teased, rising a bit unsteadily and linking her arm through mine. "What say we get outta here?"

"Good plan," I agreed, keeping my arm firmly locked with hers and feeling the slight tremor in her limbs as we walked toward the car. I cast a concerned sideways glance in her direction, but she simply smiled and patted my hand.

"It's beautiful here, isn't it?" she remarked.

I nodded and returned her smile, a silent agreement to let her off the hook for now, but I would be keeping a close eye on her over the weekend.

BY THE TIME WE'D RETURNED to the condo and showered, it was after five. My stomach rumbled loudly.

"Hey, Faith," I hollered toward the bathroom, where she was busy primping. *Southern women and their makeup. Sheesh!* "You hungry?"

"Starved."

"Where do you want to go for dinner? My treat!"

"Oh no, you don't!" she scolded, emerging from the bathroom, dressed like a Southern belle who'd collided with a circus car. Decked out in a gold-and-purple skirt, a shimmery green top, and enough makeup to rival Bozo himself, she had the nerve to give *me* the once-over, arms akimbo, a dissatisfied grimace on her gaunt face. "That'll never do," she complained with a cluck of her tongue. With pursed lips, she swept her gaze over my dark denim jeans and black-and-silver-striped halter. "I told ya to dress *festive*. Ya call that festive?" Abruptly, she whirled on her shiny gold heel and disappeared down the hall.

"What?" I chased after her. "Where are we going?"

"I've booked us dinner and a show." Her voice was muffled as she burrowed into her closet. "Voila! Put these here things on, and you'll be fine." She handed me a pair of gold-and-green elbow-length gloves, a purple ruffled jester's collar, and several strands of beads. "Oh, and these too!" She waved two gold masks. "There's been a murder at Mardi Gras," she whispered, leaning in to elbow me conspiratorially in the ribs.

I stood dumbfounded, clutching the gaudy accessories in my hands.

"Oh, for pity's sake, if ya must know, we're off to Mobile Mystery Dinners, so put 'em on, and let's go. We don't wanna be late!"

I sighed and tugged on the long gloves. There was no arguing with Faith once she'd set her mind to something.

IT WAS A SHORT DRIVE to downtown Mobile. The small theater was dimly lit but tightly packed with festively attired people. We were seated at our table with thirty minutes to spare before dinner. Meanwhile, cocktail hour was in full swing. Our waiter, wearing a feathery green mask, appeared tableside to take our drink orders.

"Two New Orleans hurricanes," Faith ordered. She pronounced it *Nawlins*. "It's a Mardi Gras classic," she added for my benefit.

"Since when did you become a Mardi Gras expert?" I teased.

"You know what they say—when in Rome, do as the Romans do," she drawled. "Well, 'round here, people *do* Mardi Gras."

"So it's like a verb, then?"

"That it is," she said, and laughed loudly.

I eyed her suspiciously. Faith had always been adventurous and fun-loving but never quite so over the top. "So what's gotten into you? This whole scene's a bit, uh, much. Don't you think?"

"Ya don't like it?" she asked, feigning hurt.

"Of course I like it. I just wouldn't have guessed *you'd* be into it."

Stan, our masked waiter and, presumably, a character in the show, reappeared with our drinks.

Faith tipped him generously. "Just livin' life to the fullest, I guess. So tell me, what's the latest with you and Lia?"

"We're giving it a go, I guess. Wading cautiously into the waters. Guess we'll see which way the current takes us."

"And how did baking day go? You didn't say much about it."

"Wasn't much to tell. She came. We baked, talked about our jobs, life with kids. We're taking things slow, getting to know each other again." I paused and tapped the side of my glass. "Lia suggested we make baking day an annual tradition again, said she'd missed it."

Faith was eyeing me intently. "So she's looking to the future with you. That's good."

I sipped on the peach-colored drink. Its tartness sucked the moisture from my mouth.

"Good, isn't it?" Faith asked, taking a pull on her own straw. "Explain to me again this whole disappearin' to Miami bit."

Stan carefully deposited two steaming crocks of creole gumbo soup and garden salads onto the table. "Your entrees will be up in a jiff."

"Well, as I mentioned on the phone, Lia's aunt's husband, Roberto, had a heart attack. So Lia dropped out of Maryland and moved south to help her aunt."

"She must have liked it there since she decided to stay."

I shrugged and gnawed on a hangnail. "I guess."

Faith narrowed her eyes. "All sounds a bit rash, don't ya think?"

"Not if you knew Lia," I said with a snort. "She was always spontaneous. Thrived on drama." I spooned the last of the spicy gumbo into my mouth just as the entrees arrived. "Aren't you hungry?" I asked Faith, eyeing her half-eaten salad and untouched soup.

"Just savin' room for my grits," she said with half a smile.

"You and your grits." I shook my head and was still laughing as Stan arrived with our entrees: a heaping plate of Louisiana chicken and Andouille sausage grits for Faith and a deep bowl of shrimp jambalaya for me. I blew gently on a small spoonful and hazarded a bite, shocked by the heat and intensity of the spices. Acid was already creeping up my throat from the gumbo. "I hope you have Tums at home," I said, my scorched throat making my words come out in a croak.

Faith ignored my Tums comment and pressed on. "So why didn't Lia tell y'all what she was doing? You'd think she'd at least wanna say goodbye to her friends. Leave a forwarding address or something. And why didn't she call you once she got settled at the Inn, tell you where she was?"

I'd asked myself the same questions many times. "She claims it all happened really fast, that it would have been too hard to say goodbye. She also said she needed a fresh start, and that meant leaving her past behind. All of it. Including me. So she just... left." I chewed at my hangnail again, and Faith swatted my hand from my mouth.

"Something 'bout that tale smells fishy to me. It doesn't add up." Faith propped her chin in her palm and drummed her fingertips against her thin cheek. "There's more to the story, don't ya think?"

"Maybe. Probably. But what can I do? Fishy or not, that's her explanation. Lia was never what you'd call rational, and she definitely wasn't a conventional thinker. I can either choose to accept what she's told me and forgive her, or I can tell her to go to hell and move on."

Faith sliced a small round of sausage into quarters, pierced one of the bits with her fork, and slid it into her mouth. She chewed slowly, deliberately, the cogs of her therapist's mind kicking into gear. "Well, you'll never truly have peace in your heart until you forgive her."

"I know." I frowned. "That's kind of what I figured." I speared a pink shrimp and popped it into my mouth.

"Besides, she's part of who you are, part of your history. And one can never have too many friends."

"Well, I have you. That's all I need."

Faith fidgeted, avoiding my eyes.

I leaned sideways into her line of sight, forcing her to look at me. "You know you're my best friend, right? Whatever happens with Lia won't change that."

Faith patted my hand. "I know."

The lights in the ornate theater flickered, and Stan reappeared, holding a carafe of hot coffee. "Last call for the bar, ladies. Show's about to start. Can I get ya anything else?" He filled our coffee cups and served us each a dish of bread pudding.

I slumped in my chair and crossed my arms. We would have to continue our conversation later. "Nothing for me, thanks."

"Another round of hurricanes," Faith contradicted, stifling a yawn.

"Two hurricanes comin' up. Would ya like a box for that?" Stan asked, gesturing toward Faith's nearly full plate. Despite her claims of hunger, Faith had done little more than push her grits around with her fork.

"No thanks, hon."

"Okay. Someone'll have your drinks out to ya shortly. Enjoy the show!"

We watched as Stan faded into the sea of servers-slash-actors exiting the room to prepare for the performance. Then I glanced pointedly at Faith's plate and raised my eyes to hers, one eyebrow arched in question.

"What?" Faith defended. "It was fillin'. Now, if you'll *excusez-moi*, I'm off to powder my nose before the show begins." She pushed back from the table and walked stiffly toward the restrooms, as tiny as a speck of dust carried on a puff of air.

THAT NIGHT, I COULD hear Faith quietly moaning and retching. At the sound of shuffling footsteps outside my door, I poked my head into the darkened hallway in time to see Faith disappear into the kitchen. She appeared ghostly in the moonlight that filtered in through the slatted blinds. I clutched my arms tightly to my chest to ward off the late-night chill and followed her. She was leaning against the sink, filling a glass with water.

"Faith?"

My voice startled her, causing the glass to slip from her shaking fingers and clatter into the sink. She retrieved the fallen glass and filled it again. Her face was deathly pale, a greenish-gray tinge lurking beneath the translucent surface of her skin.

"Hurricanes coming back to bite you in the ass?" I teased.

"I'm fine. Go back to bed."

I placed my hand against her forehead and frowned. Her brow was clammy. Wisps of faded walnut hair were plastered against her cheeks.

"Ate some bad food is all," she muttered, drifting back toward her room. "G'night." The bedroom door clicked shut behind her.

I CRACKED MY EYES OPEN and reached for the clock on the nightstand. I was surprised to see it was 10:41! My body jerked upright. *How in the hell did I sleep so long?* I hadn't slept past nine since I was in college. *Damn hurricanes.* I scrambled from the bed, retrieved a pair of jeans from my suitcase, and pulled a long-sleeved shirt over my head. I wondered if Faith was still sleeping too. My bedroom was pitch-black. With a fingertip, I retracted the blinds from the window. The sky was a heavy gray, with thick, dark, ominous clouds hovering menacingly above the bay. Soft rain had begun to patter against the windowpanes.

The condo was eerily still and quiet. I padded to the kitchen and put on the kettle. The mere thought of coffee, in all its acidic glory, burned the back of my throat. There was no sign of Faith. I crept back down the hallway and rapped gently on her closed door, but there was no answer. I turned the handle and cracked the door an inch. The hinges screeched in protest, and I peeked in. Faith was sitting up in bed, her legs as scrawny as sticks beneath the covers. She stared, eyes unseeing, at the wall in front of her.

"Faith?" I whispered. She seemed so far away. "Everything okay?"

She swallowed and nodded.

"Do you think you have food poisoning?" I drew the blinds, and weak pewter light filtered into the stale room.

"Must be some sort of virus that's got hold of me," Faith pondered aloud.

I pressed my palm against her forehead. She didn't have a fever. The kettle began to whistle. "Would you like some tea?"

"Please. And some toast too?"

"You got it." I retreated to the kitchen, retrieved two mugs, two sachets of chai, and a loaf of rye from the breadbasket. My granny always made buttered rye toast for me when I didn't feel well.

As I prepared our meager breakfast, the sea crashed angrily against the shore. The rain was coming harder now. I filled the mugs with boiling water and slid two pieces of bread into the toaster. Beyond the sliding glass doors, the wind howled, whipping the bay into a churning, frothy mass. I stepped onto the balcony and tilted my chin to the sky, letting the misty raindrops splash onto my skin. The air was humid but cool. The moisture made my shirt feel damp and sticky against my body. I retreated into the crisp chill of the condo and left the slider open a crack to let in some fresh air. Faith had settled onto the couch. She was still in her pajamas and had a blanket drawn around her shoulders. Purple smudges hung like dark crescent moons beneath her eyes.

"Guess we're not goin' for a run today," she mused.

"You think?" My voice was playfully laced with sarcasm. "Maybe we should be going to the doctor instead?"

Faith shook her head. "And ya claim Lia's the drama queen."

"Well, you don't look so good."

"Thanks a lot. You don't look so hot yourself, missy," she retorted, critically eyeing my matted hair and smeared mascara. "I just need to rest."

The toast sprang from side-by-side slots. "Want butter?" I asked, returning to the kitchen.

"Plain's fine."

I spread whipped butter onto one of the slices and carried the plate and two napkins into the family room. Then I returned to the kitchen to fetch the steeping mugs of tea.

We sat next to each other on the denim-hued couch. Mobile Bay was a roiling mass of browns, blues, and greens. The swirling colors reminded me of Jack's eyes. "I can't believe we slept so long. My flight leaves in less than three hours."

"I can't believe Stan, *our Stan*, was the murderer," Faith mumbled, nibbling her toast. "Instead of Professor Plum in the library with a candlestick, it was good ol' Stan on Bourbon Street with a wrought-iron spindle." She pronounced it *li-bree*.

I shook my head and chuckled. "Who would've guessed?"

"Well, I best get into the shower." Faith discarded the blanket and scooched toward the front edge of the cushion. She moved slowly, cautiously, like an old woman. She eased onto her feet, slowly straightened her back, then swayed precariously, grabbing my shoulder to steady herself. "Woo, head rush."

I lowered her back to the couch. Her heart was hammering against her rib cage, the vibration resounding against my arm.

"Easy there." I stood facing her, arms crossed. "What happened to resting?"

"If I'm gonna be ready to get you to the airport on time—"

"Oh no, you don't! I'm calling a cab. If you won't go to the doctor, you sure as hell aren't going to the airport!" Ignoring her protests, I snatched the cordless phone from its cradle and dialed 411. My girls would tease me mercilessly for using such an archaic method of information retrieval, but old habits died hard. Besides, my cell phone was just a little flip-top number, and I was stubbornly proud of still being smarter than my phone. A nasally prerecorded voice requested my city and state.

"Mobile, Alabama." Then, taking a wild guess, I said, "Mobile Cab Company." I listened as a live operator reeled off several options. I chose one at random and waited while the call was connected. "Or maybe I should just stay here with you a few more days until you're feeling better."

"Absolutely not. Don't be ridiculous! You've got kids at home that need you."

"Seems to me like you're the one needing some TLC."

"Looky here, Anna. I'm a grown woman. I can take care of myself. If I get to feeling worse, I'll go to the doctor. Promise," she added in response to the skeptical stare I'd leveled at her.

I sighed and booked the cab as Faith glared at me through narrowed eyes. "Well, my mama's probably rollin' over in her grave. A guest of mine takin' a cab—it just ain't right."

"What isn't right is you going out in this weather as sick as you are. I've half a mind to call one of your coworkers to check on you after I leave."

"The hell you will!" Faith argued.

But I was already dialing one of her fellow therapists, having found Faith's address book in a kitchen drawer. I left a voice message and, satisfied, sauntered back to the couch, a smug smile on my face. "Now if you don't mind, your *guest* would like to take a shower."

"By all means," Faith muttered.

"Can I get you anything else?"

"No, ya can't." She crossed her arms and pressed her lips into a thin line.

"You are the most stubborn woman I've ever met!"

"Me? Looky who's talkin'! No wonder that Lia girl skipped town without telling ya. Makes a lot more sense to me now."

Despite the jab, I was pleased to see Faith's feistiness restored and some color returned to her cheeks, I flounced to the bathroom, relieved to finally rid my hair and skin of the lingering aroma of Cajun food.

An hour later, I was freshly scrubbed and had my bags packed and waiting by the door. A cab pulled up to the curb and honked the horn impatiently.

"Well, ain't that gentlemanly?" Faith complained. "With what you're paying him, he could at least get on up here and help ya with your bags."

I refused the cab fare Faith waved in my face on the grounds that she wouldn't accept a single dime for the pricey dinner theater outing. Reluctantly, she tucked the bills into her wallet and hugged me tightly, fiercely. At least her strength seemed to be returning.

"I had such a good time. Thanks so much for everything," I said, collecting my bags. I held Faith at arm's length and peered into her disturbingly rheumy eyes. "You take care of yourself. Fluids, rest..."

"Yes, ma'am," Faith agreed, humoring me.

"And I'll be calling to check on you when I get home." I hugged my friend one last time before descending the stairs and climbing into the waiting cab.

CHAPTER 22
March 2010

T he thick, knobby bike tire was wedged between the back seat and the door of the van. I pulled and tugged, attempting to free the heavy bike. Lia had called two weeks earlier and invited me to ride the BWI Trail with her.

"Need a hand?" a sweet voice chimed.

Lia stood watching me, a mirthful smile on her lovely face. I absently wondered if these early attempts to regain our footing as friends would mimic early courtship, where everyone is on their best behavior.

"Nope, I've got it." I grunted, giving the bike another good tug. It dislodged suddenly, and the rear tire struck me in the gut, knocking the wind out of me. I threw the steel beast to the asphalt, cursing and coughing.

Lia laughed merrily. "Not the most auspicious start!"

I eyed her surreptitiously as I collected my bike from the pavement. In her tight biking shorts and form-fitting performance T-shirt, she appeared tinier than ever.

"Another six pounds since Christmas!" she boasted, having caught me staring.

"So awesome! But so unfair," I mumbled. "I've gained five since then."

"Well, not picking at the boys' lunches while I'm packing them and putting the kibosh on late-night ice cream binges has really helped. The weight just keeps coming off."

"Must be nice," I said through gritted teeth. "I eat well and work out and *still* gain weight."

"Maybe it's muscle."

"I wish. I think it's the eating. I'm swimming more, but being in the water makes me so doggone hungry."

"Doggone?" Lia questioned, brows arched.

"One of Faith's expressions," I explained.

"Is she still coming up for the triathlon in May?"

"Planning on it. Should be a piece of cake for her—except for the swim. Southern women don't like to get their hair wet," I joked.

Lia smiled. "I can't wait to meet her." She strapped on her helmet and slid a water bottle into the cage attached to the bike frame.

"She's anxious to meet you too. She's heard *sooo* much about you."

"All good, of course," Lia quipped.

I shot her a sideways glance, and she laughed out loud. "I'm just happy that my two best friends will finally get to meet each other."

Lia's head snapped up, her eyes wide. *Best friends.* I hadn't meant to say it—it had just slipped out. I blushed and dropped down on one knee to tie my shoe.

"So, this airport loop is fifteen miles?" I asked, changing the subject.

"Twelve and a half to be exact. And there's a great spot for lunch about halfway around with an awesome view of the runway."

I hadn't thought to bring lunch.

"Don't worry," Lia said, registering my frown. "I brought sustenance!" She zipped up her pack and started pedaling toward the trail. "Let's go!"

I mounted my bike and followed her. Children's laughter float-ed from the nearby playground. The sound carried on an early spring breeze that smelled of grass and damp earth. I caught up to Lia and rode beside her. Her copper hair was tied in a ponytail and threaded through her helmet, reminding me of a lick of flame danc-ing behind her.

"So get this," I began. "I reached for seconds at dinner last night, and Jack had the nerve to whisper 'hungry, hungry Anna' un-der his breath. Like I wouldn't know what he was talking about."

Lia snorted at my reference to the childhood game we'd both loved. My parents had given me Hungry Hungry Hippos for my seventh birthday—my favorite gift that year—and Lia's aunt had sent it to her for Christmas. When I met Lia, my game had long since been sold at a yard sale. But Lia had kept every single gift her aunt had ever sent, and upon discovering our mutual fondness for the chomping hippos, she'd produced the gently worn box from its hiding place beneath her bed. When it was cold outside, we would set up on the boat's small kitchen table and play for hours. On balmy days, we would sit at the boat's stern, happily noshing on Bu-gles while our hippos greedily gobbled marbles, and laugh until our stomachs hurt. At carefree moments like that, Lia would pounce, catching me off guard.

July 1988

"SO, HAVE YOU AND JACK done it yet?" Lia asked in the heat of one particularly competitive round of Hungry Hungry Hippos.

"Lia!" I yelped, splashing berry liquid down my chest.

"I take it that's a no?" My silence was answer enough. "That's what I thought," Lia muttered, disappointed.

Instead of our usual Cherry Cokes, Lia had produced two wine coolers from her mini fridge. When I hesitated, she'd rolled her eyes and reached over to crack the top of my berry-flavored Bartles and Jaymes. "Will you ever stop being such a prude? We're seventeen. We're seniors. Let's celebrate!" She clinked her bottle against mine and ducked out of the kitchen.

I took a tentative sip and followed her, secretly relishing the sweet taste of the wine. The truth was, I'd been thinking about sex. A lot. Imagining sex with Jack made my limbs go fuzzy and warm, and it made my pelvis grow heavy with desire. We'd been pushing the boundaries, rounding the bases, but I still wasn't ready. And Jack had been incredibly patient, never pressuring me.

"It's okay," he'd murmured, kissing my palm when I'd halted an intense make-out session that had strayed beyond my comfort zone. "Whenever you're ready. I'll wait for you, as long as it takes."

I'd grabbed his face with both hands and smashed my lips to his. Kissing I could do. But the subject was not one I wanted to discuss with Lia. Clearly, her views on sex were completely different from mine. Whereas she approached sex as a challenge to conquer or a sporting event to be enjoyed with multiple partners, I had always hoped that when I finally decided to have sex, it would be about love and respect, something private to be cherished. And my relationship with Jack was one that I treasured, the details of which I mostly preferred to keep to myself.

Mumbling about prudes and old maids, Lia had packed up the game and settled into her beach chair. Tipping her chin toward the sun, she gathered her long hair in one hand, exposing a round, purplish bruise above her collarbone.

"Who's that one from?" I asked with a grimace, feigning interest in her latest trophy hickey.

Lia shrugged and released her hair, letting the coils of sun-kissed locks tumble down around her shoulders. "Dunno. Some guy I met at the marina last night. He had the biggest—"

"Lia! Shh!" I interrupted, my eyes darting around. As if anyone at the marina who would hear us... or care.

Lia threw her head back and cackled, flashing the hickey again. "You *will* tell me when you finally have sex with him, though, right?"

"Sure," I said to satisfy her.

Lia slid her sunglasses down the tiny, crooked slope of her nose and peered over the rims at me. "Don't wait too long. Guys have needs. If he doesn't get it from you, he might get it somewhere else."

MY BODY TEMPERATURE spiked at the memory as we pedaled along the trail. Whether it was from desire or embarrassment, I wasn't sure. More likely, it was from chugging my way up the first of many relentless hills and charging into the morning sunlight.

Lia and I rode almost seven miles before stopping for lunch, reaching the overlook just before noon. Dozens of airplanes taxied to and fro in a continuous, meticulously orchestrated loop of arrivals and departures. Lia spread a checkered cloth across a splintered picnic table and produced two bottles of water, two almond-butter-and-honey sandwiches on whole grain, an apple, a banana, and two mini Hershey's Special Dark chocolate bars from her backpack. It was a picture-perfect spring day, with new leaves budding on the trees and young shoots sprouting from the flower beds. Oddly, an emu surveyed us from a nearby farm, craning its long neck and turning its head to give us an assessing, one-eyed stare. We ate and talked and laughed about everything and nothing, just as we'd done as teenagers, shielding our ears from the roar of the jet engines overhead. Time flexed and warped. In that moment, I was a carefree sixteen-year-old girl again instead of a married, responsibility-laden thirty-nine-year-old mother of three.

"Thanks for lunch," I said as we gathered our trash and stuffed the tablecloth into Lia's pack.

"Oh! I just remembered. I have something for you." Lia unzipped the front pocket of her backpack and withdrew a rectangular box wrapped in turquoise paper.

I eyed the box suspiciously. "What's this?"

"Your birthday present. Sorry it's late, but—"

"Lia, you didn't have to get me a present." Two weeks prior, I'd marked the occasion with my family at one of my favorite restaurants. To me, it was the perfect way to celebrate: not too much of a fuss, but I got a night off from cooking.

"I know. I wanted to."

I slowly loosened the tape on either end of the box, unwrapped it without tearing the paper—a pet peeve of Jack's—and lifted the lid. Inside was a small, soft-bound whipstitch journal with a supple saddle-tan leather cover.

I sucked in my breath. "Lia..." I began to protest then reconsidered. "It's beautiful." I sighed and lovingly stroked the buttery leather.

"Open it!" she implored.

The journal was filled with natural parchment paper. I pressed the paper to my nose and inhaled the inspiring pulpy scent. On the inside cover, Lia had meticulously inscribed a quote by E.R. Hazlip in gold calligraphy. "Friendship is a horizon—which expands whenever we approach it."

Beneath the quote, Lia had written, "To my dear friend, Anna. May we continue to expand our horizons. Love, Lia."

Blinking back the tears that stung my eyes, I reached for Lia and hugged her tightly. "Thank you."

"You are most welcome." She smiled, her expression so comforting, so warm and familiar. It seemed to bridge the gap across the miles and years between us.

TWO MONTHS AFTER BIKING the BWI Trail with Lia, I completed my first international-distance triathlon. I'd always imagined crossing the finish line hand in hand with Faith, as we'd done at the mud run in Richmond, but her winter malaise had lingered into spring and devolved into a serious sinus infection with a side of bronchitis. She'd graciously offered to transfer her bib to Lia—who'd been regularly cycling and swimming—but when I shared Faith's offer, Lia had promptly declined, cupping her large breasts in her hands and jiggling them up and down.

"These girls aren't made for running," she quipped. "I'd end up with two black eyes!"

"Ha ha. Very funny." I suggested that she could invest in a more supportive sports bra or walk the running portion of the event. But Lia insisted that the bib should go to someone who was actually fit to run the thing. Besides, her boys had a baseball tournament that weekend. So I'd gone solo.

After the race, I'd staggered into the house, consumed what remained of the previous night's pizza, and collapsed into a deep, dreamless sleep.

Now, rested and freshly showered, I was sitting on the back patio, lost in the mundane task of shucking corn. Jack and the girls had ventured out to pick up a half bushel of steamed crabs and two pounds of shrimp. I was ripping the silks from the last ear of corn when the phone rang. I considered letting it go to voice mail but thought better of it. *It might be Jack, seeking my weigh-in on medium crabs versus large or on veiny shrimp as opposed to deveined.* Sucking air in through clenched teeth, I gingerly eased myself to a standing position and lurched into the kitchen, wincing as my aching quads and overtaxed hamstrings rebelled. "Hello?"

"How'd it go today?" The weak voice that greeted me was barely recognizable.

"Faith! It's so good to hear from you! I was going to call tonight to check on you and tell you all about it."

"Well, don't keep me in suspense," she rasped.

"It was so much fun! I finished eleventh out of twenty-three in my age group. Can you believe it? We're getting ready to celebrate with a good ol' Maryland crab feast!"

"Congratulations! That's amazing!"

"Thanks. But I really wish you'd been there. You sound awful, by the way." I retrieved a bottle of sparkling water from the fridge and headed back out to the patio, tipping my face toward the late-day sun that flooded the yard. Closing my eyes, I envisioned Faith across the miles, the same sun warming her as she sat on the balcony of her condo, overlooking Mobile Bay.

"You always say the nicest things."

"You know what I mean. So what's going on with you?"

"Can't seem to shake this cold." She coughed lightly and blew her nose.

"Have you seen a doctor? Are you taking anything for it?"

"Yes, Mom." I could practically hear Faith's eyes roll over the phone. "Rest, fluids. The usual. And antibiotics for the sinus infection. Happy?"

"Yes," I said, hoping Faith would soon find relief. It had been another tough year for her, and her health had continued to take a beating. But summer was coming. It had probably already arrived in Mobile. Hopefully, the season would bring sunnier days for Faith.

"Everything all right with Lia?"

I cracked the top of my water. "Yes. Seems to be."

"That's good. Really good."

I paused, the glass halfway to my lips. There was a peculiar note to Faith's voice. But before I could prod further, the sharp, tangy aroma of Old Bay suddenly wafted out from the kitchen as Jack and the girls barreled in with a piping-hot bag of shellfish. "They're as big as my head!" Helene shrieked, jumping up and down as she described the crabs.

"At least this big," Evelyn added, holding her hands as wide as her shoulders while Kathryn smirked.

"I'll let you get to your dinner," Faith said, undoubtedly hearing the three-ring circus that had arrived. "You've earned it! Eat some shrimp for me."

"What, no crabs?" I teased, knowing full well that Faith abhorred Maryland's crab-picking tradition. I sipped my water and laid the freshly shucked corn on the oiled grill.

"Eck! No way. I hate those nasty, scavenging things. Makes my skin crawl just thinking about it."

I laughed. "Okay, okay. Just the shrimp, then. You get well soon. It wasn't the same without you today."

"You'll be just fine without me, Anna."

"What—" I began. But she was gone.

That was odd. I stood in front of the grill, its heat billowing against my abdomen. I held tongs in one hand and the silent phone in the other. I rotated an ear of corn and made a mental note to check in with Faith again in a few days.

CHAPTER 23
September 2010

The summer passed in a sweaty blur of swim meets, work, vacation, and triathlons. Jack, Kathryn, and I participated in a local sprint triathlon, and Kathryn, despite it being her first tri, managed to snag third place in her fifteen-and-under division. Evelyn and Helene also got in on the action at two youth triathlons, and the extra miles I'd logged on the BWI Trail with Lia throughout the spring and summer helped me to earn an award for my cycling split. It seemed our family had caught triathlon fever. But the fun came to an abrupt end when my phone rang on the second Monday in September.

"Mrs. Anna Wells?" an unfamiliar voice warbled.

"Yes. Who's calling, please?" I questioned, all business. I was on a tight deadline for two magazine articles.

"This is Mabel Danner. I'm a friend of Faith's. A friend of her mama and daddy's, actually." The voice cracked then, and I clutched the phone tighter, watching my knuckles turn white as I listened to the stranger gently weep. A feeling of dread bloomed in my gut.

I swallowed my fear, refusing to jump to conclusions. "How can I help you, Ms. Danner?"

Ms. Danner blew her nose, a dainty, ladylike sound only a Southern woman could manage. "I don't know if you remember me. We met when you was down to visit two winters ago. I was at the house, helping to care for Clarence—Faith's daddy—God rest his soul."

"Oh, yes. I remember." The dread now pulsed sickeningly through my veins.

Another long silence followed. "I'm so sorry to have to tell you this," Mabel sniveled, "but Faith..." A slow, agonizing minute ticked by as I watched the second hand on the clock make a full rotation. "Faith went to hospice yesterday. It's not good, dear." The soft, muffled weeping resumed.

"Hospice!" I spluttered. "What do you mean, 'Faith went to hospice'?"

Mabel sniffled and delicately blew her nose again. "She was in the hospital a short spell, but there was nothing they could do for her, seeing it'd metastasized. Poor girl went downhill so quickly."

"Metastasized?" I fought to remain calm, to control the hysteria rising in my chest. "I don't understand."

"The cancer got hold of her just like it did her mama, God rest her soul."

"Faith has cancer?" I whispered. "When? How?"

"Ovarian cancer, dear. Couple of years now. She didn't tell you?" Then, before I could respond, Ms. Danner said, "No, I'm guessing she wouldn't. She wouldn't have wanted anyone to know, to be fussing over her and feeling sorry for her."

"I'm not just *anyone*!" I cried, choking on a sob. "I'm her friend. Her *best* friend! I could have been there for her. I could have helped!" I stumbled toward the living room and sank into a chair. Images of Faith as I'd last seen her bombarded my brain: the deep circles beneath her eyes, the weakness, the vomiting, and skipping the triathlon because she was sick. *You'll be just fine without me.* Oh God! Another sob escaped from my throat, and I clapped my hand over my mouth. Warm, wet tears trickled over my fingers.

"I know the two of you were close. You should come, dear. Don't wait too long. She's at Mercy Hospice in Mobile."

MERCY HOSPICE WAS A quaint, unassuming, one-story brick structure located a block away from Mercy Medical in downtown Mobile. The vibrant gardens surrounding the building were in full, fragrant bloom under a bright, sunny sky, and the air was thick with humidity. It was a stark contrast to the cool, dim interior of the building with its purposely homey décor and musky oil scent, an admirable attempt to offset the underlying bleachy ammonia smell of the place.

Inside, voices were hushed, shades were drawn, and televisions hummed on low volume. A plump black woman with kind eyes and graying hair sat at a cherrywood desk. Birds chirped in a cage to her left, and colorful fish swam in an aquarium behind her.

"I'm here to see Faith Barrows," I announced, my calm voice belying the weakness in my knees.

"And you are?" she asked kindly.

"Anna Wells."

The woman, whose identification badge read Sylvia, tapped on the keyboard and peered at the screen. Her face remained placid, but I was certain I detected the slightest change in her eyes: a subtle flicker of the lids, a slight pinch of her brows. "Please have a seat." She gestured to a small waiting area beyond the fish tank. "Someone will be with you in a moment."

I wandered into the cozy room. Two burgundy leather couches faced each other, a vase of fresh flowers on the table between them. On the sideboard stood a fresh pot of coffee, a full tea service, and the usual array of accompaniments. A glass pitcher of iced water and a basket of assorted packaged snacks and fresh fruit completed the offering. I perched on the edge of the couch, too anxious to eat, drink, or flip through any of the magazines that lay fanned across the glass-top table in front of me. My unease had persisted since Mabel's call less than twenty-four hours prior.

Ten minutes later, Sylvia reappeared with a short, raven-haired woman at her side. I stood as the women entered the room. Sylvia, dressed in a baby-blue smock printed with tiny daisies, gave me a tight-lipped smile and retreated to the front desk.

"I'm Charlotte Burke, head counselor here at Mercy Hospice," the dark-haired woman said. "Mrs. Danner told us we could expect you today."

"Is Mrs. Danner here?"

"I'm afraid she's gone home for the afternoon."

"Oh." My voice was small and foreign-sounding to my ears. Somewhere in the building, someone sniveled and made small squeaking sounds that tore at my heart.

"Won't you please sit?" Ms. Burke invited, gesturing open-palmed toward the couch. The outline of my backside was still imprinted on the soft leather. Mrs. Burke and I sat side by side, our bodies angled toward each other, our knees nearly touching.

"Mrs. Wells... Anna. May I call you Anna?" I nodded, and Ms. Burke smiled warmly. "Please, call me Charlotte," she offered, her gaze intent.

I cleared my throat and coughed lightly into my fist. I remembered distantly, belatedly, that my daughters had been taught in preschool to cough into their elbows instead of their hands to prevent spreading germs. "How is Faith?" It sounded like a ridiculous question considering the location. "Can I see her?"

Charlotte's smile faded. She placed cool fingers on the back of my hand. "Faith passed this morning," she said softly.

Her voice was strange, incomprehensible. Her words floated past my ears and dissolved in the musky, bleach-scented air that was suddenly too warm. Stifling. My vision blurred and tunneled.

A high-pitched whine sounded briefly in my ears, and perspiration beaded my upper lip and hairline. I wondered if I might pass out. I shook my head to dislodge the dizziness that enveloped me, yet a strange tingling remained in my limbs. "I'm sorry. Did you say Faith *passed*?"

"Yes. She passed away peacefully a few hours ago. Mabel was with her."

My body was numb, rooted to the spot. My brain was sluggish and confused. "I-I don't understand," I stammered. "She just got here two days ago, right?"

"Yes. The average stay for our patients is about five days."

"But—"

"These may help." Charlotte handed me several brochures. The one on top pictured a forlorn woman peering out a window. The caption read, "Dealing with the loss of a loved one."

I stared blankly at the glossy pages on my lap.

"Is there someone I can call for you? Do you have a place to stay?"

I stood and clutched my bag with both hands. The brochures fell from my lap and scattered across the floor.

"Here's my number if you'd like to talk," Charlotte offered, extending a business card.

I brushed past her, ignoring the proffered card, and headed blindly for the exit, swiping angrily at the hot, bitter tears that scalded my cheeks.

"Mrs. Wells?" Sylvia called as I careened past her desk.

I paused, my back rigid, my eyes fixed on the front doors: my escape from this hellish place.

Sylvia appeared by my side and placed a gentle hand on my shoulder. "Mrs. Danner left this for you." My name was written in shaky scrawl across the front of a plain white envelope.

"Thank you," I whispered. I accepted the envelope and sprinted through the doors, my breath coming in short gasps. I spotted a wooden bench nestled among the flowers, shaded by a weeping willow. *Ironic choice.* I sank onto the bench, dropped my head into my hands, and wept until the sun began to cast long shadows across the garden.

THE ENVELOPE CONTAINED Mabel's address and phone number. When my tears dissolved into hitching gulps and I'd finally managed to collect myself, I called Mabel. She invited me for dinner, and even though I had no appetite, I accepted, hoping to gain a better understanding of what had happened. I felt like I'd been involved in a hit-and-run accident, my body smashed to bits by an invisible perpetrator.

An hour later, I turned onto Mabel's street in a quaint neighborhood of post-war homes. Massive, ancient trees towered over modest dwellings with meticulously kept lawns, so unlike the trendy, cookie-cutter McMansions of modern suburbia. In Mabel's neighborhood, each house was pleasingly unique. I passed a rancher with a picture window followed by a modest, two-story brick colonial and a plantation-style home with a wide front porch.

This all seems very familiar. Then I slammed on the brakes. Of course it was familiar. I was in the neighborhood where Faith had grown up, just a few blocks from her childhood home, the home I'd visited on my first trip to Mobile when I'd met Faith's father. That trip could have been yesterday or a zillion years ago. I mopped away the sweat that suddenly slicked my brow and continued slowly down the road until I reached 287 Conti Street.

Mabel's house was a one-and-a-half-story, pitched-roof white house with cornflower-blue shutters. Three dormer windows jutted proudly from the slanted roof, and the front porch was supported by six white pillars. A palm tree stood to the right of the house, and a beech tree to the left.

I parked the rental car along the curb and approached the gate that led to the tidy front yard. Mabel, white-haired and serene, sat rocking on the porch, a sweating glass of sweet tea by her side. She smiled and motioned me forward. I unlatched the gate and walked along the narrow stone path that dissected the front yard and was bordered by magnolia trees. Three worn steps led to the covered porch. Mabel stood when I reached the top, and I fell into this strange woman's comforting embrace.

After a few moments, she held me at arm's length, appraising me with wide, faded denim-blue eyes that had probably once matched the bright cornflower hue of the shutters. Mabel had clearly been beautiful once. She was still beautiful, her face lightly etched with life and laughter, her full lips painted a deep rose. *A Southern woman doesn't set foot out the door without lipstick*, Faith used to proclaim. *Used to*. A soft whimper escaped my lips.

"Thank you for coming, dear," Mabel said in her sweet Southern twang. "May I offer you some tea?" The way she pronounced it—"tay"—made me smile. It reminded me of Faith.

"Yes, that would be lovely. Thanks."

"You make yourself right at home while I fetch the pitcher." Mabel gestured toward the rockers. "It's such a fine evening, I thought we'd take our dinner on the porch if that suits?"

"That would be great, though please don't go to any trouble. I'm afraid I don't have much of an appetite."

"Nonsense. It's no trouble at all." Mabel dismissed my comment with a wave of her veiny, spotted hand. "Besides, I'd enjoy the company. Can get a bit lonely 'round here sometimes. Especially nowadays." She disappeared into the house, and the screen door banged shut behind her.

Bees, not yet retired from their day's work, buzzed lazily around the hanging flower baskets, which lightly scented the evening with their sweet perfume. I inhaled a deep, cleansing breath of the fragrant air. Children rode bikes in the street. An older couple strolled by, hand in hand, waving as they passed. The neighborhood was alive with Southern warmth and hospitality. I could definitely picture Faith growing up there.

Mabel reappeared with my tea and a plate of hot, buttered biscuits, fresh from the oven. My mouth watered despite my stomach being clenched tight. The comforting aroma eased the muscles in my abdomen, coaxing them to relax and soften like the petals of a flower in bloom. It occurred to me then that I hadn't eaten since breakfast.

"Thank you, Mabel. These look delicious."

"Please, have some. I baked 'em myself."

"Did you?" I nibbled the soft biscuit, and it melted on my tongue. "Mmm."

"Nah!" She laughed and patted my knee familiarly. "Just pulling your leg. I picked 'em up at the corner bakery yesterday morning."

Mabel reminded me of a young Betty White. I was certain that, under different circumstances, she would be quite a hoot. A companionable silence stretched out between us, but I couldn't stop my hands from shaking. I curled my fingers into fists and held them tightly against my stomach. "Faith never told me she was sick."

"Sweetie, she didn't want no one knowing. Didn't want anyone treating her differently. She was diagnosed with stage-four ovarian cancer shortly after moving here. It devastated her, but she accepted her fate with courage and grace. She refused treatment, refused to spend the last of her days getting chemo, feeling sick, and being confined to bed with her hair falling out. She wanted to *live*, Anna. You gotta understand, she watched her mama suffer for years, and she refused to travel that path herself. She wanted to live her life, whatever was left of it, and enjoy every moment, right up 'til the end."

"But I don't understand," I cried, my tears falling. "The treatments are so much better these days. Survival rates have improved. And knowing her mother died of cancer, maybe there were preventative measures she could have taken."

"Shh," Mabel soothed. "She did it her way, Anna, on her own terms. We can't begrudge her that. It was her choice to forgo treatment. It's what she wanted. She'd already lived through that hell with her mama." Mabel lowered her eyes and continued in a whisper. "Besides, by the time she was diagnosed, the cancer had already spread. Prognosis was bleak. She refused to spend her last days suffering through treatments, in and out of the hospital..."

"When I was here in February, she wasn't doing well," I confided. "She was nauseated and weak. But she told me it was just food poisoning or the flu. She lied to me, Mabel. She knew the truth, and she didn't tell me. Why would she do that, Mabel? Why would she lie to me?" The sobs were racking my body.

Mabel put her arm around me and drew me close. I rested my forehead against her shoulder and tried to absorb what she was saying. I tried to accept that Faith was gone. My dear friend was *gone*.

"Oh, Anna. Faith surely did battle the flu and every little virus that came 'round. She was feeling poorly more often than not, but she always bounced back. She was strong. A fighter. Willful, stubborn little thing right 'til the end. But she was happy, Anna. She was at peace with her decision, her destiny. How many of us can say that? Besides, what would you have done had she told you? Felt sorry for her? For yourself? Begged her to get treatment? She didn't want that. Two days before she went to the hospital, she was out walking on the beach, feeling the sun on her face and the sand beneath her feet. She only spent a few days in the hospital before hospice was called. I went to visit her, and she made me promise that if this was it—if she wasn't going home—that I would let you know. So that's when I called, per her wishes. She knew you were coming. I told her you were on your way. She wanted so badly to see you, to say goodbye. But the good Lord had other plans. Her mama and daddy were waiting up in heaven for her, and it was her time to go. So much sooner than we anticipated, Anna, but it was her time. She went quickly and peacefully, just the way she wanted."

Mabel gave me another tight squeeze and patted my shoulder before retreating into the house. I was utterly numb, as if I were glued to the rocker. As if I *were* the rocker. *I must be off my rocker!* The ridiculousness of it all suddenly struck me, and I was seized by a fit of inappropriate laughter.

When Mabel returned, a box of tissues in hand, I was doubled over, giggling hysterically. Faith had once told me that laughing and crying, given their physiological similarities, were very nearly the same. They both required the use of the stomach muscles, they could sound similar, and they both released toxins. Well, I sure as hell felt toxic, so I went with it, letting the emotions roll between laughter and tears and back again. I wept, wailed, moaned, and laughed until I was utterly spent.

Mabel sat quietly, letting me get it all out. When I finally settled down, I wiped my eyes and blew my nose loudly.

Mabel, a proper Southern lady, flinched at the honking sound. "Poor dear," she muttered, gently rubbing my back, her small hand making circles between my shoulder blades. "I have a pot roast in the oven. Will you join me for supper?"

"Thank you, Mabel. You've been so kind. But I honestly don't think I could eat a bite. I think I need to go back to my hotel room and lie down a bit."

"I understand, dear. Will you be staying in town for the funeral?"

"Yes." I bowed my head, and a few stray tears escaped from my eyes. Mercy had supplied the details. Apparently, Faith had made her own arrangements. She was to be cremated and laid to rest next to her mother and father in the church cemetery. The ceremony and burial would take place the day after next. Faith would be pleased I would have a day in between to find a suitable dress for the occasion. *Well done, Faith. Well done.*

EXHAUSTED AND DISILLUSIONED after my ordeal in Mobile, I arrived home on Friday morning to find Lia sitting on my front porch, a box of Bugles in her lap. I had no idea they still made the things. When we were teenagers, we had routinely gorged on Bugles and ice cream to cure whatever ailed us.

"What? No ice cream?" I asked, palms upturned.

Lia leaned forward and, from the messenger bag at her feet, withdrew a pint of mint chocolate chip and two spoons.

Later that evening, after Lia had gone home, Jack held down the fort while I retreated to the calm, quiet sanctuary of a hot bath. The scalding water lapped at my body and melted some of the tension from my muscles, but it did little to soothe my aching heart. Through the steamy mist, I glimpsed Jack, an apparition leaning against the doorjamb. His arms were folded across his muscular chest, and one ankle was crossed over the other.

"You are so beautiful," he said.

I smiled weakly. "Kids in bed?"

"Yep."

"Homework done? Lunches packed?"

"I've got it covered, Anna. You relax. I know it's been a hard couple of days." Jack perched on the edge of the tub and kneaded my shoulders with his strong hands.

"Lia was here when I got home," I reported.

He continued kneading. "She called while you were in Mobile, said she couldn't reach you on your cell. I told her what happened, when you'd be home. She didn't tell me she was coming by, though."

"Well, I'm glad she did. You know, Jack, life is short. I guess I've always known that, but now I really *feel* it. You know?"

He nodded solemnly, working his hands lower down my back.

"I've already lost one friend. I don't want to lose another."

Jack paused in his ministrations and leaned forward. He cupped my chin in his hand and tipped my face toward his. I could see the question and concern in his eyes.

"I mean, I already lost Lia once, and now I've lost Faith. It's kind of miraculous, actually, that Lia came back into my life when she did. I don't want to lose her again."

"Then don't." Jack kissed me lightly on the lips.

CHAPTER 24
October 2010

I was updating my calendar with everyone's activities for the month when I realized I'd missed my period. Alarmed, I scrolled back to September, and sure enough, the crimson tide should have rolled in at the end of the month. It was almost two weeks past due. If there was one thing that was as sure as death and taxes, it was my period, reliably arriving every twenty-eight days.

I cupped my breasts. They didn't feel heavier or more tender than usual. My skin was clear, and my energy levels were normal. I wasn't experiencing cramps or odd cravings. Pushing back from the desk, I ran to the bathroom and stepped on the scale. I hadn't gained any weight. I breathed a sigh of relief but, nonetheless, sat on the toilet, peed, and inspected the tissue for any telltale trace of pink. There was none. So I didn't have any obvious signs of early pregnancy, but there were no signs of an impending period either. I paced the room, racking my brain to come up with the date of the last time Jack and I had sex. Given our battle with secondary infertility, we'd paid little mind to birth control, which may have been foolish, but we had always considered pregnancy a blessing. Well, not *always*. My fear of becoming pregnant was one of the reasons I'd held him off for so long when we'd first started dating.

October 1988

I WANTED JACK SO BADLY, it hurt. But I was scared—scared it might literally hurt, scared I might become pregnant. But I was also beyond curious and dying to know what all the fuss was about. And I loved him.

At a homecoming bonfire, almost exactly a year to the date when we'd first met, Jack wrapped his arms around me from behind, kissed my neck, and whispered, "Next week. My mom and sister will be out of town. Can you get away?"

This was it. I was ready. I nodded, and Jack kissed me again, hugging me tighter. I was grateful for the flames that danced before us, warming my body and masking the heat that flushed my face and simmered in my belly.

The following weekend, Jack officially became my first. He took his time. He was gentle and kind, protective. He gazed adoringly into my eyes and brushed my hair back from my forehead as I trembled slightly beneath him. My nose was filled with the intoxicating scent of him as he held me close, caressed me tenderly, and kissed every inch of my body. It was all very sweet and romantic—everything I imagined it would be and more.

The morning after I'd been with Jack, the scent of his skin still fresh on my own, I pulled into the marina and checked my face in the rearview mirror, carefully arranging my features into a mask of nonchalance.

But Lia wasn't fooled. She yanked the car door open, took one look at me, and knew. "You little vixen! You did it, didn't you?"

Scarlet heat flooded my cheeks, but I couldn't hide the smile that crept onto my face.

"You did!" Lia shrieked. "Details. Now!"

To Lia's utter disappointment, other than a basic confirmation of her assumption, I gave her nothing.

"Come on, spill it!" she pleaded. "After all the things I've told you, you could at least tell me if he was any good!"

Blood rushed to my face again. *How would I know?* It wasn't like I had anything to compare it to.

Lia caught on and altered course. "Okay. So did it *feel* good?"

I winced but kept quiet.

It was enough to encourage Lia, and she pressed on. "Was he gentle? Did it hurt?"

"Lia, I love him." I relented. "It was beautiful. Amazing."

Lia slumped in her seat, defeated. "Could you be any more boring?" But then she smiled and gave me a big hug. "Well, congratulations. You're a woman now. Welcome to the club!"

What Jack and I had seemed different from other high school relationships. There was a maturity to it. It was something deep and pure... and scary. As the months ticked by, I was afraid to acknowledge it for what it really was: love, the true and lasting kind. *How could I possibly have found my soul mate, the love of my life, at the age of seventeen?* And though I tried to spend time with Lia, I could feel her putting up walls, putting distance between us. Her usually effusive commentary in the school store was pointedly absent, and she avoided me in the hallways. Lia was pulling away from me, like a piece of driftwood lost to the current.

IN HIGH SCHOOL, WHEN Jack and I had first started having sex, I could never relax. We always used protection, but the specter of an unplanned pregnancy still hovered over me. Once we got married, I felt free. And after Kathryn was born, Jack and I realized what an absolute gift it was, the ability to create life. We'd welcomed the news of each pregnancy with unbridled joy. But now I wasn't so sure.

I paced the bathroom and chewed my thumbnail. My desire to have a boy, to give Jack a son, was still as raw and powerful as ever. But I had to face reality. If I were pregnant, Helene would be nearly ten when the baby was born. The baby would essentially be an only child. He would grow up alone, scarcely knowing his siblings. Kathryn would nearly be old enough to be his mother, for God's sake! But, still. A boy. A *son*. I paused to caress my abdomen, a smile on my lips, then resumed my pacing, coming to a dead halt mid-stride.

Jack! What would he think of this? I would have to tell him soon. I glanced at my watch. There wasn't enough time to run to the store to buy a pregnancy test before the girls got home, and I still needed to shower. That night was date night, dinner and a movie. I reached into the shower, turned on the water, and peeled off my clothes. When the water warmed, I stepped beneath the rainfall showerhead and let the soft cascade wash over me. I would tell Jack over shanghai shrimp with garlic sauce, his favorite.

TIMING DICTATED THAT we see the movie before dinner. Ironically, the movie, *Life as We Know It*, told the story of how two people's lives were turned upside down and irrevocably changed when they became the guardians of a baby. Though Jack seemed to enjoy the movie, laughing heartily at all the appropriate moments, I couldn't quite share in his joviality. Instead, I fidgeted uncomfortably in my seat and anxiously twisted a long brown lock around one finger while chewing the nail of another.

"Hungry?" Jack teased, catching me gnawing away.

I elbowed him, hard, and tucked the bitten finger into my pocket.

After the movie, we walked the short distance from the theater to P.F. Chang's. The October evening was clear and crisp. The faint scent of woodsmoke in the air always reminded me that Halloween was near and the leaves would soon be falling. I tugged my denim jacket tighter around me and picked up the pace.

The upside to a late dinner was that there was no wait. We were seated immediately. But I was edgy and couldn't stop my knee from bobbing beneath the table. When our appetizer and drinks arrived, I took a hearty sip of my pomegranate martini and then, thinking better of it, pushed it away.

Jack gave me an appraising glance. "You seem a little... jumpy." He bit into a spring roll, devouring half of it in a single bite.

"I'm not jumpy," I defended, stilling my knee and locking my eyes onto his. "I'm—"

"Are you ready to order?" our waiter interrupted.

"Vegetarian lettuce wraps and the tuna tataki crisp," I said, miffed by the untimely interruption.

"Shanghai shrimp for me, thanks," Jack ordered predictably. The waiter collected our menus and scurried away.

"Jack—" I began.

"Anna, I need to talk to you about something," my husband said before popping the remainder of the spring roll into his mouth. He chewed slowly, swallowing it down with a healthy swig of pale ale. His eyes were unreadable. "It's just that I, uh, well, I've been thinking..."

Jack, typically confident and sure, was not one to mince words. He pushed the appetizer plate aside and reached across the table to take my cold, shaky hands into his warm, steady ones. I gave his hands an encouraging squeeze, and my own heart compressed with fear.

Jack cleared his throat and began again. "I know it's been difficult, with the infertility and all, but we haven't been taking any precautions. It's not impossible, you know, that you could still—"

"I know!" I exclaimed, nodding and smiling, overcome with happiness and relief. Jack wanted another baby. I should have known we would be on the same page.

"And the last time you were on the pill, you had trouble with headaches and dizziness. I wouldn't want you to have to deal with that again."

Pill?

"So I was thinking that maybe I should get a vasectomy."

His words were like a swift sucker punch to the gut, knocking the wind from me. My own spring roll, which I'd been nibbling, suddenly lodged in my throat. I couldn't move, couldn't breathe. My eyes sprang open, wide and watery. I clutched the napkin in my lap and somehow managed to draw a thin stream of air into my lungs, enough to instigate a spluttering, gagging, coughing fit.

Jack was on his feet in an instant, rubbing my back and murmuring words of comfort and encouragement until I finally ejected the offending morsel into my napkin.

"Oh my God, Anna! You scared me! Are you okay?"

"No, Jack! I'm not okay!" I cried. Jack was kneeling beside me so that we were eye to eye. "I'm... late."

"Late for what?" Jack's beautiful eyes, wide with concern, flickered, and I watched as dark understanding dawned in them.

"I'm late, Jack," I whispered then laid my forehead against his shoulder and wept.

Jack swallowed hard—I could hear the noise in his throat. "Do you want to get out of here?"

"Mm-hmm," I murmured against his arm and rubbed my nose on the sleeve of his shirt.

He retrieved his credit card and flagged our waiter. "I'm sorry, but there's been a change of plans," he explained. "We need to take our entrees to go."

"No problem," the waiter replied. "Your food's coming up now. I'll box it and bring you the check."

"Thanks." Jack stood and helped me into my jacket. His face had gone ghostly pale beneath the dim lights, and his lips were pressed into a hard line.

He held my hand—clutching our takeout in his other hand—as we walked in silence to the car. "Are you sure?" he asked as we drove home.

I crossed my arms defensively over my chest. "I'm sure that I'm late."

"But you're not sure if you're pregnant?"

"No," I admitted. "We didn't have any pregnancy tests at home. But I'm never late."

Jack abruptly switched lanes and hooked a right at the next traffic light.

"Where are you going?"

He pulled into a CVS lot and parked the car. "To get a test."

A tear slid down my cheek as I watched him stride into the store. Clearly, I'd been mistaken. Jack did not want another baby. In fact, it was quite the opposite. He didn't want this baby or any baby. He wanted a vasectomy!

I gazed out the window and caught a glimpse of my reflection in the side-view mirror. My eyes were puffy, my skin ghastly in the red glow of the CVS lights. I swiped at my tears with the back of my hand. I knew Jack was right. I'd known it when I was pacing in the bathroom, contemplating how old the girls would be when this baby was born, and I knew it now. *But a vasectomy?* It just seemed so... final.

Jack returned to the car, plastic bag in hand, and wordlessly backed out of the lot. When we were back on the highway, headed for home, I pivoted slightly in my seat and surreptitiously studied his chiseled profile. He was working his jaw, the muscle at the side of his face clenching and unclenching.

"How long have you known?" I asked, unable to keep the accusatory note out of my voice.

"Known what?" Jack replied, his knuckles turning white as he gripped the steering wheel tighter.

"That you wanted a vasectomy!" I shouted, the outburst bringing fresh tears to my eyes.

Jack exhaled and reached for my hand. Despite my anger, I let him interlace his fingers with mine. "Anna, we're almost forty. Christ, Kathryn will be driving a car in less than a year!" His words gave voice to my own worries and doubts. "It's time for us to move on, embrace the next chapter in our lives, not have more babies. Don't you think?"

I opened my mouth to reply, but only a sob came out. *What if it's too late? What if I'm already pregnant?*

As if reading my mind, Jack squeezed my hand. "If the test is positive, then it's meant to be, and I will love this baby, and I will love you, as I always have and always will." He lifted my hand to his mouth and kissed my knuckles. "But if it's not, I will consider it a close call, a warning. We shouldn't have been so cavalier, so careless, assuming that we just wouldn't get pregnant. Either way, I think getting a vasectomy is the right decision, the *responsible* decision."

When we got home, the girls were already in bed. I gave them each a gentle kiss on the forehead—relishing their sweet, individual scents—and trudged down the hall to the bathroom, pregnancy test in hand.

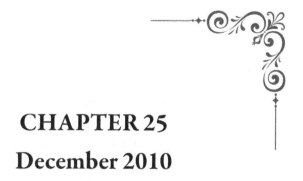

CHAPTER 25
December 2010

My knee bobbed up and down, and my hands twisted in my lap. Jack, however, was as cool as a cucumber, as if we were in a movie theater instead of the office of Dr. Ken Stark, urologist.

The late period in October had been a false alarm. The stress of Faith's sudden passing had evidently taken its toll on my body. I'd gone into the bathroom to take the pregnancy test only to discover a bright-red splotch of blood in my underwear. The relief that followed was palpable. I'd collapsed into Jack's arms, and after several in-depth, soul-searching discussions, I had agreed through a sea of bittersweet tears that he should get a vasectomy. Our days of changing diapers, watching *The Wiggles*, and going to Gymboree were a thing of the past.

"Mr. Wells?" a skinny young nurse called in a crisp, confident voice that belied her petite frame and awkward posture.

Jack's hand rested lightly on the small of my back as we followed the nurse down the hallway. I trained my eyes on the nurse's long brunette fishtail braid. She opened a door near the end of the hallway and motioned toward two black leather chairs sitting opposite an ornately carved and meticulously organized mahogany desk. "Dr. Stark will be with you in a moment," she announced before backing out of the room and pulling the door shut behind her.

My knee immediately resumed its bobbing. Jack laid his hand firmly atop my hammering leg and gave my thigh a reassuring squeeze. "It's okay." He looked directly into my eyes. "We talked about this, remember? We agreed it was the right decision."

I gulped and nodded. My mind raced through the countless hours we'd spent weighing the pros and cons of Jack getting a vasectomy. "Are you sure?" I'd asked, my eyes searching his face for any trace of doubt.

"Yes. I'm sure," Jack confirmed. "We are so blessed. Our family is complete. It's time for us to move on to the next phase of our lives." He was utterly resolute.

I pressed my lips into a thin line, and my eyes brimmed with tears. "But what about the son you've always wanted? Don't you worry that someday you'll regret not having a boy?"

"Anna, I have everything I want. I'm so grateful for the family you've given me. I am a very fortunate man." He'd planted a warm kiss on my forehead and wrapped me in his strong, comforting arms as tears trickled down my cheeks.

But I still mourned the son we would never have, the chair that would remain empty at our dinner table, the toy cars and trucks that would never get pushed around our house. And I mourned the fact that I would never nurse another baby, never feel the warmth of another newborn's fuzzy head tucked beneath my chin, never feel the flour-sack weight of another small, sleeping body nestled against my shoulder. My days of walking into a room and being overcome by the sweet smells of milk, cotton, and powder were a thing of the past. No more slobbery chins to wipe or warm, smooth bellies to zerbert. No more fat, dimpled hands to play pat-a-cake with or soft, chubby thighs to squeeze. No more silky round cheeks to kiss or tiny flat feet to press against my face.

I knew Jack was right. It was time for us to move on. But the grace and ease with which he accepted that inevitability left me feeling alone and abandoned in my grief. While he slept soundly, I often crept from our room to shed silent tears in the night while gazing helplessly at the stars as if I might find reassurance in their twinkling light. Eventually, my grief faded, becoming as dull and gray as the winter sky. But a strange anxiety had taken its place. *What if something goes wrong? What if we're making a mistake? What if we change our minds?*

Dr. Stark strode into the room, startling me with his sudden arrival. He was tall and solidly built. A salt-and-pepper goatee framed a full mouth that was cocked in a perpetual half-smirk.

"Dr. Stark," he introduced curtly, reaching out to firmly shake our hands. He settled into his chair and flipped through the pages of Jack's file. The room was silent except for the rustling of paper and the deep growling of Dr. Stark clearing his throat. Abruptly, he closed the folder and leaned forward, his fingers steepled on the desktop. "So," he began, looking directly at me. "Three girls? You okay with not having a boy?"

My throat was dry. *Is he reading my mind? Peering into my soul?* I disliked Dr. Stark instantly and resented his direct, intrusive question.

"Despite what they say," Dr. Stark continued with a chuckle, "a vasectomy is a permanent procedure. Very difficult to reverse once it's done."

"We're okay with that," Jack answered.

Dr. Stark shot a quick sideways glance at Jack before leveling his gaze at me again. "So, are you ready to go ahead with the procedure today, or do you need time to think about it?"

"We're ready," Jack said.

An uncomfortable minute passed before Dr. Stark cleared his throat again and flashed a wide grin, displaying a row of perfect white teeth. He reminded me of Bruce the shark in *Finding Nemo*, an enemy pretending to be a friend.

Dr. Stark handed Jack several sheets of paper detailing the procedure. My eyes glazed over, and I mentally checked out as Dr. Stark droned on in a bored monotone about the specifics of the procedure. Jack sat calmly beside me. I found it ironic—humorous, even—that the man who'd nearly passed out when I received my epidural now sat stoically while a stranger described in detail how he was going to slice into Jack's balls.

"Your wife can accompany you if you'd like," Dr. Stark offered.

The words jolted me from my stupor. I needed to be strong for Jack. "It's up to you," I whispered to Jack. "I'll go with you if you want me to."

"No, it's okay. I'll be fine," Jack said, though I detected the slightest hesitation in his voice.

My eyes searched his face. "You sure?"

Jack exhaled. "Yep. I'm sure."

I grasped his hands and gave them a reassuring squeeze. Jack and I were a team. If he'd wanted me to accompany him and hold his hand during the procedure, I would have. After all, he'd been there for me during the labor and birth of each of our daughters. But I was secretly relieved he'd let me off the hook. In truth, I wasn't convinced I would be the most reassuring presence, all things considered.

"Okay, then," Dr. Stark said, standing from his desk. "Jamie will get you prepped, and I'll see you in a few." With that, he was out the door, his white coat flapping behind him.

We returned to the waiting room, which was packed, and found two empty chairs against the back wall, facing the window. I stared at the rain pounding the sidewalk while Jack flipped absently through a *Forbes* magazine. The muscle clenching and releasing in his jaw was the only outward sign of his unease.

"Mr. Wells?" Nurse Jamie called, her long braid swishing as she scanned the waiting room.

Jack closed the magazine and squeezed my hand. "It's okay," he whispered. "It's the right thing." He gave me a reassuring kiss on the cheek and followed the nurse down the hall. How absurd that he was the one comforting me. Though I had to admit, his confidence was indeed reassuring.

As the minutes ticked by, my imagination went into overdrive. I envisioned Jack lying on a stiffly padded, paper-covered table, completely vulnerable as Dr. Stark pressed a scalpel into his most delicate, tender area and revoked our ability to create life. The image took on cartoonish proportions as I envisioned sprinting in slow motion down the hall, bursting into Jack's procedure room, and yelling "Stop!" only to see thin tendrils of smoke curling into the air and a wicked grin on Dr. Stark's face as I realized I was too late. I shook the image from my mind in time to see Jack strolling gingerly down the hallway. A gentle smile—or perhaps a grimace—awakened his dimples and crinkled the corners of his eyes.

"All set?" I asked, shocked by his calm demeanor. He appeared as if he'd just had his teeth cleaned instead of his scrotum cut. I joined him at the checkout window and listened carefully as the woman behind the sliding glass instructed us on the use of ice and pain medications.

"A six-pack and an ice pack. Got it," Jack said, glancing at the Vicodin prescription and shoving it into his back pocket.

"Do we need to fill that?" I asked as Jack eased himself into the passenger seat.

"Nah, I don't think so." He winced ever so slightly as he settled onto the seat and sucked in a small breath through his teeth. "But I'll hang on to it just in case."

The rain poured in thick sheets as we drove, and the windshield wipers beat a steady rhythm across the glass. Jack slipped into a light sleep, and I hummed quietly to the radio, steeling my heart

and mind against the knowledge that our futures had been irrevocably altered. The tears came again, mirroring the steady flow of the
rain.

"WHAT YOU NEED, MY FRIEND, is a girls' day out. My treat!"
Lia had offered, attempting to lift my spirits. I hadn't told her about
Jack's vasectomy, so she was operating solely under the impres-
sion that I remained grief-stricken by Faith's sudden death. That,
of course, was true. The vasectomy merely added salt to that fresh
wound.

I entered the small riverfront building, and my eyes struggled
to adjust to the dark-stone-and-wood interior. Outside, the brilliant December sunshine glinted off the snow in blinding white
arcs. The sky was a clear, crisp blue, the air icy and sharp. The cozy
warmth of the café and the aroma of freshly roasted coffee provided a welcome respite from the harsh winter day.

A hand shot up across the room, waving exuberantly. Lia was
kicked back in a plush, overstuffed chair adjacent to the fireplace.
I smiled brightly and peeled off my red chenille hat and gloves as
I walked toward her. She looked radiant and happy. In the two
months since I'd last seen her, her hair had grown longer. Loose
coppery waves tumbled in layers to her shoulders. The trendy cut
was becoming, complementing her bone structure and making her
appear more youthful than ever.

"Hey, you!" she said, standing to wrap me in a big hug. She
was wearing a pumpkin-hued sweater dress that clung to her curves,
high-heeled leather boots, and large hoop earrings.

Despite my lean, lithe figure, I had always felt dowdy in Lia's
presence. I glanced down at my creamy-white L.L. Bean sweater
and raggedy old jeans haphazardly stuffed into a pair of flat, rub-
ber-soled brown boots.

"You look great," Lia complimented.

"Thanks. You do too."

"What, this old thing?" she deadpanned. She smiled, but the humor fell short of her eyes.

An awkward silence descended as we settled into our over-stuffed, adobe-brown chairs. I rubbed my hands together and held them toward the fire. Tongues of orange and yellow flames leapt and danced behind the wire screen. "It's freezing outside," I said, stating the obvious.

"Yeah. Doesn't seem that long ago we were sweating our butts off in Harper's Ferry."

I grimaced at the unpleasant memory of swarming gnats and aggressive yellow jackets as Lia and I hiked the C&O Canal tow-path and attempted a late-October picnic alongside the Potomac. "I'm going to grab something to drink. You need anything?"

"A stiff shot of whisky?"

I gave her a curious glance. "I think you've come to the wrong place," I said with a laugh.

"How 'bout a menu, then?"

"Sure." I headed for the counter, grateful for the distraction. Something was up. I didn't know what, but Lia's obvious unease gave me the unsettling urge to commiserate, to confide in her about Jack's vasectomy despite my resolve to keep such a private matter to myself. Things were going well with Lia, and I wanted to trust her, but I was still afraid of being too vulnerable, of opening up and letting her back into my life only to have my heart broken again. If Faith were there, she would be giving me that look—one perfectly arched eyebrow raised above the rim of her ruby glass-es—and telling me to get my head out of my hiney and get over it already. But that was just it—Faith wasn't there. I knew I was still reeling from her death and that my current reticence toward Lia—and my oscillating emotions regarding our friendship—had little to do with Lia herself and everything to do with my grief over losing Faith.

But like everyone else, I was drawn to Lia. She was like the sun, emitting a gravitational force that pulled people to her and kept them in her orbit. Every fiber of my being fought to shout my news, to bare my soul and my grief to her, to lean on my oldest and once dearest friend. But I smothered the urge and resolutely wrapped my fingers around my steaming mug of chai as I retreated to our little nook by the fire, with two menus in hand.

"Thanks," Lia said politely.

We busied ourselves perusing the lunch specials as the fire crackled and popped beside us. A Jamie Cullum CD played in the background. Two frazzled women with five infants and toddlers between them temporarily shattered the peace of the café as they noisily bustled in to collect a bakery order to go. As if on cue, Lia and I both glanced up, and our eyes locked.

She opened her mouth, I presumed, to share her lunch choice. Instead, she said, "I'm leaving Neil."

"Jack got a vasectomy," I blurted simultaneously.

The shock on Lia's face surely mirrored my own as our expressions morphed from concern to understanding to empathy until we were both laughing hysterically. Lia leaned forward and gave me a hug, which I accepted gratefully. I sank into my chair, giggling and swiping at wayward tears, and Lia did the same. Then we fell into silence again. I sipped my chai. Feeling exposed, I immediately regretted my impulsive lapse.

"When I first moved back to Baltimore," Lia began, "I felt so alone, untethered. Neil made me feel safe. I met him after an Orioles game. He co-owned a bar across the street. I remember sitting on my stool, watching him work. He was charming and confident, quick with his hands and his wit. We started dating, and six months later, he asked me to marry him." Lia smiled briefly before a shadow crossed her face, chasing away the happiness. "But then the bar went belly up, and Neil changed. He wasn't used to failure, and he resented that I was suddenly the breadwinner. I think he felt threatened. He's really conservative. Traditional, ya know?"

I nodded, but truth was, I didn't know. Jack was the opposite: liberal, loving, supportive. He was an equal partner in every way. Besides, part of me was selfishly, irrationally annoyed that Lia had launched into her own tale of woe without giving a second thought to mine. I'd just dropped a bombshell of my own, and she appeared oblivious, as if she hadn't even heard what I'd said. My heart sought to comfort her, to play the supporting role I'd always played in our relationship, but my mind was stubbornly overriding any attempt to nurture or comfort. My body remained rigid, and my tongue silent. I entertained the idea of standing up and walking out, just as Lia had done so many years ago. Then I remembered the one and only time Lia hadn't put herself first.

January 1989

MY RELATIONSHIP WITH Lia was inversely proportionate to my relationship with Jack. The more time I spent with Jack, the less time Lia spent with me. When we returned to school after the holidays, she wouldn't even sit with me at lunch anymore.

"What's going on with you?" I demanded one morning as we sorted and folded a new shipment of Bay View sweatshirts in the school store.

"Jack's taken you away from me," Lia complained. She shoved a balled-up sweatshirt into one of the apparel cubbies. "Things just aren't the same between us anymore."

"That's not true!" I retorted, but Lia simply shrugged, offering no further explanation, and continued to avoid me at school.

Then, out of the blue, she called. "I think I'm pregnant," she said, crying.

For a moment, I was speechless. *What's the right thing to say in such a moment?* "Are you okay?" I closed my bedroom door, sank onto my bed, and sucked in a deep breath. "Do you know who the father is?"

"Yes. No." Lia cried harder. "Maybe."

"Don't worry. We'll figure something out. We'll get through this. I'll help you."

To my mother's astonishment, I spent the next several evenings and the entire weekend at the library. "What?" I challenged when I returned home with a stack of books in my arms.

"Nothing. I think it's wonderful that you're utilizing the library," my mother demurred. "Find anything good?"

"Yep," I replied then disappeared into my room. Behind my locked door, I scoured articles on teen pregnancy and dog-eared pages to photocopy during my next visit to the library.

Two weeks passed, but despite Lia's shocking revelation, she continued to avoid me. Annoyed, I took the uncharacteristically bold step of relocating to the far end of the lunch table—where Lia now routinely sat—and wedged myself between Lia and Kelly. "Hey, Lia. Can I, um, talk to you for a minute?"

Kelly shot Lia a curious glance but tactfully excused herself to go in search of ketchup for her fries.

"What's up?" Lia asked.

"What's *up*? You're the one who dropped a huge bombshell. I've been at the library, researching—"

"Shh," she hissed through her teeth then pressed her finger to her lips. Her eyes darted wildly and settled on Renee, who sat across the aisle from us, watching with rapt attention and undoubtedly salivating over the possibility of impending drama. "I'll call you later, okay?"

"Whatever," I said.

Renee's mirthful laughter rang out as I stomped out of the cafeteria. But my phone did ring that night.

"False alarm," Lia announced and hung up.

I promptly tossed all my research and all my photocopies into the trash.

A few days later, I arrived home from my evening shift at the Pizza Palace with flour dusting my hair and the disgusting odor of anchovies still fouling my fingers despite multiple scrubbings. Exhausted, I tossed my soiled apron into the laundry tub and tromped up the stairs to my room. "Jeez!" I yelped. My mother was sitting on my bed, clutching several sheets of paper in her white-knuckled hands. I knew instantly what she was holding, what she'd found.

"Anna," she whispered. Her hands were shaking, and her face was drained of color. My mother had always been the embodiment of beauty to me. Now she simply appeared deflated and old. I noticed for the first time the prominent veins trespassing on the backs of her hands and the fine, wispy lines framing her worried blue eyes. "Is there something you need to tell me?"

"No!" I shouted. "They're not mine. They're for... a friend." I realized how ridiculous the words sounded coming out of my mouth, even if they were true.

My mother shook her head, and her blond hair swished across her shoulders. Her eyes watered, and she pressed her lips into a tight, thin line. "Anna—"

"Mom!" I interrupted, but she wasn't having it.

"Look, I know you and Jack are crazy about each other. I was your age once—"

"They're not mine," I repeated. The words hung in the air, and anger flooded my veins. All I had to do was say the word, reveal Lia's name, and I would be exonerated. And my mother would believe me. She'd seen the way Lia had behaved at the beach and knew how boy crazy she was. But despite all the friction between us, I still felt loyal to Lia. I didn't want to betray her. My mother hesitated, doubt and hope waging war across her features.

Then a firm, determined voice cut through the air, startling us both.

"She's telling the truth."

My mother and I snapped our heads toward the sound, and my mouth dropped open. Lia stood in the doorway. Her face was pale but fierce.

"How—"

"Your dad let me in." Lia stepped into the room and inclined her head toward the papers my mother was still holding. "Those were for me. I thought I might be, but I wasn't. I'm not." She dropped her eyes to her feet, her bravado beginning to evaporate beneath my mother's disapproving gaze.

Absorbing Lia's admission, my mother nodded primly, stood from the bed, and pulled me into her arms. It felt good to be held, and I wished for a moment to stay forever in her protective, loving embrace. The minute she released me, I missed the warmth and comfort of her, the familiar scent of her. She walked stiffly across the room, placed her fingertips beneath Lia's chin, and lifted Lia's head so that she could peer directly into my friend's eyes. "Does your mother know?"

Lia wrenched her chin from my mother's grasp and shook her head.

My mother pulled Lia into a perfunctory hug, her maternal instincts kicking in. "It's getting late. What brings you here at this hour, Lia?"

"Anna, um, left her homework at my house. She has math first period, so I wanted to bring it to her," Lia fabricated, shocking me with her selflessness. She'd stuck up for me and come to my rescue even though it meant she would take the fall. No one had ever done that for me before. No one had ever put themselves on the line for me. With that single act, my connection to Lia went deeper, and the bonds of our friendship, despite our recent struggles, grew stronger.

"Well, okay. But let's make it quick, shall we?"

Lia and I nodded mutely. Seeming satisfied, my mother turned to leave. With her hand on the doorknob, she paused and glanced over her shoulder. "If you ever need to talk... either of you," she offered, though she was looking directly at Lia.

And I knew it cost her. My mother was as prudish as she was lovely. We'd never had "the talk." She'd relied on my school health classes to provide my sexual education.

I gave her a wobbly smile, and she ducked her head, an unspoken agreement between us. She took the papers with her when she left. All the articles I'd copied on abortion were still clutched in her hand.

"BUT THAT'S ENOUGH ABOUT me," Lia said suddenly, jolting me from my memory. "Tell me about Jack."

That's enough about me? In all the time I'd known Lia, such a phrase had never crossed her lips. Everything had *always* been about her: Lia's perfect SAT scores, Lia's newest conquest, Lia's latest drama, Lia's slew of admirers. I couldn't believe my ears and was flummoxed by being put on the spot. I reached into my bag and extracted a compact mirror. "Eyelash," I murmured, feigning a search for the offending lash. "Did, uh, you and Neil try counseling?" I demurred, satisfied that she'd shown concern for my situation but unsure of my readiness to discuss it further. *Be careful what you wish for.*

"Not Neil's style," Lia replied with a snort. "You know, Neil's the kind of guy who needs a dependent, submissive woman. When

I first met him, I *was* that woman. But then my career took off, and I regained my confidence. Things really went downhill when Neil lost his coaching job. He was depressed, drinking heavily, and started taking his frustrations out on me but, thankfully, not the boys. He adores them."

"What are you going to do?"

"As soon as the boys finish middle school, I'm out. Neil and I both deserve to be happy, and right now, neither of us are. There hasn't been any real love between us for a long time. If there ever was."

Lia's calm, rational discussion of such a difficult, emotionally charged situation infused me with hope. Gone were the trademark drama and exaggeration, the manipulative plays for pity, envy, or attention. Lia was simply sharing her turmoil, opening herself up to me, trusting me.

"That's a really tough decision to make. I'm sorry you're going through this, that you've been unhappy."

"It wasn't all bad," Lia said wistfully. "We cared about each other once. We created a family..." She gazed absently out the window at the snow-covered riverbank, her face ghostly pale in the refracted light. She appeared more vulnerable and uncertain than I'd ever seen her.

My heart constricted. It was as if I could feel her pain mixing with my own, and the need to share my own heartache with her, to bond and commiserate with her, was suddenly overwhelming. The words began to tumble from my mouth.

"I wanted a boy so badly for Jack," I whispered. "But after Helene was born, we struggled with infertility, and I had two miscarriages. I was devastated and so depressed. I felt like such a failure." I paused, half expecting Lia to somehow belittle my situation or launch into another tale of her own, but she didn't. She sat quietly, her hand giving mine a reassuring squeeze, encouraging me to continue. "Without a boy—a son—I can't shake the feeling that our family is incomplete, unbalanced somehow. And then I feel ashamed for feeling that way because I know it sounds so selfish and ungrateful."

"You are entitled to your feelings, Anna. It doesn't make you selfish or ungrateful. And you certainly aren't a failure," Lia soothed.

"That's what Jack says."

"You don't believe him?"

"I do. It's just..." I faltered, struggling to find the right words. "It's not only about Jack not having a son, which I know sounds ridiculously archaic, but it's also about the finality of it all. Jack getting a vasectomy closes that chapter of our lives forever. There's no turning back now. That's the part that really breaks my heart."

Lia remained silent and leaned forward, closer to me. She rested her forearms on her knees and fixed her eyes on mine. Her wordless support suffused me with courage.

I wiped my palms on my jeans and continued. "When Jack insisted it was time for us to move on, I reluctantly agreed that him getting a vasectomy was the right thing to do. And deep down, I know it was the right decision. But that doesn't make it hurt any less. I knew it would be hard, but I didn't expect to feel like this... so empty and alone."

Lia reached out and squeezed my forearm. "Anna, you are not alone. Have you told Jack how you feel?"

"Sort of, but he doesn't really get it, the whole maternal thing. You know Jack—he sees things as black and white. Decisions are clear-cut for him. He doesn't torture himself by weighing the pros and cons of everything."

"You've always been a worrier," Lia teased, attempting to lighten the mood but quickly sobering again. "But clearly, Jack is okay with having only daughters, right?"

I sank back in my chair and exhaled, the rush of air making my lips flutter. "That's what he says. I just hope he's being completely honest. I don't ever want him to have any regrets." I bit the inside of my cheek, remembering the wistful expression I'd once seen on my husband's face, the softness in his eyes as we'd watched a father and his young son playing together in the park.

"He won't," Lia reassured. She sank back too, her posture mirroring mine. "As you said, things are clear-cut for Jack. He won't have doubts or second guesses. And now that the baby years are behind you, you can focus on the girls and all the fun the teen years have to offer. Ha!" She chortled at her own joke. "But don't worry. It goes by quickly."

I cocked my head. "Your boys just turned thirteen, right?"

"Yeah, you know what I mean." Lia smiled and waved her hand through the air as if chasing off a fly. "At least that's what they say, that it goes by in a blink. Shall we order?"

CHAPTER 26
June 2011

"**C**heers!" I clinked my icy-cold bottle of Blue Moon against Lia's Corona. She'd chilled our favorite beers and even sliced the necessary citrus accompaniments—orange for me, lime for her.

My body, wet with perspiration earlier in the day, was now cloaked in a sticky layer of stale sweat. I propped my bare feet on the railing and relished a moment of stillness on the shaded deck of Lia's new townhome. The movers had done most of the heavy lifting, but I'd met Lia at sunrise to help load my Honda and her Lexus with dozens of smaller boxes and fragile items.

"Telling the kids was way harder than telling Neil," Lia confided between sips. "Nick refused to speak to me for weeks, and Nate said I was ruining his life. It broke my heart. But what was I supposed to do? Stay in an unhappy marriage? I think it's better this way than for the boys to be subjected to the daily fallout of a broken marriage."

On numerous occasions over the past few months, I'd held Lia's hand as she'd cried. I had drunk with her, distracted her with plans for a rigorous hike up Old Rag Mountain, and finally, I'd helped her move. Now we were surrounded by piles of boxes and bubble wrap, the transition complete.

"It was the right thing," I reassured her, taking a long, appreciative drink of the sweet, citrusy beer.

"I know." Lia sipped her own beer. "But why does the right thing always have to be so hard?"

I shrugged. "If it were easy, everyone would do it."

"True that!" she agreed, tipping her Corona toward me.

While Lia had been struggling to disentangle her life from Neil's, Jack and I had been working to redefine ours now that having more children was definitely—and irrevocably—off the table. I'd come to terms with Jack's vasectomy and accepted it. I knew in my heart it had been the right thing to do, and Jack was adamant that he had no regrets. But it had taken an emotional toll. The cold, dreary winter months that followed the vasectomy were a sad reflection of my mood. It was as if a storm cloud perpetually hovered over our house, blanketing our life in shadows. As Lia said, the right thing was often not the easy thing.

"When will the divorce be final?" I ventured.

"Next June. In Maryland, you can't file until you've lived separately for a year."

"It'll be here before you know it. The years are flying by."

"I know, right? The kids are getting old, but we're only getting better with age, like fine wines."

"A girl can dream!" I teased.

Lia swatted me on the arm. "Speak for yourself," she said with a chuckle, and then her face sobered. "I can't believe the twins are headed to high school."

"I hear you. Kathryn's already starting to think about colleges."

"Oh yeah? Where does she want to go?"

"So far, she really likes Delaware and Virginia Tech." I reached into what was left of a bag of chips and shoved a handful of crumbs into my mouth.

Lia squeezed more lime juice into the dregs of her Corona then licked her fingers. "What's she planning to major in?"

"Graphic design. She likes that it's creative but definitive. Kathryn doesn't like leaving things to chance."

Our conversation was interrupted by the sound of the doorbell. "Pizza!" Lia exclaimed before disappearing into the house to retrieve our dinner. "Grab me another Corona, would ya?"

I moseyed over to the cooler and fished my hand through the ice cubes while reflecting how different I was from Kathryn at her age. I had willingly tossed the dice on my future and left my very fate to chance.

May 1989

MY HAPPINESS BEGAN to crumble around me. College acceptance letters had arrived, and Jack and I had both gotten accepted to several of the same schools. Jack was thrilled, but I was panicking. It was as if I could suddenly see my whole life before me—a good life but one that was already completely mapped out. Jack and I would graduate from college, get jobs, get married, have children, grow old together, and live happily ever after. The end. At eighteen, I felt as if my whole story had already been written. *No surprises, no adventure. Do not pass go—go directly to the white picket fence.* I began to feel trapped, like a bird who was finally ready to fly but then had her wings clipped. I was also fearful of following in my mother's footsteps. My mom had married her high school sweetheart and dedicated her whole life to her family, to her husband and her children, to being the perfect housewife. Fresh laundry every day and a home-cooked meal on the table every night were her idea of nirvana. And she seemed truly content and happy with that life... with one exception.

Once, I'd accidentally overheard my mother on the phone, whispering to someone in hushed, anguished tones, wondering if, perhaps, she should have lived a little more—loved a little more—before settling down. It was a fleeting moment of weakness. A brief moment of introspection and second-guessing that I never heard my mother give voice to again. But the sound of her voice laced with wonder and regret was seared into my adolescent brain.

From that moment on, I knew I wanted to live my life without regrets. I wanted a career. I wanted to explore. I wanted to sow my oats. So I started avoiding Jack. I made excuses for not seeing him. I shunned physical contact. Jack was as dear to me as ever—never pressuring me and giving me the space I needed—but it wasn't enough. I suddenly envied Lia's freedom and experiences. The urge to be reckless and irresponsible began growing like a cancer in my body. But I was a coward. I couldn't bring myself to utter the words that would set me free. So I morphed into a total bitch instead. Jack was hurt and confused by my behavior. But instead of feeling badly about it, I leveraged those feelings to my advantage.

On the eve of our senior prom, Jack appeared on my doorstep, his eyes tight and jaw set. He insisted we talk. My heart hammered in my chest. *This is it.* I could feel it. I closed the front door behind me and walked silently beside him. We shuffled along a path to the small man-made lake that flanked Tidewater's main entrance. The sky was a beautiful cloudless blue, and children swarmed the playground. Their joyous laughter and shrieks of delight filled the air as they rushed down slides and arced through the horizon on swings. Jack walked with his hands shoved into the pockets of his stonewashed jeans. I crossed my arms tightly in front of my chest, attempting to literally hold myself together. Because, on the inside, I was falling apart. I feared that pieces of my heart and soul might actually rattle free from my body and shatter on the ground at my feet.

Jack paused under the shade of a large, blooming dogwood. Wordlessly, he lowered himself to the ground. I sank down beside him, not touching him, and drew my knees to my chest.

He plucked a few blades of grass from the earth and twisted them into knots. "What's going on?"

It was my chance to come clean, to explain what was going on inside my head and my heart. It was my chance to ask him to set me free if he truly loved me. Instead, I remained gripped by cowardice and fear. I replied with clipped answers to his questions as he struggled to understand.

"Why are you doing this? Why are you pulling away?"

"I don't know." It was a lie, but I couldn't form the words I needed to speak. I couldn't express the complicated feelings I was struggling with.

And so, that day in the park, Jack gave me what I'd been seeking: my freedom. The hurt on his face painfully carved itself into my heart. He stood and walked away, his shoulders hunched, the sun shining on his thick, dark hair.

I collapsed into the grass and sobbed until the earth beneath my cheek had become sodden with my tears. Then I walked home on numb legs. Avoiding my parents, I headed straight to the shower to scrub away my pain and self-disgust. I hoped I might emerge cleansed, fresh, and new, as if from a cocoon, so I could finally spread my wings and fly, and so I could pretend that what had just happened was for the best.

DESPITE OUR BREAKUP, Jack and I agreed we would still go to prom together. It was our senior year, after all, and the tickets were nonrefundable. Naïvely, I hoped we might still be able to enjoy a fun evening together as friends. But it quickly became obvious that Jack had hoped our breakup had been an emotionally charged rash decision, a mistake, one that prom would set right. But despite the world feeling as though it were cracking and shifting beneath my feet, I stood my ground, though it required every ounce of strength and willpower I had. Over the course of the evening, Jack grew increasingly agitated as I rebuffed his romantic gestures and avoided him as much as possible. By the end of the night, we were barely speaking to each other.

At school, word spread like wildfire that Jack and I were officially over. Throughout the spring, as I had battled my increasingly confusing and conflicting feelings about Jack, Lia had gradually moved her way back down the lunch table until she was once again sitting across from me. But things were still awkward between us. The week after prom, as we collected the remnants of our lunch, Lia dropped a note onto the table in front of me. I sat in stunned silence, suspiciously eyeing the small square of pink paper as Lia merged into the flow of students filing out of the cafeteria. I picked up the pink square, turned it over in my hands, and tapped it against the edge of my notebook. When everyone was gone, I tugged the tab of the tightly folded page and smoothed it against the table. Six words were written in Lia's trademark sparkly purple ink. The feminine colors were a paradoxical contrast to her sharp, angular print: "Meet at Keller's on Saturday?"

"SO I GUESS YOU HEARD about Jack," I said, solemnly sipping my chocolate milkshake.

Lia nodded, frowned, and commiserated for the briefest requisite moment before launching into her own tales of woe and showering me with verbal vomit about Joe, her latest crush. "I'm, like, so into him. He just seems so different, like someone I could totally be serious about." I raised one eyebrow and continued sipping as

Lia prattled on. "I mean, I might even be willing to give the whole monogamy thing a try for a guy like him."

"Well, if you really like him, don't sleep with him right away," I advised. "You know what my dad always says..."

"Why buy the cow when you can get the milk for free?" Lia mocked, rolling her eyes, and we both dissolved into a fit of giggles. It was good to laugh with her again, to be at Keller's with her again, even if she only wanted to talk about Joe.

"I say, why buy the pig?" Lia retorted with an unladylike snort.

I had missed Lia. I was completely brokenhearted over my breakup with Jack—even if I was the one who had instigated it—nearly insisted on it—but at least I wasn't alone. I still had Lia.

And while my dad may have warned about the pitfalls of giving away milk for free, my mom was the one who'd always told me that boyfriends would come and go, but friendships would last forever.

CHAPTER 27
December 2012

Flour? Check. Eggs? Check. Chocolate? Check, check.

F   I may not have been Santa Claus, but I was a firm believer in making a list and checking it twice. The last thing I wanted to do was get home from the store, realize I'd forgotten the cranberries or the shredded coconut, and have to trudge back out into this slushy mess again. It was worth standing in the baking aisle a few extra seconds and listening to the annoyingly cheery holiday music piped through the store's overhead speakers to make sure I had everything I needed. I glanced at my watch and hurried to the express checkout lane. Lia was due to arrive in less than an hour for our third annual Christmas Cookie Baking Day Extravaganza.

With my goods bagged and paid for, I hopscotched through the soupy parking lot, plopped the bags of baking goodies onto the passenger seat, and squinted through the sleet and rain that pelted the windshield as I drove home.

In high school, when Lia and I had baked Christmas cookies with my mom, the fireplace was always crackling, and hot cocoa or eggnog had filled our mugs. Snowflakes had drifted silently past the windowpanes and collected in the corners of the sills, and my mother had sung along to her favorite carols. At least that was the idyllic way I remembered it. Now that I was the adult responsible for orchestrating the controlled chaos otherwise known as baking day, I realized it had likely been too hot in the kitchen to require a fire and too hectic to enjoy sipping mugs of cocoa, and it rarely snowed that early in December. There had probably been cookie dough caked in my hair and a fine layer of flour coating every surface of our kitchen, and my mom had most likely been sweating, cursing, and barking orders instead of singing, not to mention nipping something a little stronger than eggnog. Those things I knew to be true—not from memory but from personal experience—because my mother had long ago passed the baking baton on to me so I could carry on the tradition with my own daughters.

Today, however, will be different. I pulled up to a stop and drummed my fingers on the steering wheel as I idled at a red light, a smile creeping onto my face. Today, my idyllic childhood memory would come to life as Lia and I baked side by side, sipping spiced wine and listening to a CD I'd made of our favorite Christmas songs from the eighties: "Do They Know It's Christmas" by Band Aid, "Last Christmas" by Wham, "Santa Baby" by Madonna, and "Grandma Got Run Over By a Reindeer" by Elmo & Patsy.

In the three years since Lia and I had reconnected, we'd created our own personal version of *Back to the Future:* traveling back in time—at least in our minds—and diligently attempting to fill in the gaps and reclaim the years we'd lost. We had pored over pictures and exchanged detailed stories of our college years, our weddings, and the births of our children, so we could pretend we hadn't missed the important moments in each other's lives. I'd told Lia about my raucous spring break trips to Key West and Jack's proposal the day we graduated from college, and Lia had described the birth of her twins in such colorful detail that I could almost believe I'd been there, holding one of her legs as she pushed those sweet, tiny babies into the world. We'd done our best to cover every important milestone from the past so we could pave the way to our future.

The light turned green, and the traffic crept forward. The past year had been difficult. But Lia had finally adjusted to her new co-parenting arrangement with Neil, and Jack and I had worked through the emotional turmoil of his vasectomy and were ready to embrace the next chapter of our lives. We already had several college tours lined up for Kathryn. Through it all, Lia and I had been there for each other. We had become bound to each other anew. Though Jack was my true love and soul mate, Lia had once again become my confidante and partner in crime. My best friend.

The sleet had disintegrated into delicate flakes of snow. I parked the car and dashed up the porch steps. The reusable grocery bags dangled from my arms as I struggled to turn the key in the lock. Shouldering my way into the foyer, I kicked the front door closed behind me, stepped out of my wet boots, and padded into the kitchen to unload my burden onto the granite countertop. The room was my pride and joy, with its high ceilings and tall, arching windows.

Ten minutes later, Lia stood smiling and rosy-cheeked on my doorstep. She looked both lovely and girlish with snowflakes dusting her hot-pink coat and clinging to her eyelashes.

"Hey there!" I greeted, throwing open the door and pulling her in from the cold.

Lia unwound her scarf and gave me a warm hug. "Are the kids getting out of school early today for the snow?"

"Nah. It's supposed to stop by noon."

"It's really slippery out there," she reported. "We're not getting any of this at my house."

"You do live an hour south. But just the threat of snow is enough to get the crazies out stocking up on bread and toilet paper."

"I'm guessing the store was pretty insane?" Lia surmised with a roll of her eyes.

"A nightmare. But neither rain nor sleet nor snow nor mobs of paranoid shoppers could keep me from procuring our ingredients!"

"Well done, my friend. Well done."

I marveled at how far Lia and I had come, how easy and natural our banter was. Our friendship as adults, new though it was, was deeper and more meaningful and precious than it had ever been in high school. Older, wiser, and more comfortable in our own skins, we'd managed to repair the rift between us. Despite everything that had happened, our friendship seemed destined.

Lia followed me into the kitchen and headed straight to the sink to wash her hands. Chessie and Bay danced around her feet and sniffed at her jeans, undoubtedly getting acquainted with the scent of Lia's new cat, Jolie.

"Sorry I can't pet you right now," Lia apologized, swiping her tiny foot down Bay's flank and leaving little bits of white sock fuzz on his black fur. "But I'll make it up to you later. Promise!" As if they understood her perfectly, the dogs retreated to the family room and curled up on the floor in front of the fireplace.

"I brought a new recipe with me," Lia said, extracting a folded piece of paper from her back pocket. "They're called chocolate diablo cookies. I thought it'd be fun to try. You have cayenne pepper, right?" As she unfolded the pink page, it slipped from her fingers and fluttered to the floor. "Oops." She giggled as she bent to retrieve the soft-pink paper from where it had landed between us on her snowman-sock-clad feet.

My eyes were riveted to the lined pink paper and the neat, angular writing. My mind ricocheted to the memory of the envelope that had fallen out of my yearbook and the letter that was inside. *I have something to tell you. It's important.*

"Anna? Are you okay? You look like you've seen a ghost."

"I'm, uh..."

"We don't have to make the diablos if you don't want to."

"It's not that. I just feel a little dizzy."

"Do you need to sit down?"

"No, I'm okay, I think."

"Here." Lia filled a glass with cold water from the tap. "Drink this."

I drained the glass in large, greedy gulps then wiped my mouth with the back of my hand.

"Better?" Lia asked.

"Yeah, thanks. Let's get started," I suggested, tying an apron around my waist.

TWO HOURS OF FRANTIC baking had initially served to distract me from the dark thoughts that lurked in the quiet corners of my mind, taunting me like a devil sitting on my shoulder and whispering evil into my ear.

But the endless rolling, kneading, cutting, and stirring were wearing me down. I could feel my resolve slipping and my efforts to banish unwanted thoughts faltering. To bite back the words I did not want to say, to keep from hearing things I might not want to hear, I withdrew, becoming quiet and contemplative as I went about my baking.

Lia leaned against the counter and sipped her mulled wine. "What's up?"

"What do you mean?" I asked, feigning nonchalance. I emptied half a bag of Hershey's Kisses onto the table and began unwrapping them.

Lia reached over, grabbed one of the chocolates, and defiantly popped it into her mouth. She knew I hated it when she ate the ingredients, yet I remained silent.

With a long, exasperated sigh, she slipped a batch of butterscotch cookies into the oven then faced me and crossed her arms in front of her. "Spill it," she ordered.

I wiped my flour-covered hands on my apron and crossed my own arms. "This might sound ridiculous, but is there something you need to tell me?"

Lia blanched, her eyes widening.

"I mean, something you *meant* to tell me? A long time ago?" I prompted, nervously twisting my soiled apron in my hands.

Lia's gaze shifted from the back slider to the front door, as if searching for an escape, before settling on my face again. "What do you mean?"

I knew I wasn't playing by the rules. I was digging up something from the past, something she probably didn't even remember. Hell, even *I* had managed to forget about the letter until that pink envelope had tumbled out of the yearbook. But then I'd made the decision to put the letter out of my mind—to declare it old news, ancient history—and I'd done a pretty good job of it until that damn piece of pink paper with Lia's recipe written on it had landed at her feet. It was ludicrous for me to think she would have any clue what I was talking about. *But if that were true, why did all the color drain from her face?*

To ease the tension, I forced a laugh and smiled. "Wait here a minute." I untied my apron and tossed it into the laundry room on my way to the office. I extracted the blue yearbook from the bookshelf and rifled through the pages until I found the letter.

"Here." I returned to the kitchen and handed Lia the crumpled pink envelope. "I found this a few years before the reunion, in a box of random stuff from high school. It's a letter you wrote to me the summer after we graduated."

Lia turned the envelope over in her hands. Splotches of color bloomed on her cheeks as she extracted the letter and began to read. I watched intently as her eyes moved over the page. Her brows were drawn in concentration, and her Cupid's-bow lips were pursed. Her expression remained carefully neutral, but she had less control over the slight tremble of her hands.

She shrugged, stuffed the letter back into the envelope, and handed it to me. "I have no idea what this was about."

As if on cue, the oven timer beeped, startling us both. Lia removed the baking sheets from the oven and placed them on a cooling rack before retrieving two more sheets of raw dough. "Why didn't you call me after you read this?" Her voice was thick with forced nonchalance as she slid the trays into the oven.

"I knew I'd see you today, and—"

"No," Lia interrupted forcefully. When she turned to face me, her arms were tight against her sides, her hands curled into fists. "The *first* time you read it. All those years ago, after I gave it to you. Why didn't you call?"

"I-I don't know," I stammered. Suddenly *I* was the one being interrogated. "Things were crazy, packing for college, getting ready to go to Ohio. I guess I forgot." I shook my head, determined to get the conversation back on track. "Anyway, what was so important that you had to tell me *in person* before I left?"

Lia narrowed her eyes and pressed her lips into a thin line, a stubborn expression I was all too familiar with. "I told you—I don't remember. It was twenty-three years ago. Besides, you know how dramatic I was. That letter could have been about anything. It was probably nothing."

Lia was lying. I was sure of it. She had the same expression on her face—a mixture of guilt and defiance—that she'd always had in high school when she wasn't telling the truth. The awkward silence lingered between us as we stood locked in a verbal stalemate.

Without a word, I tossed the envelope into the trash and turned my attention to the half-finished buckeyes languishing on the counter. I grabbed a wad of peanut butter and rolled it furiously between my palms. Lia stood beside me, her shoulder gently touching mine. She scooped a spoonful of peanut butter into her own palm and began molding it into a tiny ball. We worked in silence, rolling the peanut butter into balls until my flash of anger subsided. It wasn't worth it. Whatever Lia wasn't telling me, it was her truth to keep. And besides, it was old news, very old. It definitely wasn't worth fracturing the fragile new friendship we'd forged. The past was the past, and we'd put it behind us. It held no sway over our future.

"You *were* dramatic," I agreed with a roll of my eyes as I gently bumped my arm against her shoulder. I carried the baking tray to the stove and began dunking the peanut butter balls into a pot of melted chocolate. Lia retrieved the last two sheets of cookies from the oven and deposited a batch of cooled treats into a holiday tin. The entire house smelled of cinnamon, vanilla, and chocolate.

Lia exhaled, and her shoulders relaxed, the tension easing from her face. "Cookie?" She handed me a warm, gooey chocolate chip straight from the oven—a peace offering.

After the kitchen was cleaned and Lia and I said our goodbyes, she left with two tins of cookies tucked neatly beneath her arms. I made myself a mug of tea, curled up on the couch, and gazed out the window at the naked trees, sodden and dreary against a bloated gunmetal sky. The light snow had morphed again into a wet mix of rain and sleet that pattered against the window.

As I sat still for the first time all day, the oppressive weight of exhaustion and emotion set in. My eyelids fluttered, growing heavy. The urge to sleep tugged at the edges of my mind like a strong tide trying to pull me under, but I didn't have enough time for a nap—the girls would be home from school soon. Instead, I focused on the blurred image of the pine trees beyond the window and let my thoughts wander.

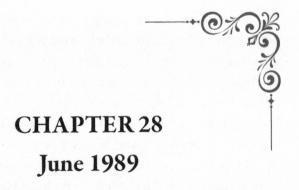

CHAPTER 28
June 1989

Becky's grandmother had offered Becky, Kelly, Kim, Lia, and me the use of her condo for the traditional week of post-graduation revelry at the beach. Though the five of us could barely contain our excitement, the reality of what lay ahead was never far from our minds. It was our last summer together before we all went our separate ways to college.

As for Jack, I purposely avoided him, though I was always aware of his presence if he was anywhere near, as if an invisible electric current ran between us. We were awkwardly cordial whenever we passed in the hallways or found ourselves at the same party, but I'd refused to tell him which college I'd chosen. I didn't want to unduly influence his decision in any way. But as it turned out, he'd also chosen to attend Ohio University as a human biology major. Since fate had seen fit to deliver us both to Athens in the fall, I was more determined than ever to keep my distance from him.

Lia, meanwhile, had been carefully plotting her plan of attack to land Joe once and for all. In an effort to demonstrate her sincerity, she'd not so much as kissed another boy since spring break. By June, we were both well-primed to let loose at the beach, unaware that the house of cards we'd so carefully built was about to come crashing down.

After all the pomp and circumstance of graduation, we finally arrived at our condo on 128th Street and wasted no time breaking out the Bugles, the Budweiser, and the bathing suits. Beers in hand, we headed directly for the pool. I was eighteen, I was at the beach with my friends, and I was headed to college in the fall. It was pure euphoria. I'd never felt so happy or free. With only a speck of shame, I realized I was glad I didn't have a boyfriend and that I wasn't tied down. I was like a caterpillar having emerged from a cocoon as a butterfly. I was ready to spread my wings and fly.

TO MY SURPRISE, JACK, Chris, and two other guys from the swim team had joined forces with four guys from the soccer team and rented a huge house in Ocean Dunes, about fifteen minutes south of us. They were rumored to be throwing the biggest, most anticipated bash of the week. Knowing that Joe—along with most of our senior class—would be there, Lia insisted we go. I was reluctant at first but ultimately agreed, and the party did not disappoint.

We could barely squeeze in through the front door because of the keg stands inside. Guys wearing nothing but ski masks streaked through the house while dozens of other partygoers skinny-dipped in the pool. A Beastie Boys song was blasting on the stereo, trays of Jell-O shots were being passed around, and a rowdy stair-diving competition was underway. The party was totally living up to its hype. I was glad Lia had twisted my arm.

Earlier in the day, we had been lounging on our condo's patio, sharing a case of beer with a bunch of guys we'd met on the beach. That was when Jack showed up, wanting to talk. I was sitting on some random guy's lap, and his arms were casually encircling my waist. Eyes blazing, Jack insisted we go for a walk.

"No," I said, my voice like ice.

The guys laughed. "We're kinda busy," one of them taunted, throwing salt.

Jack worked the muscle in his jaw, and I tried to ignore how sexy he looked when he did that. He stalked off, his face twisted with rage and his eyes thick with hurt.

The boys on our deck continued to snicker. "Better luck next time," one of them heckled at Jack's retreating form, which forged my stomach into a hard knot of guilt and self-hate. I shoved the guy's arms away, retreated to the bedroom, and cried until I fell asleep... or passed out. I wasn't really sure which.

Several hours later—anxious to get to the party and make her move on Joe—Lia roused me from a deep, dreamless slumber and dragged me into the shower. The robin's-egg-blue afternoon had given way to the cotton-candy hues of early evening. The five of us, pumped up on rum and Cherry Coke, had sprinted a block down Coastal Highway, arms linked, to catch a bus to the party. For a dollar each, we could ride all day.

Nervous about running into Jack, I dove into the melee once we arrived and attempted to make myself invisible by fading into the crowded corners of the house and the dark shadows of the deck. An hour and several shots later, I began to relax and let my guard down, working up the courage to mingle—a mistake that set the next fateful events into motion.

I was laughing and dancing to the thumping beat of a Young MC song when Jack's friend Chris appeared beside me, grim-faced. He grabbed me by the arm and pulled me into the hall. "What are you *doing* here?"

I giggled and covered my mouth as a hiccup escaped. "Dancing. What's it look like?"

I tried to pull away, but Chris squeezed tighter, his fingers digging into my flesh. His plain boyish features, typically placid, were pinched with disgust. "He doesn't deserve this," Chris said, his lip curled in anger as he dragged me farther down the hall and stopped in front of a closed door. "He wants to talk to you. Hell if I know why. But he keeps asking for you." Chris opened the door and shoved me inside.

The room was dark and stank of something sour and sickly sweet, like sweat and rotting fruit. In the weak moonlight slanting in through the blinds, I could just make out the shape of a body slumped on the bed. I walked tentatively across the room, my eyes straining to adjust to the dim light, and sat on the edge of the mattress. The springs creaked beneath me.

Jack rolled onto his back and gazed at me with glassy, red-rimmed eyes. His emerald-flecked irises gleamed in the moonlight that fell across his face. A slow, lazy smile played on his lips. He reached for me and pulled me close. We hugged tightly, and for a moment, I melted into his arms. My alcohol-altered mind registered the embrace as a goodbye, as acceptance that we were finally letting each other go. My breath caught in my throat, and my eyes burned. But when I tried to pull away, Jack held tight.

"Don't go. Stay with me," he murmured. His breath was putrid, his skin sticky with the pungent smell of alcohol and sweat. As he struggled to sit, lifting himself clumsily onto one elbow, I realized he was extremely drunk.

The stale, airless room was closing in on me. I couldn't breathe. My emotions were a tangled mop of yearning and disgust, self-loathing and regret. I twisted free from his grasp and stood abruptly. "No." I shook my head and backed toward the door.

"Please stay," Jack repeated, his arm outstretched, reaching for me.

"I can't." I turned and fled. With my hand on the knob, I hazarded one backward glance. Jack had collapsed against the pillows and flung his forearm across his eyes. I fought the urge to rush to his side, to nurture and care for him, to bring him water and a cool rag for his head, to tell him I was sorry and that I loved him. Because I did love him. Instead, I slammed the door and ran down the hall, away from the dark, claustrophobic room, away from the love of my life, and into the bright, raucous mass of sweating, gyrating, dancing bodies in the living room. With tears in my eyes, I ran past the jocks in the kitchen who were chanting "drink, drink" as some loopy girl dropped to her knees to gulp beer from a bong. I ran past prone figures passed out on the deck and couples making out in the dark. And I ran smack into Joe—Lia's Joe.

Joe reached out to steady me. Beer sloshed out of his plastic cup and drenched my shirt. "Whoa," he said, gaping at me as he held me at arm's length. "Where's the fire?" He slipped an arm around my shoulders and hugged me to his chest.

I could feel the heat of his body beneath my cheek. The wet fabric of my shirt pressed between us clung to my stomach, and I began to tremble.

"Are you okay? What happened?"

That tiny bit of compassion and humanity broke me, and my heart began a free fall in my chest. I sobbed drunken tears, soaking the front of Joe's shirt as he rubbed my back. He let me cry until the torrent began to slow, then he grabbed my hand and led me away from the chaos of the house and toward the relative calm of the pool deck. We sat facing each other on a pair of rickety plastic chairs. Joe offered me a sip of his drink, which wasn't beer but something fizzy and bitingly sweet. I gratefully accepted and imbibed in long gulps until it was gone. His eyes widened, and he edged closer. He removed the empty cup from my hand and lobbed it toward a nearby trash can, expertly sinking it. I collected myself then, keen to the fact that I was sitting knee to knee with Lia's crush, the guy she'd been relentlessly pursuing for months, the guy she had forsaken all others for, the guy she claimed to love.

"Have you seen Lia?" I asked.

"I dunno. I think she's around here somewhere."

"She's probably looking for you," I hinted, smiling weakly.

"Why?"

Duh. "Because she likes you." Boys could be so obtuse.

"Oh. Well, I'm, uh, not really interested."

I shrugged. "Your loss," I said, standing to go.

Joe stood, too, and the top of his head crashed into my chin.

"Ow!" I yelped, my hand flying to my mouth, checking for blood where I'd bitten my lip.

"Sorry." Joe chuckled as he tenderly patted his crown.

As I lowered my hand from my mouth, Joe abruptly leaned in and kissed me. I was stunned, momentarily rooted to the spot, as his warm, generous mouth covered mine, making my sore lip sting. The world began to spin, and my eyes flew open. I jumped back, swaying on my feet as my brain went fuzzy and I struggled to concentrate. Dazed, I saw Lia standing on the deck, frozen in place. Her eyes were wide, her mouth agape. I knew instantly she'd witnessed the kiss. I lurched toward her, wanting to explain, needing her to understand, but she bolted into the house.

"Let her go," Joe advised, his fingers encircling my wrist.

Ignoring him, I yanked my arm free and pushed into the crowd, frantically searching for Lia. My heart hammered in my chest. My ears were ringing, and my head pounded in tandem with the thumping bass. Adrenaline coursed through my veins. Lia was so short that it was easy for her to disappear. I couldn't find her anywhere.

Without warning, the room tilted, and my mouth watered. I dashed out the front door and heaved into the nearest bush. The sharp branches scratched my face as I emptied the contents of my stomach in a long, steaming stream.

Kelly and Kim magically appeared as my stomach lurched one last pitiful and unproductive time. They hauled me to my feet by my elbows, and the three of us stumbled toward Coastal Highway to catch the bus back to our condo.

"Where's Lia?" I panted.

Kelly shook her head, her long ponytail swinging.

Kim shrugged. "Dunno."

"Probably hooking up," Kelly added as she and Kim whooped and slapped high fives.

No one else knew about Lia's feelings for Joe, no one but me, and I was too drunk and sick and hurt to explain, to tell them how wrong they were.

I didn't remember boarding the bus or how long we waited for it to arrive, but I was grateful to sit on one of its torn vinyl seats, even though it scratched the backs of my thighs and made my legs sweat. Gingerly, I rested my throbbing forehead against the window as we bounced down the highway, the first rays of morning light beginning to paint the horizon.

WE WERE PACKING THE van when Becky and Lia slunk in the next morning with red eyes, rumpled clothes, and clumps of sand in their hair.

"Slept on the beach," Becky mumbled through a yawn.

Lia refused to meet my eyes. She disappeared into the bathroom, fine grains of sand raining down as she walked, like pine needles falling from a dying tree.

"Lia didn't want to come back," I overheard Becky whisper to Kim.

A few hours later, when the van was loaded and ready to roll, Lia claimed shotgun, leaving Becky, Kelly, and me to sit in the back. We rode in silence as the Ocean City skyline receded behind us. Each of us were lost in our own sleepy, hungover musings as we endeavored to choke down our greasy breakfast sandwiches. I chewed absently, my Egg McMuffin a lump of disgusting mush in my mouth. On the radio, Bret Michaels crooned about every rose having a thorn.

July 1989

MY WILDLY ANTICIPATED week of freedom at the beach had left me empty and depressed. I spent my days sulking in my room and my nights working at the Pizza Palace. Occasionally, Kelly or Becky would drag me to the pool, and I reluctantly went on a few dates. But mostly, I was just sad, low, and feeling sorry for myself. Weeks passed, and the sharp heat of early summer mixed with the oppressive humidity of July, turning the once bright-green blades of grass a wilted, dismal brown.

On one particularly muggy day, a knock at the door, followed by Tank's frantic barking, jolted me from a fitful nap. I flung open the door and was astonished to find Lia on my doorstep. In her hands, she held two thick milkshakes from Keller's. I could see that one of them was chocolate topped with a fluffy mound of whipped cream and drizzled with hot fudge, just the way I liked it. Cautiously optimistic, I stepped onto the front porch and accepted the frothy treat. Lia and I sipped and swayed on the porch swing in silence. I relished the feel of the chilly liquid as it slid down my throat and doused the sweltering heat in my belly. Suddenly, Lia threw her head back and belted out a maniacal laugh, an unsettling departure from her trademark melodious giggle. The wild gleam in her eyes made her appear insane.

"What's so funny?" I asked.

An amused smile remained perched on her lips. "We did it again."

"Did what?"

"Let a boy come between us."

I took a vigorous pull on the straw. Despite the heat, the thick shake was still impossibly difficult to draw upward, and my cheeks ached with the effort. The flowers in the surrounding beds were stooped and bent, beaten into submission by the relentless midday sun.

"I'm sorry," Lia blurted.

I stared at her. Lia rarely apologized to anyone about anything. In fact, "make no apologies" was one of her favorite mottos. But she did indeed look sorry. In fact, she looked not only sorry but concerned, stressed out. A deep vertical furrow was etched between her brows, and the corners of her mouth tugged downward. She stared ahead, her catlike eyes vacant and tired.

"Sorry for what? Joe?" I was confused. *What exactly is she apologizing for? Shouldn't I be the one apologizing?*

Lia threw her head back and cackled again. "First Jack, then Joe." She shook her head, and her wavy, sun-kissed hair bounced across her freckled shoulders.

"I didn't kiss him," I whispered, recalling the hateful glare in Lia's eyes when she'd caught Joe with his lips pressed to mine.

"I know," she said. "It doesn't matter. But it's still no excuse..."

"For what? Us not talking?"

"No. Not that. Never mind." Lia pursed her lips and exhaled as her fingers fidgeted with her straw. "I'm just sorry is all. For what I... for everything."

She wasn't making any sense, but I didn't care. I slung my arm around her shoulders and gave her a squeeze. "I'm just glad you're here."

"Me too," she agreed with a sniff, her eyes watering. "I couldn't imagine leaving for college without seeing you again, without patching things up between us. We still have a month before I go. Let's not waste it."

August 1989

THE REMAINDER OF THE summer was a dizzy kaleidoscope of fun, and by the time Lia had her bags packed for Maryland, we were inseparable once again. I was over the moon to have my best friend back and my life restored to order. I missed Jack, but I tried not to think about him. I hadn't seen him or talked to him since the beach, but I'd heard that he was lifeguarding at the swim club in Annapolis. Visions of him in his bathing suit, displaying his muscular torso and sculpted arms, often invaded my mind, and I wondered if he was dating anyone. The thought of him with someone else made my heart ache. But I reminded myself that breaking up with him had been the right thing to do. It was better that way, to go off to college unencumbered and start a new chapter in my life without any attachments. At least that was what I kept telling myself.

True to form, Rose had hopped a bus to New Mexico for some hippie fest, leaving Lia with well wishes and the rusted-out beater of a car as her transportation to college. Lia fretted over how to fit all of her things into the car, so I offered to help her move, and it was a good thing I did. Despite Lia's modest collection of personal belongings, the El Camino was packed to the gills.

On moving day, temperatures climbed into the triple digits. With sweat beading my forehead, I loaded my car with Lia's overflow and followed her as she drove to College Park. The Camino belched a steady stream of foul-smelling fumes in its wake. I'd imagined that Lia's dorm would be similar to my own soon-to-be new home in Ohio: a quaint brick building nestled on a scenic rolling green. In reality, Lia's dorm was a sixteen-story concrete tower housing freshman science, math, and engineering majors. The behemoth high-rise lacked air-conditioning, and in some cruel twist of fate—or an upperclassman's sick idea of a joke—the elevators were out of service. A sign reading Sorry for the Inconvenience—the understatement of the year—was posted in the lobby. Yellow caution tape was stretched across the double bank of elevator doors. Given that I had to work that afternoon, we chose to tackle the stairs rather than wait for the elevators to be repaired.

We carried the first load of Lia's belongings into the dorm, and my best friend made a show-stopping entrance as usual. The boys practically tripped over their tongues as they gaped at her. Dressed in a short white denim skirt and red crop top that accentuated her trim waist and ample breasts, Lia was undoubtedly a vision, a mirage in the shimmering heat, a cool drink of water in a sweltering desert. As usual, I went unnoticed as I cooked inside my knee-length pinstriped shorts and green T-shirt.

Amidst mass chaos and profusely sweating, swearing parents, Lia and I hauled her belongings up the crowded stairwell, and my claustrophobia mounted with each trip to her tenth-floor room. Lia, typically a ball of boundless energy, was uncharacteristically subdued, huffing and puffing as we carted her bags and boxes. She paused often to catch her breath as we ascended the stairs, and her face paled, taking on a sickly greenish tinge.

"Are you okay?" I asked, noticing the dark half-moons smudged beneath her eyes.

"Fine," she said. "Just tired."

By the time we delivered the last load, we were both exhausted, dehydrated, and dripping with sweat. Our clothes were plastered to our sticky bodies. I lifted my arm to wipe the sweat from my brow and nearly blinded myself as the sun shining in through the west-facing window glinted off my watch. "Shit!" I said under my breath, noticing the time. It had taken much longer than I'd expected to haul all of Lia's crap to her room. Though I would have preferred to hang out and explore the campus with her, I would be late for work if I didn't leave immediately. Rush hour was already kicking into high gear on the Capital Beltway. "I've got to go!"

Lia and I hugged each other tightly and whispered tearful goodbyes. "Good luck!" I said, hurrying toward the door. "Promise me you'll write? And visit me in Ohio after the holidays?"

"I promise!" Lia yelled as I scurried down the hall.

As I ducked into the stairwell, I heard Lia cry out, "Wait!" Her footsteps pounded down the hall, and her sweat-dampened strawberry hair streamed out behind her. "I almost forgot!" She shoved a soggy pink envelope into my hand. "You need to read this. It's important. Okay?"

"Okay," I replied, confused. Lia had scrawled my name on the front in sparkly purple ink. I stuffed the envelope into the pocket of my shorts, gave Lia another quick hug, then fought my way down the crowded, stifling stairwell.

When I finally reached my car, I stopped to catch my breath, grateful for the tiny puff of air that wafted across the parking lot. I reached into my pocket to withdraw my keys, and out tumbled the envelope, which fluttered to the ground on that tiny breeze. I snatched the rumpled paper from the scalding pavement and—curiosity getting the best of me—hastily tore open the flap. My eyes quickly scanned the page: "I'm sorry for all that's happened between us... can't write everything I need to say... I have something to tell you... It's important..."

My mind churned as I tried to make sense of the jauntily scribbled words before me. Then, somewhere on campus, a chiming clock tower jolted me back to reality. It was four o'clock. *Shit.* I shoved the letter back into the envelope and unlocked the car. No way would I make it to work by five. I tossed the letter onto the passenger seat, where it landed on top of my yearbook, which was still in my car from when Becky had finally gotten around to signing it a few weeks ago. I shifted the car into reverse, but as I pulled up to a red light and stomped on the brake, the letter catapulted to the floor. With a groan, I bent over the stick shift to retrieve it and slipped it between the pages of the yearbook. The light turned green, and I merged into a sea of taillights four lanes deep. The letter was out of sight, out of mind, and instantly forgotten.

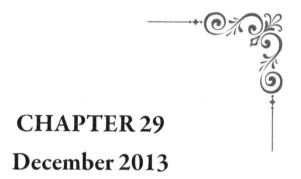

CHAPTER 29
December 2013

The aroma of freshly baked cookies made my mouth water, but I didn't dare eat another. I would have to run five extra miles to burn off the half dozen or so I'd already scarfed during the morning's baking festivities with Lia.

I filled a glass with water and gazed out the window. A languid winter sun hung low in the sky, its weak light just beginning to melt the dusting of morning snow that clung to the naked tree limbs and frozen blades of grass.

It was hard to believe an entire year had passed since my last baking day and that my firstborn—now officially an adult—had already completed her first semester of college. I sipped the tepid water then poured what remained onto the parched soil of my wilting corn plant before the cookie tin caught my eye again.

"Oh, what the hell," I muttered, slipping my fingers beneath the loosely wrapped foil and snatching a warm concoction with cranberries, oatmeal, dark chocolate, and macadamia nuts. The cookies were pure decadence. *Kathryn will love these.* My tongue darted out to swipe a stray crumb from the corner of my mouth. Though she'd made me promise not to include any fattening snacks in the care packages I sent to her at Virginia Tech, Kathryn happily accepted the boxes of dried fruits, nuts, pretzels, and Twizzlers I mailed each month.

"These are okay," she'd explained of the Twizzlers, "because they are low fat. Gotta avoid the freshman fifteen," she'd quipped, patting her flat stomach as we'd shopped for towels and bedding last summer.

My heart had simultaneously been swollen with pride and shattered by loss when we'd left Kathryn at the Blacksburg campus four months ago. Jack had held up admirably except for that first day after we'd settled Kathryn into her dorm. We'd said our goodbyes and were on our way home when we passed a fraternity house with a banner flapping from an upper-floor window. It read, "Don't worry, Dad. We'll take care of her." Neither of us uttered a word, but Jack had turned a sickly shade of gray.

Now I paced from the kitchen to the front door, checking the time and listening for the telltale crunch of gravel. Waiting for Kathryn to arrive was like the proverbial watched pot. *Will she be the same? Will a semester of college have changed her?* Christmas was still six days away, but I was already as giddy as a kid on Christmas morning because Kathryn was coming home *today*. Jack and I had done our best to adapt to the empty space left by Kathryn's absence. We stayed busy with work and with Evelyn and Helene—helping them with homework and shuttling them from one sport or activity to the next—but we still missed Kathryn desperately. With her return, our family would feel complete for the first time in months.

For dinner, I'd made Kathryn's latest favorite—baked tilapia with homemade mac and cheese, cooked carrots, and buttermilk biscuits. Evelyn and Helene were due home from school within the hour, and Jack had arranged to leave the office early so we could all eat dinner together. Afterward, we would have the cookies for dessert then package the extras to deliver to our neighbors in the morning, a family tradition we'd started when Kathryn was three years old. I could still picture her as we walked from door to door that first year: Kathryn's warm breath forming small puffs of moisture in the frigid December air, her unruly mop of brown hair cascading down her back, and her round cheeks rosy as she clutched the bags of cookies in her small, gloved hands. The memory of those precious years forced a single tear from the corner of my eye, and I wiped it away hastily. Kathryn would not want to see me cry. Despite her kind and gentle exterior, she was as tough as nails on the inside, driven and determined. She'd worked hard on her application to Virginia Tech and had leapt joyfully around the house upon receiving her letter of acceptance to the College of Architecture and Urban Studies.

Chessie and Bay suddenly leapt to their feet and tore toward the front door, barking and thrashing their tails, alerting me to the approaching car. I followed the dogs into the foyer and threw open the door, sending the bells on the wreath jingling, and watched breathlessly as my beautiful daughter emerged from the car. She was no longer a chubby-cheeked three-year-old but a tall, graceful young woman with long chestnut hair that hung in thick, wavy tendrils to her waist. Tears sprang to my eyes at the sight of her.

"Mom!" she called when she saw me standing in the doorway. She retrieved a rolling suitcase and a duffel bag from the trunk and walked toward me. The girl Kathryn was carpooling with trailed in her wake. She was pale and waif-like, with jet-black hair and thick eyeliner.

"Are you crying?" Kathryn admonished, spying my watery eyes. "You should be happy to see me, not sad."

"I *am* happy to see you! You have no idea!" I exclaimed, hugging her tightly, resisting the urge to lift her into my arms and carry her into the house the way I'd done when she was a toddler. Instead, I held her at arm's length and admired every inch of her. She was as lovely as ever, despite the dark smudges of eyeliner and thick mascara that made her appear much older and far more sophisticated than the fresh-faced eighteen-year-old we'd delivered to campus.

"Mm. Smells good," she said, catching a whiff of the sweet and savory scents wafting from the kitchen. "I'm starved."

"Well, dinner's just about ready. I made your favorite."

"Tilapia?" she asked.

"Of course."

Kathryn squealed with delight, the child that remained within escaping in the unchecked moment.

I peered over her shoulder at the slip of a girl lingering near the stairs.

Kathryn caught my gaze and collected herself. "This is Clare." Kathryn had often spoke of the art history major who lived on her floor and to whom Kathryn had grown quite close. It was immediately apparent where Kathryn received her cosmetic inspiration.

I smiled at the girl. "Hi, Clare." Taking in the tiny hoop perched at the end of one precisely arched eyebrow and the tiny gem that twinkled in the crease of the girl's nose, I could only hope that Kathryn would not be similarly influenced by Clare's taste in facial accessories. "Nice to meet you." I gave the girl a brief hug, recoiling slightly as her delicate, protruding shoulder blades pressed into my forearm. "Will you join us for dinner?"

"Thanks, but I can't," she said. "My mom's expecting me home." The surprisingly precise, well-timbered words floated from the girl's mouth, carried like a song on the breeze.

"And where is home?" I prodded.

"Philly. I'm spending Christmas with my mom and then heading to Jersey to visit my dad."

"Well, that sounds nice. Please tell them I said hello and wish them a merry Christmas for me."

"Will do," Clare said. Then she turned to Kathryn. "Pick you up at two on New Year's?"

"Perfect!" Kathryn exclaimed.

"New Year's Day?" I asked, my smile fading. "Your dad and I were planning to drive you back to Tech, maybe spend a few—"

"New Year's *Eve*," Kathryn corrected. "There's a huge party at the Fiji house!" She smiled brightly at Clare, and the two girls bumped their fists together before pulling their hands back, fingers splayed.

"It's going to be prime!" Clare exclaimed.

"You two don't strike me as the fraternity party types," I observed, recalling the dreadful banner.

Clare bit back a smile, and Kathryn treated me to another eye roll. "A party's a party, Mom. Doesn't matter who's throwing it!"

"True that!" Carla replied with a grin. She touched two fingers to her forehead in an awkward farewell salute and retreated to her car, her legs as skinny as twigs in her black jeggings.

"Merry Christmas!" Kathryn called after her.

"Drive safely," I added.

"Always such a mom," Kathryn muttered, shaking her head disapprovingly.

"I'll always be your mom, Kathryn."

Clare honked the horn and peeled out of the driveway. I rubbed my arms to generate some heat as we watched her go, her little red Ford Fiesta disappearing into the trees. "Let's go inside," I suggested, grabbing Kathryn's duffel from where she'd dropped it on the porch. "It's freezing out here!"

Kathryn wheeled her suitcase into the foyer before turning to face me. "Oh, and by the way, it's Kat."

THE NEXT DAY, AFTER seeing Evelyn and Helene off to school, I set out to run some errands. Kathryn was still asleep. I tried to hide my annoyance, not because Kathryn was sleeping the day away, but because it was precious time we could have spent together. When I arrived home two hours later, lugging armloads of groceries into the house, she was nowhere to be found. Neither were Chessie or Bay for that matter. I was prepping the filling for the night's dinner—stuffed peppers, another of Kathryn's favorites—when she barreled in through the back door, dogs in tow.

"Well, hello there, sleepyhead," I greeted.

Kathryn tugged off her wool hat and mittens and flung them onto the couch. "Hey, Mom." She slung an arm around my shoulders and reached past me to grab a banana from the fruit bowl.

"Where've you been?"

"I took Chessie and Bay for a walk down by the stream."

"By yourself?"

"Mom," Kathryn grumbled, rolling her eyes.

"It's pretty secluded on that path, you know?" My eyes flicked to the window above the sink, taking in the thick, barren trees bordering the yard, the carpet of dead leaves obscuring the trail, and the ominous flint-gray winter sky. I pictured Kathryn as the only ray of light on the dreary trail, the single accent of color in a black-and-white photo.

Kathryn fixed me with a gaze. "You know I go hiking by myself all the time at Tech," she said matter-of-factly.

"No, I did not know. Maybe that's not such a good idea, Kathryn."

"Kat," she reminded me. "And it's fine, Mom."

The college administrators had enlightened us to the challenges of reintegrating a newly independent young adult into home life. Their warning had been quite clear. *They will have become accustomed to living on their own, not having to answer to anyone. It will be a delicate transition for all.*

Capitulating to this new reality, I changed the subject. "I'm making another one of your favorites for dinner tonight." I proudly displayed a dish of red, yellow, and green peppers stuffed with brown rice and cheese.

"Looks great, Mom," Kathryn said. "But I'm going out tonight."

"Oh." My shoulders slumped, and I pressed my lips into a tight line.

Kathryn peeled the banana and took a delicate bite. "Brooke's having a party."

"Brooke Abramson?" I asked skeptically. "I don't recall the two of you being particularly close in high school."

"We weren't, but that's beside the point." She bit off another small piece of banana and tossed the remainder, half eaten, into the trash. "A lot of my friends will be there."

Defeated, I let out a long, frustrated sigh. "What time will you be home?"

She shrugged and filled a cup with water. "Dunno. Late."

"Kathryn, I'd like to have some idea when to expect you."

"*Kat*," she reminded me again, her voice laced with irritation. "I don't know, Mom. You don't have to wait up."

"It's not like I'll be able to sleep until I know you're home safely."

Kathryn crossed her arms and jutted her hip. "Mom, you do realize I've been coming home whenever I want for, like, four months now. I don't need to check in with anyone. I'm an adult."

"An adult who still relies on her parents for tuition, room, and board."

"What does that have to do with it?" she asked, indignant.

"It has to do with you showing common courtesy to your family when you're home. There may not be anyone at school who worries about you or cares whether you come home or not, but I do, and so does your father. If we don't know what time to expect you, how do we know you're not—"

"Lying in a ditch somewhere." Kathryn shook her head. "Do you realize how morbid that sounds?"

Ignoring her, I guided the conversation back to the issue at hand. "So what time?"

"I said I don't know. Jeez! By three, I guess."

"*Three*!" I exclaimed. "What can you possibly be doing until three in the morning?"

Kathryn leveled her gaze at me, allowing me a moment to ponder the possibilities, and the corners of her lips twitched upward at my dismay. "It may be earlier," she conceded. "But you're the one who wants to pin me to a time."

"Two o'clock," I said.

"Two-thirty," she countered.

Our eyes locked. We were two strong women, and neither of us were willing to back down.

"Fine," I agreed, knowing that Jack would be sleeping like a baby while I lay awake, fretting.

She smiled and kissed me on the cheek. "Don't worry, Mom. I'll be fine."

"Where are you going now?" I asked as she disappeared down the hall, trying to hide my disappointment that she was leaving again.

"To take a shower. Jess will be here in an hour to pick me up. We're headed to the mall and then out to dinner before the party."

I ripped a piece of foil from its container, wrapped it tightly over the dish of stuffed peppers, and shoved the whole thing into the fridge. We would order pizza instead.

THE DELICATE COEXISTENCE I'd achieved with Kathryn in deference to her newfound independence came crashing down again the day before she was scheduled to return to school.

"A bunch of us are headed to Ram's Head Live for a concert," Kathryn announced from the powder room where she was applying an extra coat of mascara.

"When will you be home?" I asked, steeling myself for another battle.

"Dunno," she said with a shrug as she waltzed into the kitchen. In a fitted black top and distressed jeans, she looked effortlessly stunning.

"Kathryn—"

"Kat." She tossed the mascara into a small leather knapsack then slung the bag over her shoulder.

"*Kat*. We've been over this already. You know I'd like to have some idea when to expect you."

"Mom, I am not a baby," she replied, her whiny tone indicating otherwise. "I haven't had a curfew for months."

"I realize that, *Kat*. But now that you *are* home and I know you'll be out—in the city no less—I'll worry about you. As I told you before, I won't be able to sleep until I know you're home safely."

"I don't even know for sure if I'm coming home."

I raised my eyebrows, incredulous and at a total loss for words.

"We might stay overnight, especially if no one feels like driving. Jessie's brother knows someone who has a condo in the city," she rambled, skimming over the obvious fact that they planned on drinking.

"You're not twenty-one, Kat. You're eighteen. It's illegal to drink." I cringed inwardly at my hypocritical words. I'd certainly had more than my share of alcoholic beverages before I was twenty-one. It was definitely a "do as I say, not as I do" moment, but I couldn't help myself—Kathryn was my daughter.

Kathryn crossed her arms. "Exactly. I'm eighteen. An adult. Old enough to make my own decisions."

"And old enough to go to jail if you break the law," I reminded her.

She remained silent, her gaze flicking impatiently to the clock. I wished Jack were there to back me up. Kathryn had always been a daddy's girl, but I knew Jack would be on my side. We had always presented a united front when it came to parenting decisions. But it would be another hour before he left the office, plus an additional thirty minutes by the time he picked up Evelyn and Helene from indoor soccer practice on his way home.

"As a courtesy to your dad and me, at least check in and let us know your plans."

Kathryn pressed her lips into a hard line. "I'll try to remember," she muttered.

"It's what a respectful, responsible *adult* would do."

Kathryn flushed crimson, but she did deign to call that night to let us know she was safe and staying in the city until morning.

The next morning—a mere two hours after she'd arrived home from Baltimore—she was headed back to Blacksburg with rumpled clothes and eyes heavy with fatigue. Jack and I stood on the front porch, waving and shivering in the cold winter air, our breath coming out in small arctic puffs, as Kathryn climbed into Clare's car.

The minute the little red Fiesta was out of sight, my brave façade crumbled, and I buried my face in Jack's chest and sobbed. He hugged me tightly, resting his chin atop my head. If I weren't mistaken, I heard him sniffle once or twice, too, his breath catching in his throat. Our daughter, our firstborn, was leaving us for the second time in four months, and it hurt as much as it had the first time, perhaps more. For the first time in my life, I could truly understand how difficult it must have been for my own parents so many years ago when I'd left for Ohio.

———— ⟋⟍⟍ ————

September 1989

THE BEAUTY OF THE ATHENS campus was breathtaking. The dull grays and browns that had blanketed the town when I'd first visited in the dead of winter had been replaced by lush green lawns, magnificent oak trees, and vibrant flower beds still bursting with summertime glory. Meandering pathways curled around stately brick buildings that were fronted by intricately carved white pillars and nestled idyllically along the banks of the Hocking River.

I wrote to Lia, gushing about the gorgeous campus, the lively uptown scene, and the abundance of cute boys. It was as if I'd died and gone to college heaven. And I reveled in the joy and freedom of living independently and carving my own path in a new place.

My first college party coincided with my first college make-out session with a local, corn-fed boy. Tim was nice. He had nice manners, and it was nice to kiss him, but there was no passion, no fireworks. We went on a date—a hayride to a bonfire. We roasted marshmallows and drank from bota bags filled with hot toddies. We had a nice time. But I didn't see him again after that.

I did, however, see Jack. He was leaving the aquatic center, undoubtedly having just finished swim practice, his hair still wet from the shower. I ducked behind a tree so he wouldn't see me, but I could not hide from the fire that burned in my belly. Jack was so much more than just nice.

Since I'd met my prince in high school, I was apparently destined to meet a string of frogs. After Tim, the parade of slimy amphibians included a drunk frat boy who kept trying to shove my hand down his pants, an initially charming and handsome Southerner who was quick to show his true sexist, racist colors, and an aggressive jock who would not take "no" for an answer. I eventually had to knee him in the nuts to get my point across.

I did, however, have a one-night stand that rocked my world. Kyle was gritty and rugged and aloof. He wore a black leather jacket and boots, and he tooled around town on a motorcycle. We met at an off-campus party. He had a longish flop of brown hair that fell across his forehead and a sly smile, like he was keeping a secret, which I found extremely sexy. Intrigued by the two Chinese characters tattooed on his forearm, I reached out and traced them with my finger. I was just tipsy enough to be bold. Kyle awakened something wild and reckless inside of me.

Back at my dorm, he took his time. Kyle was slow and gentle and explored every inch of my body. I was extremely tense and self-conscious at first, until he whispered, "Relax. You're gonna enjoy this." And I did.

As the rosy light of early morning crept into my room, Kyle silently stepped into his jeans, shrugged on his leather jacket, and kissed me on the forehead, leaving me to fall into a deep, satisfied sleep. Occasionally, I would see Kyle around campus. He would wink at me and flash a knowing grin, but we never spoke again. Kyle had taught me more about my body and what it was capable of than I ever could have imagined, and he made me feel womanly and worldly and experienced. For that, I would be forever grateful.

I wrote to Lia about all of these adventures. But for all the letters I sent to her, I only ever received one in return. It was stilted and formal, like reading a page from the campus brochure. She wrote about Maryland's redbrick Georgian buildings and the campus arboretum tours. Only a few snippets of the real Lia were woven in. And despite all the juicy tidbits I'd sent her way, the only thing she wanted to know was if I'd read her letter. She wanted to know why I hadn't met her at Keller's before I'd left for Ohio and why I hadn't called.

When I read that, I sucked in a breath and chewed the inside of my cheek. *The letter*. I had forgotten all about it. After I'd helped Lia move into her dorm, she'd chased me down and handed it to me as an afterthought. In my hurry to get to work on time, I'd ripped it open, scanned it briefly, and tossed it inside my yearbook. It had remained there as I'd busily packed my belongings and prepared for my own move to college in the days that followed. There hadn't been time to meet at Keller's before I left, and when I'd tried to call Lia, her roommates said she wasn't home. They must not have given her the message. Then I'd arrived in Athens and gotten swept up in college life—in my own life—and I honestly hadn't given the letter another thought. I figured whatever Lia had wanted to talk about, we would talk about later. I figured it wasn't that important. I guessed I had figured wrong.

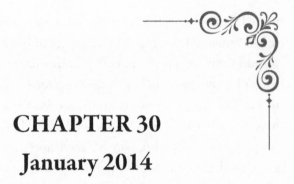

CHAPTER 30
January 2014

"How was your holiday?" Lia asked between sips of wine. "It was great!" I replied with false cheer. Even the rich, peppery cabernet had failed to lift my spirits. A new tavern had opened in Ellicott Mills, and Lia and I had agreed to meet on Wine Wednesday to check it out.

She cocked her head and pursed her lips, waiting.

"Okay. It was awful," I admitted. "It was so *hard*. I was thrilled to have Kathryn home, but it also broke my heart a little, how much she's changed already. And it's only been one semester!"

"It'll get easier," Lia said, placing a soothing hand on my arm. "What you need is a diversion. Can you get away?"

"What do you have in mind?" I dipped a celery stick into a heaping bowl of homemade hummus and stirred. I hadn't eaten since breakfast, but I had no appetite.

"Skiing! Seven Springs is having a great deal right now."

"It would definitely help take my mind off Kathryn," I mused. Her leaving again was like having a Band-Aid ripped from a still-raw wound.

THREE DAYS OF SHREDDING the slopes with Lia was exactly the elixir I needed. Lia and I fell into an easy routine of skiing in the morning, heading back to the condo for lunch, then skiing again until sundown. Afterward, we would retreat to the lodge, uncork a bottle of red, and sit in the soft leather chairs in front of the roaring stone fireplace overlooking the snow-covered mountain.

"So, how does Kathryn like school?" Lia asked, topping off our wine glasses.

"She's flourishing. Totally loves it. But what's not to like, right? Beautiful campus, complete independence of the best kind, with Mom and Dad still footing the bill."

"It *is* beautiful there," Lia agreed, her eyes fixed on the flickering flames.

"You've been to Blacksburg?" I asked, surprised.

She appeared momentarily stricken. "I have clients in Christiansburg," she explained, referring to the town twenty miles east of campus.

"Huh." I sipped my wine and shifted my gaze toward the slopes, where a handful of night skiers were still making their way down the mountain. I wondered why Lia had never mentioned Christiansburg before, knowing that Kathryn was at Tech. "Let me know next time you go, and I'll go with you," I said, watching her closely. "I can visit Kathryn while you're meeting with your client."

"Sure. Road trip. That'd be fun. Like Thelma and Louise." Lia smiled tightly, and the hairs on the back of my neck stood on end.

I had the odd but distinct feeling Lia was hiding something from me. Maybe if I followed up on my request to travel to Christiansburg with her, I would figure out what it was.

A loud ruckus suddenly shattered the tranquility of the lodge as a dozen people dressed like jesters, kings, and clowns tumbled into the room.

A cocktail waiter sidestepped toward our chairs, making room for the rowdy group to pass.

Lia tugged the sleeve of the waiter's shirt. "What's going on?"

I gazed at the shiny green, gold, and purple of the group's costumes and the strands of colorful beads dangling from their necks. I knew the answer before the waiter replied.

"Mardi Gras party," he said.

"Oh, that's right!" Lia said with a laugh. "That is this week, isn't it?"

I knew it was too dark in the lodge for Lia to notice the tears that had gathered in my eyes as I remembered Faith and the evening I'd spent with her at the Mobile dinner theater, trying to solve the mystery of the murder at Mardi Gras.

"I think we should be drinking hurricanes instead of wine, don't you?" Lia asked, standing from her chair. "Can I get you one?"

"Sure," I said to Lia's retreating form. "Why not?" I leaned back in my chair and used a cocktail napkin to dab my eyes.

Lia was halfway to the bar when another group of revelers crashed into the room. Decked out in swim caps, goggles, Speedos, and Mardi Gras beads, the six men dashed across the lodge on their way to the pool. The cacophony rose as they made their way through the room. As the group dashed past my table, I realized why. One of the men was sans Speedo, his pale backside taking the bar patrons by surprise as he streaked by. I shook my head and chuckled, but the laughter died in my throat as I remembered the last time I'd seen men parading around in Speedos.

October 1989

MY FIRST TWO MONTHS at OU were a rush. I worked hard and played harder. I pretended I was having the time of my life, that I was enjoying the full "college experience," but in reality, I felt empty and lonely. I'd made friends, but I still missed Lia. But most of all, I missed Jack.

Ohio was a big enough campus that I didn't see Jack often, though I would catch occasional glimpses of him here and there as he ducked into a classroom or out of a bar. As a student athlete, Jack lived on the west side of campus. Conversely, my life as a journalism major kept me on the south side. Sometimes, when I was feeling especially low, I would venture across the main green to the aquatic center and watch from the safe anonymity of the hallway as the swim team practiced. With my forehead pressed to the glass, I would scan the sea of Speedo-clad bodies for Jack's muscular legs and broad torso.

It was during one of those reconnaissance missions that I saw her. Blond, lean, and lovely, the girl rested her hand lightly on Jack's arm as she laughed at something he'd said. Their pool-dampened bodies angled toward each other. My heart sank like a leaden object tossed into the deep end.

TWO WEEKS AFTER SPOTTING the blond girl on the pool deck with Jack, I was seated in the nosebleed section of the psychology lecture hall when they walked in. Talking and laughing, they selected seats next to each other in the middle section. I didn't hear a word the professor said the entire hour. My mind, as well as my gaze, was fixed on the two heads dozens of rows in front of me—one wavy and dark, one smooth and blond—that remained bent together throughout the lecture.

My stomach was a fist of regret, and my body was coiled like a snake, ready to strike for the exit the minute the professor dismissed us. But to my horror, instead of leaving through the lower level doors in which they came, Jack and *that girl* began to ascend the stairs. I slumped in my seat, praying I wouldn't be noticed, and hastily flipped open my notebook. I tried to appear engrossed in my reading. I wished I could disappear.

"Anna?"

The voice slayed me. My insides dissolved into jelly. I didn't want to look up. I didn't want to see his eyes—his stunning, breathtaking eyes—but I had no choice. I sucked in a deep breath and struggled to arrange my features into a mask of surprise.

"Oh. Hi!" My voice was squeaky and unnaturally high.

"I thought that was you!" Jack said, flashing his heart-stopping smile. "How's it going?"

"Fine. It's, uh, fine," I lied. "How are you?"

"Um, good. Great!" he said, his eyes boring into mine. I felt like he could see right through me, right into my very soul, as if all my thoughts and feelings and indiscretions were laid bare before him.

That girl subtly cleared her throat and shifted her weight, her shoulder gently brushing Jack's arm.

"Oh, uh, Anna, this is Holly. Holly, Anna."

"Hi," Holly said, all lightness and sunshine. Her skin was flawless. She had wide gray eyes, and her white-blond hair was pulled back into a high ponytail. "Nice to meet you," she chirped, the picture of Midwestern perfection.

"Well, I better get to class," I said, standing abruptly, the notebook tumbling from my lap.

"Yeah. Us too." Jack concurred, following Holly up the stairs. "See you around."

Us.

AGAINST ALL ODDS, THE next time I saw Jack—other than during my weekly hour of torture otherwise known as Psych 101—was on Halloween. The infamous Court Street Block Party drew thousands of costumed revelers to campus, effectively doubling the town's population overnight.

It was an unseasonably warm night for late October, and my Raggedy Ann costume was hot and itchy. My Raggedy Andy counterpart had ducked into a restroom, leaving me on the sidewalk to marvel at the thousands of people that swarmed the cobblestones in creative costumes I never would have dreamed of—a drunk deck of cards, puppies from *101 Dalmatians*, and the fallopian swim team, to name a few.

I was viciously scratching beneath my red yarn wig when someone grabbed me from behind and pressed something hard and dull into my ribs. "Give me your wallet," a deep voice growled.

I gasped and whirled to see a tall man looming over me. He was dressed in green from head to toe. In his hand, he held a green squirt gun. A green ski hat covered his head, and a green bandana obscured his face, but I would have known those eyes anywhere. *Jack.* I dropped my gaze to his chest. Gang Green was written in large black letters across the front of his green T-shirt.

I laughed. "Good one." I had no idea how he'd recognized me, dressed as I was, among the thousands of people swarming the street. "You come up with that all by yourself?"

"No, it was Hol—" Jack caught himself before he said her name.

"So where's the rest of your *gang*, anyway?" It came out snarkier than I meant for it to.

Just then, Holly bounded up to Jack. "There you are!" she exclaimed. Even her blond ponytail was dyed green. "I've been searching everywhere for you! The rest of the gang is headed to see the band." She hooked her fingers into air quotes around the word "gang."

"Holly, you remember Anna?" Jack prompted.

"Oh, yeah. Hi," she said, finally noticing me.

"I'll catch up with you in a minute," Jack said to Holly, surprising her and me.

Holly shot one quick glance in my direction, her smile faltering only a little before catching herself. "Okay. See you in a few!" She bounced up on her toes and planted a quick peck on Jack's cheek.

Jack watched Holly as she disappeared into the masquerading crowd, and his eyes darkened with something akin to regret.

"She's, uh, really pretty," I said. Sorrow weighed heavily on every cell in my body. "And really nice too." Bitter tears stung my eyes.

Jack reached for my hand. "But she's not you."

AFTER REPEATEDLY TRYING—AND failing—over the next month to reach Lia by phone, I decided a letter would have to suffice. In a few short weeks, the semester would be over, I would be home for winter break, and I could tell her face-to-face. But I couldn't wait that long. I grabbed a sheet of paper from my desk drawer and excitedly scribbled the good news—Jack and I were back together, for good this time. There was no doubt in my mind. He was "the one."

CHAPTER 31
March 2014

Spring break was still a week away, but I'd already started stocking up on Kathryn's favorite foods. I'd just plopped a bag of frozen blueberries into the grocery cart when my cell phone rang. I was delighted to see the 540 area code.

"Hi, sweetie! Your ears must be burning."

"Why? Are you talking about me?" Kathryn asked with a chuckle.

"Not talking about you. Thinking of you, though."

"Oh yeah? What about?"

"About whether two cartons of ice cream will be enough or if I should get three?" I laughed. "You know I like to spoil you when you're home."

"Whatever you get is fine." I could practically hear her eyes roll over the phone. "That's kinda why I'm calling, though."

"About ice cream?"

"No..."

"Is everything okay?" I asked, alarmed by the odd tone of her voice.

"I'm fine, it's just... about spring break."

Unwilling to delay the inevitable, I forced down the lump of dread that had risen in my throat. "Is there a change of plans?" I asked, my voice climbing to an unnatural octave.

"Um, yeah. I'm going to be staying here instead of coming home."

I remained silent, knowing my voice would betray me, and waited for Kathryn to explain.

She cleared her throat. "Clare thinks we should stay on campus for a few days to find an apartment for next year."

Clare thinks. I clenched my jaw and felt my nostrils flare as I exhaled.

"You know, to get a jump on things?" Kathryn continued. "And then we're planning to spend the rest of the week at Norris Lake."

"Norris Lake? In Tennessee?"

"Yeah. There's a guy in my dorm whose parents have a house there. A bunch of my friends are going."

I stood speechless in frozen foods. I couldn't forbid her to go. *Could I?* Nor would I beg her to come home.

"Mom? Are you there?"

"Yes, I'm here," I said, my voice husky. I swatted angrily at a traitorous tear making its way down my cheek. "That sounds like fun, sweetie," I managed to squeak.

Kathryn's voice brightened immediately. "Thanks, Mom!" she gushed. "I'll really miss seeing you guys, but I totally want to go on spring break with my friends. Tell Ev and Lene I said hi. Love you!"

"I love you too," I managed. "Be careful—"

But she was already gone.

TWO WEEKS LATER, THE phone was ringing as I elbowed my way in through the front door. My arms were weighted down with bags of groceries, and Chessie and Bay tap-danced at my heels. "Okay, okay," I acknowledged. "I know you need to go out."

Before I could reach the kitchen, Kathryn's sweet voice was on the answering machine, sounding breathless and excited. "Hey guys, great news. Call me!"

I heaved the grocery bags onto the kitchen island and opened the back door for the dogs. Chessie and Bay raced across the yard, startling several deer that were grazing along the tree line. The dogs gave a spirited chase before abruptly dropping to squat. I watched as Chessie frolicked in the grass and hoped she was simply scratching her back and not wallowing in deer excrement.

Risking muddy paws and offensive odors being tracked into the house, I left the door ajar so the dogs could return at will. I had exactly thirty minutes to get dinner on the table so Evelyn and Helene would have time to eat before their respective lacrosse and gymnastics practices, but I was eager to return Kathryn's call. I dialed her cell and put the call on speaker. The shrill ringing filled the kitchen as I unpacked and washed the vegetables. By the third ring, my heart sank. I must have just missed her. I'd resigned myself to leaving a voice message when Kathryn picked up the call.

"Kathryn! I'm so glad I caught you," I said, pulling a cutting board from the cabinet. "So what's the big news?"

"We got it!" she exclaimed.

"Got what?"

"The apartment. It's perfect!"

I paused, the knife in midair. "That was fast," I said, pushing the cubed peppers aside and starting on an onion.

"Aren't you excited for me?"

"Of course I am," I answered, though she knew I preferred that she live on campus for another year. "Tell me about it."

"Well, it's two bedrooms, and it's near the BT stop, so it will be really easy to catch the bus to class."

"How much does—"

"Oh, hey guys!" Kathryn interrupted, greeting someone. Before I could ask who, I heard a high-pitched barking in the background.

"Is that a dog?" I asked, surprised.

"Yeah. That's Hokie. He's the cutest thing ever. I can't wait for you to meet him."

My eyebrows shot to my hairline. "Whose dog is it?"

"Mine. And Clare's, of course."

"Of course," I added with a touch of sarcasm. "When did you get a dog, and how are you possibly keeping it in your dorm room?"

"Dustin is keeping him for us until we move into the apartment."

My head was starting to spin. "Who's Dustin?"

"Oh. He's a friend of the guy whose house we stayed in at Norris Lake. Hokie was a stray or abandoned or something. He hung around all day and slept on our deck every night. He's the sweetest thing. We just couldn't leave him there. I think he's still a puppy."

"A puppy is a lot of work."

"It'll be fine. Clare and I will share responsibility for him."

"Financial responsibility as well? Puppies are expensive too. The vet bills, food—"

"I know, Mom," Kathryn interrupted, a hint of irritation creeping into her voice. "That's why I got a job, to help pay for him. And to gain work experience."

"A job?" Just then, Evelyn and Helen came busting into the house with two friends in tow.

"Hey, Mom!"

"Hi, Mrs. Wells," the friends chorused.

"I told Ashley and Madeline we could give them a ride to practice," Evelyn announced. "Can they eat dinner with us?"

"I hadn't really expected company—"

"Thanks, Mom," Evelyn said, giving me a quick kiss on the cheek before grabbing two apples from the fruit bowl and heading down the hall with Ashley.

"Is that Kathryn?" Helene asked, bouncing up and down excitedly.

"Hey, baby sis. What's up?" Kathryn's disembodied voice filled the room. I'd forgotten she was on speaker.

"Hey, Kat!" Helene grabbed the phone and pressed it to her ear. She'd easily adopted her sister's nickname. Giggling, Helene walked outside, joining Chessie and Bay on the patio, her friend Maddie in tow. Helene pulled the French door closed, presumably so I wouldn't eavesdrop on her conversation.

I resumed my chopping, adding mushrooms and zucchini to the mix, and muttering under my breath about dogs, kids, jobs, and apartments. Ten minutes later, Helene and Maddie waltzed back into the kitchen. Helene extended the phone toward me, and I inclined my head toward the countertop, indicating for her to put the phone back on speaker since my hands were covered in bits of vegetable and raw shrimp.

Helene obliged and yelled into the air, "See ya later, alligator."

"After 'while, crocodile," Kathryn replied.

"We'll be in my room doing homework," Helene informed me as she snatched a handful of peppers from the cutting board and dashed down the hall. I pulled four extra kabob sticks from the drawer to accommodate the two extra mouths and began skewering the vegetables and shrimp.

"Those girls," Kathryn said, laughing. "I miss them!"

"They miss you too. We all do."

"So, where were we?" she asked.

"Dog, apartment, job..."

"Right. The apartment allows dogs, so Hokie will only be with Dustin until summer, and the apartment actually costs less than you're paying for room and board."

"What about food? Have you factored that in?"

"Yeah, I figured about fifty dollars, maybe seventy-five."

"A week?"

"No. Per month."

I barked out a laugh. I couldn't help it. "Sweetie, if you were surviving on fifty dollars a month in food, we'd be seeking housing that specialized in eating disorders."

"Mom!" Kathryn admonished.

I shook my head, chuckling. I supposed that was all part of growing up—learning how to survive in the real world and how expensive it was to live in it. "So when do we get to see this apartment?"

"I'll give you the grand tour when you're here next month."

"Sounds good. You know, your sister has her learner's permit. She's excited to be our chauffeur next time we hit the road."

"Ev behind the wheel? Watch out!" Kathryn laughed, a lovely, musical sound that warmed my heart. She was usually so serious. It was nice to hear her laughing and relaxed. "Well, I'm supposed to be somewhere in ten minutes, so I have to get going."

"That's fine. I've got to get these kabobs on the grill and get your sisters to practice. Talk soon?"

"Sure. Love you."

"I love you too," I said into the silence.

I rinsed the knife, leaned my back against the sink, and closed my eyes. My head was still spinning. I took long, deep breaths to soothe my frayed nerves and racing pulse. A memory of Chessie and Bay as young dogs bloomed in my mind, and I was reminded of the training walks I used to take with them, when their rapidly growing bodies had surpassed their manners. The dogs would be walking along beside me, beautifully obeying my heel command, when a squirrel would suddenly dart into our path. Just when everything seemed to be under control, the dogs would lunge forward while I tried with all my might to restrain them.

With a sigh, I realized that the frustration I'd felt then was similar to the frustration I was feeling with Kathryn. Like Chessie and Bay, Kathryn was simply doing what was natural, leaping excitedly toward the things she wanted. Yet I was still struggling to hold on to the leash, trying to restrain her and keep her from pulling away from me.

I collected the colorful kabobs, carried them outside to the grill, and neatly arranged them on the grate before carefully brushing them with a generous amount of olive oil. As the vegetables slowly began to char, I rotated each kabob, remembering that although it was natural for dogs to chase squirrels, I'd also read that dogs could sense—and would react to—my tension. So I'd learned to remain calm when unexpected critters appeared, and when I relaxed my grip on the leash, the dogs relaxed too. And so it would go with Kathryn. The tighter I held on to her, the more she would pull away from me, and I didn't want that tension between us.

The sun was just beginning to sink behind the treetops. I applied another coat of olive oil and, satisfied, removed the kabobs from the flames and stepped back from the grill. I sank onto a nearby chair and watched as an invisible hand painted the early evening sky. I set my mouth into a firm line and resolved that I would remain calm no matter what Kathryn threw at me next. It was time for me to relax my grip.

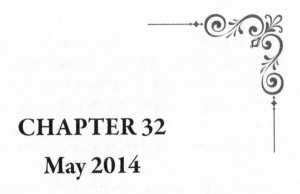

CHAPTER 32
May 2014

Jack sat in the front passenger seat on the way to Blacksburg to oversee Evelyn's driving. Before we'd even left our neighborhood, Ev ran a stop sign and nearly hit an approaching car. Then, just as we'd merged onto I-81 South and I'd started to relax, Evelyn abruptly changed lanes and moved directly into the path of an eighteen-wheeler that was barreling down on us. I inhaled sharply, making a hissing sound as I sucked air in through my clenched teeth and clutched the headrest, bracing for impact.

"Mom!" Ev scolded. "That doesn't help. I'm trying to concentrate."

"And I'm trying to stay alive!" I retorted.

Jack remained stoically silent, though I noted with satisfaction that the color had drained from his naturally bronze face. "Make sure you turn your head and look before you change lanes," Jack advised in his deep, soothing voice. "You can't always rely on your mirrors. Watch this." He put his hand on the wheel to keep it steady. "Keep your eyes on the rearview mirror and tell me what you see."

Evelyn obeyed Jack's instructions and flicked her thickly lashed sea-green eyes toward the overhead mirror. "Oh my God! That car disappeared!"

"Exactly. The mirrors have blind spots, so you have to turn and look."

Evelyn swallowed and nodded, clearly more nervous than she was letting on. Beside me in the back seat, Helene slept soundly. Her head was pressed into a pillow that rested against my shoulder, and earbuds were shoved firmly into her ears. She was oblivious to the fact that we'd twice come within inches of our lives.

My mood darkened as we made our way through Christiansburg. Kathryn had already informed us that she was not coming home for the summer.

"Get this!" she'd exclaimed on the phone last week. "I landed this choice internship designing brochures and advertisements for a local real estate company, and I'll be creating a new website and company logo too. I'll earn course credit *and* get paid!"

"Congratulations, honey," I'd replied, infusing my voice with false enthusiasm, remembering my pledge to remain calm and relax my grip. Getting paid to earn college credit and gain work experience while still a freshman was indeed a coup, but I would have paid her salary myself if only she'd come home for the summer. The ache of missing her left an irreparable, gaping wound in my chest.

"I was here first, remember," Jack had gently reminded me, trying to humor me out of my despair. I knew he sometimes feared I would slip into the darkness of depression again, so I'd tried to reassure him that just as going off to college was a rite of passage for Kathryn, it was a rite of passage for me as a mother to learn to let my children go. And to mourn their leaving.

We pulled up to Kathryn's dorm—a forbidding, six-story stone structure—and easily found a spot in the temporary parking area. The campus was nearly empty, the majority of students having already made their summer exodus. The four of us—stiff from the long drive—tumbled out of the car and shambled into the cool, sterile lobby. Helene and I elected to ride the elevator to the fourth floor while Jack and Evelyn opted for the stairs.

"Beat ya!" Ev exclaimed as Helene and I joined her and Jack in the hallway.

"Pure luck," Helene retorted, scowling at her sister.

"Whatever," Ev muttered under her breath.

Undoubtedly hearing the commotion in the hallway, Kathryn flung her door wide and greeted us with open arms. "You're here!" she cried. "And in one piece," she added, smirking at Evelyn, who narrowed her eyes at the insult.

"Very funny," Ev remarked, nonetheless wrapping her arms around her big sister's neck.

Helene flung her arms around them both, creating what the girls called a "sister sandwich." The sight of my three girls laughing and clinging to one another brought tears to my eyes. If only I could freeze the moment and preserve it indefinitely.

Kathryn tugged her sisters into her room, and Jack and I followed. My arms were dead weight at my sides, aching to hug Kathryn, to hold on to my firstborn and never let her go. When, at last, she walked into my arms, my tears began to fall.

"Mom, you promised," she whispered, but I was certain her eyes were misty as well. She stepped away with a smile and sprang toward her father, her long, dark ponytail bouncing, and suddenly she was five years old again, leaping into her father's arms. Jack was outwardly stoic, as usual, happy to let me be the emotional one, while he played the role of the more chill parent. But I knew better. I saw the twitch of his lips as he smiled and the pinch at the corners of his eyes as he worked to keep his feelings in check.

"I'm all packed and ready to go," Kathryn announced, gesturing toward the boxes and suitcases stacked neatly on her side of the room. Clare's half was still in disarray, with clothes spilling out of suitcases, books and shoes scattered everywhere, and an open bag of Fritos on the desk. Kathryn followed my gaze to the train wreck on her roommate's side of the room and giggled. "Clare's still packing. She and her mom went for coffee."

"Shall we?" Jack rubbed his hands together, his eyes sweeping over the room.

"Let's do it!" Kathryn lifted a large box from the bed and passed it to Jack.

"Time to get this party started!" Evelyn exclaimed, grabbing a suitcase and a backpack.

Kathryn handed me a shoulder bag and a small box, instructed Helene to grab a stack of pillows, and proceeded to load Jack like a pack mule.

"To the stairs, then?" he asked, winking at Evelyn, who was similarly weighed down with bags and boxes but still determined to take the stairs. She claimed it was in the name of fitness, though we all suspected she harbored a secret fear of elevators.

"Last one's a rotten egg!" Ev shouted.

THE TWO-STORY BRICK apartment building was only a five-minute drive from the heart of campus. To my dismay, Kathryn's unit was on the ground floor.

I nervously eyed the sliding glass doors that opened onto a small courtyard at the back of the building. "I'd feel more comfortable if you were on the upper level."

"Mom." Kathryn rolled her eyes. "It's fine. It's Blacksburg, not Baltimore."

"Well, keep it locked, okay?" Jack added, to which Kathryn shrugged and agreed.

I bit my tongue to keep from reminding her that crime happened everywhere as I did a quick survey of the rest of the apartment. The hard, cold floor was a dull-gray linoleum, and the walls were a dingy eggshell. The ceiling, however, had been freshly stomped in bright white paint, adding a touch of light and flair to the otherwise uninviting space. The kitchen was small but efficient, with dark laminate cabinets sans knobs and white countertops with gold flecks.

"This one's mine," Kathryn said, indicating the smaller of the two rooms situated across the narrow hallway from the bathroom. Her room featured a double bed with just enough space at the foot for the tiny closet door to fold out. A small square window on the opposite wall allowed a thin ray of light to slash across the room, and a battered metal desk was positioned to the right of the window.

"Charming," I muttered, my lips curling in distaste. It was hard to imagine Kathryn living in such a cold, sparse space. Her dorm room, by comparison, was cozy and vibrant, one of many dotting a long, lively hallway filled with fellow students. At the apartment, Kathryn would have only Clare for company. And Hokie.

As if reading my mind, Kathryn piped up. "Dustin is bringing Hokie by around four o'clock."

"Kathryn and Dustin sitting in a tree, K-I-S-S-I—"

Kathryn silenced Helene's childish taunt with a pinch to the arm.

"Ow!" Helene complained, rubbing her shoulder.

"Dustin's just a friend," Kathryn corrected, though I wondered if that was true.

I left the girls to their sisterly bickering and found Jack in the kitchen. He'd started unpacking a box of dishes we'd brought from home and was neatly stacking plates and bowls in one of the overhead cabinets. Helene, having escaped her sister's wrath, spruced up the scratchy navy-blue couch with Kathryn's multicolored throw pillows while Evelyn arranged bath towels in the hall linen closet.

Wordlessly, Kathryn and I made another trip to the car to fetch the remaining suitcases and boxes.

"It'll be much nicer once we get all of our stuff moved in," Kathryn opined. She seemed happier and more upbeat than usual. Her cheeks were rosy, and her eyes appeared bright and lively. The hint of a smile played on her lips. I wondered again if Dustin might be the reason.

"Of course it will," I said, unconvinced. Though I had to admit, Kathryn's room was already markedly improved by the addition of her deep indigo comforter and shag throw rugs.

When the last box was unpacked and all the clothes were hanging in the closet or neatly folded on the shelves, we headed to Macado's for lunch. As usual, I was dazzled by the restaurant's dizzying array of movie memorabilia. Multiple superheroes clung to the walls, an enormous King Kong dangled precariously from the ceiling, Fay Wray was clutched tightly in the ape's grasp, and Marilyn Monroe greeted us at the door, her white dress blowing skyward and her blond head tossed back in eternal ecstasy.

The hostess eyed our group. "Five?"

"Five," I confirmed, beaming.

"Right this way." The perky blonde led us to a booth surrounded by plastic palm trees and prehistoric birds. A gigantic *T. rex* was perched menacingly overhead.

Jack ordered a schooner of IPA, took a big swig, and passed it to me. I gulped at it greedily, but the bitter ale made my throat burn and my eyes sting. Still, I helped myself to another sip, more gingerly this time. The bitterness generated an involuntary grimace and a welcoming warmth in my abdomen. Jack covered my hand with his, stroking my knuckles with his thumb. He knew how hard it was for me to let go.

As Kathryn chatted excitedly about the conference she would be attending in Roanoke, a persistent ringing began in my ears, drowning out the surrounding commotion of the busy restaurant. I could see Kathryn's lips moving, but I could no longer hear what she was saying.

This is it. I'm losing her. I was desperate to hold on to my daughter, but I could feel her slipping through my fingers like fine sand through the hourglass of time. And there was nothing I could do to stop it.

Jack's hand was on my knee, his reassuring squeeze a lifeline, keeping me afloat, keeping me from sinking into the depths of my despair.

"Mom?" Kathryn was watching me with wide-eyed concern, as if she were the adult and I the child. "Are you okay?"

Get a grip, I scolded myself. *Don't ruin the weekend. Kathryn has her own life now. You have to let her go. You promised yourself you'd ease up.* "Of course," I said weakly. "I understand. You have responsibilities, your own life..."

Just then, our food arrived, and everyone dove in. The rigors of the move had taken their toll, but I merely picked at my veggie wrap. I chewed slowly, the food thick in my mouth and hard to swallow. While we ate, Ev regaled everyone with the play-by-play of her last lacrosse game, and Helene had everyone doubled over with laughter as she described her gymnastics teammate's leotard ripping open at the seam as she executed her vault, exposing the girl's bright-green frog-print underwear.

"She said it was her lucky charm! That it makes her leap higher!" Helene howled, prompting uproarious laughter from the table.

I felt dazed, as if I were eavesdropping on the conversation of strangers, and my smile was slippery. I was an outsider in my own family.

WE'D JUST RETURNED to Kathryn's apartment when someone rapped a merry tune on the front door. "That's Dustin!" Kathryn yelled. She flung the door open and threw her arms around the neck of a short blond boy.

I eyed the newcomer suspiciously. *Could this diminutive scrap of a boy possibly be the cause of Kathryn's rosy glow and perky demeanor?* I highly doubted it. Dustin was admittedly adorable but extremely short, his mop of curly hair just reaching Kathryn's nose. He was slightly built, and his wide, inviting grin was framed by a sparse, patchy beard that made him appear to be an adolescent boy desperately trying to resemble a man. He wore baggy shorts that hung below his knees and a pair of red Chuck Taylors on his feet. A tie-dyed Grateful Dead T-shirt completed the ensemble.

Kathryn had always favored the tall, clean-cut, athletic type—everything this boy was not—but I could understand why she was drawn to him. A warmth emanated from his mischievous denim-colored eyes that I immediately liked. I pictured him being like a brother to Kathryn, a boy she could trust, a boy who would protect her in a brotherly way, despite the hint of longing and adoration I detected in his gaze as his eyes followed Kathryn around the room. *Maybe there is more to it after all. What do I know?* I was just the mother.

"Mom, Dad, this is my friend Dustin."

Jack stepped forward, looming over Dustin. He reached out to shake the boy's hand, a wary, appraising look in his eyes. "Dustin," he said formally.

"Nice to meet you, Mr. Wells," the boy replied, confidently meeting Jack's eyes.

I gave Jack a knowing glance and greeted the boy with more warmth. "It's wonderful to meet you, Dustin."

"Likewise," Dustin replied before Ev and Helene rushed to the door, instantly overwhelming him and the medium-sized dog sitting patiently by his side.

"And this," Kathryn introduced with a wide smile, "is Hokie."

At the mention of his name, the rust-brown dog sprang to his feet, furiously wagging his tail. His front paws, which were both white, as if he'd stepped in a puddle of paint, tapped an excited rhythm on the concrete floor. Dustin unhooked Hokie's leash, and the dog dashed around the apartment, exploring every room and sniffing every surface. The dog's chest also had a patch of white fur to match his paws. After a thorough investigation of the new place, Hokie eagerly lapped water from the stainless-steel bowl Kathryn had produced from under the sink and curled up on the couch in a fading triangle of sunlight. I had to admit, the idea of Kathryn having a dog gave me some measure of comfort considering her new ground-floor accommodations.

"So what do you think?" Kathryn asked proudly.

"He's awesome!" Ev enthused, lovingly stroking the dog's fluffy fur.

"Chessie and Bay will love him," Helene decided, scratching Hokie under the chin.

"He's had his shots? Been checked out by a vet?" the ever-practical Jack asked.

Kathryn blushed deeply and dropped her gaze to the floor.

Dustin shot a quick glance in her direction and cleared his throat. "Uh, yeah. We had Hokie checked out by the vet when we got back from the lake. He's good to go."

Kathryn's marked reaction to Jack's question did not go unnoticed, and she flushed a deeper shade of red under my inquisitive gaze.

"Well, uh, I gotta roll," Dustin said, rescuing Kathryn from further scrutiny, at least for the moment. "Catch you downtown later?" he asked her.

"Not tonight, but I'll call you tomorrow," Kathryn promised, walking her friend to the door.

"Cool." Dustin treated Kathryn to a boyish grin, and a knowing gleam lit his eyes. "Nice to meet y'all." His slight Southern twang and good manners reminded me of Faith. After another quick handshake with Jack and a nod in my direction, Dustin was out the door.

"Is that your *boyfriend*?" Helene teased.

"Dustin? No way! We're just friends."

"Too bad," Ev said. "He's kinda cute."

"And really nice too," Helene added.

"And I think he likes you," Ev observed.

"He does not!" Kathryn denied. "Not like that anyway. He's more like a... brother," she explained, confirming my assessment.

"Is someone *else* your boyfriend, then?" Helene persisted, her prying question returning the color to Kathryn's face.

"Ah, nope. No boyfriend," Kathryn stated, her voice tense. "So what should we do now?"

Jack stood from where he sat on the couch and stretched his long arms toward the ceiling. "How 'bout we take Hokie for a walk?"

At the word "walk," Hokie went from completely zonked to fully alert. He was on his feet in an instant, his body rigid with excitement as his tail thrashed enthusiastically.

Helene giggled as Hokie licked her face. "I think Hokie likes the idea!"

Kathryn exhaled, and her face relaxed. She retrieved Hokie's leash from the closet and clipped it to his collar. "Let's go!" she said, making a beeline for the door.

ALL TOO SOON, JACK, Evelyn, Helene, and I were back in the car, heading north and watching Virginia Tech and the Blue Ridge Mountains fade in the rearview mirror. I quickly swiped away a tear that had slid hot and fast down my cheek. I'd been brave while saying goodbye to Kathryn after breakfast, but as we barreled down the interstate, heading for home, a fresh wave of disappointment consumed me, bringing a rush of unwelcome tears to my eyes.

As if reading my mind, Jack reached over and wordlessly grasped my hand, intertwining his fingers with mine. Ev and Helene were sound asleep in the back seat, no doubt exhausted from staying up until the wee hours with Kathryn, laughing, reminiscing, and generally relishing their sisterhood.

During our breakfast at Mill Mountain Coffee, Kathryn's cell phone had chimed incessantly. Most of the messages she glanced at and dismissed. One, however, made the color rise in her cheeks, and she excused herself from the table. I watched from the corner of my eye as she hovered next to the industrial, stainless-steel coffee grinder showcased in the Mill's large bay window, with a silly smile plastered on her face. She twirled a long, dark lock around her finger and whispered in hushed tones. A ruddy flush crept up her neck and settled prettily onto her cheeks. She was positively glowing.

"Who was that?" Ev blurted as Kathryn returned to the table, with a slight skip in her step.

"Oh, just a friend," she murmured, slipping the slender phone into the back pocket of her jeans.

We all waited silently, expectantly, for her to elaborate. Kathryn met our curious stares directly but shifted uncomfortably in her chair as she dished up some nonsense about a party that night at a friend's house.

"Uh-huh," Ev said, unconvinced. She would have pressed her sister for details if our plates of bagels, omelets, and pancakes hadn't arrived at that precise moment.

Kathryn took full advantage of the timely distraction to change the subject. "So, Helene, are you excited to start swim team next week?" she'd asked.

And then we were in the car, waving goodbye to Kathryn as she stood on the sidewalk in front of the Mill, her thick, shiny hair blowing in the spring breeze.

As we drove, I agonized over how long it would be before I saw her again, and a dreadful sense of déjà vu washed over me. Suddenly, I was eighteen, frantically searching the marina for Lia, crestfallen with the knowledge that she was gone and bewildered as to why she'd left. It was agony, wondering if I would ever see her again.

December 1989

LIA WAS STRANGELY EVASIVE when I arrived home from Ohio for winter break. She didn't call or stop by the house, and when I went to the marina, she was never there. She'd also never responded to the letter I'd sent to her in November about Jack and I being back together.

One particularly dank and dreary afternoon, I zipped my coat to the neck, braced myself against the frigid breeze blowing off the bay, and walked down the dock to Lia's boat. The marina was eerily quiet, save for the occasional mournful cry of a gull. I wiped a circle of dirt from one of the cabin windows with my gloved fist and peered inside. The cabin was empty, but the crumpled Coke cans in the trash, an open box of Bugles on the kitchenette table, and a light left on in the head served as evidence that she'd been there.

When two more weeks passed with no word from Lia, I began to worry. *What if something is wrong? Maybe she's sick or hurt.* I decided I'd better drive over to the marina again and check on her. Ducking my head against the whipping wind, I tromped down the dock and stopped dead in my tracks when I arrived at Lia's slip. Two strangers were perched on the bow of the boat, acting as if they owned the place. A skinny man and rotund woman, both bundled in tattered down coats, lounged in the beach chairs Lia and I used to sit in. Their booted feet were propped up on the railing, and they each held a fat joint. *Perhaps they're Rose's friends?*

"Hi," I said, clearing my throat. "Is, uh, Lia here?"

"Lia who?" the man grumbled.

"We don't know any Lia," the woman called out before being consumed by a phlegmy coughing fit.

My pulse sped up, and my heart hammered in my chest. My imagination ran wild. *What if these crazy people kidnapped Lia or killed her? Maybe they threw her limp, lifeless body overboard to be devoured by bottom-dwelling scavengers so they could claim the place as their own.* I fled down the pier and across the parking lot into the Harris Marina Mart where Old Man Louie stood behind the shabby, worn counter, puffing away on a cigarette.

"Have you seen Lia?" I demanded.

"Nope. Haven't seen hide nor hair of that girl. Left an extra month's rent and a note saying she was terminating her lease, effective immediately. Not so much as a goodbye for her old friend Louie."

"That makes two of us," I commiserated, slumping into a nearby booth. The red vinyl seat was sticky and cracked. Bits of foam padding belched from the seams and lay scattered on the weather-worn floor. "So she's just... gone? You don't have any idea where she went or if she's coming back?"

Louie shrugged. "Haven't a clue, girlie." He tipped his head back and blew a string of smoke rings into the air. His unkempt beard ran down his neck and disappeared into the yellowed collar of his stained T-shirt. "Can I get you a drink? Something to eat?"

I fingered the fake ID in my pocket but suppressed the urge to order a beer or a shot of tequila. "No forwarding address?" I pressed, hopelessness seeping into my voice. My chest was heavy. Feelings of fear and abandonment squeezed my lungs, making it hard to breathe.

Louie shrugged again. His cigarette dangled precariously from his thin, chapped lips. "Nada." He turned his bony back to me and proceeded to dry the clean glasses with a dirty rag.

As I plodded back to the car, I shoved my fists into my coat pockets. The maddening reality pressed down on me like the g-force that pinned me to my seat on a roller coaster, making my cheeks ache and my chest cave in. I reached out to steady myself against the hood of the car. I was dizzy, and my head was spinning. I refused to accept the truth that had already decimated my heart.

Lia was gone.

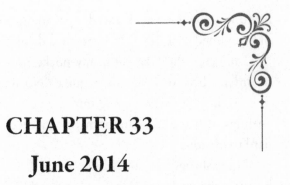

CHAPTER 33
June 2014

"It's perfectly natural," Lia insisted of my feelings about Kathryn. Jack was sympathetic, but no matter how kind and understanding he was, he could never fully appreciate what I was going through. I felt as if my maternal bonds—the very fibers of my soul that linked me to my daughter—were being ripped to shreds, and I longed for the empathetic compassion I would find in a fellow mother. A blissful smile lingered on Lia's face as the massage therapist rubbed lavender-scented oil into her shoulders. "I never realized gardening could be such hard work," she said with a groan, switching subjects as the therapist kneaded her lower back.

"So you don't think I'm overreacting?" Unlike my own therapist—whose primary technique involved digging her elbow into my scapula—Lia's massage therapist deftly employed a flurry of effleurage strokes to melt the tension from her muscles.

"Not at all. It's like what that author Elizabeth Stone said: 'To have a child is to forever have your heart go walking outside your body.' We love them, guide them, and protect them as they navigate the world, but who guides us? Who protects us? We survive it however we can. That's all I could do. Survive." Her voice was groggy, as if she were on the verge of sleep.

I stared at her. "What do you mean?"

"About what?" she said, stifling a yawn.

"Your kids are younger, Lia. I don't expect you to understand what this is like yet. I just need you to be here for me. I can't lean on Jack all the time. You know how guys are—they want to be problem solvers. They want to fix things. But this isn't something Jack can fix. I just have to work through it on my own."

Lia was quiet for so long, I thought maybe she'd fallen asleep after all. But then I noticed the subtle furrowing of her brow and the way her fingers worried the edge of the white sheets. "I just meant all the difficult decisions we have to make. As mothers. As women. We do the best we can. We make the hard choices, and we move on. We survive. That's all."

Lia's odd reply triggered an uncomfortable yet familiar sensation: a fist of dread in my belly and the whisper of a feather on my neck. I had the strange, niggling feeling that Lia was keeping something from me.

"How do you feel?" my massage therapist asked, patting me roughly on the shoulder. *Like I've been trampled by a horse.* I envied how Lia's therapist delicately cupped Lia's head between her hands and whispered, "Thank you. We're all finished." My therapist's vigorous touch, combined with my frayed nerves, raw emotions, and underlying sense of unease only served to heighten my agitation rather than ease my stress.

Lia stretched languidly on her padded table.

"Take your time. Take some deep breaths," her therapist advised before slipping silently out the door. My therapist had long since made her hasty departure.

"I'm starved," Lia said. As if on cue, her stomach rumbled loudly. "Lunch?"

"Sure, whatever," I replied and began to dress.

LIA DUG INTO HER VEGGIE burger with gusto. "That massage sure gave me an appetite," she said between bites.

I picked at my own salad, not that Lia had noticed.

The vegan deli was a short walk from the spa. It was a gorgeous day, and we had taken our time getting there, meandering along the tree-lined sidewalk that passed in front of a potpourri of quaint boutiques, bakeries, and street vendors. Lia had stopped occasionally to try on a pair of sunglasses or slip a handwoven straw bag over her shoulder, making idle chatter along the way. The deli was on the corner of a long strip of shops. Small wooden tables with red umbrellas sat on a crushed gravel patio bordered by bubbling fountains and flowering shrubs.

"You say things like that a lot, you know," I blurted.

"Like what?" Lia asked, polishing off her burger and starting in on our basket of kale chips.

"Like alluding to having done something or experienced something that you clearly have not, at least not to my knowledge."

Lia absently waved her hand in the air and sipped her organic green tea. The gesture rubbed me the wrong way, like she was blowing me off, like I had no idea what I was talking about. I straightened my back and squared my shoulders, determined not to let her off the hook this time.

"I'm not making this up," I pressed. "And the more I think about it, the more I realize how much I still don't know about you, about your life. I'm happy that we've reconnected, and I treasure our friendship, but it's just... this feeling I have sometimes when I'm with you, like you're hiding something from me."

Lia's cold indifference pulsed across the table like an outstretched arm pressing against my chest, holding me at bay. Then a sudden longing for Faith surged warm and hot through my body, and Faith's familiar, comforting presence washed over me, taking my breath away. It was as if she was *there* with me, guiding me, protecting me. *Warning me.* Suffusing me with strength. Then the feeling was gone, flowing away from my body like an ebbing tide.

"I won't go there again," I said, my voice hard and my hands shaking.

"Go where?" Lia asked, baffled.

"I won't tolerate you playing games with me. I've been completely honest with you. I've let you into my life again, into my heart again, but I'm not sure I trust you. I feel like you're keeping me at arm's length, which is ironic," I mused with a snort. "I thought it would be me keeping you at a distance. But it doesn't work that way, you know? Our friendship *won't work* that way."

Lia dabbed the corners of her mouth with her napkin. "Sometimes it's better that way, Anna," she postulated, refusing to meet my eyes.

And I knew I'd touched on something real. Fleeting and delicate but real. I wasn't imagining it. My words had reached out and grasped the edge of truth, and the realization emboldened me.

"What aren't you telling me, Lia? What are you hiding? Sometimes the things you say don't make sense. You said you went to Miami to help your aunt, but I still don't understand why you couldn't tell anyone about it. You also said you wanted to leave the past behind and start a new life. But if that's true, why did you move back to Maryland? And why, after all these years, did you decide to reach out to me again? It just doesn't add up."

Lia fidgeted with her napkin. Her pained expression was a window to her internal struggle. When she finally glanced up, I could see the storm of indecision had passed. The clouds of doubt had vanished, and her expression was clear and unguarded. I peered into her green eyes, still beautiful and bright despite the fine spray of crow's feet etched at the corners, and I knew the veil had been lifted. I braced myself for the truth.

"Anna—" And then her phone rang. Flustered, she reached for her bag and rummaged through its contents. With an apologetic shrug, she withdrew a sleek pink metallic phone and pressed it to her ear.

As the person on the other end spoke, the color drained from her face, and her phone clattered to the ground.

THE NEXT DAY, AS WE made our descent into Phoenix, Lia dug her fingernails into the back of my hand, leaving little half-moons on my skin, and squeezed her eyes shut. I leaned away from her and pressed my forehead against the cold oval pane, watching out the window as the arid landscape rose to meet us. Lia didn't speak until we were safely buckled in the rental car and heading north out of the city toward Sedona.

"She was my mother, but I didn't know her at all," Lia mumbled as she gazed out the window. "And now she's gone."

"I'm so sorry, Lia. I know this must be hard for you."

Her face was impassive, but her eyes spoke volumes. I had no clue how hard this was for her. I could not begin to imagine what it was like to have a mother who had betrayed me and always put her own needs before mine, a mother who'd never been there for me and who was now gone forever.

We rode in silence, watching in subdued awe as we passed dozens of giant saguaros that had miraculously sprung from the sunbaked earth. They soared skyward and stood sentry over fields of barrel cactus and bear grass. The area's legendary red rocks loomed majestically in the distance, dominating the landscape as we made our way to the small town of Clarkdale, thirty-eight miles outside of Sedona, near the Sycamore Canyon Wilderness. The vibrant, earthy colors of the land—red rocks, orange clay, craggy brown mountains, and green cacti—set against the azure southwestern sky formed a breathtaking tapestry that overshadowed the fine layer of dust that seemed to coat every surface and cling to the very air.

Eventually, the paved road gave way to gravel and then dirt as we approached a wooden arch erected near a narrow, trickling stream. The squatters' camp was located fifty yards to the left of the arch, discreetly sheltered by soaring rocks, ponderosa pines, and yucca palms. As we approached, we saw a motley crew of hippie-types gathered in a circle, their hands clasped and heads bowed. We parked the car in a dirt clearing and sat motionless, watching the spiritual gathering in progress and listening intently as the group sang songs and chanted in an unfamiliar tongue.

Eventually, a rail-thin woman with rust-colored skin and waist-length raven hair generously threaded with silver broke away from the group and strode toward us. As she drew near, we could see the pain etched on her leathery face. Her eyes were red-rimmed and watery. Her dirty, tear-streaked skin was stretched tautly over her sharp cheekbones. She had a high, wide forehead and a proud, prominent nose. Her dark hair fell in knotted clumps, dreadlocks gone awry.

The woman stopped a few feet short of the car and eyed us warily. "I'm Toski," she rasped, her bony arms hanging limply at her sides. "You are Emilia?" Doubt creased her face.

Beside me, Lia released a long, shuddering sigh. She leaned forward, removed her sunglasses, and met the woman's eyes. "I'm Emilia."

"Ah. It is clear you are the daughter. You favor her," Toski said matter-of-factly. "Come. We've been waiting for you." She beckoned us to follow.

We scrambled from the car and walked stiffly and fearfully, shoulder to shoulder, as if we were walking toward the gallows instead of a peaceful gathering of weathered beatniks. "She's the one who called," Lia whispered into my ear, inclining her head toward the woman.

As we neared the group, the low, murmuring voices grew quiet. Two men, their bare backs a boneyard of jutting shoulder blades and spiny vertebrae, released their gnarled hands and stepped backward, welcoming us into the circle.

Lia gasped and became limp at my side. I clasped her hand tighter. In the center of the circle, a thick stump of wood supported a clay urn. Native American images of Kokopelli, Kokopelmana, and Paiyatamu were intricately carved into the urn's surface, and locks of silvery russet hair, shiny river rocks, and tiny beeswax candles surrounded it. Several stick-framed photos and personal mementoes leaned against the stump, adorning the shrine.

Toski moved to the center of the circle and stood beside the urn. From her shirt pocket, she produced a scroll secured with twine. Once she had freed the tie and unrolled the parchment, she began to read:

Do not stand at my grave and weep.
I am not there. I do not sleep.
I am a thousand winds that blow.
I am the diamond glint on snow.
I am the sunlight on the ripened grain.
I am the gentle autumn's rain.
When you awaken in the morning hush,
I am the swift uplifting rush
of quiet birds in circled flight,
I am the soft stars that shine at night.
Do not stand at my grave and cry:
I am not there. I did not die.

"Hopi Indian Prayer," Toski explained as she deposited the scroll into a small, simply crafted wooden box at her feet. "Rozene went in peace from this earth, daughter," Toski said, her eyes locked on Lia's.

"How—" Lia began but was quieted by Toski's raised palm and somber expression.

"But she had no peace in this life," Toski continued. "And no peace with you, her only child. On the eve of her death, she put this, her box of treasures, into my hands so that I might see it safely to your keeping." Toski bowed her head and extended the box to Lia. "Askwali. Thank you for being here today."

I released Lia's hand—my mind a jumble of confusion and concern—and watched, mesmerized, as Lia accepted the box with shaking hands. Her face was wet with tears.

"Askwali," she repeated.

Toski dipped her head in acknowledgement and drifted silently from the circle, which instantly disintegrated as the other members of the group, following Toski's lead, quietly faded into the jagged outcroppings of rocks and scrub and disappeared into their makeshift shelters.

Lia sank to the ground, the wooden box in her lap, and lifted the lid. With trembling fingers, she sifted through an array of crystals, a glass marijuana pipe, three joints—one of which she slipped into her pocket—a Conch Out business card, multihued feathers attached to strips of leather, a small piece of animal hide, shark's teeth, snake skins, and a tiny pink crocheted baby bootie. "Mine," Lia whispered. There was also a tarnished silver ring with a turquoise stone, which Lia slipped onto her finger, and two photographs. One photo was a black-and-white image of a stern-faced man and woman standing rigidly in front of an old farmhouse. "Rose's parents," Lia explained. "I never met them."

The other was a more recent photograph. Lia held the slightly blurry photo up to her face and stared at it wide-eyed. Fresh tears spilled from her eyes, and I watched helplessly as she hugged her knees to her chest and wept. The photo slipped from her fingers and fluttered to the ground. A gentle breeze swept it beyond my reach. I crawled on hands and knees to retrieve it.

"That was the last time I saw her," Lia murmured. The palms of her hands were pressed to her face, muffling the heart-wrenching words.

The photo was limp and wrinkled, the edges softly worn. I peered closely at the picture, at Lia's radiant young face, and the two women who stood smiling beside her. One of them had long red hair, and the other was platinum blonde with short, spiky locks. All three women had fair skin and matching green eyes. Nestled in Lia's arms was a tiny infant. Its fragile newborn head, topped with a thatch of dark hair, was gently cradled in Lia's palm.

I stared slack-mouthed at the photo. My gaze darted from Lia to the picture and back again.

Lia's hands fell to her lap. She fixed me with an intense, pleading gaze. Finally, she spoke slowly, searching my face, as her fingertip grazed the worn edge of the photograph. "This is the real reason I went to Miami."

WE HIKED TO A NEARBY cliff overlooking the town. Lia lit the joint she'd pocketed from Rozene's box—Rozene, Toski had explained, was the Native American word for rose—and inhaled deeply.

"I almost didn't have him," Lia whispered, her eyes unreadable.

I remained still, waiting for her to explain, but she lapsed into remote silence again.

"Is that what you wanted to tell me in that letter? That you were pregnant?"

She took another long drag and let the pleasant, potent fumes simmer in her lungs before exhaling a pungent cloud of herb-scented smoke. We watched as the hazy tendrils swirled skyward and languidly dissipated. Lia's profile was illuminated by the setting sun, which cast her face in shadow. She passed me the joint. "I was so scared, Anna. I never thought it would happen to me, you know?" She laughed bitterly and shook her head. "God knows I took too many chances, rolled the dice too many times. I guess my luck finally ran out. You were always the practical one. I thought if we could get together—if I could work up the courage to confide in you—you would know what to do." Lia's rueful grin was chased away by an ugly snort that sent us both into a fit of giggles.

But beneath the laughter, I knew I'd failed my friend, and my heart squeezed with regret.

"But I didn't hear from you. And then you were gone. Off to Ohio," Lia continued. "I went to a Planned Parenthood center near campus to get an abortion, and I couldn't do it. Whatever mistakes I'd made, they were *my* mistakes. They had nothing to do with the innocent baby growing inside of me. I went back to the dorm and cried myself to sleep. I stayed in bed for days."

I reached for her hand. "I'm so sorry I wasn't there for you."

Lia shook her head dismissively. "My roommate thought I was sick, asked if there was someone I could call. And that's when it hit me. Aunt Ivy. I blubbered like an idiot and told her everything. She agreed to help but only if I promised to stay in school and finish my education. She said her husband, Roberto, wasn't well and that she could use the help anyway. So as soon as the semester was finished, I headed south and lived at the inn with my aunt and Roberto. And believe it or not—despite everything—I was happy there. Really happy. And Roberto was the closest thing I'd ever had to a father. I named the baby after him."

We sat and smoked in silence, immersed in our own private, hazy reveries. "What about Robert's real father?" I asked gently.

"Not in the picture," Lia replied with abrupt annoyance, stubbing the joint out on a rock. "Neil was Robert's father," she continued, her voice hard and defiant. "He legally adopted Rob after we got married. It's one of the reasons Robert hates me, though."

"Surely he doesn't hate you," I soothed, my words beginning to soften and slur.

Lia's face crumbled, and a tear leaked from the corner of her eye. She angrily swiped it away with the back of her hand. "Rob and Neil never really connected. They were like oil and water. Neil always made Robert feel like he wasn't good enough, especially after the twins were born."

"Does Robert know Neil isn't his real father?"

Lia's expression darkened. "I would have told him myself one day, when he was ready. But Neil beat me to it. One night, when Rob was in high school, he and Neil got into a huge fight, and Neil—that asshole—told him. He had no right! I would have left him then and there if it weren't for the twins. But that's when I knew for sure I *would* leave him. It was just a matter of time.

"Robert was distant after that. I couldn't really blame him. I'd lied to him for so many years, let him believe Neil was his father. But I knew what it was like to grow up without a father, and I didn't want that for him. Rob was so young when Neil adopted him. I didn't think I'd have to worry about it until Robert was older, maybe with a family of his own. In hindsight, it was a mistake not to tell him. I don't think he's ever forgiven me."

"Where is he now?" I ventured.

"He graduated from high school, went to UVA, and never came back."

"That's what the college administrators told us when Kathryn started Tech. 'They're never coming back.'"

Lia met my gaze. Her green eyes were glassy and red as she searched my face. Then, without warning, she leapt to her feet, extended her arms, tipped her head back and began spinning in circles with her eyes closed, laughing maniacally.

"Lia, stop! You'll fall!" I yelled, fearful that she would lose her footing and tumble ass over teakettle right off the cliff. My alarm only incited her further, and she spun faster, cackling wildly. Feeling desperate, I tackled her, grabbing her around the waist and forcing her backward, away from the edge.

Together, we stumbled and fell into a patch of sandstone, dirt, and ferns. With her arms pinned to her sides, Lia had skidded face-first into the red soil and came up spluttering, a reddish-brown smear on her cheek. I gaped at her in wide-eyed horror, hoping she hadn't cracked her skull on a rock. But a single glance at my terrified expression sent her into peals of laughter, and she began to pluck bits of fern and desert grass from my hair. Relieved, I lay back on the rocks beside her. Giggling, we admired the crimson southwestern sky as it darkened to rich shades of indigo and violet.

Lia grasped my hand as we lay motionless, our backs pressed into the rapidly cooling earth. "I don't know if Robert will ever forgive me, but I hope you will."

I squeezed her hand and held it tightly. "I already have."

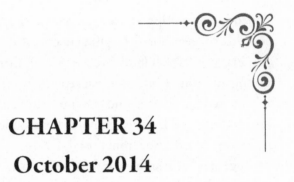

CHAPTER 34
October 2014

The heat of summer pressed relentlessly into fall. The foliage along the Blue Ridge Mountains remained stubbornly green, stalling their transformation into the vibrant patchwork tapestry of autumn. But I paid little notice to the passing scenery. The only colors on my mind were the rich dark brown of Kathryn's hair and the golden glow of her summer-bronzed skin. Other than a brief weekend visit in late August, we hadn't seen her in five months, a span of time that was hard to fathom. The anticipation of seeing her again created a twirling coil of nerves in my stomach. Jack exited onto Prices Fork Road, made a left onto University City Boulevard, and drove directly to her apartment.

At our knock, Kathryn flung open the door and bounced up and down like a child, a welcome greeting far removed from her usual reserve. Dressed in a pair of dark-gray hiking shorts, a jade-green tank top, the waterproof hiking boots we'd given her on her birthday, and a funky pair of knee-high compression socks, she was the perfect mix of sporty, fashionable, and stunning. Her dark-brown hair tumbled in shiny waves over her shoulders, her eyes were bright and alert, and her skin was clear and flushed with the healthy glow of youthfulness and time spent outdoors. But her radiance was more than skin deep. A palpable sense of peace, purpose, and fulfillment emanated from her. The cautious, wide-eyed girl we'd delivered to campus just over a year ago had blossomed into the confident, self-assured woman who now stood before us.

"I'm so happy to see you!" Kathryn exclaimed, stealing the very words from my mouth.

I swept her into my arms, inhaling her familiar scent of vanilla and sunshine. "It's so good to see you too. We've missed you so much. You look beautiful."

"Aw, thanks," she said, blushing slightly as she tucked into Jack's embrace.

His throat worked to form words I was sure he didn't yet trust himself to speak. "How are you?" he finally managed as he lovingly cupped the back of her head with his large hand.

"I'm good, Dad. Really good." As she stepped back, I saw that her eyes were misty, another atypical display of emotion from our stoic eldest daughter. The two of them were cut from the same cloth. Kathryn was the spitting image of her father and had been since the day she was born.

He pulled her to him again. "I'm so glad. So what are we gonna do today?" he asked, releasing her.

"I hope you brought your hiking shoes!" she said, a mischievous gleam in her eyes.

Jack and I shot each other an apprehensive glance that made Kathryn giggle with delight.

"The campus is crawling with people for the family weekend, so I thought we'd get out of Dodge. I'm thinking Dragon's Tooth. It's the best! My favorite hike."

At the word "hike," Hokie leapt to his feet, his tail wagging excitedly. Kathryn bent down and stroked the dog's fur. "It's Hokie's favorite hike too, isn't it, boy?" The dog wiggled enthusiastically beneath her hand, and it warmed my heart to see the mutual and obvious affection between them. Though Kathryn never said so, I assumed that she missed Chessie and Bay and that Hokie filled the doggie void in her life.

"Let's do this thing!" Jack rallied, rubbing his hands together. "After that long car ride, I'm ready to stretch my legs and get some fresh air."

FORTY MINUTES OF TWISTING and turning along narrow country roads had left me trembling and nauseated. By the time we arrived at Jefferson National Park, I would have agreed to hike Mount Everest if it meant I would be free from the car. I staggered out of the back seat and grimaced at my green-tinged reflection in the side-view mirror. Kathryn offered me a bottle of water and a hard sourdough pretzel, which I gratefully accepted.

We followed her to the information kiosk at the rear of the lot. "Ten minutes of hiking this beast, and you'll have forgotten all about your queasy stomach," she teased.

We retrieved a trail map from the wooden box attached to the kiosk. Hokie, anxious to be free of his leash, began turning in circles at our feet. The Dragon's Tooth trailhead, located just beyond the kiosk, was the beginning of a steady uphill climb that, despite the easy footing on the smooth, hard-packed earth, set my hamstrings and calves on fire. I gulped deep lungfuls of air and struggled to keep pace with Jack and Kathryn. Though I was fitter than I'd ever been in my life, I was no match for Jack's strong, powerful stride or Kathryn's youthful energy. After more than a mile of climbing, we turned right onto the white-blazed Appalachian Trail heading south toward Dragon's Tooth. A rock monolith of Tuscarora quartzite stood proudly atop Cove Mountain. The smooth dirt suddenly gave way to a treacherous, rocky trail that clung to the edge of the mountain and became so steep that a series of iron steps had been embedded into the rock.

"This is my favorite part," Kathryn said, flashing a wicked smile as she launched herself up the steep steps. "It's Dragon's Back, the spine of the mountain."

As I scrambled after her, my foot skidded on a loose outcropping of rock, and Jack grasped my elbow to steady me. I could feel his hot exhalation on my neck and was slightly comforted by the fact that I wasn't the only one breathing heavily.

"This must be payback for something," I muttered. "Do you think she still holds a grudge from the time we grounded her in tenth grade?"

Jack laughed. "I think she's just showing off."

"Are we there yet?" I hollered at Kathryn's back.

"Almost! There's a great overlook up ahead before we pick up the Spur Trail to the top."

When we caught up to Kathryn, she was leaning against a rail at the edge of the overlook where the mountain gave way to a sheer rock face that disappeared into thin air. The sight of her standing so close to the cliff's edge made me gasp.

"Isn't it gorgeous?" She gestured toward the sweeping view of Roanoke Valley rolling out in sprawling green waves behind her.

"Beautiful," I agreed, staring directly at my daughter.

"Are you trying to kill us?" Jack asked, his breath finally slowing.

"Nope. Just trying to keep you young. Less than half a mile to the top," Kathryn announced, bounding away from us again.

Finally, after two hours of rigorous hiking and an elevation gain of 1,505 feet, we reached a wide, flat clearing. In the center was an outcropping of several canine-tooth-shaped quartzite spires thrusting skyward. The tallest "tooth" reached nearly thirty-five feet above the surrounding rock. I rotated in a slow circle, taking in the magnificent 360-degree view that absolutely made up for the grueling climb.

"Pretty cool, huh?" Kathryn asked as I admired the landscape. "But you have to follow me if you want your lunch!" she teased, walking behind one of the teeth where she wedged her foot into a crevice and hoisted herself up the side of the rock.

"Oh, no way!" I exclaimed, realizing that she meant for us to scale the sheer rock to the tippy top.

"C'mon, you can do it!" she encouraged. "You can't come all this way and not climb the Tooth. I promise you it's worth it."

And so, against my better judgment and with Jack standing behind me to catch my fall, I shoved my foot into the crevice and followed the path Kathryn had taken to ascend the rock. My heart hammered in my chest. "This is insane," I muttered under my breath. My limbs shook from fear and exertion, and my palms were sweaty.

"Don't look down," Kathryn advised from her perch at the top.

"Don't worry, I won't!" Then my foot lost purchase, and my shin scraped along the rough surface of the rock as my body careened sideways.

"Whoa!" Jack said from below as his strong hands gripped my calf. "You okay?" he asked as he guided my leg toward a new, invisible foothold.

I wedged my toes into the small crevice and gritted my teeth. "Fine," I said, summoning all my nerve and upper body strength I didn't know I had to hoist myself upward. I didn't think I had ever worked harder for anything in my life. Even childbirth may have been less rigorous. It had definitely been less frightening. At last, I reached the top of the Tooth, with Jack close behind. I sank onto the sun-warmed rock and closed my eyes, sending up a small prayer of thanks that I'd made it with all limbs intact.

"Now that's what I call a hike!" Jack enthused.

The three of us sat huddled on our narrow spire like birds perched in a nest, higher in the sky than any human should have been, and on such a small slab of stone, it felt as if we were suspended in midair. Gazing at the horizon gave me vertigo, and my stomach roiled with fear.

"You'll get used to it," Kathryn said as I closed my eyes and pressed my palm to my abdomen.

Deep breaths, deep breaths. I'd just begun to relax when I was struck with a horrifying thought that sent my stomach cartwheeling again: *What goes up must come down.* I shoved my fear aside and focused my attention on the food Kathryn was producing from the depths of her backpack.

With her usual easy grace, as if we weren't suspended atop a mountain where one unfortunate lapse in balance would send us plummeting to our deaths, Kathryn spread a small tie-dyed bandana onto the rock and topped it with three wrapped sandwiches, a bag of pita chips, a container of carrot sticks, apples, chocolate chip cookies, and a small thermos of green tea.

Kathryn poured the tea and handed us each a cup. "Cheers!" she said. "You guys are troopers."

"So how'd you find this place?" Jack asked.

"Jay brought me here. He's in the Outdoor Club. We hike the Tooth as often as we can."

"Jay?" I asked between bites. The fearful churning of my stomach had been overtaken by ravenous rumbling.

Caught up in the adrenaline and exhilaration of the moment, Kathryn realized her slip a moment too late and blushed scarlet to the roots of her hair. "Oh. Jay?" She shrugged, feigning nonchalance. "He's just this friend of mine."

Jack bit into his sandwich and raised his eyebrows expectantly, waiting for details, while Kathryn chewed.

"*Just* a friend?" I questioned, suspecting there was more to the story.

Kathryn shied away from my inquiring gaze but couldn't hide the slow smile that slid across her face. "He's awesome," she admitted, her words tumbling out in a rush. "I met him last spring, and we *were* just friends, at first, but then it was different. I guess you could say we've officially been together four months now." She hooked her fingers into air quotes at the word "officially" and giggled, a delightful, bubbly sound so unlike Kathryn, our serious, studious daughter.

"Four months?" Jack questioned.

"Why haven't you told us about him?" Doing the math, I became convinced that it wasn't just her internship that had kept her on campus and away from us this summer—it was this boy. This *Jay*. I bit my tongue to keep from making a snarky comment I would regret.

"I'm telling you now," Kathryn pointed out.

"Will we get to meet him?" I asked. Part of me hoped the answer would be yes, but the other part selfishly hoped it would be no. It was our weekend with our daughter, and I wasn't keen on sharing her.

Kathryn glanced away again. "No, I don't think so. I'm not really ready for the whole meet-the-parents thing yet. Besides, he has to work this weekend."

"Where does he work?" Jack asked before polishing off the rest of his sandwich.

"At the vet office. That's where I met him, actually. When Hokie went in for his checkup."

We all peered over the edge of the tooth to where Hokie lay blissfully panting in the shade. Kathryn had tethered his leash to a small sapling, and a bowl of fresh water lay by his side.

"So how are things with you and this guy?" I asked.

"Things are good." Kathryn smiled demurely at her lap, the color rising in her face again. "I like him a lot."

The look on her face took my breath away. With her long, dark lashes sweeping over her rosy cheeks and a coy, secretive smile playing on her lips, it was an expression I recognized immediately, one I was intimately familiar with. It was the expression I'd worn in high school... when I was falling in love with Jack.

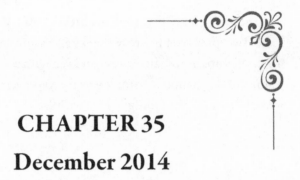

CHAPTER 35
December 2014

It was Lia's turn to host our annual cookie-baking festivities. Her house, always cheerful and cozy, was particularly inviting on such a bitterly cold day. Lia was waiting at the door when I arrived. I hurried inside, shrugged out of my red coat and hat, which were lightly dusted with fine, powdery snow, and gratefully accepted the warm mug of mulled wine she offered.

"I thought you'd never get here," Lia complained good-naturedly.

"Traffic was a mess, people freaked out by the snow." I shook my head in mild annoyance as I followed her up the stairs. *Just drive, people,* I'd muttered under my breath most of the way to Lia's, making a mental note to head home well in advance of rush hour.

By noon, we were elbow-deep in cookie dough and had moved on from mulled wine to spiked eggnog. Lia had laughed delightedly when I revealed my suspicions about Kathryn being in love.

"Did you get to meet him?" she asked.

"No. Kathryn said he was working, but I think she just wasn't ready to make introductions yet." Using a rolling pin, I manipulated a ball of dough with more vigor than necessary.

Lia raised one ruddy eyebrow. "Give her time. If it's the real deal, you'll meet him. And go easy on the dough, would you?"

I'd spread the dough so thin that it had torn in three places. With a sigh, I gathered the ragged mess into my hands, patted it with flour, and reshaped it into a ball.

"Remember, you want to roll it, not kill it," Lia instructed.

In retaliation, I snatched a dish towel off the table and snapped it at her hip. With a yelp and a quick sideways hop, she dodged the blow by the skin of her jeans. I smiled, happy to see her in good spirits. Though her relationship with Rose had been a rocky one, the surprise news of her mother's death had hit Lia hard. It had been a difficult few months for her.

"Jingle Bell Rock" began playing on Pandora, and Lia reached over to crank up the volume just as two quick, cursory raps sounded on the front door.

"Expecting someone?" I asked.

Lia shrugged, her eyes wide with surprise. Downstairs, the front door sprang open, ushering in a burst of fresh, cold air. "Hey, Mom!" called a deep voice from the foyer below. "I'm home."

Mom? Certainly Nicholas and Nathan aren't home from school so early. And that's not the voice of a teenage boy. This voice was deeper, more masculine and confident, the voice of a man. I shot a startled glance in Lia's direction.

She stood frozen with her hands in midair. Her fingers were caked with thick mud-colored goo from the peanut butter balls she'd been rolling.

Heavy footfalls sounded on the stairs, as if someone were bounding up them two at a time. A mop of shiny dark-brown hair came into view at the top of the landing. I held my breath as an exceptionally handsome young man—tall and lean, with finely chiseled features and broad, muscular shoulders—strode into the kitchen. He smiled warmly at Lia, plucked a peanut butter ball from the tray in front of her, tossed it into the air, and caught it neatly in his mouth. A satisfied smile curled his lips as he chewed.

"Robert!" Lia exclaimed. "What are you *doing* here?"

"Finished up early at work. Thought I'd surprise you." He slung an arm around Lia's rigid shoulders, careful to avoid her goopy, up-lifted hands, and used his free hand to grab a warm cranberry oat-meal cookie from the cooling rack. "And I was hoping to catch the guys for a quick match." He gave her shoulders a squeeze and plant-ed a kiss on the top of her flour-dusted head.

As he turned to leave, he caught sight of me standing speechless behind the table where I'd been decorating sugar cookies. "Oh, hey," he said, looking directly at me for the first time. He had a charming, boyish smile, and deep dimples creased his cheeks.

Time stood still as I gazed at this boy's—this *man's*—smooth golden skin, high, prominent cheekbones, and long, straight nose. The tip of his nose was the slightest bit crooked and flushed a del-icate pink from the frigid winter air that still clung to his clothes. My gaze traveled over his face and settled on his eyes, which were a rich, velvety brown flecked with bits of emerald and ringed in sap-phire. Those eyes were unbelievably, achingly familiar. They were the same young eyes that had once gazed into mine before they'd grown adorably creased and crinkled with years of laughter, eyes that were now aged and weathered by a life well-lived.

The man-boy moved closer, his arm outstretched to shake my hand. At the same moment, I tore my eyes from his haunting, mes-merizing gaze and extended my own arm, palm out, to halt his ad-vance. Our fingers collided, and a shot of energy ran up my arm, as if I'd been electrified. My head snapped up. For a split second, I was sixteen again, reaching into a cooler to grab a Coke, my fingers brushing against those of a boy who'd reached for the same one. Time warped and flexed. It was as if I were looking straight into the youthful face and mesmerizing eyes of the boy I'd fallen in love with. It was as if I were looking directly at *Jack*.

I couldn't breathe. I closed my eyes to erase the image from my mind, and my body went numb. The old-fashioned glass of spiked eggnog slipped from my fingers and shattered on the tile floor, sending shards of glass skittering in all directions. The shock of the crash made time lurch forward again. My lungs were burning from lack of oxygen. I sucked in a gulp of air, and the sticky, half-chewed cookie in my mouth lodged in the back of my throat, blocking my windpipe. My right hand flew to my neck as the other hand grasped the back of a chair for balance.

The man-boy's inconceivable eyes widened in alarm, and he took another cautious step toward me. Shaking my head frantically, I backed away and finally pulled enough air into my lungs to cough with enough force to send the wet glob of dough flying past my lips. It landed with a splat on the floor near Lia's feet.

"What... how..." I sputtered.

Lia slowly lowered her arms to her sides and absentmindedly wiped her peanut-butter-caked hands on her apron. Her eyes cleared, and the slightly dazed expression was suddenly replaced by a sharp, defensive look. "Robert, this is my friend Anna," she said, jutting her delicate chin in my direction. "Anna." Her eyes fixed steadily on mine. "This is my son."

"So I gathered," I muttered, regaining a smidgeon of composure.

"Nice to meet you," Robert said politely, extending his hand again.

I stared at the outstretched hand before me, strong and masculine, with clean, neatly trimmed nails. Rather than take it, I casually wiped my lips with the back of my hand, straightened my spine, and squared my shoulders. Robert slowly lowered his arm and furrowed his brow, a confused look in his eyes. *Those eyes!*

Mindful of the glass still littering the floor, I stepped gingerly around the boy and crossed the tile to retrieve a napkin. I scooped up the discarded glob of chewed cookie and deposited it into the trash bin beneath the sink. "Likewise," I finally whispered, staring at Lia. My voice sounded strange, strangled. "If you'll excuse me?" I beelined for the upstairs bathroom. When I reached the upper landing, I paused to listen as the hushed sounds of Lia's high-pitched voice and Robert's baritone mingled with the swish and clink of glass being swept and discarded.

Turning slowly toward the bathroom, I caught my reflection in the mirror. My clammy skin was ghostly pale. Strands of disheveled hair stuck to my forehead, and a fine mist of flour coated my fore-arms. With shaking hands, I turned on the tap as hot as I could stand it and vigorously lathered and scrubbed with peppermint-scented soap, carefully removing the bits of dough that clung to my rings and fingernails. Then I switched the tap to cold and repeated-ly splashed my face. The shock of it made me gasp. Finally I turned off the water and patted my cheeks and hands dry with a fluffy pink towel. I looked again in the mirror, but it was Jack's handsome face that danced before my eyes. My husband. The man I loved with my whole heart and trusted with my entire soul. Yet the truth that stood before me in Lia's kitchen mocked that trust and made me question everything I'd ever believed. Though my mind struggled to solve the riddle of what I'd seen, and my heart fought against the shock and disbelief I felt, the painful truth throbbed in every ounce of my being. Gripping the edge of the sink, I hung my head in de-spair as my insides twisted with grief. The boy I'd met downstairs was not only Lia's son. He was Jack's son too.

WHEN I WAS CERTAIN Robert had left, I crept silently down the stairs on shaky legs. The upbeat holiday tunes Lia and I had been so merrily singing along to had been replaced by the suitably melancholy notes of a saxophone rendition of "White Christmas."

The living room was warm and pleasantly suffused with the aroma of freshly baked cookies. Lia sat on the taupe suede couch. An open bottle of Bailey's Irish Cream—the first alcoholic drink we'd shared when we'd snuck it from Becky's parents' liquor cabinet during a Halloween party our sophomore year—stood on the low, round table in front of her. She sipped slowly and thoughtfully. Her eyes were fixed on the frosty windows and the slate sky heavy with the promise of fresh snow. I'd hoped to sneak past Lia and slip out the door unnoticed, but a creaking floorboard betrayed me.

Her head swiveled in my direction, and she sprang to her feet. "Anna." Her voice was husky, her eyes pleading.

"Don't!" I shouted and raced down the stairs to retrieve my coat and hat from the rack behind the door. As I shoved my arms into the coat and my feet into my boots, I could hear Lia's quick, light steps on the stairs above me. I flung open the front door, and her small fingers grasped the sleeve of my coat. Her touch seared me. I imagined the heat of her hands singeing my skin through the thick wool. I wrenched my arm from her grasp and lurched over the threshold. My vision was blurred by the bitter tears gathering in my eyes.

"Anna, please!" Lia wailed, following me outside in her socks.

"No, Lia!" I screamed, fumbling with my keys as my chest heaved. She reached for me again, but this time, when I tried to twist away, my foot slipped on a patch of ice, and I landed hard on my backside. The contents of my bag spewed forth and littered the driveway.

Lia dropped to her knees before me and clasped my wet cheeks in her tiny hands, forcing my head upward.

My eyes bored into hers. I'd never felt such pure hatred.

"Please listen," she begged. "I can explain."

"How can you possibly explain this?"

Her face crumpled, and I shook my head free, my lips curling into snarl.

"You can't!" I screamed. "You can't explain it, and you can't lie your way out of it! Not this time! I saw him with my own eyes, Lia. I *saw* him."

"It's not what you think." A desperate whimper escaped her lips.

"How could you possibly know what I think?" I challenged with a hiss.

Lia reached out to steady me as I struggled to stand, but as I jerked away, my feet lost purchase again. "Ow!" I hollered as my hip made contact with the low stone wall bordering the dormant flower beds.

"Anna!" Lia yelped, leaning toward me.

I shoved her angrily. "Stay away from me!" I screamed, but she came at me again.

I balled my fists and pummeled her. She grabbed my wrists with surprising strength and forced my hands to the ground. I swung my leg, and the heel of my boot connected with her thigh, making her cry out. I wrenched one of my hands free and struck her again, knocking her off balance, but before I could scramble away, she wrapped her arms around my waist and tugged me backward, causing us both to topple over into the snow. I let out a guttural screech and twisted away, not giving a damn about the scene we were making in her front yard. Then I pivoted on my knees to face her and unleashed twenty-five years of pent-up anguish and rage in a flurry of punches and slaps as the tears flew from my eyes and snot streamed from my nose.

Lia ducked and covered her head with her forearms, willingly submitting to my abuse and bearing the brunt of my anger. As the adrenaline drained from my body and my blows faltered, Lia rose and grabbed my wrists again. I protested and thrashed weakly until the storm that had seized my body finally dissipated, leaving me physically and emotionally spent.

Exhausted and panting, I raised my burning, puffy eyes to hers. "Robert. He's Jack's?"

Lia pressed her lips into a hard line and averted her gaze, causing hot flames of fury to lick at my insides again.

"Just answer me, goddammit! Tell me the truth! For once in your fucking life, just tell the truth!"

Lia met my eyes and at least had the decency to look both devastated and ashamed before cutting me to the core with a single word. "Yes."

A horrifying and unwelcome image of Lia in Jack's arms came unbidden, and betrayal curdled in my stomach. I suddenly pitched forward and heaved on the pristine snow. The pain was physical and overwhelming. I wrapped my arms around my waist in a pitiful attempt to hold myself together and keep my very soul from shattering. As I rocked back and forth on my knees, I became aware of a low keening sound. It took a moment before I realized the sound was coming from me.

Lia's blurry image swam into focus. As she faced me, the two of us kneeling in the snow, I imagined kicking her in the teeth, running her over with my car, and driving away without looking back. What I did instead was collapse against her chest and let her hold me as I wept.

I didn't know how long we remained that way, with Lia's body draped protectively over mine, but her small frame was useless against the powerful sobs that wracked me.

I curled into a ball and laid my head in her lap as I spluttered and hiccupped, my whole body shuddering. "Y-You lied to me. You've both lied to me for so long. I feel like such a fool."

Lia's cold fingers worked to brush back the hair that was stuck to my wet cheeks, and then her hot breath was on my ear. "He doesn't know," she whispered through her own tears. "Jack doesn't know."

I SAT STIFFLY ON THE edge of the overstuffed chair facing the couch and accepted the proffered glass of Bailey's on the rocks. I drained the contents in one gulp. Wordlessly, Lia refilled my glass before replenishing her own. She sat back with a sigh, tucking her short legs beneath her. I anxiously tapped my neat bare fingernails against the glass, fighting every frayed nerve in my body that was screaming for me to leave before Lia began speaking the words I could never un-hear. Words that would change everything. Words that would rewrite my history and irrevocably alter my past as I knew it. But I couldn't move any more than I could get warm. Ice flowed through my veins. Despite the roaring fire and the heavy blanket wrapped around my shoulders, my teeth chattered uncontrollably, and my body shook. I was temporarily outfitted in a soft pink gingham pair of Lia's flannel pajamas while my own clothes, saturated from our tussle on the snow-covered lawn, tumbled in the dryer.

My limbs were heavy, and my mind was numb, as if I'd been drugged. I sat silent and immobile. My eyes were fixed, unseeing, on the bottle of Bailey's standing sentry on the table between Lia and me. The slightest touch, even a single puff of air, might have turned me to dust.

"Robert," I finally mumbled, the word heavy in my mouth. I struggled to wrap my mind around the existence of this boy, Jack's son. My *stepson*. I tilted my empty glass at Lia, the remaining ice cubes clinking, demanding. She obligingly filled the stout glass and watched intently as I tipped my head back and sent the contents down my throat, lighting a fire in the pit of my stomach. I licked my lips and eyed her warily, recognizing her expression. Her mind was clicking away, the wheels turning and calculating. It dawned on me that she was trying to decide what to say, how much to tell me. "Just get it over with."

Her eyes were distant, her brow furrowed as she remembered. "It was an accident," Lia began.

Once the floodgates opened, the words spilled out, saturating the room, dragging me under, drowning me.

Lia took a deep breath. "I saw you kissing Joe at that party during beach week. You knew how I felt about him. I couldn't believe you'd do that to me. I saw the two of you kissing, and then I only saw red. I ran into the house, and it was chaos, everyone drinking and dancing and hooking up. I was furious. And horny. I hadn't been with anyone in months. I grabbed the first beer I could find and chugged it. And then I felt sick. My mouth started watering, and I knew I had to get to the bathroom before I hurled all over the floor."

I frowned and narrowed my eyes at Lia. "What does any of this have to do with Jack?" I wished she would get to the point and stop dragging it out.

Lia swirled the contents of her drink, took another sip, and averted her gaze. "The bathroom was pitch-black. I couldn't see a thing. When my eyes adjusted, I realized it wasn't a bathroom. I could just make out the shape of someone lying on a bed."

It was my turn to drink and look away. My insides contracted. I had a sick, sinking feeling I knew what was coming next.

"Anna, we don't have to..." Lia pleaded.

"Tell me," I demanded. "Just get it over with. I deserve to know."

Lia's shoulders slumped, and a fat tear splashed onto her pants. "I didn't know who it was. His face was turned away. I moved closer, tripped on something, stumbled against the bed. He grabbed my wrist and pulled me forward."

I hung on every sick, twisted sentence Lia uttered. Dread coiled into a violent ball in the pit of my stomach, and my body trembled. I needed to hear the rest, yet I couldn't bear to hear another word.

Lia's voice became devoid of emotion, her words a dull monotone as she continued. "I lost my balance and landed on top of him. I could feel him against me and decided a quick lay with... whoever it was... would make me feel better, take my mind off you and Joe. So I unzipped his shorts." Lia's voice cracked, and her lip trembled. "And he slurred something about knowing I'd come back. I had no idea what he was talking about." She swallowed and wiped away a tear with the back of her hand. She dropped her voice to a whisper. "He shoved the pillow away, and... I saw his face."

For a split second, Lia looked directly at me, shame and regret turning her eyes into hard, dark stones. Her face crumpled, and the tears started falling steadily. I was crying, too, but I couldn't feel the tears. My whole body was numb.

"He whispered your name," Lia admitted. "And all I remember is feeling jealous and angry and hurt. You and Jack weren't even together anymore. You'd dumped him. So what difference did it make? I was drunk and horny, and I didn't care that it was Jack. I just wanted to get laid."

I'd never hated anyone as much as I hated Lia at that moment. Her next words were like salt in an open, weeping wound.

"When Jack realized it wasn't you, he tried to push me away. But it was too late. I leaned over the edge of the bed and puked on the floor. I felt vile and disgusting. I hated myself. I wished I could take it back, but I couldn't. Jack passed out cold, and I got the hell out of there as fast as I could. I never told anyone."

THE SNOW HAD TURNED to sleet and rain. Lia tried to convince me to stay, to let the salt trucks work their magic on the slippery roads, but I refused. I couldn't breathe. I had to get out of there.

With a foggy brain and a heavy, aching heart, I somehow managed to navigate the slushy roads and pelting rain as the wipers beat back the sleet that pummeled the windshield. I didn't remember leaving Lia's house, and I didn't remember driving home—it was all a blur—but I did remember that night in June twenty-five years ago. Jack had been drinking heavily and reached for me. I'd avoided him and pushed him away. I remembered Joe kissing me and how wrong it had felt, and I remembered Lia seeing us and being pissed. It had all been a big misunderstanding, and I'd wanted to explain. But I hadn't been able to find Lia anywhere, and she'd never come home that night. Now I knew why.

As the miles ticked slowly by, I was consumed by a fathomless emptiness that ran deep and wide, like I'd been hollowed out from the inside, as if the soft, vulnerable parts of my being had been scooped out and tossed away. I longed for the blind happiness and naiveté I'd possessed just hours before, and I longed for Faith. I'd never felt more alone.

I ENTERED THE DARK, empty house and tossed my keys onto the hall table. The key ring slid across the slick, polished surface and came to rest in front of my wedding photo. I picked up the crystal frame and peered at Jack's loving, familiar face and his remarkable eyes. *Why didn't you tell me? Do you even remember?*

I replaced the photo and haphazardly kicked off my boots, heedless of the melting snow that dripped from the rubber soles, leaving a puddle on the hardwood. The kitchen, which faced south and was usually bright and sunny, was cloaked in darkness and gloom, compliments of the thick clouds that blanketed the winter sky. I crossed my arms against the chill and glanced at the clock.

It was 4:30. Jack and the girls weren't due home for another hour. *Enough time for a hot bath.*

I twisted the tap on full blast and stripped off my clothes, noticing for the first time since leaving Lia's house that I was still wearing her pink flannel pajamas. My initial instinct was to toss them into the laundry basket. Instead, I balled them up and marched naked through the house and into the garage, where I stuffed the garments deep inside the trash can and slammed the lid shut.

The hot, steamy air in the bathroom was a welcome respite for my gooseflesh. I dipped my toe into the scalding water and hissed through my teeth as I sank into the tub. The painful heat on my skin was a welcome exchange for the cold agony that filled my empty core. I leaned back and closed my eyes, but rather than the blissful escape I hoped for, the tub became a torturous think tank. I was helpless against the thoughts that crashed through my brain and stabbed at my heart. *It was too late... jealous and angry... just wanted to get laid... never told anyone... he doesn't know...*

I shuddered and bolted upright. Beads of sweat dotted my forehead and upper lip. It all made sense now: the note Lia had written, begging me to meet her at Keller's, insisting she had something important to tell me. The reason she had distanced herself from me and then disappeared altogether was suddenly so clear. She had been pregnant... with Jack's baby. The realization sent a fresh wave of pain and nausea crashing through me. *But did Jack really not know? The son he'd always wanted, he'd actually had all along. And how could Lia keep such a secret? How could she have kept Jack from his son all these years? How could she!* I raged inwardly then sank back against the tub, cowed by what might have happened if he had known.

Unable to relax—my mind and body jittery from the combination of adrenaline, despair, and confusion—I uncorked the plug and let the steaming bathwater drain from the tub. Without bothering to towel off, I stepped into a pair of sweatpants and tugged a sweatshirt over my head. I padded numbly to the kitchen, distracted and unmotivated, and scrapped my original plans to broil tuna steaks for dinner. I tossed the fish back into the freezer and retrieved a frozen pizza instead. I preheated the oven, opened a can of black olives, and set to chopping raw vegetables. In the silence of the kitchen, the sudden chime of the oven signaling it had reached the proper temperature startled me, and I pressed the knife into the flesh of my finger instead of the stalk of celery.

"Shit!" I hollered and stuck the bleeding digit into my mouth. While I searched upstairs for a Band-Aid, all hell broke loose in the kitchen as my family tumbled into the house.

"Yay, pizza!" Helene yelled.

"Smells good in here," Jack commented.

"Mom, can Ashley come over? Dad said it's okay with him if it's okay with you," Evelyn bellowed.

With the arrival of the Family Circus, the house was restored to its usual chaotic state—bright, loud, and buzzing with energy. I slowly descended the stairs, stopping halfway to take in the scene. All the lights were on. Jack was hanging up his coat in the hall closet while the dogs danced around his legs. The girls opened and closed the refrigerator, pulling juice, grapes, and cheese from the shelves. Ev chatted on her cell phone, and Helene hastily unpacked her backpack and raced to the computer before Ev could call dibs. The sight of my family lit a small, dim glow of warmth and hope deep inside my body. I inhaled a deep, steadying breath and descended the remaining stairs.

"Hey," Jack said as I entered the kitchen. He slid his arm around my waist and kissed my cheek, which was still flushed from the bath.

I tensed beneath his touch.

Jack drew back and held me at arm's length, peering closely at my face. "You okay?"

"Of course," I lied, avoiding his eyes. "Why?"

"Because you only get this"—he leaned in to kiss the furrowed space between my brows—"when you're worried about something."

I shook my head and extracted myself from his embrace. The pizza still had two minutes to cook, but I ignored the timer and pulled the pie from the oven to cool.

"So can she, Mom?" Evelyn pressed.

"Can who what?"

"Can Ashley come over? She has the last *Twilight* movie on DVD, and I'm dying to see it."

"Sure," I said, welcoming the distraction. "If it's okay with your dad."

Evelyn frowned. "I already said it was okay with him—"

"Ooh, can I watch too?" Helene called from the living room.

"No!" Ev shouted.

"Girls!" Jack scolded. "Quiet down." He reached for the bowl of olives, plucked one from the dish, tossed it in the air, and caught it in his mouth.

An image of Robert doing the same exact thing with a ball of peanut butter blindsided me, and the pizza cutter I'd just pulled from the drawer slipped from my shaking fingers and clattered to the floor. I shrieked and jumped back from the cutter like it was a venomous snake about to strike. In my mind, I saw only shattered glass on tile rather than an intact pizza cutter spinning on hardwood.

The dogs hurried to my aid, disappointed to find only a harmless pizza cutter at my feet. Evelyn paused midsentence to stare wide-eyed, and Jack moved toward me, arm extended, just as Robert had done amidst the broken glass. I fled from the kitchen and locked myself in the powder room, where I buried my face in my hands. *What am I going to do? Should I tell Jack? And if I do, what will happen to my family?*

Jack knocked on the door, his voice thick with concern. "Anna?"

"I'm fine. I just need a minute." I wondered what Faith would have thought of this mess, and I was suddenly consumed by longing for my friend. "I knew I shouldn't have gone to that damn reunion," I muttered, my eyes cast heavenward.

When I finally emerged from the powder room, my family, who only minutes before had been laughing and happily chatting, had fallen silent as they'd gathered around the dinner table. I carefully arranged my face into a pleasant expression and helped myself to a slice of pizza I had no appetite for.

"So, tell me about your day," I entreated.

The girls eagerly complied, their sentences tangling together as they regaled Jack and me with detailed anecdotes, restoring the normal vivacity to our family meal.

After dinner, as I bagged the leftover veggies and Jack washed the pizza tray, I noticed Helene standing in the center of the kitchen, turning in a slow circle, arms akimbo.

"Looking for something?" I asked.

"Yeah. The cookies," she replied, her accusing eyes scanning the countertops. "Didn't you bake with your friend today?"

I whipped my head around to scrutinize Jack's face, as if a mere reference to Lia might trigger some reaction from him, but he simply kept scrubbing. "Yeah," he concurred. "A chocolate-dipped coconut macaroon would sure hit the spot."

"Oh," I said with a shrug. "Would you believe I forgot them? Left them right on her countertop." I couldn't bring myself to say her name.

"Mo-om!" Helene admonished, extending my name to two peeved syllables.

"Really, Mom?" Ev piped up, sticking her head around the corner, her cell phone pressed to her ear again. "Ash and I were looking forward to a cookie feast during the movie."

"Well, then, I guess you'll have to settle for Chips Ahoy," I replied nastily and stalked out of the kitchen, leaving them all to stare in slack-jawed disappointment.

IN BED THAT NIGHT, I lay on my back, staring up at the ceiling, listening to Jack breathing deeply and peacefully beside me, and I wondered, for what must have been the millionth time, what I should do.

If I tell him, it will crush him. Jack was a stand-up guy. If he knew he had a son, he would want to do the right thing. *And what, exactly, would that be?*

But this newfound knowledge I possessed was too powerful, too huge and dangerous. I feared it might eat me alive if I kept it inside. I needed to talk to someone. *But who?* Tears filled my eyes as I thought of Faith. If she were there, she would know what to say, what to do. I rolled onto my side, my back to Jack. I'd never kept anything from him, and this secret had already become an insurmountable wall between us. *Keeping something like this from him makes me no better than Lia. It makes me a liar, just like her.* And that was exactly what this would be—a lie of omission.

But what will the truth cost me? I curled into a ball and squeezed my knees to my chest. *I can't do it. I can't tell him.* It would devastate him to know he'd had a son all this time, a son who, like him, hadn't known his father. I couldn't imagine hurting him like that, causing him so much pain and regret. Somehow, I would have to find the strength to bury that information deep within my soul and pretend

I'd never seen that boy with Jack's eyes or heard the unbelievable, horrifying words Lia had uttered. It was a secret I must keep. The burden was now mine to bear just as it had been Lia's burden for so many years. I resented that it was a burden we now shared. But I resolved, for the sake of my family, that the truth must be left untold.

CHAPTER 36
February 2015

I was engrossed in an article on the reintroduction of gray wolves to the Northern Rockies when an insistent knocking trampled on my solitude. Miffed by the intrusion, I stalked to the front door, prepared to berate a trespassing solicitor, and was shocked to find Lia standing on my doorstep with a half-dozen yellow roses clutched in her small gloved hand. I slammed the door in her face.

"Anna?" she called, knocking again.

I stood with my back pressed against the door. My pulse hammered, and blood thundered in my ears. Immediately after the shock of discovering the truth about Robert, Lia had let things simmer. But since Christmas, she'd been calling incessantly, leaving messages that I promptly deleted and ignored. I never imagined she would show up at my house.

"I'm not leaving until you talk to me."

My mind raced. I made a snap decision and grabbed my coat from the closet and my keys and bag from the table. "Fine!" I shouted, storming out the front door. "But not here."

"Where, then?" she asked, having the gall to sound annoyed.

"Follow me."

I stomped to my car, backed out of the garage, and floored the gas pedal. I was pleased to hear tiny bits of gravel ping against Lia's Lexus as I peeled out of the driveway. Lia watched slack-jawed from the porch. I knew she had her beloved car detailed monthly, and I hoped to hell I'd chipped the pristine white paint.

I had no idea where I was going. Fumbling blindly through my bag, I located my phone. I didn't want to call Jack on his cell—I knew he would be able to hear the lie in my voice—so I called home and left a message telling him I'd gone out to run some errands.

As I drove down Main Street, with Lia following closely behind, the bright-green awning of the Junction Tavern caught my eye. Recalling that the Junction served breakfast all day, I hastily steered into the lot, parked the car, and stalked into the tavern.

"How many?" the hostess asked.

"Two," I said. The bells on the tavern door jingled as it opened behind me, ushering Lia in on a gust of cold, dry air.

"This way."

Lia and I sat glaring into each other's eyes as the waitress poured ink-black coffee and withdrew a notepad from her apron. "What can I getcha?" she asked, her wrinkly, weathered hands clutching the notepad and a pen.

"Just coffee for me," Lia said.

I almost ordered a mimosa but, deciding it was too festive, ordered a Bloody Mary instead. The tart drink would complement the bitter tang in my mouth. The waitress sighed and turned on her heel, undoubtedly displeased that we were not ordering a proper breakfast while occupying a prime table in her section during the busy brunch hour.

"How dare you show up at my house like that?" I whispered through clenched teeth.

"You wouldn't take my calls," Lia replied in kind.

I anxiously tapped a sugar packet against the scarred wooden table. "Why are you here? What do you want?"

"I want to talk."

I stared at her, dumbfounded. "I have nothing to say to you."

Lia lowered her eyes and her voice. "I'm sorry, Anna. So sorry. But I miss you."

I stood abruptly from the table and nearly knocked over my chair. "I don't care how you feel!" I snatched my coat from the back of my chair and shoved my arms into the sleeves. "We're done here!"

"Anna, wait!" Lia shouted. "Don't go!"

Several nearby diners gaped at us, their expressions curious and eager, deftly attuned to the impending drama. I flushed, horrified by the sudden realization that someone I knew might be among the patrons. My eyes darted around the dim, wood-paneled tavern, searching for familiar faces. Finding none, I sank heavily onto the chair and crossed my arms and legs defensively.

Lia slowly lowered herself into her chair, her eyes trained on my face, as if any sudden movement might set me off. "I know I don't deserve your forgiveness—"

"Damn right you don't!"

"But just hear me out. Okay?"

I ground my molars and gave a curt nod.

"I made a mistake," she continued. "A huge mistake. One I've lived with my whole life. When I missed my period after beach week, I didn't think anything of it. It wasn't unusual for me to miss one sometimes. It didn't even occur to me that I could be pregnant. I hadn't been with anyone in months until..."

My nostrils flared, and my eyes blazed. I dared her to utter Jack's name.

Lia shook her head and continued, a hesitant hitch to her voice. "But when I missed it again the next month, I knew something was wrong. When the pregnancy test came back positive, I panicked. And then it hit me whose it was." Regret rendered Lia's lovely face quite ugly.

I opened my mouth to protest. Lia had slept with so many guys in high school. *Am I just supposed to believe her?* Maybe the baby wasn't Jack's. Maybe she was lying. Then I thought back to that fateful day nearly three months ago, to that boy with Jack's eyes suddenly appearing in Lia's kitchen, and my heart constricted. I couldn't deny what I'd seen when I'd peered into that boy's face. He was definitely Jack's. I clenched my jaw and leaned heavily against the chair, and my shoulders hunched forward.

"Sure I can't getcha anything else?" our waitress prodded as she delivered my Bloody Mary.

Lia and I shook our heads. The waitress frowned, slapped the bill facedown on the table, and scurried off to serve more profitable patrons.

Lia and I sat in silence. She stared into the dark depths of her coffee while I hazarded a sip of my drink. The tart, potent spices burned my throat, and the acidity made my already queasy stomach churn in protest. I shoved the drink away in disgust.

"I didn't know what to do." Lia's eyes were pleading, anguished. "I considered getting an abortion. Then I thought about my own mother, who'd been in the same situation—a pregnant, unwed teenager—and how if she'd chosen to abort me... well, I wouldn't exist. And while my life's not *perfect"*—she spat the word at me—"I'm still glad to be *alive*. So I couldn't do it. No matter the cost." Lia jutted her chin in her familiar defiant way, hardening her features.

My shoulders slumped forward. Lia exhaled loudly and leaned back in her chair, her defeated posture mirroring mine. "I didn't know how to tell you. And I knew you'd think I was lying." She shot me a sharp, accusing glance. "So I wrote that letter, the one I gave you when you helped me move into my dorm. I knew I had to tell you to your face, but I was scared. I also didn't want to completely blindside you."

At that, I let out a loud, derisive snort and recrossed my arms.

"So I wrote that I had something important to tell you. I hoped it would prepare you to expect something... significant."

My patience was wearing thin. "Lia—"

She held up her hand. "Let me finish."

I glared at her. *Let's get this over with once and for all.*

"My plan was for us to meet at Keller's, and I would tell you. I knew you'd be furious, that you'd hate me. Hell, I hated myself. I regretted betraying you, and I regretted taking advantage of Jack when he was hurt and vulnerable and thought I was you. But I couldn't change what happened. I tried to console myself with the fact that you and Jack weren't together anymore, that he wasn't your boyfriend when it happened. But after I gave you the letter, you never called. You went off to Ohio, and then two months later, you wrote the words that slayed me—that you and Jack were back together. You wrote that he was 'the one.' And I knew it was true. You and Jack were meant to be together, and I'd be damned if I was going to ruin your happiness. You loved Jack, Anna, but I loved *you*. I couldn't bear the thought of hurting you. So I bolted. I moved to Miami, and it seemed like the perfect solution. Things were going well at the inn. But then Uncle Roberto took an unexpected turn for the worse and died suddenly of a massive heart attack."

Lia, always a good storyteller, had my attention. Her tale had so entranced me that I'd nearly forgotten her reason for her telling it. Remembering, I narrowed my eyes and held her gaze as she continued speaking.

"Aunt Ivy, Benita—the innkeeper—and I were devastated. But we were a good team. We persevered. I was happy in Miami with my aunt and my son. Robert was my sunshine, my reason for being. It was impossible to imagine my life without him."

A dark shadow passed over Lia's face, twisting her lovely features into a mask of pain and despair. "Then everything changed," she whispered. "I remember it like it was yesterday, the sirens, the sick feeling in my gut. I ran from the inn, toward the flashing lights and the people hovering near the intersection." Her eyes filled with tears at the memory, and she continued her tale in a soft monotone. "My aunt was broken and bleeding in the middle of the street. The car that hit her was flipped on its side, its windshield cracked. Another car had jumped the curb and crashed into a building. Smoke was coming out of the hood, and a horn was blaring. People were crying and screaming. A paramedic checked my aunt's pulse and shook his head. Another one draped a cloth over her body."

I resisted the urge to cover my ears, as if I could squeeze Lia's words—and the sounds of horns and sirens and wailing—from my head. I reached for her hand, but she pulled away. Her face hardened to stone.

"They say she died instantly. Without pain." Her voice caught in her throat, but she straightened her spine and continued. "I graduated from Miami a month later, went through the motions of walking across the stage, accepting my diploma. Aunt Ivy had willed the Conch Out to me. I had a job lined up with Lockheed Martin, and Benita to look after Robert, but without my aunt, Miami could never be home. Lockheed granted my request for a transfer. I packed everything I owned into Aunt Ivy's car, which she'd also willed to me, and headed north. I rented an apartment near Baltimore and started my new job with Lockheed. A month later, I met Neil."

"Well, that's quite a story, Lia. But I really don't understand what any of it has to do with me." I rose from my chair and hooked my purse over my arm. I'd done my part. I'd let her say her piece, and now there was nothing more to say. As Lia had pointed out, neither of us could change what had happened. *What more does she want from me?*

"Don't you see? I made a huge mistake, and I'm so sorry for what happened. But I took responsibility for my actions, and we all went on to live our lives. I made things right the only way I knew how."

"By lying? By keeping Jack's son from him all these years? By denying Robert the opportunity to know his real father? No wonder he hates you," I said, going in for the kill. It was a low blow.

"He doesn't hate me. That was—"

"Another lie. Of course."

"What would you rather I had done, Anna?" Lia hissed through clenched teeth, her tiny fists balled on the tabletop. "Would you really have wanted me to tell Jack about his *son*? Do you really think he still would have married you?"

"He sure as hell wouldn't have married *you*!" I retaliated, but hearing Lia give voice to my own fears and doubts shook me to the core. It was as if the ground was shifting beneath my feet, tilting me off balance.

"Jack loved you, Anna, but he's an honorable man. His conscience would have ripped him apart, tearing him between his love for you and his sense of obligation and responsibility toward his child. He would have wanted to do the right thing, and you know it. Maybe he *would* have married me. How would you have liked that? Is that what you would have wanted?"

My arm shot out, and I struck her, hard. The flat of my hand connected with her cheek, and her head snapped sideways. Lia covered her face. The apple of her cheek bloomed magenta beneath her palm. My own hand was stinging from the blow. My arm was not my own—it belonged to a stranger, a soap-opera actress. I'd never slapped anyone in the face before.

Lia's eyes, wide and watery, were on mine. Suddenly, I was overcome with hilarity, like a madwoman whose final tether to reality had snapped. I doubled over, hysterical, and my body heaved with inappropriate laughter. For once, I'd rendered Lia speechless. I howled even louder.

The manager appeared at our table, with our scowling waitress at his side, and asked us to leave, seeing as how we were both "quite finished with our brunch." His nasal voice and snooty comment, so egregiously out of place in the blue-collar tavern, made me positively convulse.

"Quite finished!" I bellowed.

Lia, jolted from her stupor by my outburst, suddenly chimed in. "Yes, quite!" She burst into a fit of giggles, and the two of us stumbled from the tavern, gasping for breath.

Outside, the cold February air was like smelling salts to my senses, snapping me back to reality and leaving me limp and exhausted. I sank onto a nearby bench, my limbs like lead. Lia sat beside me, our knees touching. She held both of my hands in her own. My larger, capable hands dwarfed her smaller, childlike ones.

"Jack never loved you," I murmured, struggling to block from my mind the images of Jack and Lia together that constantly invaded my head and tortured me with their very existence.

"I know. But I still believe he would have struggled to do the right thing, whatever that was to him. And I'm pretty damn sure it would have broken your heart and destroyed your happiness to know Jack and I had a child together."

I remained silent, my eyes fixed on my lap, my breath coming out in small, visible puffs. A shiver ran through my body, and I pulled my hands from Lia's grasp.

"Thanks for hearing me out," she said. "I'll go now."

I watched with a heavy heart as Lia gathered her coat around her and walked away, her small frame hunched against the sharp breeze. Part of me was relieved to see her go—hopefully out of my life for good this time—and part of me longed to call her back.

What am I supposed to do now? How can I simply go on with my life, as Lia had done for so many years, pretending not to know what happened, pretending that Robert doesn't exist? The burden of this secret, this knowledge, accidentally though it may have been discovered, was now mine to carry too. It was my secret to share with Lia. The weight of it felt so unfair and overwhelming.

My phone suddenly buzzed against my hip, making me jump. I reached into my coat pocket to retrieve the phone and glanced at the screen. My editor was calling. *How can I possibly focus on work at a time like this?* I saved the message and willed my frazzled mind to remember to send a reply later. My screen saver appeared, a family photo taken during the holidays. I let my eyes sweep over the image, memorizing every detail: Kathryn's radiant smile, as if she were lit from within; Evelyn's mischievous bunny ears floating above Kathryn's head; the lively glint in Helene's eyes and the smudge of chocolate at the corner of her mouth from the

buckeyes she'd just polished off; Jack kissing me on the cheek, his arm slung around my shoulders, holding me close.

A lump rose in my throat as I imagined how my life might have been different if Lia had revealed her secret all those years ago, if Jack had known he'd had a son. *How would the course of our lives have been altered?* Perhaps my three precious girls wouldn't even exist. The mere notion sent a chill down my spine. I gazed across the street to where the remains of a mangled takeout box lay. The abandoned Styrofoam container had been run over by a car, and its state of wreckage seemed symbolic of what my life might have been like if Lia had made a different choice. I gazed at the image of my family, my whole world, my every reason for being—happy, healthy, and laughing—and true forgiveness cast its first ray of light.

I reflected on all the recent sleepless nights I'd lain awake in bed, wavering between honesty and secrecy, the truth tormenting my conscience and weighing on my heart. I knew it was a lie of omission to keep such a devastating secret from Jack. But night after night, I bit back the words, sharp and toxic, like tiny sea urchins that pierced my tongue and scratched my throat as I swallowed them whole, choosing to remain silent. And now, gazing at the image of my family, I knew I'd made the right choice.

A sudden rush of understanding and compassion, thick and raw, engulfed me. For the first time, it dawned on me that Lia's choices—every choice she'd made since discovering she was pregnant—were driven by a selflessness that I was just beginning to comprehend. What Lia had done, she'd done for Jack and me, so that we could move forward with our lives and live happily ever after, unburdened by past mistakes. And for Robert, she'd chosen life—his life over her own—and given him the best one she could, all at the expense of her own happiness.

I bolted upright from the bench, my knees shaking, my lips quivering. "Lia!" I shouted. She was in the parking lot and had just opened her car door.

Lia paused, her back to me, then turned slowly, her face expressionless.

I sprinted from the bench and stood gasping a few car lengths away from her. "Thank you. For telling me. And for... well... thank you."

She stood like a statue, unmoving. One corner of her mouth twitched upward, the ghost of a smile haunting her lips, before she ducked into her car.

CHAPTER 37
April 2015

I woke with a pounding headache. Despite the beautiful spring day, which dawned sunny and warm, I shivered beneath my comforter, my muscles achy and weak. Easing myself from the bed, I was struck with a wave of nausea that sent me sprinting to the bathroom. I made it just in time. With a trembling hand, I lowered the toilet lid over the remnants of last night's Mexican dinner and flushed it away. Sitting on the edge of the sunken tub with my head in my hands, my skin flushed and clammy, I waited for the dizziness to pass.

Why today? Jack and I were heading to Virginia Tech for the spring family weekend at Tech. I'd been counting the days to our return to Blacksburg, not only because we would get to spend time with Kathryn—who we hadn't seen in four months since she was home for Christmas—but we were also going to meet Jay. He was no longer just Kathryn's boyfriend but, as she'd confessed over the holidays, the man she was in love with.

The absolute certainty and unusual candor of Kathryn's confession had surprised me at first. But when I remembered that beautiful fall day in October when Jack and I had hiked Dragon's Tooth with her—the light in Kathryn's eyes, the warmth and wonder in her voice when she'd first told us about Jay—I realized I'd already known she was in love. And I wanted to meet the man who had captured her heart.

I tottered back to bed and lay down atop the covers. No longer shivering, my fiery skin had exploded into a drenching full-body sweat.

Jack entered the room, whistling. One glance at me, and his broad smile vanished. "You look awful."

"Gee, thanks," I muttered.

Jack placed one large palm on my forehead, and his frown deepened, etching lines of concern into his skin. "You're burning up."

With what felt like enormous effort, I pushed myself up to a sitting position and leaned back against the pillows. "I really want to go," I whimpered.

"We'll reschedule," Jack decided. "I'll call Kathryn and ask her if there's another weekend that would be good for us to visit."

I nodded weakly as Jack left the room, undoubtedly in search of Kathryn's phone number. I didn't have the energy to beckon him back and tell him I knew the number by heart or that Kathryn was on speed dial on my cell phone, which lay in the drawer of my bedside table. I leaned my head back and closed my eyes.

WHEN I FELT THE PRESSURE of Jack's hand on my swaddled thigh, I opened my eyes and blinked against the new brightness that lit the room. I glanced at the clock and saw that it was 9:22! Though I was certain only minutes had passed, it had actually been almost two hours.

"Jack!" I exclaimed, my voice raspy. "We were supposed to leave twenty minutes ago. Why didn't you wake me?"

"You're not going anywhere. You're sick, remember?"

"I'm fine," I lied, swinging my legs over the edge of the bed and regretting it instantly. I rushed to the bathroom and knelt in front of the toilet yet again. My empty stomach churned and cramped, ejecting little more than a thin stream of bile for all its effort before devolving into a series of dry heaves that left my body exhausted and trembling. I wobbled back to the bed, where Jack tucked me in like a child and kissed me on the forehead.

"By the time I got off the phone with Kathryn, you were knocked out. Thought you might need these when you woke." Jack inclined his head toward the table. A glass of water, a pack of saltines, and a bottle of ibuprofen stood on my nightstand.

"Thanks," I said, helping myself to the ibuprofen and a few cautious sips of water, hoping it would stay down. "So what did Kathryn say about another date?"

Jack averted his eyes and resumed rubbing my leg through the covers. "Not 'til the semester's over, babe. She's working next weekend, and then she'll be studying for finals." Jack said the words so quietly, I could barely hear him.

"So we won't see her until June!" I wailed.

"I'm sorry. I know how much you miss her."

That's the understatement of the year. "You could still go," I ventured.

Though the suggestion made perfect sense—there was no reason Jack shouldn't go to Tech and spend the weekend with Kathryn—it still pained me. Jack and I had always made the trek to Blacksburg together. And if I were being totally honest, the idea of Jack getting to see Kathryn while I was stuck at home, sick in bed, filled me with irrational jealousy. I couldn't help it that I was feeling completely selfish and sorry for myself. I tugged absently at a loose thread on the hem of my nightshirt.

"I think I should stay here and look after you," Jack argued, likely sensing my inner turmoil.

"No," I whispered, shaking my head. "You should go." My watery eyes bored into his. "There's no sense in you staying here." I could see the relief on Jack's face despite his effort to hide it. "If you leave now, you can still make it in time for lunch," I urged.

"Are you sure?" he asked, his expression cautiously optimistic. "You'll be all right?"

"I'll probably just sleep most of the day anyway. Tell Kathryn I miss her and love her."

"I will." Jack kissed me on the forehead again and stood to go. "I'll leave a note for the girls to check in on you when they get home from school. Get some rest."

That wouldn't be a problem. My eyelids were already growing heavy.

I WAS CURLED UP ON the couch, watching *Seinfeld* reruns with Ev and Helene, when the phone rang. "Hey there," I whispered, my throat still tender.

"How's my hot mama doing?"

"Ha!" I exclaimed through a bark of laughter that dissolved into a hacking cough. "Though I guess hot would be a somewhat accurate description."

"Still running a fever?" Jack asked.

"Yep. Though not as high as it was this morning. But enough about me. I want to hear about your day. How's Kathryn?"

She's fine. We met for lunch at Macado's, and then she took me to Harrisfield Plantation. We got to tour the house, and a period interpreter described life on the eve of the American Revolution."

"Sounds like fun," I lied. History held little allure for me.

"Oh, and I met Jay today."

I sat up straighter on the couch, my heart suddenly racing. "*The* Jay?"

"The one and only. He seems like a really nice guy."

I was simultaneously excited that Jack got to meet Jay and envious that he'd met him without me. "Details, stat!" I practically shouted into the phone and instantly regretted it as my head and throat throbbed in protest.

"It started raining while we were at the plantation, so instead of hiking around Pandapas, we went to the BreakZone to shoot pool. Jay met us there. I cleaned up on billiards, but Jay totally schooled me in darts."

"That's all fine and dandy, Jack, but what's he *like*?" I demanded.

Jack's tone grew serious. "He's a good guy, Anna. Intelligent, respectful, witty. He seems really into Kathryn, and she's obviously crazy about him."

My eyes welled with tears. My baby girl, my firstborn, was in love. I tried to picture her and Jay in my mind and struggled to create the image. "What does he look like?" To my frustration, the only photos I'd seen were from Kathryn and Jay's trips to Norris Lake and Snowshoe. Their hats, sunglasses, and ski goggles made it impossible for me to form a clear image in my mind.

Jack chuckled. "According to Kathryn, he's 'hot.' Does that help?"

I wasn't about to let him off the hook that easily. "Specifics, please," I prodded.

"He's tall. Not quite as tall as me but maybe six feet? Dark hair. Fit. The kind of guy you'd picture Kathryn going for."

An image began to take shape in my mind. "So then what? After darts?"

"We headed to Backstreets for pizza and beer."

"Beer?" Kathryn wasn't yet twenty.

"Well, Jay and I had one."

"Jay's old enough to drink beer?"

"Yeah. I think he's a year or two older than Kat."

"Oh. Then what?"

"It stopped raining, so we walked to the rec fields to catch the rugby game. Tech versus Clemson."

Clemson. My brother would have loved seeing his alma mater in action. I missed him. He and his wife, Amy, had recently moved to Colorado Springs and were in the process of adopting a brother and sister from Ecuador. Too much time had passed since we'd seen them. I made a mental note to give Jeff a call as soon as I was feeling better.

"Anna? You still there?"

"Yeah, sorry." I shook my head and ordered my fever-addled brain to keep up with the conversation. "Anyway, since when is Kathryn into rugby?"

"Apparently, a handful of guys from Jay's water polo team play. It was pretty fun to watch. Those guys are hardcore!"

I swallowed my envy and smiled at Jack's enthusiasm. Clearly, he'd had a good day. And it was nice that he was getting to spend some one-on-one time with Kathryn. "So what are you doing now?"

"The kids started talking about heading downtown, so I begged off, waved the white flag."

"What's the matter, old man? Can't hang with the college kids?"

"Not a chance. I'm beat. And Kathryn has another full day lined up for us tomorrow: farmers' market, hiking McCoy Falls, then a tailgate before the lacrosse game against Maryland. Big rivalry, apparently. Jay's meeting us after work for dinner and a concert on the green."

"Sounds like fun." I sighed, fighting against the jealousy that was rearing its ugly head again. Feeling sorry for myself, I coughed loudly, trying to incite a little sympathy.

"It would be a lot more fun if you were here," Jack soothed.

A comfortable silence lingered between us before a sudden genuine coughing fit wracked my body. *Karma, baby.*

BY SUNDAY, I FELT MARKEDLY better, aside from the lingering weakness in my limbs and the congestion that had taken up residence in my lungs. My fever had broken during the night, and I'd woken in the wee hours of the morning in a pool of my own sweat, a development that drove me to my first shower in nearly three days. The shower had the excellent effect of restoring a good bit of my humanity. It was as if I'd literally scrubbed the sickness from my body along with the perspiration.

Jack called at ten that morning to let me know he and Kathryn had just finished breakfast and that he would be on the road within the hour. Though his words were straightforward, he'd sounded rushed, eager to get off the phone. I paced the house, waiting for what felt like an eternity for Jack to get home and shed some light on his mysterious call.

Five hours later, Jack swept into the house, deposited his suitcase at the foot of the stairs, and joined me on the couch, where I sat mindlessly flipping through a *Yoga Journal* magazine. He seemed flustered and agitated. His expression alternated between a goofy grin and a worried grimace. I fought the urge to grill him but decided he would tell me what was on his mind when he was ready.

It wasn't until after we'd finished our Chinese takeout—wonton soup only for me—said goodnight to the girls, and retired to our own bedroom that Jack finally opened up.

"I have something to tell you," he said, flashing a quick smile before snatching it back, carefully rearranging his features into a neutral expression.

"I know. I can tell. The fact that you haven't told me yet is killing me. Should I be worried?"

"No, not at all. I didn't mean to worry you." He took my hands in his. "It's just that, well, what I have to say will probably come as a bit of a shock. I know it took me by surprise."

"Okay..." I braced myself for the worst. My traitorous mind tormented me with thoughts of Lia calling Jack and revealing her secret. *Our* secret. So far, I'd held tight to my resolve to keep mum about Robert's existence. I was confident that it was the right decision for my family to spare us all from the inevitable heartbreak and pain the truth would inflict. But the fact that Lia still held the power to unravel my family with a single phone call and a few whispered words rattled me to the core.

Jack led me to the cozy sitting area in our bedroom. "You might want to sit down for this," he suggested. The color drained from his face, leaving him unusually pale. "In fact, I'll sit with you."

Perched on the edge of the chaise lounge, we faced each other, our knees touching. Jack grasped my hands, drew them both to his mouth, and kissed my knuckles, which had blanched with anxiety in his grip. His lips were warm and determined. The unexpected intimate gesture caused an exquisite mixture of fear and desire to course through me. I squeezed my eyes shut and clenched my teeth, stopping short of grinding my molars, which was like nails on a chalkboard to Jack.

"Anna, it was an interesting weekend. I really wish you'd been there."

I nodded, encouraging him to move along and get to the point.

"Jay seems like a great guy."

"So you said."

"I think you'll really like him."

"Well, hopefully I'll get to meet him soon."

"Oh, I think you will," Jack replied too quickly.

"You think Kathryn is really in love with him, then?"

"Definitely. More to the point, I think the feeling is mutual. In fact, I know it is."

I tilted my head. "How do you—"

"Anna," Jack interrupted, his words suddenly coming in a rush. "Jay asked for my blessing. He wants to ask Kathryn to marry him."

"What!" I gasped, and my compromised, congested lungs burned, frantic for air. "They're too young! Kathryn's only nineteen! What's the hurry? She has to finish school!" I spluttered.

"They won't get married until after she graduates," Jack explained.

"He told you this?"

"Yes. But he does plan to propose. And soon."

I stood and began to pace the room, anxiously gnawing a hangnail. "But they've only been dating, what, a few months?"

"A year, actually."

My mind was reeling. "What did you say to him?"

"I was taken so off guard. Though it's not nearly as surprising when you see them together—"

"Jack!" I stopped pacing, and my eyes bored into his. "What did you *say*?"

"I said I wanted to talk with you first, but if it were up to me—and it's really not—I'd say yes. So yeah. I guess I gave him my blessing."

I realized I'd been holding my breath and exhaled loudly in one long, quavering rush. "Are you crazy? How could you, Jack?" I cried, a sob catching in my throat. "She's only nineteen, for God's sake."

"Anna, it's an antiquated notion, don't you think? Jay asking me? It was simply a kindness, a gesture of respect. He and Kathryn are adults. They don't need our permission to get married."

He was right, of course. Shocked into silence, I knotted and twisted my hands in my lap. My brain was bombarded with a highlight reel of images: Kathryn staying on campus last summer, Kathryn going to Florida for spring break, Kathryn going skiing with friends, Kathryn headed back to campus early to celebrate New Year's. Only now this boy, this *Jay*, was present in every image, and I realized, in retrospect, he'd been there all along. And though I'd known Kathryn had a boyfriend—and she'd admitted that she loved him—it had never dawned on me that it was so *serious*. I sank onto the chaise and dropped my head into my hands.

Jack's fingers, insistent beneath my chin, urged my head upward, tilting my face toward his. "I was younger than Kathryn when I knew I wanted to spend the rest of my life with you."

"But I haven't even met him yet," I argued, my voice pitiful to my own ears.

"But you will."

My vision was swimming, making my lap blurry. A tear escaped from the corner of my eye and splashed onto the back of my hand. My palm was sweaty against my bare leg. "I just don't want her to rush into anything. I don't want her to make a mistake, one she might regret."

"She's going to make mistakes," Jack reasoned. "It's part of life. But Kathryn's an adult now, Anna. They're her mistakes to make."

I looked away, swiping at the tears that streaked my cheeks.

"I think you'll feel differently once you've met him." Jack rubbed a soothing palm up and down my back. "If he's truly the guy he seems to be—and I think Kathryn's a pretty good judge of character—then maybe it's not a mistake. Maybe it's meant to be."

"You're right," I murmured. "This is just so hard. It's so sudden and unexpected." I reached for a tissue and blew my nose. "I wish Faith were here."

"I'm here," Jack reminded me. "We're a team, remember?"

"I know." I lowered my eyes and pressed my shaking hands to my thighs.

Jack pulled me close and wrapped his strong arms around me, and I melted into his comforting embrace. Peeking up at his face, I found in his eyes the reassurance and strength I needed. "So our baby's getting married?"

"Well, Jay hasn't asked her yet, but I'm pretty sure she'll accept. So, yes, our baby's getting married. And we should be happy for her. We need to give her our support and, since we're being asked, our blessing."

The lump that had risen in my throat prevented me from speaking. I pressed my face into Jack's chest and hugged him tighter, willing myself to be happy for Kathryn and resolving to meet Jay as soon as possible. I would call Kathryn and get a date on the calendar. Having a specific goal to set my sights on made me feel the tiniest bit better, a little more in control.

"Everything's going to be okay." Jack kissed the top of my head. "I've got some work to catch up on. You okay if I go hole up in the office for a bit?"

"Sure," I murmured, finding my voice again. "I think I'll take a bath." Although I'd already showered that morning, a hot bath suddenly beckoned. I needed some time to think, to absorb everything Jack had said.

"That sounds like a good idea," Jack agreed, kissing me again before retreating to the office.

In the bathroom, I stepped out of my underwear and tugged my sports bra over my head. I tossed both into the laundry bin and turned the tap on hot. I added a dash of lavender bath salt and, when the tub was almost full, lowered myself into the scalding water. I wrapped my arms around my legs and rested my forehead on my knees, hissing through my teeth as the water seared my skin. It felt like penance for not being happier for my daughter.

But despite Kathryn's obvious joy and contentment over the past year and Jack's stamp of approval on our prospective son-in-law—*son-in-law!*—my maternal instincts were going haywire, sounding the alarm and triggering a sense of foreboding that I couldn't shake. Despite the heat rising from my skin, I shuddered beneath the warm water. I reached forward, opened the drain, and stepped out of the tub into the steamy embrace of the bathroom. From the rack behind the door, I retrieved a towel and wrapped it tightly around me, wishing the soft, absorbent fibers could wick away the unease that lingered beneath my skin.

CHAPTER 38
June 2015

We pulled into Kathryn's parking lot just past noon and knocked on door 2A. On the other side of the door, I could hear Hokie's nails clatter on the linoleum as he sprinted down the hall. A shadow passed over the peephole, followed by the rattle of the chain and click of the bolt before Kathryn flung open the door.

She flew into our arms. "I'm so happy to see you!" We embraced in the hallway, the three of us momentarily locked in a group hug before stepping apart.

Kathryn was more radiant than ever. Her cream-colored halter top complemented her glowing, sun-kissed skin. Her dark, shiny hair spilled over her bare shoulders.

"Aw, sweetie, I've missed you so much. You look beautiful." Despite my best efforts to remain stoic, tears welled in my eyes.

"Come in!" Kathryn invited, surprisingly misty-eyed as well. "I just made a pitcher of sweet tea." Clearly, living in southwestern Virginia was rubbing off on her. Not only had she made sweet tea, but she was dangerously close to pronouncing it "tay." *Just like Faith used to.*

"I'd love some," I replied, watching as she poured, her back to me. I gazed at her lovely, flawless skin and the flat, lightly toned space between her delicate shoulder blades, the space I used to rub when she was little. My palm would gently circle that very spot to help soothe her to sleep. She handed me a tall glass filled with the sweet amber liquid and tapped the rim of her own glass against mine, making the ice cubes clink.

"Cheers!" she exclaimed, her wide smile transforming her face into a mask of pure joy. "Dad? Tea?" she called.

Jack and Hokie, who'd greeted us with his rope in his mouth, had retreated to the living room for an energetic round of tug. "I'll take a beer," Jack said. Catching my glance, he added, "What? It's five o'clock somewhere, isn't it?"

Clearly, it hadn't crossed his mind that Kathryn, still two months shy of her twentieth birthday, shouldn't *have* beer in her fridge. I realized, of course, this was completely unrealistic thinking on my part.

Not skipping a beat, Kathryn cracked the refrigerator door and peered inside. "Corona or Yeungling?" she inquired. "Oh, and we still have a few Dogfish Head too."

"I'll take one of those," Jack replied, referring to the latter.

Kathryn expertly poured the brew with just the right amount of foam into the frosted glass. *When did she learn to do that?*

We sipped our drinks and laughed and chatted as if our lives weren't about to change. On the phone, Kathryn had hinted at having some news to share, her perky, upbeat words hanging over my head like an ominous cloud. For me, this day couldn't have come a moment too soon. It was high time I met Jay and, if possible, impressed upon both of them that time was on their side. There was no need to rush into anything.

"You guys hungry?" Kathryn asked, glancing at her watch.

"Starved," Jack replied.

"Good. I told Jay we'd meet him at Macado's at one thirty."

Tiny pangs of hunger had been nagging me for the past hour, but at the mention of Jay's name, my stomach tightened uncomfortably, and my appetite waned.

"Mom, are you all right?" Kathryn asked, regarding me closely, worry creasing her brow. The expression was an exact replica of Jack's. "You're a little pale."

"I'm fine. Just hungry."

"Well, let's get you some lunch, then." Kathryn linked her arm through mine. She'd pronounced it "git."

"To Macado's!" Jack directed. His boyish enthusiasm eased my worry, as did the comforting feel of his palm on the small of my back, but it also felt a bit like I was being walked to the plank.

MACADO'S HAD OPENED a new outdoor patio. Our table was surrounded by Venus flytrap replicas from *Little Shop of Horrors* and shadowed by a large cardboard cutout of Edna Turnblad from the musical *Hairspray*. Kathryn sat across from us, jackhammering her knee and drumming her fingertips on the tabletop until I was as nervous as she looked.

"Ants in your pants?" Jack teased.

Kathryn stilled instantly. "No, I'm just anxious for Jay to get here. I can't wait for you to meet him, Mom." Her hand flew to her mouth, and she redirected her nervous energy toward chewing her already gnawed fingernails. I frowned, recalling my unsuccessful attempts to break her of the nasty habit as a child. With what seemed like a Herculean effort, Kathryn forced her hand into her lap.

A perky young waitress with braided pigtails appeared at our table. "What can I get y'all?" she asked in a deep Southern accent that reminded me of Faith.

We requested waters all around and informed our wait-ress—Mandy, her name tag read—that we were still waiting for one more person to arrive.

"All righty, then. I'll be back in a sec with y'all's waters." Mandy spun on her heel, her pigtails flying out to the sides, just as a *ping* sounded beneath the table. Kathryn dove for her bag and withdrew her phone. As she read the text, her face fell, and then her thumbs were flying over the miniature keyboard. Dropping the phone back into her bag, she took a deep breath and glanced up at us. A ner-vous, slippery smile transformed her face.

"Jay's in surgery—"

"Surgery!" I exclaimed. "What happened? Is he okay?"

Kathryn laughed. "He's not *having* surgery, Mom. He's per-forming it. Assisting, actually."

Seeing my confusion, Kathryn continued. "He's a veterinarian, remember?"

I shook the cobwebs from my brain. *Did she tell me that?* I was certain she hadn't, or surely I would've remembered. *Wouldn't I?* Small snippets of lost conversation began to crystalize in my foggy mind. *Took Hokie to the vet... met this guy...*

"You said you met Jay at the vet clinic. I don't recall you saying he *was* the vet."

"I told Dad," Kathryn protested.

I shot Jack an accusing look. He dismissively shrugged his large, well-defined shoulders and sipped his water.

"Anyway," Kathryn continued, "Jay is studying to become a vet. He has one year left to earn his DVM and will start a full-time in-ternship at the clinic this fall. We're thrilled! It's quite an honor to be awarded such a coveted post."

And there it was again: *we*. "Is he not joining us for lunch, then?" I asked.

"He's not sure. There were some unexpected complications, so the surgery's taking longer than expected. He said we should go ahead and order—"

"Great!" Jack interrupted. His stomach had been rumbling ferociously for the past fifteen minutes.

"*And* he said I should go ahead and tell you." She smiled, the expression spreading slowly across her face, transforming her features into an endearing, childish mask of nervous excitement.

Jack froze beside me. My mouth dropped open, and my eyes widened. *Is this really happening? Here? Now? Before I've even met the guy?* I swallowed hard, attempting to hide my disappointment and annoyance. I didn't trust myself to speak so I averted my gaze to the menu. The lunch specials swam before my eyes.

"Tell us what?" Jack asked, feigning ignorance.

"The *news!*" Kathryn exclaimed as she fumbled through her bag beneath the table.

Jack gave my knee a hard squeeze, and I fixed my eyes on Kathryn.

Her face was flushed, and her smile was wide, the veritable definition of "ear to ear." Her eyes were shiny and bright, an iridescent blue green, and her arms stilled beneath the table. Without warning, she thrust her left hand toward us. "I'm engaged!" she shrieked, attracting the attention of our fellow diners, who began to clap and shout their congratulations. The applause transformed Kathryn's rosy blush of excitement into a deep scarlet of pleasure.

The ring was classic and sensible, befitting a couple still finishing their college educations. And though the size was not ostentatious, the quality was impressive. The princess cut solitaire glittered brilliantly in the bright afternoon sunlight, taking my breath away.

"Congratulations, sweetheart," Jack said, pushing back his chair and rounding the table to sweep Kathryn into his arms.

Mandy, drawn by the ruckus, bounded over and stood waiting, expectant. "Champagne!" Jack ordered upon seeing her.

"I'm sorry, sir, but we don't have—"

"Your best bottle of wine, then."

"You got it!" Mandy said with a smile, undoubtedly pleased by the positive effect this would have on her tip.

Knowing this moment was coming didn't protect me from the shock of it. I was struck speechless. Kathryn making her announcement without Jay and before I'd even met him had taken me by surprise, but her pure joy and happiness were palpable, and I was quickly swept into the excitement.

"Well, Mom, what do you think? Aren't you happy for me?"

"Of course I am," I said as Jack pulled me into a three-way hug with him and Kathryn. And though my heart indeed swelled with joy for my daughter, I worked to shield it from the warnings my mind hurled like javelins, threatening to burst our happy bubble.

Mandy, flanked by the restaurant manager, reappeared with a bottle of Cabernet Franc for our inspection. Reluctantly, we stepped apart. My cheeks and Kathryn's were wet with tears. At Jack's misty-eyed nod of approval, the manager uncorked the bottle and poured a sample for him.

Jack swished the ruby liquid in the glass, inhaled deeply, and took a discerning sip. "It's good," he proclaimed, and the manager proceeded to fill all three glasses.

If there was any concern as to whether Kathryn was of age to drink, no one mentioned it. *And rightly so.* She was a woman of nearly twenty who was engaged to be married. *To hell with the drinking law!*

I drained my glass and regretted it instantly. On an empty stomach, the alcohol, combined with the rising heat of the day, rendered me light-headed. "Can we order now?" I pleaded.

"Absolutely!" Jack bellowed. He selected a trifecta of appetizers from the menu.

"Right away," the manager replied with a slight, awkward bow that I found immensely humorous given that we were surrounded by man-eating plants and a looming cardboard likeness of John Travolta in drag.

I began to laugh hysterically.

"What's so funny?" Kathryn asked.

"Oh, nothing. Everything!" I giggled again, feeling as if my sanity was slipping away, like soft, fine sand through my fingers. I refilled my own glass and clinked it against Kathryn's. "To Kathryn and Jay! Congratulations, honey."

"To Kathryn and Jay," Jack echoed.

I drained the glass once more. "But I still need to meet this man of yours."

"You will. He'll be here as soon as he can. You're gonna love him."

"If you love him, then I'm sure I will too," I agreed, though whether that statement was to reassure her or me, I didn't know. "But are you *sure*, Kathryn? You're so young. You don't have to rush—"

"We're not rushing, Mom. I've been with Jay for more than a year. I know he's the one, so why should we wait?"

Mandy reappeared with a busboy in tow. The large tray hefted onto her shoulder was loaded with heaping plates of cheese quesadillas, muchos nachos, seafood potato skins, and a basket of blue-corn tortilla chips with healthy sides of salsa and guacamole.

"Can I getcha anything else?" Mandy asked, surveying the food-laden table.

"Nope. We're good for now. Thanks," Jack replied.

I sipped the peppery wine and tried to imagine Kathryn as a bride, walking down the aisle, but the image was murky. It dawned on me then that I still had no clear picture in my mind of what Jay looked like, Jack's meager description notwithstanding.

"Jay proposed at the very top of Dragon's Tooth," Kathryn said, interrupting my thoughts. She dropped her chin into her palm. A lazy smile slid across her face, and a dreamy expression softened her eyes. "It was so perfect. Extremely romantic."

WE SPENT THE NEXT HOUR munching, dipping, and sipping while Kathryn chattered excitedly about ideas for the wedding—where to have it, who to invite, and the kind of dress she wanted.

"Either a halter or strapless. Or maybe one with a sweetheart neckline and cap sleeves. Nothing too fancy. And royal blue for the bridesmaids. Or ivory. That would look really clean and classy, don't you think?"

I was dazed by the amount of consideration she'd given her wedding already. "Anything you decide will be lovely. Just don't make us climb that damn tooth for the ceremony, okay?"

Kathryn laughed, her eyes dancing at the mention of the Tooth. "I won't."

"I'm going to hit the ladies' room while you settle up," I said to Jack. "Meet you out front?"

"Sounds good," Jack replied, retrieving his wallet.

When I emerged from the restaurant—my belly full, my bladder empty, and my lips freshly glossed—I spotted Jack and Kathryn in the parking lot, talking to a tall, dark-haired man. With his back to me, I could see that he was almost but not quite as tall and broad as Jack. His dark hair was damp and wavy, as if he'd just stepped out of the shower, and his arm was around Kathryn's waist. He must have said something funny, for as I approached, my heart racing and my stomach twisted in anxious knots, Jack tipped his head back and laughed. Then he clapped the man on the shoulder. Kathryn, all smiles, bounced up on her toes and kissed the man on his cheek, which was lightly shadowed with stubble.

"Mom!" Kathryn exclaimed as I walked toward them. "I'd like you to meet Jay Martin. Jay, this is my mom, Anna."

Jay turned and greeted me with a wide smile. The muscles in his tanned forearm rippled as he extended his hand. "Nice to meet you, Mrs.—"

"Oh my God!" I gasped, backing away. "You're, he's..." I spluttered, my mind racing, my mouth unable to form a coherent sentence.

Jay cocked his head to the side, and his smile faltered slightly. I could see the question in his dark, striking eyes. Emerald flecks blazed in the sunlight as he gazed at me. "Do I know you?"

"*Know* her?" Kathryn asked, puzzled. "How could you possibly know my mom?" She shifted her gaze from me to Jay, waiting for an explanation.

Jack was immediately at my side. "Are you okay? You look like you've seen a ghost," he whispered into my ear.

I opened and closed my mouth a few times, like a fish washed ashore, but no sound came out.

"I know I've seen you somewhere before," Jay said, taking a step closer.

Instinctively, I took another step back and collided with Jack, which caused my bag to slip from my shoulder and land with a loud *thwack* on the pavement. The bag tipped, scattering its contents across the blacktop, and the small mirror I carried for contact lens emergencies cracked, littering shards of silver at my feet. Kathryn lunged for a tube of lipstick that was skittering toward the underside of a parked truck, and Jack saved a pack of breath mints from rolling into the sewer. Jay and I simultaneously knelt to pluck the broken mirror from the pavement and bumped heads on the way down.

"Ouch!" I hollered, rubbing my temple.

"I'm sorry—" Recognition dawned in Jay's eyes. *Jack's eyes.* "My mom's house... that's how I know you. You're my mom's friend."

Jay and I stood just inches apart. His expression was one of pleasant remembrance. Mine was a mask of shock and horror.

Kathryn put her hand on Jay's arm. "Your mom and my mom are *friends?*"

Then, through the ringing in my ears, I heard the confusion in Jack's voice as he asked, "How do you know Jay's mother?"

I sprinted across the parking lot and hurled into the bushes.

"SMALL WORLD, EH?" JACK commented casually.

I rested my forehead against the comforting coolness of the window and watched the highway speed by beyond the glass. The thick green trees bordering I-81 blurred and sharpened with the ebb and flow of my tears.

"What's the big deal?" Jack asked in response to my silence, an edge to his voice. "So what if he's Lia's son?"

Helpless rage bubbled in my stomach. "Because if Kathryn marries Jay, Lia will be a part of my life forever! She'll be Kathryn's *mother-in-law*," I said through gritted teeth. "*That's* the big deal."

"But Lia's your friend, right? Didn't the two of you patch things up?"

"Sort of," I conceded. "But that doesn't mean I want her to be part of my *family*."

"But Kathryn loves him, Anna. Isn't that what really matters? You and Lia will just have to get past your differences."

"It's not that simple, Jack. Jay—" I snorted. "And that's another thing. *Jay.* When I met him, Lia called him Robert."

"That is odd," Jack agreed.

"Damn right it is!"

"Well, I'm sure there's a perfectly reasonable explanation, one we might have learned if you hadn't overreacted and insisted we leave." The edge to Jack's voice grew sharper. The image of Kathryn and Jay standing dumbfounded in the parking lot as we drove away, their faces twisted in shock, hurt, and confusion, was undoubtedly etched in his mind as it was in mine.

I was unused to Jack taking that tone with me. "I don't feel well." And it was the truth. My stomach twisted and clenched, and my head pounded.

Jack placed a large hand on my forehead then wiped his palm on his shorts. "You don't have a fever, but you're clammy as hell."

Thankfully, the tenderness was back. I didn't like it when Jack and I were at odds with each other, and I couldn't begin to imagine what would happen if he knew the truth about Jay. Robert. Whatever! *But I have to tell him, don't I?* The truth always came out eventually. I would have to tell him before he found out some other way. *But how the hell can I tell him such a thing? "Hey, Jack! That boy? Jay? He's your son."*

Then the most disturbing part—the hulking, grotesque monster that I was trying to ignore—shoved its way to the forefront of my mind: Kathryn was unwittingly engaged to her half brother. My stomach cartwheeled, and my mouth filled with saliva.

"Stop the car!" I yelled.

"What? We're going seventy miles an hour—"

"Just stop!"

Jack pulled into the right lane and eased onto the shoulder, slowing as quickly as possible without skidding or fishtailing. I pushed the door open while the wheels were still rolling and vomited again. The last remnants of my lunch splattered onto the road.

I wiped my mouth with the back of my hand, slammed the car door shut, and leaned my head against the seat.

"Okay?" Jack asked.

"Fine," I lied. Nothing was fine. Nothing was fine at all.

"DID YOU KNOW?" I SCREAMED into the phone. My accusation was met with silence. "Did you know your son, *Jay*, was dating *my daughter*? That he wants to *marry* her?"

I'd paced the kitchen that morning, waiting for Jack to leave for work. The instant his truck was out of sight, I'd punched Lia's numbers into the phone, swearing under my breath and praying she would pick up. Ev and Helene were due home from a sleepover at their friend's house in less than an hour.

"No," Lia whispered. "I mean, I knew he had a girlfriend, that it was serious. I never thought—"

"No, you never do think, do you? Do you have any idea how absolutely *fucked up* this is?"

She went silent again. "Does Jack know? Did you tell him?"

"That Jay is his son? Hell no! And that's the way I would have kept it. But now I don't have a choice, do I? Now I'll have to tell him, and it will break his heart. And Kathryn's too."

"I'm sorry, Anna. I never could have imagined this—"

"Oh, shut up, Lia. Just shut up!"

She did as I commanded, and the silence was deafening. Then the little niggling bit that had been taunting me resurfaced. "By the way, you said your son's name is Robert?"

"It is. Well, sort of. He's named after my uncle, Roberto." As usual, Lia was speaking in riddles.

I sighed loudly, expectantly, and waited for her to continue.

"Like I told you, when I moved to Miami, I felt like part of a family for the first time in my life. Before Robert was born, I took my aunt and uncle's last name—Martin. Roberto is my son's middle name."

"So Jay is his first name?"

Lia's next words were scarcely a whisper. "For a while, I think I'd convinced myself I really didn't know who his father was. It was just easier that way, to pretend I didn't know. But when Rob was born, he looked *exactly* like—"

I ground my teeth together. "Just say it!"

"Fine! Like Jack! He looked exactly like Jack, okay? When I saw my baby's tiny face, I couldn't deny the truth. My aunt was standing beside me, holding my hand, and I remember thinking to myself, *this is Jack's son*. But I must have said it out loud because then my aunt said, 'What a perfect name. He looks like a Jackson.'" Lia let loose a long, shuddering exhalation. "My son's name is Jackson Roberto Martin."

Lia paused, allowing the full implication of her statement to hit me like a sledgehammer. I let out a maniacal cackle. "Jackson! Is that supposed to be funny? Like some kind of sick joke?"

Lia ignored my outburst and forged ahead with her story. "I knew I could never call him that without immediately thinking of Jack. Or you. Or what I'd done. So I've called him Robert—or Rob—since the day he was born."

Bitter tears were streaming down my face as I imagined a tiny version of Jack, the baby boy I'd always dreamed I would hold in my arms. Instead, the world had conspired against me, and the only son Jack would ever have had been born to my best friend. My *former* best friend. And now that baby boy was engaged to my daughter. Kathryn was engaged to be married to her *half brother*. The situation was completely twisted beyond belief. But I was still confused. "But you said Neil adopted Robert."

"He did."

"Then why isn't Rob's last name Nelson? Like yours?"

"Neil and Rob's relationship was... complicated. The two were like oil and water. To say they never really got along would be putting it mildly."

I grunted and paced the kitchen, glancing nervously at the clock and growing impatient for Lia to get to the point already. "And..."

"When Robert found out that Neil was not his real father, he was furious. But he was also relieved. It was like a weight had been lifted from his shoulders, like everything finally made sense."

Morning light slanted into the kitchen, drawing me to the window. Outside, a pair of wrens splashed carelessly in a puddle before flying away. I envied their weightlessness and freedom, and I wished that I could fly away from the nightmare I was living.

"Rob said his entire relationship with Neil had been based on a lie," Lia continued. "And he no longer wanted to be connected to Neil in any way. When he turned eighteen, he had his name legally reverted to his birth name. I didn't agree with the decision, but I couldn't stop him. He was an adult. He also started going by Jackson."

"Ooo-kay. But that doesn't explain why Kathryn calls him Jay."

"Beats me. When he played club basketball at Virginia, his friends nicknamed him Dr. J. Then he actually decided to become a doctor, so I guess it stuck. That's probably why Kathryn calls him Jay, but maybe you should ask her yourself."

"Don't you dare tell me what I should do!" My head was spinning. It was difficult to wrap my mind around everything Lia was telling me. "So Robert, or Jackson... I mean *Jay,* or whatever the hell his name is, knows Neil is not his father, but you never told him who his real father is?"

The line was filled with another long pause. I turned from the window and leaned against the sink, chewing the inside of my cheek until I tasted blood.

"I told him I didn't know," Lia finally said. "As much as it hurt to lie to him, to imply that I was—"

"A slut?" I hurled the epithet on purpose, to hurt her.

Lia continued in a voice as cold and as hard as ice. "I told him I'd been young and stupid and had unprotected sex with boys I didn't know during the summer he was conceived. Ultimately, I lied to my son to protect him. But as you already know, I also lied to protect you."

"Well, a lot of good that's done, Lia. Thanks for nothing! It's one thing to screw up your own life, but now you've managed to screw up everyone else's too. Congratulations. You've really outdone yourself this time."

I slammed the phone into its base, disconnecting the call, then slid down the side of the kitchen cabinet and onto the floor. Dropping my head into my hands, I let out a shuddering sob, the pressure behind my eyes ebbing away as the tears flowed between my fingers.

I STARTED AVOIDING Kathryn's calls. When she left a message, I would listen to it over and over again just to hear the sound of her voice.

"Why don't you just talk to her?" Jack asked.

"I can't."

"Why are you doing this, Anna? Our daughter is trying to plan a wedding, and she needs her mother. She needs *you*."

As the summer wore on, hot and humid as a baby's breath, Jack's confusion morphed into anger in direct proportion to Kathryn's frustration. I pleaded with Jack to tell Kathryn I was sorry to have missed her call, that I'd been out or was on a deadline for work, but Jack was growing weary of making excuses for me, and our disagreements were regularly escalating into heated arguments.

During one particularly nasty shouting match, Helene snatched her phone from the kitchen counter and disappeared into her room, locking the door behind her. Later, I overheard her telling a friend, "My parents are fighting again," and it filled me with anguish. I was withholding the truth from my family to protect us, but left untold, the truth threatened to destroy us anyway.

In my heart, I knew we could not go on like that much longer. Jack had always been my rock, and I needed him more than ever. Without his support, I was weakening, faltering. My carefully constructed walls of secrecy were collapsing, suffocating me, and the burden I carried clawed at my conscience. I was becoming desperate, and my family was suffering. The stakes had been raised. I no longer had a choice. I would have to tell Jack the truth. And soon.

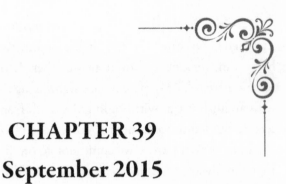

CHAPTER 39
September 2015

It was after midnight when the last guest finally departed. Feeling something akin to happiness for the first time in months, I hummed to myself as I made the rounds to collect the empty bottles and trash that littered the back yard. Jack and I had hosted a small Labor Day barbeque for a few neighbors and some of Jack's coworkers. The forecast had promised rain, but the menacing clouds that hovered in the morning sky had gradually dissipated. The adults had spent a lovely evening relaxing by the firepit while the girls and a dozen of their friends engaged in competitive rounds of cornhole and dashed through the yard, playing flashlight tag.

Jack came up behind me and wrapped his arms around my waist. I leaned against him, enjoying the feel of his strong arms around me and the warmth of his breath against my neck. The tension of the past few months had rendered us unusually distant, and I realized how much I'd missed him. Pressed against his body, I could *feel* how much he'd missed me.

"Nice party," he whispered into my ear.

"Yeah, it turned out okay. I think everyone had fun."

"I think you're right. It's nice to see a smile on your face again."

I tucked my head into his shoulder and tilted my chin toward the star-studded sky, watching the satellites hurl through space, tiny pinpoints of light streaking across the ink-black night.

"Kathryn called," Jack said, some of the lightness ebbing from his voice. "She said she's left three messages about setting a date to shop for wedding dresses, but you haven't returned her calls."

I pulled away from him and resumed my cleanup duties. Jack retrieved a beer from the cooler, popped the top, and took a long swig, scanning the patio for the firepit cover. Once he located it behind the grill, he placed it atop the tiny flames that danced in the bowl, smothering the life from them.

"I can't."

"Why the hell not, Anna? This is ridiculous! Isn't wedding planning one of the things mothers live for? What's the matter with you?" Jack's voice pulsed with anger, and his accusing tone ignited my own fury.

"Me? What's the matter with *me*? I am not the problem here, Jack. The wedding is the problem. She can't marry him."

"Why not? I know she's young, but your parents were young. Hell, *we* were young. And we're all happily married. It'll be okay."

"No, it won't be okay!" I couldn't keep the growing hysteria from my voice.

"She's a grown woman, Anna. This has to be her decision."

"You don't understand, Jack. She *can't* marry him. She can't marry Jay!" The tears started falling. I dropped the trash bag to the ground, and soiled napkins and paper plates spilled onto the grass. An evening breeze swept through the backyard and scattered the litter across the lawn, mocking my efforts to keep my life tidy.

"What's wrong with Jay? I know you hate that he's Lia's son, but that's no reason to hate *him*. I like him. And more importantly, Kathryn likes him. She *loves* him. He's a—"

"He's your son!" I wailed, my fingers splayed in front of my chest. My body was rigid with fear. "How can you not see it, Jack? He looks just like you!"

"What did you say?" The venom in Jack's voice belied the fear and uncertainty that haunted his face. He took two long strides across the patio, grabbed me by the shoulders, and gave me a gentle shake. His blazing eyes bored into mine, the gem-toned flecks glowing like an animal's in the night. "What did you just say?" he shouted.

I held my ground. The fact that Jay was Jack's son was only half the story. The other half—whether Jack remembered screwing Lia, whether he truly did not know Lia had become pregnant and had his son—was about to be revealed. There was no turning back. I steeled my heart and soul for the discovery. "Jay—*Jackson*—is your son. Yours and Lia's." I held his gaze, demanding the truth, fearful of the acknowledgement I might find in his eyes. Instead, there was only confusion.

Jack drew his thick brows down over his startling eyes. "What do you mean, *my* son? Mine and *Lia's*? That's ridiculous! Impossible!"

An unwelcome image of Lia and Jack, locked in an embrace, sliced through my brain, and my breath caught in my throat. "Lia said that you, that the two of you, during beach week—"

"That's a damn lie!" Jack whirled and flung his beer bottle into the firepit. It shattered against the ceramic edge, and I screamed. The ruckus roused Chessie and Bay, who rushed to my aid, barking urgently.

"Stay back!" I yelled at them. Broken glass was scattered across the patio and winked in the moonlight, threatening to slice the dogs' paws as they ran toward us.

Jack grabbed the dogs by their collars and dragged all 160 pounds of them, splay-legged and skidding, into the house and slammed the French doors with such force that they bounced open. "Damn it!" he yelled, yanking the doors shut again.

My legs had turned to jelly, so I lowered myself onto the knee wall. My whole body was trembling. Jack pulled up a chair and sat facing me. His piercing eyes were narrowed to slits, and his mouth was twisted in pain. His whole face contorted into a frightful mask of rage. "Tell me *exactly* what she said to you," he demanded, his nostrils flaring.

With a quivering voice, I recounted Lia's version of what had happened at the beach, about her becoming pregnant and moving to Florida to live with her aunt, about her having a baby—Jack's son—who knew he was adopted but who never knew his real father, and about Lia's decision to keep her son's paternity a secret to protect us all. As I spoke, I watched Jack's features morph from anger to shocked disbelief to heart-wrenching sorrow.

Jack made a guttural noise. He dropped his forehead into his hand and massaged his temples with his thumb and middle finger. "I was crushed when you left me that night at the beach, that you wouldn't stay with me." Jack's voice was a low, haunted whisper. "When Lia came into the room later, I thought it was you... at first. That you'd come back. And then she... we..."

A deep scowl creased his face, and his jaw began to quiver. "I knew that I shouldn't... that she wasn't... But I was hurt. And drunk. And it felt..." His voice broke. "I'm so sorry, Anna, so sorry. But I didn't know that she was, that she'd become *pregnant*." He choked back a sob and covered his face with both hands.

My eyes filled with tears, my heart breaking to see him in so much pain. I moved to sit beside him on the chair and rubbed his back, my palm making soothing circles between his large, shaking shoulders.

He sniffed and looked up at me with anguished, red-rimmed eyes. "The next day, I was so hungover. I wasn't even sure if anything had happened. I mean, I knew she'd been there, but I couldn't remember if we... if I... It was all a blur." Jack shook his head, and his shoulders heaved. "But a *son*. All this time, I've had a son, and she never told me. Why wouldn't she tell me something like that, Anna? How could she keep him from me for all these years?"

His face crumpled—collapsed in on itself the way a tin can did when it was stepped on—and I couldn't take it anymore. I pulled him toward me, and he laid his head in my lap. Jack sobbed like a baby, and I cried with him while protectively curled around his body like a snail's shell shielding the fragile being within.

WE WOKE AT DAWN, ENTWINED and shivering on a lounge chair. A yellow plastic tablecloth, damp with dew, was wrapped tightly around us. We'd stayed on the patio all night, huddled on the chair, crying, consoling, and clinging to each other. The truth had hurt us badly, but it hadn't broken us.

"How long have you known?" he whispered as the morning sky faded from deep indigo to soft lavender.

"Since December. Jay stopped by Lia's house unexpectedly. I took one look at him, and I knew." I recalled the first time I'd laid eyes on the living, breathing younger version of my husband, the boy with the same dark hair, golden skin, and startling eyes but with Lia's high cheekbones and pointed chin.

"I have a son." Jack's voice was laced with amazement and wonder, but his eyes were filled with hurt. "Why didn't you tell me?"

"And then what, Jack? What good would it have done? Lia chose to keep him a secret from you, from us, for all these years, and now Jay is a grown man. Do you think you can just waltz into his life and tell him you're his father? Besides, I couldn't bear to tell you. I didn't want to be the one to break your heart, to hurt you like that."

"Too late for that," he said as fresh tears welled in both our eyes. "I just want to know him, Anna. I want to know my son."

We sat quietly for a long time, pondering a future in which we would carry this burden with us forever, like a dormant virus lying in wait to rise and attack from the inside. "Maybe someday, Jack. Somehow, some way, maybe you can know him, and he can know you. But not now. Not like this."

I used the back of my hand to swipe a stray tear that trickled down my cheek, then my thumbs to remove the wetness that collected at the outer edges of Jack's eyes. "We have to protect our daughter now. We have to think of Kathryn. I don't want to jeopardize our relationship with her, but we have to tell her. And once we do, once we're responsible for tearing her and Jay apart, she'll never forgive us."

"But she can't marry him," Jack finally agreed, resolute. "He's her half brother, for Christ's sake."

I nodded into his chest as relief washed over me. Jack and I were once again united in our resolve to prevent Kathryn's marriage and to protect our daughter from making a huge mistake.

Jack threw some fresh wood into the firepit, and I padded into the house, briskly rubbing my arms against the early-morning chill, to start the coffee. After checking on Evelyn and Helene, who remained blissfully sprawled across their beds, deeply ensconced in the specific type of all-consuming sleep reserved for the young, I returned to the patio to find Jack staring into the dancing flames of the newborn fire. I handed him a mug filled to the brim with piping-hot black coffee. Then we sat shoulder to shoulder, hip to hip, as I sipped from my own steaming mug.

"How do we do this?" I wondered as I gazed at the fire, feeling its mesmerizing pull.

"I don't know. Kathryn is strong-willed. If we flat-out tell her we oppose the marriage without giving a good reason—without telling her *why*—she'll marry him anyway, and then she'll resent us for trying to ruin her happiness."

"Maybe she won't marry him," I speculated.

Jack raised a skeptical eyebrow.

"Maybe this problem will somehow resolve itself."

"That's mighty optimistic of you." He snorted and sipped his coffee, his gaze fixed on the rapidly brightening horizon. He absently rubbed his lightly stubbled chin, making a scuffing sound, then furrowed his brows, etching ruts into the skin of his forehead.

"Jack? What is it?" I placed a comforting hand on his arm and looked into his narrowed eyes. "What are you thinking?"

"About what you said, about the problem resolving itself. It made me remember... something."

I forced myself to remain silent as the cogs of Jack's mind churned with the effort to retrieve the memory. Suddenly, the planes of his face smoothed, and his jaw, rigid with tension, relaxed. "Once, when Kathryn called this summer, and you were avoiding her"—Jack shot me a brief, accusing glare—"she was having doubts."

"She was?" I asked, disbelieving.

"Well, not doubts, exactly. Concern. That marrying Jay, as happy and settled as he is at the clinic, might mean staying in Blacksburg, which is not exactly a hotbed of opportunities for a graphic designer. I didn't think much of it at the time, but maybe she *is* having second thoughts. Maybe she will decide they should slow things down a bit and postpone the marriage."

I bobbed my head in agreement. I knew it was unrealistic—cowardly, even—to hope that the problem might resolve itself. But the idea of it was heady, hard to resist. At the very least, a postponement might buy us some time.

"Maybe we can give her a little nudge in that direction," I suggested. The idea was growing, blossoming, and taking on a life of its own. "But she'll have to think it's her idea." I began to pace the patio, tightly gripping the coffee mug between my hands. "She's coming home in a few weeks. We can talk about the responsibilities that come with marriage, about how hard it might be to stay focused on finishing school, about how it might affect her career..."

Jack frowned and squeezed his knees with white-knuckled hands. As if he could feel the weight of my stare on the back of his neck, he reluctantly lifted doubtful eyes to mine.

"Do you have a better suggestion?" I asked.

He shook his head and hunched his shoulders. I sank down on the chair beside him and stared morosely at the fire as he reached over and intertwined his fingers with mine.

I looked into Jack's troubled eyes, at his handsome face, and at his full lips pressed into a thin, tight line. "It's not a conversation we can have over the phone."

"I know." Jack parted his lips and released his breath in a rush.

I leaned over and kissed his cheek, feeling the muscles of his jaw work beneath my lips. "We'll feel it out when she's home. If we don't sense any doubts, if they're determined to move forward, then we'll have to tell her the truth."

Jack squeezed my hand tightly, though his fingers could have just as easily been wrapped around my heart.

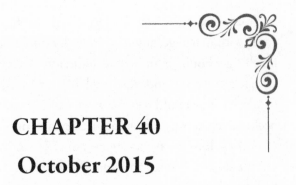

CHAPTER 40
October 2015

Jack circled the Pier 5 parking lot six times before lucking into a spot. As I stepped from the car, the cool, fishy breeze blowing off the harbor whipped my hair into a frenzy. I hugged my wrap tightly around my shoulders and interlaced my fingers with Jack's as we followed the dimly illuminated yellow pine boards to the waterfront restaurant. Ev, tottering ahead in stiletto sandals, and Helene, wearing a flimsy spaghetti-strap top, appeared impervious to the chill.

Instead of us making our annual trek to Blacksburg for the fall family day, Kathryn had decided to come home. Jack and I intended to use the weekend to expose some rift in her relationship with Jay and sow seeds of doubt. That knowledge created an oppressive heaviness in my body. The feeling was reminiscent of when I'd let the girls bury me at the beach. The wet sand had pressed down on my limbs and chest, making it difficult to breathe. The sensation made me shiver, and Jack squeezed my hand.

"Cold?"

I nodded and hugged my wrap tighter as I edged closer to Jack. I had the distinct feeling that if I were to stumble and fall into the dark, dank bay, I would sink directly to the bottom like a stone.

The restaurant's classic décor of handcrafted walnut wood and beveled stained glass was warm and welcoming. A dapper older gentleman stood rigidly at the host stand.

"Seven o'clock reservation for, uh, Martin," Jack announced, stumbling over the name.

"Ah, yes," the host confirmed. "Right this way, sir."

We followed the host through the center of the main room and into a semi-private dining area. The air was redolent of butter, shellfish, and the sharp tang of Old Bay. Kathryn and Jay were seated at the center of a wide oval table. Their heads were bent together in conversation, and an open bottle of wine sat in front of them. The sight of Kathryn—stunning in a peach-colored dress that set off her glowing olive skin—leaning over to plant a kiss on Jay's lips stopped me in my tracks. It was as if I were looking at myself, twenty-five years younger, kissing Jack.

Lia was seated to Jay's right, chatting and laughing with her twins, Jay's half-siblings, Nathan and Nicholas. Neil, apparently, had not been invited.

Feeling like an interloper to the party, I squeezed Jack's hand and fought to control my hammering heart. Though I'd known Lia would be at the dinner, my body automatically tensed at the sight of her. We hadn't spoken in more than three months, not since our last phone call in June when I'd hung up on her. *Calming breaths. Take deep, calming breaths.*

"Mom! Dad!" Kathryn exclaimed, leaping from her chair. "I'm so glad you're here!"

"Nice to see you again, Mr. and Mrs. Wells," Jay said, extending his hand to Jack, who, like me, stood rooted to the spot.

From the corner of my eye, I saw Lia lift her arm to signal our waiter. The gesture jarred me from my stupor, and I nudged Jack with my shoulder.

He cleared his throat and plastered an awkward smile on his face. "Likewise." He shook Jay's hand. "Please, call me... Jack."

"Jack it is," Jay agreed with a laugh. The sound was jovial and hearty, much like Jack's laugh. If Jay noticed that Jack held on to his hand and looked into his eyes for a beat too long, he didn't let on.

Then it was Jack's turn to nudge me. "Oh, hi again. And it's, uh, Anna," I spluttered, smiling so forcefully, my cheeks ached.

"Thanks so much for coming. It's great to have both families together," Jay said.

Families. My legs shook as I stepped closer to the table.

Before I could sit, Lia rose from her chair and walked toward me. She gave me a stiff hug and a kiss on the cheek, which I received coolly. Then, to my horror, she hugged Jack. He stood rigidly during the brief embrace. "Small world, isn't it?" she said to no one in particular.

The siblings all greeted one another as we settled into our seats around the elegant table. Jay and Kathryn easily held court. They laughed and held hands as they regaled us with tales of how they'd met, Jay's work at the clinic, and their plans for the future. They practically completed each other's sentences. It was abundantly clear, I noted with remorse, how absolutely smitten they were with each other.

I also noticed that Kathryn wasn't the only one who couldn't keep her eyes off Jay. Her sisters were eyeing him intently too. I shifted uneasily in my seat, wondering if they recognized—and God forbid, might comment on—Jay's resemblance to their father.

A waiter appeared and began filling our wine glasses. When he made to fill Evelyn's, I covered her glass with my hand and gave a subtle shake of my head, earning a disappointed scowl from my seventeen-year-old.

"I ordered a bottle for the table," Lia explained cheerfully.

After Jack and I had suffered through but survived our emotional, heart-wrenching Labor Day weekend, I'd called Lia and left a terse voice mail, wanting her to be clear on our position before seeing her.

"Jack knows. Because we love our daughter and don't want to hurt her the way you've hurt us, we don't plan to say anything. Yet. So we'd appreciate it if you'd keep your mouth shut as well. We don't anticipate this being a problem as you've proven yourself quite good at keeping secrets."

Lia hadn't responded to my message, but I could tell from one look at her—the person I'd once known as well as I knew myself—that she was on board with our plan, possibly to a fault. She was smiling, and her eyes were sparkling. It was as if she couldn't be happier that Jay and Kathryn were engaged, as if the situation were perfectly normal. Seeing her like that made my blood boil.

"To Jay and Kat," Lia announced, raising her glass, addressing the couple by their preferred monikers with ease.

"I can't believe you're getting married," Ev said to her sister.

"I can't believe it either," I muttered louder than I'd intended.

"Mom!" Kathryn admonished. She interlaced her fingers with Jay's and looked at me expectantly. "I mean, you're happy for us, right?"

I lowered my eyes and sipped my wine.

"Of course we're happy for you. It's just—" Jack flinched as I poked him in the ribs.

"You don't want them to get married?" Helene asked. She plucked the cherry from her Shirley Temple and used her teeth to free it from its stem.

"It's not that," Jack said. "It's just that—"

"You're so young!" I interrupted. "I mean, what's the rush, right?"

"Aw, you two weren't much older than they are," Lia said as she peered at me over the rim of her glass, one eyebrow raised.

What is she doing? I bit back a snarky reply as our waiter approached to take our orders. Then I silently thanked Jay's brothers for turning the conversation to sports. Ev and Helene joined in, and the four teens regaled the table with bloopers from the soccer field until our entrees arrived.

Still seething from Lia's comment, I kept one hand curled into a fist in my lap as we dined on pan-seared American red snapper, crumb-coated Atlantic cod, mouthwatering baked sea scallops, and succulent king crab. Across the table, Kathryn and Jay leaned into each other, whispering, laughing, and sharing each other's food, and I belatedly, reluctantly recognized the evening for what it really was: an engagement party.

Though Jack tried to be discreet, he couldn't keep his eyes off Jay. Meanwhile, my attention bounced between Jack and Kathryn. Jack was wild-eyed, like the intact slabs of fish on our plates, with beads of sweat dotting his upper lip and brow. Kathryn lit up the room with her radiant glow and her glittering diamond. Throughout dinner, Lia kept her eyes mostly on her plate. The happy, oblivious chatter of our children shielded the table from the awkward, uncomfortable undercurrent that lapped at its edges.

"Mom, you've been awfully quiet," Kathryn observed as the waitstaff cleared our dishes from the table. "Is everything okay?"

"Um, sure." I sipped my water and dabbed primly at the corners of my mouth.

"Your mom's always been a bit of a wallflower," Lia chimed in with a dismissive flick of her wrist.

Kathryn shook her head, her smile growing wider. "I keep forgetting you two were friends in high school." She pivoted toward me and leaned her body against Jay's arm. "I mean, can you believe it? I'm engaged to your *best friend's son*. How random is that?"

Kathryn giggled and drank her wine. "Could you ever have imagined?"

The forced smile fell from my lips. "Never," I assured her, shooting Lia a look of contempt.

"She could be a bit of a spoilsport too," Lia added with a wink, throwing fuel on my growing fire.

I reached for the bottle of wine and refilled my glass. "Well, someone as wild and free as you were *would* think that, wouldn't they?"

Jay cocked his head and furrowed his brow. "What do you mean?"

"I don't think she meant anything *bad* by it," Kathryn replied with an awkward chuckle.

Lia narrowed her eyes and sipped her drink. "Well, what exactly *did* you mean by it, Anna?"

The wine began to fizz and hum in my veins, and my cheeks flushed with anger. Lia was challenging me, baiting me, and I couldn't resist taking a bite. "Oh, you know, she had her share of fun in high school. Didn't she tell you? She was *very* popular, especially with the boys."

"Mom!" Kathryn exclaimed, a look of shock on her face.

Jack coughed loudly into his fist and gave my knee a hard squeeze beneath the table. The rest of the kids had gone still and mute, watching wide-eyed as they tuned in to the escalating drama.

Jay narrowed his eyes and pressed his full Jack-like lips together. "That's not a very nice thing to say, Mrs. Wells."

"She didn't mean anything by it," Kathryn retorted.

"She never does," Lia added. "Perfect little Anna. Always so quick to judge."

"No one's perfect," Kathryn said to Lia.

"You don't need to take that tone with my mom," Jay scolded as a waiter tentatively served him a piece of chocolate cake.

"She's being so... condescending to my mother."

Jay bent his head toward Kathryn and lowered his voice. "Your mother kinda deserved it."

"What!" Kathryn stabbed her fork into her cake. "No one deserves to be disrespected."

"Exactly. Don't you agree, Lia?" I looked pointedly at Jack and interlaced my fingers with his. His palm was cold and clammy. "*Everyone* deserves to be respected. Not taken advantage of. Not *lied* to." Somewhere in my wine-induced haze, I realized I was crossing a dangerous line.

"Speaking of lying..." Lia began.

"Who's lying?" Evelyn piped up from the end of the table.

"Quiet, Ev," Helene whispered.

"Don't you dare," I said to Lia, my voice hissing through my teeth.

Kathryn rose from the table. "Are you calling my mom a liar?"

Lia smirked and polished off her wine. "Takes one to know one, right, Anna?"

"That's enough," Jack said, his hand slicing horizontally through the air.

Jay's hands, which had been lying flat on the table, curled into fists. "Please don't raise your voice to my mother."

Kathryn crossed her arms over her chest. "Your mother started this."

"No, she didn't, actually," Jay argued, wiping his mouth with his napkin as he rose to his feet.

Kathryn's eyes widened. "You're taking her side over mine?"

Jay's features hardened. "This isn't about taking sides. She's my *mother*."

"And I'm your fiancée, soon to be your wife!"

Lia thumped her empty wine glass on the table and stood abruptly, her napkin tumbling to the floor. "Rob, don't!"

All eyes pivoted to Lia, whose own eyes had grown wide. She looked like the proverbial deer in the headlights.

"Who's Rob?" Helene asked Nate, who was sitting beside her.

Nick pointed at Jay. "He is."

Helene and Ev stared at Nate, who shrugged and slurped his Coke.

Kathryn slowly pivoted to face Jay. Her lovely face had transformed into a mask of confusion. "Why are they calling you Rob?"

"I can explain," Jay said, reaching for Kathryn's arm.

Kathryn twisted sideways, out of Jay's reach. "Explain what? I thought your name was Jay. You told me your name was Jay!" Kathryn's voice had become shrill, and her eyes blazed.

"It is," Nick contributed helpfully.

Nate laughed and shook his head, as if it should have been obvious. "His friends call him Jay, but Mom has always called him Rob. You know, for Roberto."

"Roberto?" Ev questioned before licking a glob of chocolate from her fork.

"No, I don't know!" Kathryn exclaimed. She grabbed her purse from where it hung on the back of her chair and slung it over her shoulder. "Why haven't you told me this before?"

Jay shrugged helplessly. "I guess it never came up."

"Well, what else never 'came up'?" Kathryn asked, hooking her fingers sharply around the words. "What else don't I know about you?"

Jay took a step toward Kathryn. "You don't understand."

Kathryn lurched backward. "You're right. I don't understand. I don't understand any of this, Jay, Rob... *Roberto*! Whoever you are! I thought I knew you! Maybe I don't know you at all."

Jay's face softened, his eyes pleading as he stepped cautiously toward a rigid and visibly shaking Kathryn. "Kat, it's me. Look at me."

He cupped Kathryn's chin in his hand and lifted her face toward his. "You do know me. You know who I am. And I love you."

Kathryn shook her head free as tears began to tumble from her eyes. "This is too much. Everything is happening too fast. I can't do this."

Though it was what I'd wanted—or what I'd *thought* I wanted—I felt the color drain from my face as Kathryn slid her engagement ring from her finger and placed it gently on the table. I heard Jack swallow loudly beside me and saw his Adam's apple bob in his throat.

Beyond him, a sorrowful, horrified expression had hijacked Lia's face. "Kat, Rob..."

Kathryn's head snapped in Lia's direction at the unfamiliar, inflammatory name.

"Let's calm down and take a breath."

"Stay out of it, Mom," Jay said, slicing his hand through the air in a gesture that was eerily similar to the one Jack had made.

Lia snapped her mouth shut and sank into her chair, glaring at me. I tore my eyes from hers and stared at my daughter, my heart breaking at the sight of her pained expression and crumpled posture. "Kathryn, sweetie. Maybe—"

"Mom, don't. I can't." Kathryn shrugged into her sweater and looked up into Jay's anguished face, her eyes wet with tears. "I'm sorry, Jay." She choked back a sob and fled from the room, leaving Jay standing, shocked, next to her empty chair.

After a long, agonizing moment, Jay straightened his spine, squared his shoulders, and slipped his arms into his jacket. With his thumb and forefinger, he plucked Kathryn's ring from the table. The diamond caught the light and cast the room in an array of glittering, refracted stars. He stared at it in awe, as if pondering how it had ended up on the table instead of on his fiancée's finger.

"Will there be anything else?" our waiter asked cautiously from the archway.

"Just the check, please," Jack said, his voice flat and morose.

The intrusion seemed to jolt Jay from his disoriented stupor. He tucked the ring into his jacket pocket, withdrew his wallet, and extended a credit card toward Jack.

Jack waved it away. "It's on me."

I draped my wrap around my shoulders and laid a shaking hand on Jack's arm. "I'm going to check on Kathryn."

"No!" Jay said loudly. "I mean, I'll go. Thank you, Anna, Jack, for dinner. Evelyn, Helene, it was nice to meet you."

"Nice to meet you too," the girls replied as Jay half-heartedly engaged in a complicated hand-shaking ritual with Nick and Nate.

"Little brothers, I'll see you around." Then he backed away from the table and headed toward the door, where Lia intercepted him.

"Maybe you should wait. Give her some space."

Jay held Lia by the shoulders and looked into her eyes. "No, Mom. I'm going." Then he kissed her on the cheek and was gone.

Jack slid his arm around my waist and pulled me close. I closed my eyes and swallowed the sour taste that rose in my throat from the toxic mix of guilt and relief that swirled in my gut.

Lia turned stiffly to her boys. "Nick, Nate, I'm going to hit the restroom before we leave. Meet you by the front door?"

"Great. I wanted to check out that saltwater tank anyway," Nick said.

"Can we go too?" Helene asked.

I nodded and watched silently as the four kids collected their coats and scurried out the door with Lia following them.

At the threshold, she hesitated, her spine rigid, her shoulders square. She pivoted slowly and stepped back through the archway into our private dining room, fixing her eyes on Jack. "I'm sorry.

For the beach, for taking advantage..." She stepped closer, wobbling slightly on her heels. Her eyes darted in my direction before landing on Jack's face again. She swallowed hard and continued in a whisper. "For not telling you about our son." A tear leaked from her eye, and she batted it away, her expression growing fierce. "But I was eighteen and scared. And the two of you were in love. I didn't know what else to do."

Jack's jaw twitched, and he dropped his eyes to the floor.

I released his hand and stepped closer to Lia. "And what were you trying to do back there?" I asked, jerking my head toward our table, which was littered with the chaotic detritus of our meal. "Are you okay with them being together? Are you *happy* about it?"

"I'm not happy about any of this!" Lia exclaimed, her voice rising. "I'm not happy that I had a shitty mom and a shitty childhood. I'm not happy about the choices I made, and I'm not happy about what happened with Jack. I'm not happy that I got pregnant at eighteen, though I don't regret a single second of my son's life! And I'm not happy that I couldn't tell him the truth about his father." She shot Jack a nervous, sideways glance. "I'm also not happy that the woman my son loves is his... is your daughter." Lia's arms hung limply at her sides as some of her bravado ebbed away. The implications of her last statement were clear to us all.

I took another step closer. "So what are we going to do about it?"

Jack signed the check and tucked his wallet into his coat. "Looks like we won't have to do anything. The engagement's off."

Lia held her ground and my gaze, ignoring Jack. "What *can* we do?" Her eyes filled with tears. "Besides, there are worse things, right?" A slippery, hesitant smile slid onto her face, and an odd bark of laughter escaped from her lips as she stepped through the archway. "After all, love is love."

SUNDAY BRUNCH WITH Kathryn was an excruciating affair. When we'd left the restaurant the night before, I'd spotted her and Jay at the end of the pier, their bodies little more than awkward silhouettes backlit by the restaurant's lights.

Seeing us heading toward the car, Kathryn had pried herself from Jay's insistent arms and dashed after us, her sandals swinging from her fingertips. She climbed into the back seat with her sisters and rode home in silence, save for the occasional hiccupping sob that escaped her lips and her sisters' whispered words of comfort.

Emotionally exhausted, I hadn't managed to drag myself out of bed early enough to go to the store. The result was a frantic morning of delegating tasks so we could pull together a decent meal. Jack was dispatched to retrieve coffee and juice. Evelyn made a run for bagels and scones. And Helene made a fruit salad while I chopped veggies for the casserole. I'd hoped we would be able to eat on the patio, but the warm front that had moved through left a steady, dreary rain in its wake.

With less than an hour before Kathryn was due to head back to Blacksburg, I dashed upstairs for a quick shower. While towel-drying my hair, I peeked into Kathryn's room and was surprised to find her still curled up in bed.

"Kathryn?" I pushed the door wider and padded toward the bed. The room smelled of wet cotton and stale sweat. I sank down beside her, the worn bedsprings creaking beneath me, and rubbed her back. "Sweetie, you should probably get up. Brunch is almost ready, and we'd like to spend a little more time with you before you go."

Kathryn made a small, pitiful noise and slid away from my touch. Her blanket was balled in her fist, and she rubbed the soft fabric against her upper lip, the way she'd done when she was little.

"Your dad and I can drive you back if you want."

"No," she said flatly, uttering the first word I'd heard her speak since she'd fled from the restaurant. "Jay will drive me."

With what seemed like enormous effort, she pushed herself up to a sitting position and leaned against the headboard with a shuddering sigh. A towering pile of used tissues littered her nightstand, and her peach sundress was heaped on the floor. She rubbed the bare space on her left finger where her engagement ring had perched the night before.

I placed my hand over hers, and her face crumpled. "Maybe it's for the best," I said softly.

A fat tear slid down her cheek and splashed onto my wrist. She withdrew her hand from mine. Her eyes were puffy and red, purple half-moons hung from her lower lids, and her nose was rubbed raw. "Look at me, Mom," she cried, snatching the last tissue from the box and blowing her nose. "Does this look like it's for the best?"

She threw back the covers, staggered into the bathroom, and turned the tap on full blast, though I could still hear her weeping behind the closed door.

The sound shredded my heart, and a lump rose in my throat. "Kathryn?" I retraced her steps to the bathroom and knocked lightly on the door. The rush of water went silent, and I leaned my head against the doorframe. "I know how much you're hurting, but it's okay to take your time. You're only twenty years old. You have your whole life ahead of you."

"Go away!" Kathryn shouted.

I backed away slowly, my limbs moving with great effort, as if I were underwater, and I wandered numbly down the stairs and into the kitchen. Evelyn and Helene sat at the table, tapping away on their phones. The fruit salad, bagels, and scones were neatly arrayed in front of them.

"It smells great in here," Jack said as he bustled in from the mud room. A carton of orange juice was tucked under his arm, and a cardboard tray of coffees wobbled in his hands.

I stepped closer to relieve him of the coffees.

Jack glanced at me, and the smile fell from his face. His eyes swept over the kitchen. "Where's Kathryn?"

"Upstairs."

"Good." His shoulders sagged with relief. "I was worried I'd missed her."

"Missed who?" Kathryn asked as she entered the room. She was wearing jeans and a baggy long-sleeved shirt that bore a veterinary clinic logo. Her face was splotchy but scrubbed clean, and her hair was shoved into a messy ponytail. A backpack was slung over one shoulder, and a duffel bag was clutched in her hand.

"You." Jack extracted a coffee cup from the tray and handed it to her. "Vanilla soy latte, just the way you like it."

Kathryn dropped the bag to the floor and accepted the cup but didn't drink from it.

"Shall we eat?" I asked, pulling the casserole from the oven.

"Sounds great. I'm starved." Jack sat down and poured Helene a cup of juice.

I cut the casserole into neat squares and carried the dish to the table. "Are you going to join us?"

Kathryn remained rooted to the spot, staring blankly at the cup in her hands. "I'm not hungry," she mumbled.

Jack pulled out the empty chair beside him. "Then just sit with us."

Kathryn walked, trance-like, to the table, and slumped into her seat. I served her a piece of casserole and watched, hopefully, as she lifted her fork, but she merely poked the tines into the egg and shoved the pieces around her plate.

"I made sure to add blueberries," Helene said, pushing the bowl of fruit salad toward her sister. "I know how much you like them."

"Thanks, 'Lene." Kathryn's attempt at a half-smile faltered, and fresh tears welled in her eyes.

Just then, the doorbell rang. Chessie and Bay raced through the foyer, barking enthusiastically. The five of us sat staring at each other, but nobody moved.

"It's Jay," Kathryn whispered. She used her napkin to wipe away the tear that slid lazily down her cheek.

When the bell chimed again, Evelyn stood from the table. "I'll get it."

We listened from the kitchen as Ev opened the door and greeted Jay. "Do you want something to eat? We have plenty."

"Uh, no, Ev. But thanks. We need to hit the road. I'm scheduled for the afternoon shift at the clinic."

Wordlessly, Jack retrieved Kathryn's duffel and backpack and headed for the door. The rest of us followed reluctantly in his wake. As usual, the sight of Jay took my breath away. He was so much like Jack—both in manner and appearance—it was like I knew him completely. Which would have been a relief under different circumstances because, clearly, Jay was a good man. He was smart, handsome, and successful. And he loved Kathryn. By all counts, they were a good match... if I ignored the fact that they were half-siblings. The thought made me throw up in my mouth a little.

"For the road," Helene said, handing Jay a scone she'd wrapped in a napkin.

"Thanks." He accepted the proffered scone and treated Helene to a small, tight smile that quickly faded as he shifted his gaze to Kathryn. "Ready?"

Kathryn hugged us each in turn then knelt to scratch the dogs behind their ears. Her face reddened with the effort to hold back her tears.

When she stood, I pulled her into my arms, hugged her tightly, and whispered into her ear. "I love you so much, Kathryn. Everything's going to be okay. You'll see."

She nodded into my hair and then stepped back. I held her at arm's length and looked into her eyes, but the hurt I saw there tore through my already tattered heart.

Jack hugged me to his side, and I could feel his heart thumping loudly against his ribs. We watched from the porch until Jay's car disappeared from sight.

After Kathryn and Jay had gone and the rest of my family had melted back into the house to clean up the dishes and play *Mario Kart*, I closed the front door and leaned heavily against it. *Mission accomplished.* The bitter words hung in my mind like the thick gray clouds that had blanketed the morning sky. Against all odds, Kathryn had called off her engagement. *It's what we wanted, right?*

I slid to the floor as my heart and mind waged war against each other. On some basic, intrinsic, *cerebral* level, I understood that it was wrong for Jay and Kathryn to be together. It was my *heart* that wasn't convinced.

Love is love, Lia had said.

I closed my eyes and exhaled slowly. When I opened them again, the sun was peeking out, casting tentative rays of light through the dissipating clouds and transforming the raindrops that clung to the screen into dazzling prisms. Standing to peer through the window, I marveled at how quickly things could change. I pressed my fingertips against the glass and steeled my resolve. *This too shall pass.*

Kathryn was hurting now, but she would be okay. She was strong, smart, and sensible. At twenty years old, she still had her whole life ahead of her. Calling off her engagement was the right thing to do. By the time she came home for Christmas, she would have put this all behind her and moved on. I hoped.

CHAPTER 41

December 2015

Kathryn arrived home for Christmas, sullen and gloomy, after completing her finals.

"What's wrong?" I asked. I'd found her lying on her bed, idly flipping through a magazine.

She sighed and rotated onto her back. "I miss him."

"Good grief, Kathryn, he'll be here in a few days."

As the lowest man on the veterinary totem pole, Jay had to stay in Blacksburg to man the clinic until it closed on Christmas Eve.

"I know." Her eyebrows pinched together, and her lips curled into a childish pout. "It's just, we're together almost all the time. When he's not around, it's like I'm missing a piece of myself. You know?"

Yes, I know. I sighed and sat on the edge of Kathryn's bed just like I used to when she was a little girl. She would lie on this very bed—with its lavender comforter and white eye lace trim—sulking over a fight she'd had with her sisters, puzzling over the injustices in the world, or simply drawing in her sketch pad. She'd always been an introspective, independent girl, a bit of an old soul. But she'd blossomed since going to college, and even more so since meeting Jay.

"How *are* things with Jay anyway?" My dark, tormented side shamelessly hoped that something might have changed since

Kathryn called two weeks ago to share the "good" news that the engagement was back on. I wondered if Lia knew. I hadn't spoken to her at all since the dinner debacle.

After Kathryn returned to Blacksburg with a broken heart, Jack and I had called often but were seldom able to catch her on the phone. On the rare occasion that she would pick up, she insisted she was doing fine and moving forward. When I would ask about Jay, she would say, "I don't want to talk about it," and change the subject, though her voice sounded more chipper than I would have expected given the circumstances. She'd also declined to come home for Thanksgiving, claiming that she needed to study. Then two weeks ago, we'd gotten the call.

"You were right, Mom," she'd explained in a breathless, excited voice. "Things were moving too fast. The stress was really getting to me, and I guess I just freaked out a little. On the way back to Tech, Jay explained everything, you know, about his name, and it was really no big deal. After that, we decided to just take things slow, focus on each other and our relationship and all the reasons we got engaged in the first place."

The likelihood of uncovering any small crack or fissure in Kathryn and Jay's newly solidified relationship that might signal its imminent demise was slim to none. In fact, the mere mention of Jay's name made Kathryn's face light up like a Christmas tree. From the moment Jack and I had received the call, we knew we no longer had a choice. We had to tell her the truth.

"Things are amazing. And it just keeps getting better. I really love him, Mom. He's my best friend."

He's a lot more than that. I straightened my back and sniffed piously. "You know, you can't let him be everything to you, Kathryn. It's not healthy. It's important to never lose sight of yourself," I advised, recalling the wisdom I'd gleaned from my sessions with Faith. "If anything ever happened... if things didn't work out—"

"Why would you say something like that?" Kathryn interrupted, indignant.

"You just never know what life's going to throw at you." My eyes searched her face. "You have to be prepared for... the unexpected."

Kathryn laced her fingers over her abdomen and gazed up at the tiny glow-in-the-dark moon and stars organized into various constellations that still adorned the ceiling. A small, reticent smile graced her lips.

I kissed her on the forehead as I stood from the bed. "Besides, it will be nice to spend some time with you alone." I paused at the door and hesitated before continuing. "And there are some things we need to talk about."

I left her gazing up at the ceiling, as if she could tease the secrets of her future from the glow-in-the-dark stars that winked down on her from above. That strange half-smile still graced her lips.

KATHRYN'S MOOD DARKENED when she received a text from Jay that he would not make it home for the holidays after all. "Two equine emergencies, a dog that was hit by a car, and a box of kittens abandoned on the clinic's doorstep," she read from her phone as we were all relaxing in the family room.

"Isn't there anyone else that can help?" I asked, though this new development was, to me, a blessing in disguise. It would give us the extra time we so desperately needed.

"The rest of the staff has already left for the holiday," Kathryn explained. "Jay's already had to recall one of his assistants from Lynchburg, but he still won't be able to leave."

"Well, you'll get to see him soon, right? After New Year's?" Jack offered helpfully, though it seemed to be exactly the wrong thing to say.

Kathryn's temper leapt like the flames in the fireplace. "I'm not waiting until after New Year's Eve to see Jay!" she screeched. "I want to be with him for the holidays. I'm heading back to Blacksburg tomorrow after dinner."

"You're leaving on Christmas Day?" I asked, incredulous.

"Kathryn, you see Jay all the time," Jack began. "We would like to spend Christmas with you. Your family—"

"Jay *is* my family. My *fiancé*, in case you forgot." Kathryn stood in front of the fireplace, her hands balled into fists. The flickering flames illuminated her silhouette but cast her face in shadow.

Jack and I exchanged a helpless glance. I reached for his hand, and he interlaced his fingers with mine. It was now or never. We had to tell Kathryn the truth, that Jay was her half brother. The news would crush her. She might not even believe us. She would definitely hate us. Not only would Christmas be ruined, but I had the sinking feeling that Kathryn might never forgive us for what we were about to say.

"About that," I began and faltered, my voice catching in my throat.

Jack squeezed my hand tightly. "We have to, Anna. We have no choice."

Kathryn's eyes darted from Jack's face to mine. "What are you talking about?"

"Kathryn, please, sit down," Jack entreated. "There's something your mother and I need to discuss with you."

Kathryn strode silently to the armchair facing us and sat with her elbows on her knees, drawing my attention to the hole in her jeans. It drove me crazy that she always wore jeans with holes in them. But that was nothing compared to the hole we were about to punch through her heart.

"What?" Kathryn asked. Her jaw was set defiantly, and her eyes were a curious mixture of trepidation and anger.

"It's about Jay," Jack began.

"What? You like him, don't you? You gave him your blessing to marry me last spring. Remember?" She glanced first at Jack and then, accusingly, at me, as if what was about to happen would be my fault. *As if.*

"Kathryn, that was before... we got to know more about him," Jack continued.

"What could you possibly know that you don't like? He's perfect. In fact, he's just like you, Dad. He reminds me so much of you."

My sharp inhalation caught her attention, and she swung her head in my direction, her long, dark ponytail flying out behind her. "Didn't you always say I should find a man like my father? Well, I did. I found him. He's honest, hardworking, smart, successful, funny, not to mention drop-dead gorgeous—"

"Why, thank you," Jack interrupted with a lame and ludicrous attempt at humor. There was nothing remotely funny about the situation.

Kathryn ignored him. "And he loves me. So what's not to like? What's the problem?" Kathryn's voice was growing shriller by the minute.

"Kathryn, you're so young. Why do you need to rush into marriage?" I hedged.

"We're not rushing. We've been together for almost two years now, engaged for more than seven months. And we're not too young. By the time we get married, I'll be almost as old as you were when you married Dad. And Jay is *older* than Dad was."

Jack stood and began pacing the room. "Bottom line is, we don't want you to marry him, Kathryn. You *can't* marry him. I rescind my blessing."

"*What?*" Kathryn shrieked. "You can't be serious! Why would you say such a thing? Why can't you just be happy for me?"

Jack opened his mouth to speak, and I shrank back against the couch, frightened of what was coming, of words we could never take back, words that would crush our daughter and quite possibly damage our relationship with her forever. But Jack snapped his mouth shut, shook his head fiercely, and began pacing again. His internal struggle—evidenced by his anguished face—was clearly as painful as mine.

I breathed deeply and summoned all the courage and strength I could muster. "Kathryn, we don't approve of this marriage. We can't. Jay is..." My eyes welled with tears,

and my resolve ebbed away. I just couldn't say it. "There are things you don't know," I muttered instead.

Kathryn sprang from the chair, her eyes blazing. "I can't believe this. I can't believe you're doing this to me. On Christmas Eve, no less!" she shouted. "Here's what I do know—Jay is my best friend. I'm my best self when I'm with him, and I don't ever want to be without him. We love each other." Kathryn was the one pacing now.

Jack had come to sit beside me, his hand gripping mine again. This was not going well, and we hadn't even gotten to the worst of it.

"And I'm going to marry him whether you like it or not. I don't need your permission, but I thought I'd at least have your blessing, your support. You're my parents! I thought you'd be happy for me. And I need you." At that, her voice cracked, and her lower lip quivered. She sank into the chair. "I need you now more than ever." She whimpered and hung her head. Then she began to weep.

I went to her and knelt before her. "We love you, Kathryn, so much, and we want you to be happy. We're on your side always. But we want what's best for you, and we won't let you get hurt. We have to protect you." My own tears were flowing freely now.

"Why do you think I'll get hurt? What do you need to protect me from?" Kathryn sniffed, anguish pinching her face. "Do you know something I don't?"

"Sweetheart, why can't you just wait?" Jack pleaded. He was wavering, unable to give voice to the words we so desperately needed to say. "Can't you postpone the wedding, at least a little while longer, just to be sure? If you and Jay are meant to be—"

"We are meant to be, Dad. I love him. And I don't want to postpone the wedding. I won't." Kathryn bit her lower lip, her eyes welling with fresh tears. "I can't."

"But why?" I implored. If she would only agree to postpone, it would buy us more time to figure things out and find the right words to explain.

Kathryn sighed. Her anger dissipated, and a small half-smile crept onto her lips. It was an expression I'd seen before—the one that had flitted about her face as she'd lain on her bed, gazing up at the glow-in-the-dark stars. She reached into the pocket of her sweatshirt and withdrew a small, thin box. "This is why," she whispered, handing me the box. "I was planning to give this to Jay for Christmas, but I guess you need to see it too."

Jack came to stand beside me and put his hand on my shoulder. Puzzled, I slowly lifted the lid. Inside, nestled on a bed of cotton, was a white plastic stick. A pregnancy test. It was positive.

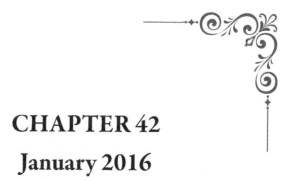

CHAPTER 42
January 2016

After Kathryn revealed her pregnancy to us, Jack and I had held her in our arms and outwardly cried tears of joy. Inside, we wept with worry and despair.

"How far along?" I whispered through trembling lips.

"About nine weeks." Kathryn slumped against the sofa and draped one arm protectively across her abdomen. That dreamy expression was on her face again. "Must have been that night we made up."

Jack had moved to stand in front of the fire. His back was to us, and his arms were crossed. He remained silent.

I cleared my throat. "You weren't using protection?" My question, deservedly, earned Kathryn's scorn.

"Of course we were! But accidents happen."

When her eyes filled with tears again, I scooched closer, put my arm around her, and pulled her close.

"But I would never consider my baby an accident," she said, her voice softening. "It's more serendipitous, I guess."

"Have you seen a doctor yet?"

Kathryn sat up straight and looked me in the eyes. "Last week. Everything's fine."

Jack sank onto the couch behind me, still not saying a word.

Kathryn smiled, and her eyes glittered with unshed tears. "I heard the heartbeat. The doctor said at nine weeks, the baby is almost an inch long, like the size of a small strawberry." She sniffed and wiped her nose with the back of her hand. "I'm due at the end of July."

I grabbed hold of Kathryn's hands and hung my head as silent tears fell onto my lap. *A small strawberry.* The notion made it almost impossible to think of abortion as an option.

Jack reached around from behind and pulled Kathryn close, wrapping us both in his strong arms.

What have we done? We've waited too long. Will the baby be okay? Will it be born with birth defects as a result of Kathryn and Jay's shared genetics? I resolved then and there to learn everything I could about the true risk involved. Knowledge was power after all. Maybe the situation wasn't as dire as it seemed.

IRONICALLY, WITH JAY'S help—he reiterated that he would be working around the clock at the clinic through the end of December—we convinced Kathryn to stay home with us for Christmas. Jack and I shamelessly preyed upon Kathryn's status as an engaged—and pregnant—young woman to point out that this might be the last holiday we would get to spend together with just the five of us.

On New Year's Eve, she packed her bags and headed back to Blacksburg, anxious to ring in the new year with her fiancé and share her news.

For Jack and me, the month of January dissolved into a black hole of research. We spent several panicked, anguished weeks poring over articles and laws regarding consanguinity. There was a plethora of scary information on the increased risk of half-siblings—who shared a quarter of their genetic material—passing on a recessive disease to their children.

However, there was also evidence that many incest laws were, in part, socially rather than biologically based. We scoured reports on the various cultures that encouraged first-cousin marriages and whose offspring from those unions seemed unaffected. Recent studies had also shown that the risk for first cousins, who shared an eighth of their genetic material, to pass on diseases to their children was less than three percent higher than that of unrelated people.

The research brought us some measure of comfort, but I still fretted during the day—unable to concentrate on work—and slept fitfully at night, tossing and turning until the wee hours of the morning.

"What do you think Lia thinks about this?" I asked Jack one morning as he was preparing to leave for work. We knew from Kathryn that Jay had proudly and happily shared the news of the pregnancy with Lia a few days into the new year.

"I don't know." He shoved his arms into the sleeves of his black wool coat and kissed me on the forehead. "Why don't you call her and find out?"

"Fat chance," I replied as he headed out the door.

I ran my finger around the lip of my coffee mug and stared at the phone. Ev and Helene had the day off from school and were still undoubtedly sleeping soundly in their beds. Other than telling Jack, Lia, and me, Kathryn and Jay had decided to keep the news of the pregnancy to themselves until after the next ultrasound.

"Just to make sure everything's okay," Jay had said. His words, spoken over the phone, had chilled me to the bone.

"And because we'll know by then if it's a girl or a boy," Kathryn added with a chortle.

I was taking a sip of my coffee when the phone rang. The sharp, jangling sound pierced the morning quiet and startled me from my stupor, causing the brown liquid to splash onto my white sweat-shirt.

"Shit," I murmured as I padded to the phone, dabbing at the stain with a napkin. I glanced at the caller ID and froze. *Lia.*

My limbs were made of stone. Unable to move, I listened as the answering machine invited callers to leave a message. At the last minute, I snatched the phone from its cradle. "Hello?"

"Congratulations, Grandma."

I slammed the phone down and stood seething. *How could she joke about this?* A minute later, the phone rang again. I clenched my hands into fists and didn't pick up.

"Anna, I'm sorry," Lia said into the machine. "I shouldn't have said that. I know it's not funny." *Damn right, it's not.* "Are you still there? Will you please pick up? I have something important to tell you."

My breath caught in my throat at those words. An image of Lia's letter, the one from so long ago, swirled in my brain. The pink paper, the purple ink. *I have something important to tell you.* The last time I ignored those words, the consequences had been devastating. I would be damned if I let history repeat itself.

My knuckles ached from the force of my grip on the phone. "What do you want?"

"I met with a genetic counselor. He told me some things I think you'll want to know."

I breathed deeply, not trusting myself to speak, and waited for Lia to continue.

In the silence that hung between us, Lia pressed on. "I *know* you, Anna. I know you've probably been worried sick—"

"When?"

Lia hesitated before answering. "Can you meet me at Keller's on Friday?"

"I'll be there at noon."

I SPOTTED LIA INSTANTLY. She sat in a quiet corner booth, looking as lovely as ever in an ice-blue sweater. Her strawberry hair curled around her shoulders. A string of bells attached to a leather strap clanged against the door as it closed behind me. Lia smiled and gave a half wave. I shoved my own thick, dark hair behind my ears and slid into the booth. The Bay View-blue vinyl seat creaked beneath me. Two highball glasses of what appeared to be orange juice rested atop damp cocktail napkins. But I knew better.

"Mimosa?" I asked, taking a sip.

"Screwdriver."

I winced at the unexpected bite of vodka. "As in 'we're screwed'?"

"Funny. But not exactly." Lia slid a thin sheaf of papers toward me. "Besides, the coffee here sucks. Tastes like burnt sand."

I pushed my drink aside and lifted the stack of papers, peering closely at the charts and graphs and highlighted sections. "I see you've done your homework."

"I'm sure you have too. There was a surprising amount of info and stats on consanguinity—both good and bad. And scary. You know how the internet is."

"Yes. I know."

"Well, one of my clients recently won a grant to design biomedical equipment. I'd been hired to help them staff and oversee a team of engineers. When Jay told me the news... about the baby... I remembered that one of the engineers had studied genetics in grad school. One quick phone call, and I had the name and number of a prominent medical geneticist in Baltimore. I was shocked she agreed to meet with me on such short notice."

I twirled the straw between my fingers. "Good to have friends in high places, I guess."

Lia sipped her drink, which was more clear than orange, and continued. "As it turns out, a certified genetic counselor in her department had conducted extensive research and written an article on consanguinity." Lia flipped to the second page and tapped on a graph that was a jumble of lines, dots, and numbers. "The researcher extrapolated the data and determined that half-siblings have approximately a five percent greater risk above the general population for passing on significant congenital defects."

"In English, please." I'd always been awestruck by Lia's brilliant mind. The way she pointed to the graph and talked me through the data instantly transported me back in time. Suddenly, I was sixteen again, struggling with math, and Lia was trying in vain to make me understand sines, cosines, derivatives, and coefficients.

"You're hopeless," she'd said back then, laughing and shaking her head.

As if she were remembering the same thing, she smirked and flipped to a page that had several sentences marked with yellow highlighter. "Basically, it means that Kathryn and Jay's baby has a ninety-five percent chance of being okay." She leaned back and gave me a small smile.

I slumped against the booth. My limbs were heavy with relief, but my mind was dizzy with line graphs and statistics. The information had given me not only peace of mind but also the delicate fluttering of hope. I grabbed my drink and drained half of it in one gulp.

"I appreciate you meeting me." Lia slipped her arms into her coat. "I know it's a lot to take in. But my plan is to stick with the status quo and keep my mouth shut, to move forward with... let's just call it cautious joy."

I tapped the papers against the table, reordering the pile into a neat stack, and handed them back to Lia.

"Keep it." She extracted her car keys from her bag. "I have a copy at home."

I reached across the table and placed my hand over hers. "Thank you."

Her eyes filled with tears. "I know you and Jack still need to talk about this, but I hope you both take a deep look into your hearts before making any decisions you might regret."

She reached for the sunglasses perched atop her head and lowered them over her eyes like a protective shield. "I, for one, know what it's like to live with regrets." She walked toward the door, with her hands shoved into her coat pockets, and pushed it open with her hip. "And I don't recommend it."

The door swung shut behind her with a jingle of bells.

That night, I watched Jack closely as he read. His head was bent over the geneticist's article, his brows furrowed in concentration, his jaw working with emotion. When he finished, his eyes were wet, and he swallowed hard. A single bob of his head was the only reply I needed.

And so, after endless days of exhaustive, frantic internet research and hours of heart-wrenching soul-searching, we hung our hats and our hopes on the data that Lia had unearthed from the genetic counselor. We decided that our secret should be left untold. *What good would it do anyone now to know the truth?* The baby—our grandchild—was already on its way. If Kathryn and Jay's relationship were revealed, a marriage would be illegal or annulled, and the baby deemed illegitimate. In fact, if Kathryn and Jay were made aware of their relationship and decided to proceed with a wedding anyway, the very fact of their knowledge would then render their actions criminal. So given the situation, ignorance was definitely bliss. The truth would not set us free. It would, instead, deliver only pain and sorrow to our daughter at a time in her life that should be filled with unconditional love, joy, and happiness.

A WEEK LATER, UNABLE to sleep, I wandered into my office and flicked on the light. For Christmas, Helene had given me Liane Moriarty's latest book, *Big Little Lies*. I plucked it from a shelf that was nearly full of books still to be read and glanced at the title. *Could be the story of my life.* With a snort, I tucked the book under my arm, climbed the stairs, and quietly slipped into bed next to my sleeping husband to read. After an hour, my eyelids were finally growing heavy. I reached for my bookmark, but it slipped from my fingers and fluttered to the floor, landing out of reach in the space between my nightstand and the bed's headboard.

"Shit," I swore beneath my breath. I slid open the drawer of my nightstand and was silently rifling through it in search of my favorite leather bookmark when I saw something that made my heart skip a beat. It was tucked behind the balled-up, discarded sock I'd used to help treat a stubborn case of plantar fasciitis.

I pushed the sock aside and withdrew the buttery-soft journal Lia had given me for my birthday the first time we'd ridden the BWI Trail together. For an entire year, I'd diligently written in the journal every night, filling the thick parchment with my innermost thoughts, goals, and memories. I flipped to the first entry and noted the date: April 1, 2010. *Six years ago.* Faith was still alive, and Kathryn was only fifteen years old. *If only I knew then what I know now.*

I turned back one more page and gazed at Lia's inscription. She'd included an E.R. Hazlip quote: "Friendship is a horizon—which expands whenever we approach it." I slid my fingertips across the words she'd written, feeling the indentations they'd left in the paper. I closed the journal and replaced it in the nightstand drawer. I knew what I had to do.

The next day, I phoned Lia to share the decision Jack and I had made. When I was greeted by her voice mail, I knew a simple message would suffice. "Congratulations to you too."

Her reply, written on pink paper in her trademark purple scrawl, arrived in my mailbox a few days later:

"As I'd always intended, this truth will be left untold so that the ones we love will not be hurt. The burden of this secret is something I've carried alone for decades in the hope of protecting the two of you, and my son, from unnecessary pain. Now it is a burden we share, one that, along with the marriage of our children, will bind us together forever—something that our friendship alone was not strong enough to do. Perhaps blood is thicker than water after all? All I ever wanted was for you to be happy, Anna, and now that's what I want most of all for our children. It's what they deserve, especially now that the universe—and destiny—has seen fit to bring them together."

CHAPTER 43
May 2016

Kathryn was a radiant bride. Indeed, the dress she'd found in Blacksburg—the first one she'd tried on—was perfect. A clever seamstress had let out the sides of the bodice and added a stretchy lace appliqued panel to accommodate her growing breasts, and the empire-waist gown skimmed lightly over her swelling belly. From the side, it looked like she was hiding a tiny volleyball beneath her dress. Once the fatigue, heartburn, and nausea of the first trimester had subsided, Kathryn's pregnancy progressed uneventfully. The twenty-week ultrasound had revealed a healthy, thriving baby girl.

The sunset ceremony on the lawn of Snowshoe's Mountain Lodge offered a breathtaking view of the Cheat and Back Allegheny Mountains. The bowl-shaped convergence of the ridges cradled the resort, which was perched atop the second highest point in the state of West Virginia. The irony of half-siblings getting married in West Virginia was not lost on me.

From my front-row seat, with Jack holding tightly to my hand, I soaked in the beautiful scenery and surveyed the elegant row of people who stood before me. Evelyn, Helene, and Clare, dressed in royal-blue silk and clutching ivory-rose-and-hydrangea bouquets, looked as if they might burst with pride and happiness as they stood alongside their sister and friend. Nathan, Nicholas, and

Dustin, Jay's best friend—the mutual friend who'd introduced Kathryn and Jay—rounded out the bridal party.

At the pastor's cue, Jay cleared his throat and began reciting his vows. His deep, resonant voice was clear and confident.

"I, Jackson Roberto Martin, take you, Kathryn Dianna Clark, to be my wife, my constant friend, my faithful partner, and my true love from this day forward. In the presence of our family and friends, I offer you my solemn vow to be your faithful partner in sickness and in health, in good times and in bad, and in joy as well as in sorrow. I promise to love you and our daughter unconditionally, to support you in your goals, to honor and respect you, to laugh with you and cry with you, and to cherish you for as long as we both shall live."

I'd been trying to hold it together—and doing a pretty good job of it—until Jay added "our daughter" to his vows and placed his hand lovingly and tenderly upon Kathryn's belly. At that, I wept openly, but I wasn't alone. There wasn't a dry eye in sight. Beside me, Jack sniffed and coughed into his hand. Behind me, my mother and sister-in-law blew their noses loudly, making honking, unladylike sounds that Faith surely would have disapproved of. *Oh, how I wish Faith were here.* At that moment, an errant gust of wind swept across the lawn. The warm, sweet-scented breeze lifted the hair from my neck and dried the fresh tears that filled my eyes, and I realized that Faith was indeed with me after all. She would always be with me.

As Kathryn launched into her own vows, I leaned forward and hazarded a glance at Lia, who was seated in the front row on the groom's side. Her cheeks were pink and dewy with tears, and she clutched a mangled tissue in her lap. She must have sensed my gaze because she turned her head and met my eyes. She smiled—a wobbly, watery expression—and I smiled back.

In February, after receiving Lia's letter, I'd called to suggest that we resume our monthly lunches at Keller's—we had a wedding to plan after all—to which Lia had readily agreed. And when Kathryn had asked me to come to Virginia over spring break to help her choose her wedding cake and flowers, I'd invited Lia—with Kathryn's enthusiastic approval—to come along. Our road trip to Christiansburg—the one I'd once posed as bait to try to catch Lia in a lie—had finally come to fruition, only under far different circumstances.

What passed between Lia and me now—as we held each other's gaze and our children exchanged rings and promised to love each other forever—was a silent acknowledgement of the agreement we had made: that our secret would remain untold. Kathryn being pregnant had changed everything. It was no longer just Kathryn and Jay's future at stake but the future of their unborn child, of the tiny life growing inside of her.

The reception was held in the lodge's ballroom, where we dined on decadent passed hors d'oeuvres of seared tuna, shrimp puffs, and bacon-wrapped sea scallops and a dinner buffet of salmon, chicken cordon bleu, wild rice pilaf, and sautéed green beans. The open bar contributed to the festive atmosphere, and we danced the night away to cover tunes and original music performed by a popular local band.

Just before midnight, we all joined together—150 of our closest friends and family members—to toast the happy new couple, or rather, new *family,* before they swept out of the lodge under a shower of rose petals and were whisked away in a horse-drawn carriage to their mountaintop villa. A more exotic honeymoon had been postponed in deference to Kathryn's impending due date. Meanwhile, the newlyweds would spend their first week as husband and wife relaxing at their villa and being pampered by the resort staff.

"They're going to be okay," Jack said. He slipped his arm around my waist and gave me a reassuring squeeze as we watched the carriage recede in the distance.

Then Lia was beside me. Staring straight ahead, she spoke the words I knew in my heart to be true. "We're *all* going to be okay." She reached for my hand, and I held on tight. "Besides, love is love, right?"

I looked into Lia's familiar green eyes glittering in the moonlight and smiled. "And friendship is a horizon."

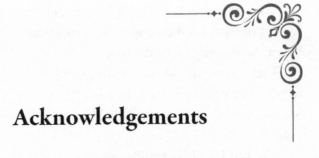

Acknowledgements

I once read that if you write nonfiction, people will try to find ways in which the book is not true, and if you write fiction, people will try to find ways in which the book is true. So to answer the question I have already been asked several times: no one in this book is real; I have not written about anyone I know. The characters are all creative composites of multiple traits and personalities I have encountered throughout my life, and writing this book has been a wild ride through my imagination.

My journey to publication has been nearly a decade in the making, and I've been extremely fortunate to have so many people who've encouraged and supported me as I've walked (and sometimes sprinted, sometimes crawled) along this path.

I'd like to thank the Women's Fiction Writers Association for being my first writing home. Being named a finalist in the WFWA Rising Star Contest helped to breathe new life into this book and propel it to the next level and also gave me a huge lift when I needed it most. Through WFWA I have found not only my tribe but also boundless support and inspiration among its many talented and passionate members. I'd especially like to thank Cara Sue Achterberg for reaching out when I hit my writing low, for talking me off the quitting ledge, for telling me to keep writing, and for being such a compassionate friend to humans and animals alike.

I'm also grateful for the Carroll County Chapter of the Maryland Writers Association, where I first cut my teeth on sharing my writing with others and began to envision becoming a published author. To the recently discovered Wednesday writing group: I'm thrilled to have met a group of local writers, and our weekly gathering at the library has added some much-needed structure to my writing routine; Wednesday is now my most productive day of the week!

To my ERReads, A Likely Story, and Panera neighborhood book clubs: I appreciate our shared passion for reading and relish our lively and respectful discussions about books.

Much gratitude must also be bestowed upon my first and earliest readers: Matt Leimkuhler, Jen Kullgren and Kari Cozzolino; your tolerance and patience with that early draft is commendable, and your thoughtful and gentle suggestions were a revelation. To Jen and Kari and also to Gretchen Laufer and Chuza Bolger; thanks for showing me that true friendship is indeed a horizon.

A huge and heartfelt thanks goes out to Red Adept Publishing for believing in me and my book. To Lynn McNamee for her shrewd business acumen, her impressive industry knowledge, her "punny" posts, and for not giving up when her first message to me was zapped by a random lightning strike! To my amazing editors, Alyssa Hall and Neila Forssberg, for your keen insights and guidance, and for pushing me to make my book the best it could be. I learned a lot from you both. To my witty mentor, Erica Lucke Dean, for her attention to detail, her lifesaving advice and for answering my many questions.

To Jennifer Klepper and Barbara Conrey, my fellow WFWA members, RAP sisters, and Mid-Atlantic dwellers; a perfect trifecta in many ways! Where would I be without you? Jennifer, I can't begin to thank you for paying it forward and leading the way through this publishing maze. I am in awe of your intelligence, knowledge and kindness. And Barbara, I feel like I've known you forever; you are one of the most generous people I've ever met, the embodiment of a rising tide that lifts all boats. I'm so happy we get to experience this debut journey together.

To the 2020 Debuts: I am beyond grateful to be part of this exceptional group. The support, knowledge, talent and encouragement that abounds is like nothing I've ever experienced, and with you I am not alone. Together we vent, learn, share, uplift, commiserate and celebrate. I couldn't imagine going through this debut year without you!

And finally, and most importantly, to my family: to my mom, Nancy Gladwell, for setting the bar for motherhood sky high and for reading to me every day and teaching me to love books; to my dad, Rick Gladwell, for his unwavering love of family and for always believing I could achieve anything. Thanks to you both for setting such a positive and admirable example of love, marriage, and family and for making such a happy childhood home for my brother, Rick, and me. I love you, and I'm so grateful for your unconditional love and support.

To my daughters, Isabelle, Erika, and Allison: you have beautiful spirits that shine from the inside out. You inspire me and make me proud every day, and I cherish the way you love and care for each other. Being your mom is such a privilege and a pleasure; it is the best thing I've ever done, and it has fulfilled me in ways I never could have imagined. I love you with every inch of my heart.

To my husband, Matt: the stars were aligned when we met, and our hearts recognized each other from the beginning. Thank you for your infinite love and encouragement, for being such a great dad, for working so hard, for making this incredible life possible; for everything. All I want is you. I love you tons.

About the Author

Sherri Leimkuhler is a multitasker extraordinaire. She has written professionally for more than twenty years but is a Jill of many trades, with experience in sales, marketing, public relations, event planning, aviation, and yoga instruction. Her health-and-fitness column, "For the Fun of Fit," appears bi-weekly in the *Carroll County Times*.

When not writing or doing downward dog poses, Sherri enjoys hiking, kayaking, trail running, traveling, wine tasting, and curling up with a good book and a steaming cuppa. She is also a competitive triathlete and a two-time Ironman finisher.

Sherri lives in Maryland with her husband, three daughters, and two Labrador retrievers.

Read more at www.sherrileimkuhler.com.

About the Publisher

Dear Reader,

We hope you enjoyed this book. Please consider leaving a review on your favorite book site.

Visit https://RedAdeptPublishing.com to see our entire catalogue.

Don't forget to subscribe to our monthly newsletter to be notified of future releases and special sales.

Made in the USA
Monee, IL
25 March 2022

93532450R00256